JOSH HAYES
EDGE OF
VALOR

AETHON
BOOKS

EDGE OF VALOR

©2019 JOSH HAYES

Print and eBook formatting, and cover design by Steve Beaulieu. Artwork provided by Florent llamas.

Published by Aethon Books LLC. 2019

This novel is dedicated to the men and women who serve and put their lives on the line—past, present and future. For your service, you cannot be thanked enough.

To those who paid the ultimate sacrifice; you will never be forgotten.

ACKNOWLEDGMENTS

As I sit here, considering everything that has gone into this project, the idea that the novel is actually finished is still difficult to grasp. Edge of Valor has been a project almost eight years in the making, and the work is much different now than when the grand idea came to me.

I can remember the time and place when the inspiration for the first scene hit me, and now looking back on the multiple iterations of the story, I'm truly amazed that it finally came together.

First and foremost, I need to thank my wife, Jamie. I don't know how many times I found myself in the middle of conversations, or doing dishing, or laundry, or just sitting on the couch being lazy while the kids cause ruckus and mayhem, and the lightbulb would go off. "That's it!" And I'd be off to write a note.

Jamie: I love you very much. Your patience, understanding, confidence, and encouragement has been incredible. I couldn't have finished this project without your love and support.

Scott Moon: for the hours of conversations that typically started with, "Hey, let me bounce this off you." We may or may not have worked out the issues, but without your sounding board, this novel would never have happened. Your friendship is invaluable. "Scariest environment imaginable."

To my editors, Steve Beaulieu and Rhett C. Bruno: your comments and corrects were invaluable, and made this book so much better than I could have produced on my own. I can't thank you enough, even if Steve has a thing against paper.

And you reader: thank you for picking up this novel. I hope that when you read this story, you enjoy reading it as much as I did writing it.

CHAPTER 1

Freeman Street,
Entertainment District
New Tuscany
2 April 2607

"Two blocks out. I'm sure the spotters can see you now," the voice in his link's cochlear implant told him. *"You sure about this?"*

"I'm sure." Fischer gave the driver a sidelong glare, their eyes meeting in the rearview. The older man, sporting a salt-and-pepper beard and the galaxy's worst combover, held Fischer's gaze for a moment, then turned his attention back to the street. It definitely wasn't the first time he'd driven a fare to this part of town, and he obviously knew better than to ask questions, which suited Fischer just fine.

Fischer lowered his voice so the driver wouldn't hear. New Tuscan cabbies were known to keep their client's business confidential, but that didn't mean there wasn't one who wouldn't miss the chance to earn some favor with the local law. "Any sign of cops?"

"None," Tensley Jones said. *"And nothing on the network."*

"What about the encrypted?"

"Hey now, what do you take me for? Tapping into the response network is illegal. I could lose my ship. Hell, they might even lock me away on Taltorgan for something like that."

"Yeah… so how's it look?"

"It's clear. You think this traitorous bastard is going to show?"

Fischer allowed the barest hint of a smile. His friend might not have been the most stand-up citizen, but for all his faults, the man was loyal, and his patriotism was unparalleled. "No reason not to."

The cab's repulser pads kicked up a cloud of dust as it pulled to a stop.

"We're here." The cabby didn't bother looking back, and without another word, the car's door slid open, letting the hot New Tuscan air flood the passenger compartment. Even two hours after sunset, it was still hot. It was always hot.

Oh, but it's a dry heat, Special Agent Jackson Fischer told himself, mimicking his wife's repetitive remarks about his current duty station. Dry or not, New Tuscany's spring was still unpleasant, but it beat being stationed on a warship for months at a time.

He tapped a tip into the terminal on the seatback and climbed out of the cab. Undercarriage marker lights danced over Fischer's boots as the door slid silently shut behind him. Repulsers hummed and the cab lifted away.

The Starmaker Tavern was half a block up, its glowing neon-purple sign flickering amidst a myriad of other floating adverts. A muscle-bound bouncer stood near the entrance, keeping close tabs on the crowds as they passed. It'd be difficult for any trained observer to think the Starmaker was anything but a front for criminal activity.

"Looks like they've changed door guy," Fischer muttered under his breath so only Jones could hear.

"Maybe he has a sick grandmother he's got to take care of."

Music reverberated through the walls of several bars along the street, creating an amalgamation of thumping bass rhythms and incomprehensible lyrics.

"You know, you can still back out," Jones said.

"Not a chance."

"Alriiight. I'm just saying, you get caught in there, it's your ass, not mine. Have you considered the fact that Feringer might not even show?"

"He'll show," Fischer said. "And by this time tomorrow, I'll be accepting Carter's apology."

"Ha! That'll be the day."

Fischer weaved his way through the crowd, fighting the urge to check his six, scan the rooftops, peer down alleys. Situational awareness was something the Academy drilled into its recruits from day one, but constantly checking one's surroundings, especially while everyone else was completely oblivious to anything not in their personal bubble, was a sure way to get pegged by anyone actually paying attention.

As if Jones had been able to read his mind, the part-time smuggler said, *"Looking good. Still, no activity on the scanners and the spotters are still just standing there. Doesn't look like they've made you... yet."*

"That's very reassuring, thank you."

"Hey, no problem my friend. I'm here for you."

Fischer stopped in front of the barrel-chested doorman. "How's the scenery?"

The bouncer grunted. "Depends on what kind of party you're after."

Fischer gave an exaggerated shrug. "Eh, a little of this, a little of that."

"Twenty." The bouncer held out a small handheld pad, his eyes scanning the streets.

Fischer flicked his left wrist, activating his link. The semi-transparent, orange-hued display rotated into position above his forearm. With the swipe of a finger, Fischer triggered his e-wallet and sent the payment over. The bouncer's link chirped, and he jerked his head toward the door. "Don't cause no trouble. I'm not in the mood for any shit tonight."

"Thanks, pal." Fischer gave the man a three-fingered salute as he passed.

Inside was much like every other bar Fischer had ever visited. Dim, pale lights illuminated a central square bar where a few patrons sat in relative silence, nursing their choice drink. Others sat around tables, eating food that Fischer was sure couldn't be healthy for human consumption. Gaming tables were set up near the back, where a handful of patrons drank and yelled good-natured insults at each other.

The booths arranged at the far ends of the space weren't well lit, partially concealed by extremely fake-looking plants. Fischer selected one with clear avenues to the exits and watched out of the corner of his eyes as the only waitress approached.

"Can I get ya?" she asked with little interest. She was well past her prime, wearing clothes that a woman thirty years her junior probably shouldn't have been wearing. Her blue hair was messy, as if it hadn't been washed in a few days and her mascara was in need of a good touch-up.

Jones spoke in his ear. *"Is she hot? She sounds hot. I hear Tuscan girls get down like nobody's business."*

Fischer ignored his friend. "Starmaker's Light... deluxe."

The waitress eyed him for a long moment, looking him up and down, considering. Fischer wondered if the phrase he'd been given had been changed, but finally, she scratched something on her datapad.

"You want your deluxe with or without mixer?"

"With."

She nodded, making another mark. "I'll get it in."

"That's right you will," Jones said.

When the waitress was out of earshot, Fischer said, "Damn it, Jonesy, you're killing me."

"What? I was just curious! We should've wired you for picture too."

"There's not much to see, trust me."

A few minutes later the waitress brought Fischer's drink. Foam splashed onto the table as she set the clear glass down. "One deluxe."

"Thanks." Fischer scrutinized the pale yellow liquid, forcing himself not to grimace.

"Those are on special tonight; two for one," she said pointing at the glass, her link glowing around her arm. "You want to open a tab?"

"Sure."

"So, what kind of mixer you lookin' for?"

He rotated the glass. His stomach turned as the acrid smell reached his nostrils. "The long-distance kind."

"Interesting choice," the waitress made a point of scrolling through her link.

"I've got an appointment," Fischer said.

She looked up from the display, eyebrows raised. "Oh?"

"Mr. Penington."

"Penington..." She repeated, continuing to scroll. A second later, she nodded. "I'll let him know you're here."

"I appreciate it."

She left him alone with his drink, which he pushed across the table.

"It's piss isn't it?" Jones asked.

Fischer cleared his throat. "Do people actually drink this

stuff?"

"Hey, not everyone can be a classy bourbon guy like you."

"If by classy, you mean not wanting to catch a disease from whatever that shit is."

"I've had worse, I promise you. You'll live."

"I'll pass."

He watched the patrons in the back playing virtudarts. A group of heavy-set worker-types were losing to a couple of older women, and judging by the number of empty glasses on their table, they weren't too happy about it.

One slammed his half-empty glass down as his opponent threw yet another bullseye, sending a good portion of his deluxe splashing across the table and the floor. He snatched the darts from his partner's hand and took his position at the line.

Wavering slightly as he adjusted his footing, he centered himself on the projection on the back wall. The multi-colored board flickered slightly, surrounded by floating numbers and the names of the other players. He brought his shooting arm up, and his friends burst out laughing as he staggered to one side. He steadied himself against a table, cursed, then returned to the throwing line.

He raised his hand into position as a virtual dart materialized between his fingers. The board flashed from red to green and yellow letters appeared at the top wishing him good luck."

Good thing those aren't real, Fischer thought, disguising a half-grin by rubbing his cheek.

The man's first dart barely hit the board, a flash of orange that vanished just outside the boundary marker. He cursed again as his friends' laughter grew louder and brought up another dart. He took a moment to aim, then threw. The second one hit on the opposite side of the board, landing in the "10" box. The board flashed green and yellow, and the number appeared above the dart.

The group cheered. One slapped him on the shoulder, congratulating him as he brought up his last dart. The thrower shrugged his friend off, aimed, and threw.

"Don't like the deluxe either, eh?"

Fischer looked up as a tall man with close-cropped brown hair came around the side of the booth. His brown leather jacket hung open, and Fischer caught a glimpse of the small pistol tucked into the man's belt. Whether intentional or not, alarm bells sounded in the back of Fischer's mind. This was not the man he'd been expecting.

"Smells like piss."

"Tastes worse. You mind?" The man gestured to the bench across from Fischer.

"No." Fischer hesitated, then motioned for the man to sit.

Balancing a half-empty drink in one hand, he extended the other. "Nice to finally meet you, Tom."

Fischer took the hand, bells still ringing in his mind. "Do you prefer Douglas or Doug?"

The man pretending to be Douglas Feringer shrugged. "Either way. My mother always used to call me Douglas when I got in trouble, but... she's gone now, so I guess it doesn't really matter."

"Doug then."

The man nodded. "I didn't think you were going to show."

Ironic, Fischer thought. *Considering the real Feringer didn't.* "Gotta make a living somehow."

"You okay, Fish?" Jones asked in his ear.

"Don't we all," Fake Feringer said, taking a sip. "Don't we all."

"I have to be honest though, I'm not sure I really like meeting in person like this," Fischer said. "Too many opportunities for the wrong kind of people to listen in."

"I'm on my way," Jones said, picking up on Fischer's meaning.

Fake Feringer set his glass down, then waved a hand through the air. "Fucking cops. They never come down here. Not even the hard up ones. Too many…" He trailed off, looking up at the ceiling. "… incidents."

Fischer sniffed. "Incidents, huh? You kind of sound like one."

Fake Feringer's face went still, his eyes locking on to Fischer's. "You saying I'm a cop?"

"Are you?"

The man considered Fischer for several beats, as if he could peer through his eyes and into his soul. Finally, a half grin spread across Fake Feringer's face. "Are you?'

Fischer gave the imposter a matching grin. "Can't ever be too sure, can you?"

Fake Feringer snorted and shook his head. "No, no you can't." He finished off his drink in one long pull, then carefully set the empty glass on the table between them. He nodded to Fischer's drink. "You mind?"

"It's yours. Two for one if you want another."

"That's my kind of deal."

"Okay, I'm here," Jones said.

"Speaking of deals," Fischer said, glancing around the bar, then finally back to Fake Feringer. "I'm sure you won't mind if I asked to see the specs before releasing the credits."

The imposter finished his sip, wiped his mouth with the back of one hand and said, "Why would I mind?"

"BTRs aren't cheap. Some people get kinda touchy about stuff like that."

"Pride," Fake Feringer said, pulling out a lightweight datapad. "Its great most of the time. Let's people know you're not a pushover. But sometimes, it just gets in the way."

He tapped in a command, then held it out for Fischer to see. Half the display showed a wireframe diagram of a Jumpspace Beam Transmission Relay, its cylindrical body slowly rotating on its axis. The other half contained several lines of text identifying make and model and other technical information Fischer didn't understand.

Fischer took a moment to read over the rest of the specs. "That's pretty impressive. Must have been a bitch liberating them."

Fake Feringer shrugged. "A bribe to a custom guy here, threaten a warehouse worker there. These things sell themselves."

"Yeah, I guess they do."

"So," Fake Feringer said, slipping the pad back into the inside pocket of his jacket. "What's the URT need with military grade relays? I mean I know why they need them, but in your position, I'd think weapons would be a higher priority."

Fischer raised an eyebrow. "My position?"

The imposter laughed. "The URT." He shook his head. "With all the shit you've been taking from the Pegasi lately. I mean, they've practically started a war without firing a shot. How many worlds they occupy now?"

"A couple." Fischer knew the exact number, but the conversation was starting to go places he didn't want to tread. He canted his head to one side. "You ask a lot of questions."

Fake Feringer lifted his hands from the tabletop, palms out. "Hey, just being friendly. You just want to get to it, let's get to it." He slid a credit chip onto the table. "Fifteen."

"Fifteen?"

"Each?"

"We discussed twelve."

"Shit happens," Fake Feringer said with a shrug. "Costs go up. Security fees, transportation, you know how it is. This economy's a bitch."

"I can get the units from Hammersmith for half that."

"Maybe. But they'd be shit. These are top of the line, straight from the manufacturer, never been used before." He raised a finger. "And untraceable. I'd be willing to bet Hammersmith can't beat that."

Fischer considered the man, giving the impression he was mulling the deal over. As price went, fifteen million for military grade BTRs was a stellar deal, especially when accounting for the manpower and logistics in transporting a yacht-sized piece of equipment through system without being detected. He reminded himself to check the transit logs for the last month. Chances were, the freighter would be there.

"Well?" Fake Feringer asked. "Do we have a deal?"

"They just pulled the bouncer off the entrance," Jones said. *"Two cars pulled up out back. Looks like they're loading someone into the second one. I'm guessing it's Feringer."*

Fischer stole a glance toward the bar, where the bartender was leaning over, talking with two other men. The group playing darts had stopped their game and were now clustered together in quiet conversation. Another two men at the far end of the bar had full mugs, both looking at a screen Fischer couldn't see. He left his gaze on them for a moment longer and just as he looked away, the eyes of the nearest man turned his direction.

That was quick, Fischer thought. *No honor among thieves.* "I'm only concerned about one thing."

"Six more just went in through the back," Jones said. *"Loomis is tracking the car."*

"Yeah," Fake Feringer said. "What's that?"

Fischer brought his gaze back to the imposter. "What did you do with Douglas Feringer?"

The imposter froze and time stood still. Fischer flicked his wrist, sliding his Fleet Intelligence badge onto the table.

Fake Feringer twisted, hand reaching for his waistband. "Fucking co—"

Fischer lashed out, fist smashing into the man's nose. There was a wet crack, and the imposter let out a painful cry. His head snapped back, smacking into the back of the booth.

"Now Jonesy!" Fischer lunged forward, practically diving across the table, sending both empty glasses flying. He drove one fist into Fake Feringer's face, connecting hard with back of the imposter's hand as it came up to defend his destroyed nose. The hand cushioned Fischer's punch, but the distraction was all he needed. He grabbed for the man's weapon, sliding forward, pushing the bench back. His fingers wrapped around the gun just as they toppled backward onto the floor.

Fischer pulled the weapon free as he rolled over Fake Feringer. He stopped himself, turning as the imposter scrabbled to his feet, then Fischer lunged again, ramming his shoulder into the man's chest.

Fake Feringer gave out a loud "oomph" as he stumbled back into the wall. Fischer hit him again, connecting hard with his gut, trying to knock the wind out of him. His second punch did the trick, and the imposter dropped to a knee, gasping for air.

Fischer stole a look over both shoulders. At the bar, the man who'd made eye contact with Fischer slid off his stool, reaching, eyes locked on Fischer. His partner next to him was already on his feet and moving. The group by the virtudarts was spreading out as well.

Too many.

He maneuvered himself behind Fake Feringer, twisting the man's arm up at a painful angle. He pinned the imposter's wrist between his shoulder blades and wrenched.

"Ahhh!" Fake Feringer screamed, lifting up on his toes.

Fischer brought the pistol up, switching between the bar group and the dart group. "Don't even think about it! Fleet Intelligence, we've got the place surrounded."

The men at the bar froze. The closest stopped, mid-drawl, and said, "You're making a huge mistake."

Fischer leveled his sights on him, shaking his head. "It doesn't have to go down like this. We can all go home tonight."

In his periphery, the bar group was continuing to fan out, trying to flank him. He eyed the had-been-drunk man, now spry on his feet, pistol held in stone-like fingers. Fischer shifted his position so Fake Feringer would be between them and the man's aimed weapon.

"Don't."

The man froze, eyes filled with hate. "You're a dead man, law. Just don't know it yet."

"Put it down, or your boy here gets the first one." Fischer put the barrel to Fake Feringer's head, just behind his ear.

"Put it down," Fake Feringer ordered.

The man hesitated, obviously considering his options, but didn't drop his weapon.

"Damn it, Wilson! Put the fucking thing down!" Fake Feringer shouted.

Slowly, the man bent and set his pistol on the floor, never taking his eyes off Fischer.

"That's better," Fischer said. "Now, I'm going to walk out of here, and I'm bringing your boss with me, and you all are just going to stand back and relax, and when we're gone, feel free to have a couple of those godawful beers on me. Everyone on the same page?"

Fischer sidestepped away from the ruined booth, taking care to keep Fake Feringer as a shield. "Jonesy, where you at?"

"Right above you."

Fischer felt the floor begin to vibrate and heard the muffled thumping from Jonesy's sprinter.

"Hear that?" Fischer asked as the thugs looked up at the ceiling. He continued toward the front door. "That's an FI assault shuttle. I'm telling you, it's not looking good for you guys. Best thing would be just to relax."

"You're a dead man, law," The drunk dart thrower repeated.

"Yeah, you said that already."

"You're making a big mistake," Fake Feringer said, his broken nose distorting his words.

"I get that a lot."

He reached the door and stopped. "Now, I'm going to let your hand go for just a second. It'll go a lot easier for you if you don't fucking move, got it?"

Fake Feringer sniffed and nodded.

Fischer released the imposter's hand slowly, then when he was sure the man wasn't moving, he reached back and twisted the handle.

Fischer "Now, that wasn't that—"

Fake Feringer slammed his back into Fischer. Pain shot through Fischer's head as his skull smacked against the doorframe. Stars flashed in his vision and the room spun.

"Kill the bastard!" Fake Feringer screamed, throwing himself forward, away from Fischer's grasp.

Half dazed, Fischer twisted himself around the doorframe as multiple gunshots rang out. Wood splintered, spraying in all directions as Fischer tumbled out of the bar, landing on the pavement outside.

He rolled into several passersby, knocking one down with a cry of surprise and pain.

"The hell?" a man shouted, backing away.

"Get back!" Fischer yelled as more shots erupted from inside the Starmaker Tavern.

The cacophony of gunfire sent the crowd outside into a panic. People screamed and took off in random directions, bumping into each other, causing even more chaos.

Hot air blasted him from above. Landing lights blinked on, bathing the street in bright white light, turning it from night to day.

Fischer scrambled to his feet. Sparks erupted from a passing car as bullets riddled its side. Its repulser pads flared as the driver increased power and turned away from the incoming fire. The driver, obviously panicked, missed the car parked on the side of the road and slammed into it, sending it careening off the street and into the glass storefront of a coffee shop.

People ducked, screaming as glass shattered and sprayed.

"Jonesy get your ass down here!" Fischer shouted over the chaos. He moved behind a red sports car, using its sleek lines for cover and brought the pistol up, covering the door.

"I'm coming, I'm coming. Keep your pants on."

Dart Thrower appeared in the door, his pistol back in his hand, eyes searching. He brought his free hand up, blocking the light from the sprinter's landing lights, then raised his pistol.

Fischer squeezed off three rounds. The first took the man in the shoulder, spinning him back through the door. The other two smacked into the frame, splintering the wood.

The wind kicked up behind Fischer as the sprinter descended to the street, the ramp under the cockpit already hanging open.

"Come on!" Jones shouted.

Fischer checked the door once more, then sprinted for the ramp.

Several shots rang out, and sparks erupted from the sprinter's hull. Fischer ducked, twisted, and returned fire, sending a spray of bullets back at them.

"I got 'em!" Jones said.

As Fischer's boots hit the steel ramp, an earsplitting *bap bap bap* echoed around him. Pressure waves from the sprinter's nose gun pounded against him as he climbed up the ramp.

The deck shifted underneath him. When he reached the small cargo bay, Fischer grabbed a rail next to him and pulled himself away from the opening.

"I'm in!"

The sprinter's engines roared. Fischer turned back to watch the street drop away. The front of the bar, now burning, was covered in smoke. What he could see had been almost completely destroyed by the ship's cannon.

"Jesus, Jonesy, you didn't have to obliterate the place."

"Hey, I can drop you back down there if you want?"

"I'm okay, thanks."

Fischer backed away from the ramp as it closed with a hydraulic whine. He slapped the handrail with his palm, wincing as a sharp pain shot through his arm. "I had him! I had him, and I fucking lost him!"

"Eh, you'll get him again," Jones said.

"I have to figure out who he was first," Fischer said, heading to the ladder near the back of the bay. "Where's Feringer?"

His question was met with silence.

"Jonesy?"

"We lost him, brother."

"Son of a bitch."

At the top of the ladder, Fischer pulled himself into the ship's bridge. Tensley Jones sat in an elevated chair, the base of which sat at Fischer's shoulder. Greg Loomistripoli sat at the most forward station, working the ship's tactical controls.

Fischer put a hand on the base of Jones's chair. "How's the traffic now?"

Jones had one hand pressed against his earphone, the other held the ship's flight controls. "Well, they aren't quiet anymore, I can tell you that."

Jones's voice echoed in his implant. He tapped the link's interface on the back of his left hand, shutting it down. "Shit."

"Any idea who that clown back there was?" Loomis asked over his shoulder.

"No clue." Fischer climbed into the co-pilot seat opposite Jones's and strapped himself in.

"Your boss isn't going to be happy about this."

Fischer checked the time on his watch. "It's not my boss I'm worried about."

Jones laughed. "Carissa going to kick your ass?"

"When she sees the news and puts two and two together, yeah… shit's going to hit the fan."

"You didn't tell her you were coming out here?"

Fischer tilted his head and said, "What do you think?"

"You're a brave man."

"I owe you one."

"One?" Jones said with a smile. "More like a hundred."

CHAPTER 2

Fischer's Apartment
Blue Lake City, New Tuscany
3 Apr 2607

The distinct lack of background noise alerted Fischer to the danger before he saw it. He turned away from the morning news, saw disaster approaching, and even as he started across the kitchen to avert it, knew it would be too late.

"No!" His fingers were centimeters from the bowl when it tipped, spilling milk and cereal across the table. The liquid, stained red and yellow and orange, ran over the edge, flowing to the floor below.

Fischer grabbed the bowl, biting his lip in an effort to hold back the string of curses threatening to explode forth. He eyed the culprit with a knowing stare, projecting his displeasure, but the target of his frustration didn't seem to be bothered in the slightest.

"Da Da," Maddie said, banging her pink spoon against the table, splashing milk.

Careful not to snatch—Carissa had chided him more than

once about *snatching*—Fischer gingerly *took* the spoon from his daughter. "No, no, Maddie. We don't spill our cereal."

"Da Da." She smiled.

Straightening her bowl in one hand, spoon in the other, he fought the urge to smile back at his sweet girl's face. "You're ridiculous, you know that? You aren't going to get away with that forever."

"Mmmm," Maddie said, pointing at him.

"No." Fischer shook his head. "You're not."

"You're not what?"

Fischer turned, keeping the right side of his face where he'd face planted into the doorframe concealed as Carissa entered the kitchen, naked, damp hair still wrapped in a towel. He forgot about the bowl and spoon and the mess waiting to be cleaned. "Now, that's just not called for at all."

Carissa gave him a look of mock concern. "I'm sure I have no idea what you're talking about."

"You know exactly what I'm talking about."

She lifted her nose and closed her eyes as she passed him. "I'm just getting ready for work."

"Sure you are." He tossed the bowl and spoon into the sink and leaned forward, gazing hungrily over his wife. Even after giving birth, she still maintained the same athletic body she'd rocked in college. His eyes lingered on her. He bit his bottom lip and shook his head. *Ridiculous.*

She opened her eyes and saw the mess. "Now what is going on here?" She squatted down in front of Maddie, who sat secured in her booster, and used the edge of her towel to wipe milk from the girl's face. "Daddy gave you a bowl of cereal, didn't he? Even though Daddy knows you can't be trusted with things like that."

"I—" Fischer started. His cochlear implant emitted a soft chime, and a small holographic panel appeared over the back of his hand. Dan Carter, Division Chief for ASI's New Tuscany field office was calling. *A little early, isn't it, boss.* He reached to tap the panel, then hesitated, thinking better of it. The ass chewing he knew was coming could wait. He swiped the link panel away, ignoring the call.

"Oh, it's okay," Carissa continued. "Mommy doesn't have anything better to do before work, does she?"

"Da da."

Carissa stood, glaring at Fischer. "The least she could do when I'm defending her is say the correct name."

Fischer turned a bit more. "What can I say? She's a daddy's girl."

"Mmhmm. This morning she is, tonight she won't be."

She moved past him, swatting his shoulder at the last minute. Fischer gasped and recoiled, reaching up to protect himself.

Carissa froze, frowning. "What's wrong?"

Fischer straightened. "Nothing."

She lifted his shirt, revealing the dark bruise still spreading across his upper back and shoulder. "What the hell did you do?"

Fischer turned away, yanking his shirt down over the injury. "It's nothing, really."

"Nothing? That thing is enormous!" She grabbed his face and turned it toward her. "Your eye. I thought you said it was only a surveillance op?"

"It was!"

"Bullshit, Jackson. I know better. What happened?"

Before he could stop them, his eyes flicked to the small display on the counter behind his wife. She turned in time to see the camera view switch from the reporter standing on the side of the road, smoke rising behind him, to an aerial shot of the Starmaker Tavern, its front entrance completely demolished.

The fire had consumed most of the building, turning the front of the bar into little more than a charred skeleton. Several first responders were still combing through the rubble as fire drones still hovered above the building, spraying fire suppressant on the remaining portions of the building. A line of ambulances sat on the street a block away, and Fischer grimaced as the camera zoomed in on one of the medical crews, treating one of the women who'd been playing virtudarts. They'd wrapped a blanket around her shoulders, her hair was matted and dirty, her face smeared with dirt and grime.

Carissa pointed at the counter where a holodisplay now showed Emma Monroe, host of IND63's Early Morning Show. "That! You did that? Tell me that wasn't you!"

"Well, technically…"

Carissa held up a hand. "Jackson Everett Fischer, I don't want to hear it from you. I really don't. I cannot believe you." She turned back to the display, watching as the Tavern was projected in three dimensions. "Is that the Black District?"

Fischer didn't answer. She turned, a look of horror on her face. "It is! What the hell is Carter thinking, sending you in there?"

"It wasn't Carter's deal," Fischer said, immediately regretting it. Carissa's face darkened as she realized what that meant. She opened her mouth to respond, but he cut her off. "Listen, it was supposed to be an easy, in-and-out deal. Admittedly, it got a little out of hand."

"A little out of hand? You could have been killed."

"I'm fine, really."

Carissa glared at him. "You promised."

Fischer felt the air leave his sails. He looked down at the floor. "I know. Look, I'm sorry. But I had a lead on this…"

"I don't care. Jackson. You can't go charging into shit like this anymore. You've got a family now. You can't just…" she trailed off, eyes still focused on Fischer, as if she'd just made the connection. "What do you mean it wasn't Carter's deal? You didn't go in there by yourself, did you?"

Shit, Fischer thought, his stomach turning. "No. Look I told you, it was just a—"

"If you weren't there by yourself, who'd you take with you? Was Woody with you? Don't tell me you dragged her along."

There wasn't any hiding it. *She knows already,* Fisher told himself. "I—"

His wife's face turned to stone. "You told me…"

Blood pounded in Fischer's ears. He opened his mouth to explain but no words came. His stomach lurched at the sight of his wife's hurt expression, and he knew there wasn't anything he could say to make it right.

"You lied to me." Her voice was a whisper now.

"I didn't, I…"

Carissa held up a hand, silencing him, then turned away. "No, I can't do this right now."

She left him with only the sound of the Early Morning Show playing in the background. He turned back to Maddie, who despite their argument, was still smiling. She waved at him. "Da Da."

He smiled back. "Mommy isn't happy with Da Da right now."

The newsfeed finished its story on the Starmaker, switching back to the anchors sitting in plush leather chairs, each one appearing on his countertop like invited guests.

An older, white haired man, sat with his legs crossed, holding a pad in one hand, shaking his head as his co-anchor capped off the previous story. He wore a baby blue suit and bright yellow shoes that flashed every time he moved. "That's just terrible."

"It really is, Larry," the woman, dressed in a tight, purple and black, low-cut dress said. "I know it's called the Black District for a reason, but you'd think the local police would be able to get a handle on the activity in the area eventually."

Larry nodded. "You'd think."

The woman turned to face the camera. "In other news, and

kind of on the opposite end of the spectrum, our own Senator Beilman, has doubled down on his stance for limited government and freedoms for the people."

Fischer shook his head. "It's crazy that it's even necessary to have that position."

"That's right, June," Larry added. "It's been his platform ever since being elected to the Alliance Senate four years ago—a stance, he says, that has served him and his constituents well."

The feed switched to a new clip. Marcus Beilman, a middle-aged man, with thinning auburn hair and goatee, gripped the edges of the podium with both hands. His conservative black suit didn't yet show the signs of office like his counterparts in the Alliance—it still fit relatively comfortably.

"There are some among my colleagues that would prefer you have no freedoms at all, that to ensure your security and safety, you must give up certain liberties and rights. I believe you should have both freedom and safety, liberty and security. At what point does sacrificing our privacy become too much? Yes, there are evil people out there in the galaxy, people which our brave men and woman of the military and police forces fight against day in and day out, but those people have always been present in society. It's nothing new. We will continue the fight against them and hold the line between chaos and prosperity."

The feed switched back to the anchors.

June continued, "Beilman's speech comes a day after Senator Kramer presented his plan for enhanced military controls for system security around New Tuscany, a plan that would effec-tively require all JumpLane traffic to submit to inspection by Naval personnel. 'My New Safe Plan,' Kramer says, 'is a step toward guaranteeing the safety of the people who've elected us to do so.'

"There are others, like the group Revolution 52, whose oppo-sition to the Senator's ideas go a step further than simply voicing their opinions over the—" She paused, frowning, hand moving to her ear.

Larry turned and looked offstage, obviously as confused as his co-anchor. He turned to face the camera a moment later, took a moment to compose himself, then said, "I'm sorry, viewers, we have to interrupt this story, to bring you breaking, exclusive news from the Rim. But we must warn you, the footage you are about to see is unedited and may be disconcerting to some viewers."

What looked like a large apartment building was on fire, a large gaping hole had been ripped out of the structure's exterior. Drones fought fires on several levels and rescue rovers helped handfuls of survivors from the rubble. He didn't recognize the local police units, but the military shuttle that passed in front of the camera he knew immediately.

What the hell did the Pegasi do now?

"We are receiving unconfirmed reports that the explosion has killed more than fifty and several hundred more remain injured on the border world of Stonemeyer. Information exclusive to Interstellar News Direct indicates that this horrific disaster is only one of many tragic incidents to occur on the planet in the last week, starting with an apparent military action by the Holloman Alliance Military.

"We've reached out for confirmation, but so far have received no response. Several sources on the ground, however, have indicated that in the early morning hours of 26 March ESC, several Alliance military personnel were observed engaging local security forces around the Holloman Embassy. That, however, has also not been confirmed."

Fischer's eyebrows knitted together as the footage switched, showing what he guessed was the Embassy. The complex filled almost four city blocks. Well-manicured lawns, trees, and decorative landscaping surrounded a modern six-story structure, all of which was protected by an eight-foot security wall topped with plasma fence. There were definite signs that a battle had played out across the bailey. Fischer reached and spun the holo, rotating the view. On the street, just outside the perimeter, he could see the remains of some kind of dropship, still smoking.

"A source within the Pegasi Peacekeeper detachment assigned to Stonemeyer has confirmed that there was an incident but declined to elaborate as their investigation was still in the very early stages."

"This is bad," Fischer whispered to himself.

His link chimed again as Carter's name rolled into view over the back of his hand. Fischer glanced down at the name glowing above his skin and sighed. He accepted the call.

"Fischer," he said, muting the newsfeed.

"Jackson where the hell have you been? I've been calling."

"Sorry, I was—"

"Forget it, I need you in the office five minutes ago. Drop whatever you're doing and head this way, Woody's already on her way."

"Look boss about last—"

"I don't want to hear about it," Carter said, cutting Fischer off. "Just get here."

The link disconnected, the panel over his hand vanishing.

"Da Da."

Fischer smiled at his daughter. "At least you're not mad at me."

Maddie slapped the table with both hands, saying something only she could understand.

"Exactly."

CHAPTER 3

Alliance Security and Intelligence,
New Tuscany Field Office
New Tuscany
3 Apr 2607

Fischer throttled down as he made his final approach, eyes only partly focused on the landing platform's mark lights. Rain pounded against the gravbike's forcefield, making lavender ripples across the energized bubble. Fischer hated the rain, but hated the New Tuscany heat even more, and welcomed the overcast skies and cooler temperatures.

The gravbike's repulser pads kicked up a torrent of water and wind as he flared slightly, descending down to the platform. A second later, he kicked the bike's stand into place and swiped the back of his hand across the bike's controls, using his link to key in his lock code. A small display flashed red and the bike went into standby mode.

He dropped the forcefield, allowing rain to beat against his helmet and leather jacket as he dismounted.

A shadow played across the pad as a compact gray cab landed

three stalls away. Its engines spun down, settling on its pads. The side door slid open and Aniyah Eliwood, Fischer's partner, climbed out.

"What are you, crazy?" Eliwood shouted, jogging away from the shuttle, her jacket held above her in a vain attempt to block the rain.

Fischer held both arms out. "What?"

She shook her head. "You are crazy!"

She ran past, heading for the building's entrance. Fischer laughed and followed. Once inside, she shook her jacket off. Her shoulder length auburn hair was pulled back in a messy ponytail. She brushed water off her black suit coat and trousers and folded her jacket over one arm, glaring at him.

Fischer pulled his helmet off and unzipped his jacket. "A little water never hurt anyone."

"You know the rain has been known to play hell with those things, right? Two people fell right out of the sky last year because of fouled intakes."

Fischer swiped the back of his hand over the square panel next to the door security panel, allowing his link to interface with the security protocols. The lock opened with a soft click, and he held the door open for his partner.

"Flukes. Bikes were poorly maintained. The riders were amateurs. Or both. It's perfectly safe."

"Uh huh, and what does Carissa say about it?"

Fischer laughed. "She's fine with it."

"Sure, she is."

The Agency lobby was empty, save for a single reception desk, which at this early hour, was unmanned. The Alliance Crest, a ringed planet flanked by wings with a starburst rising above it, was emblazoned on the far wall. The Alliance Security and Intelligence Agency motto, *SECURUS VERITATI STELLAE* written beneath it, "Secure truth, as the stars lie."

Eliwood swiped the back of her hand over the scanner next to the door. The lock clicked open, and she led them through. Unlike the lobby, the Alliance Security and Intelligence Central Operations Division's main offices were bustling with activity. Agents, analysts, technicians, section supervisors, were all in the middle of what looked like full-blown panic. Some shouted questions, others called back answers, and still others rushed between sections collecting papers to shuttle to another section.

Eliwood hesitated. "What the hell is going on?" She looked over her shoulder as she started through the chaos. "Did Carter tell you anything?"

"Nothing."

Nathan Campbell, lead agent for Western Region, Analysis Division, looked up from where he stood over an analyst who was busy reading lines of text on the screen in front of him. "Where have you guys been? Carter's been screaming for you for an hour."

"Got here as quick as we could," Eliwood answered without stopping.

"What the hell's going on, Nate?" Fischer turned and walked backward for the agent's response.

Campbell shook his head. "Shit's hit the fan, that's what."

Fischer frowned. "Okay?" He turned back around and followed Eliwood through the maze of desks, picking up bits and pieces from a dozen conversations as they made their way to Carter's office at the far end of the floor.

A potential attack. A failed mission. Dead Marines. Images from the newscast flashed through Fischer's mind, and he started to put the pieces together. It was worse than he thought.

Carter's office door opened before they reached it and Allison Blair, section lead for Sector 3 exited. She eyed Fischer and Eliwood, shook her head, and said "Good luck" under her breath.

Daniel Carter looked up from behind his desk, the glow of his link's holopanels reflecting off his face. He did not look pleased. "I'll call you back."

He tapped his link.

The Division Chief looked like he hadn't slept in a week. He hadn't shaved, making the goatee he usually sported look more like a poorly kempt beard. His bald head glistened, sweat running down his caramel colored skin. His tie was undone, hanging loosely around his neck, the shirt collar unbuttoned.

"Where the hell have you two been?" Fischer started to answer, but Carter waved him off. "Get in here! Close the door."

"What's going on, boss?" Eliwood asked, tossing her jacket over the back of one of two chairs facing Carter's desk.

Carter didn't answer immediately. Instead, he sat rubbing his face with both hands. Rain pelted the windows of his corner office, which unlike most division chiefs, was completely devoid of any decor, plaques, or pictures. A single pewter baby shoe sat on his desk, datapads covering it.

"And weren't we supposed to be going padless?" Eliwood said.

"Not now, Aniyah, please." Carter pinched the bridge of his nose, then swiped a finger on the back of his hand, and a holo-projection appeared on the wall to his left.

I knew it, Fischer thought. Images of the burning building he'd seen on the news footage earlier appeared, shot from several different angles and times. Fire drones floated over the building, coving it in yellow spray foam.

For the first time, Fischer noticed it was actually two separate buildings, one had fallen into the other. Carter moved to the wall, swiping several images away until he found the one he wanted.

"The Klausmeyer Building, Calibri City on Stonemeyer," Carter said, tapping his link again. A holographic planet appeared in front of the ever-changing stream of images, rotating slowly on its axis. Seeing the confusion on their faces, Carter continued,

"Never heard of the place, huh? Don't blame you, this morning was the first time I'd ever heard the name. Colonized in 2467, joined the URT in 2501. Pulled out of the URT three years ago, declaring themselves truly independent with no connection to the URT leadership at all. It's currently under Pegasi military occupation."

Eliwood grunted, crossing her arms. "You mean *peacekeeping*."

"Which side of the URT?" Fischer asked.

The United Rim Territories spanned one of the biggest areas of known space in the galaxy. The URT's founders proclaimed it as the last "truly independent" holdout of humanity, though in truth, it was nothing more than a collection of loosely organized planets, extracting money from whoever and wherever they could. The URT bore more resemblance to the Wild Wild West of Old Earth than anything else.

On the galactic map, it was situated directly between the Pegasi Empire and the Holloman Alliance, making the systems it contained highly valuable targets for annexation for both superpowers.

The Holloman Alliance, of which New Tuscany was one of the founding worlds, consisted of five member worlds and while relatively small, it was one of the wealthiest star nations in the galaxy. It held mutual-aid treaties with many of the non-aligned worlds along their side of the URT, providing security in exchange for access and travel through their systems.

It was in the URT core systems where the Alliance and Pegasi Empire played most of their games. Over the last twenty years, there'd been countless confrontations and engagements between the two, but never anything that would've been a full-scale conflict. And despite those conflicts, the Alliance had never officially declared war on the Empire, both governments content with letting the hostilities continue ad nauseum.

For its part, the Empire would've preferred war to the occasional confrontations. The Most High Emperor Sasidon ruled over his people with an iron fist, demanding sacrifice and service from every single one of his subjects. His regime, unlike previous emperors, had proven to be much more expansionistic in their pursuits, and over the last five years, had annexed—or conquered—many of the non-aligned worlds on their side of the URT. It was only a matter of time before all-out war commenced, and when it finally did, it would be devastating.

"It's right smack dab in the middle," Carter said. He flicked his finger again, and a small fleet appeared orbiting the planet, the Pegasi Crest, rotating slowly. "Which makes this extremely problematic."

"How long do they think the 'peacekeeping' line's going to work?" Eliwood asked, miming air quotes.

"For a long as we let them," Fischer said.

"Bastards are going to land on the wrong planet one day and get their asses kicked all the way back to their side of the galaxy." Eliwood shook her head. "For the life of me, I don't understand why the Alliance doesn't do anything to stop them. It's not like we don't have the firepower to get our point across."

"It doesn't have anything to do with firepower," Fischer said. "It all comes down to will. They have none. The only senator with enough balls to even suggest such a thing won't because he knows it'll get shot down on the Floor before it's even brought to a vote."

"Kramer's not the only one who thinks getting rid of the Pegasi is a good thing," Eliwood said.

"No, but there's a lot more who don't want to see this come to war," Fischer said. "War is bad for more people than it's good for."

"Regardless," Carter said, nodding to the wall of images behind him. "This incident is going to be the headline and lead story for every news outlet in the galaxy. We need to be on top of it and be ready for anything."

"So, what's so special about this Stonemeyer place?"

"Other than its position?" Carter asked. "Nothing. They have a relatively small population, and a history of remaining neutral, in regard to us and the Pegasi. They don't export much—some alcohol and solid fuels mostly. I do know we've been pushing hard for annexation for a couple of years, for obvious reasons."

"What's the hold up?" Fischer asked. "I mean, most of the non-aligned worlds tend to lean away from the Pegasi on general principle. Seems like they're between a rock and hard place. I'd think that decision wouldn't be difficult."

"You'd think that," Carter said. "But I honestly have no idea. I have Campbell and Task Force 3 working on those concerns as we speak. For now, however, none of that matters. The only thing that matters for us is this."

The planet and Pegasi warships vanished, leaving only the streaming images of death and destruction. Carter flicked a finger, and another building appeared, Fischer read the tag at the bottom of the image.

"The Alliance Embassy? Who in their right mind would attack our Embassy?"

"We did."

CHAPTER 4

Carter's Office,
ASI Division Headquarters
New Tuscany
3 Apr 2607

The images on Carter's wall showed sections of blasted perimeter walls, scorched earth, destroyed windows and several smoking holes in the side of the building. The compound was crawling with what looked like local police forces and Pegasi military. Most of the locals had been relegated to the outer perimeter, while the larger, better-equipped military assessed the battle damage.

Before Fischer could ask, Carter raised a hand. "I know what you're going to say, and let me just tell you, I don't know any of the details. We received a very short, very basic brief from *Vision's* CO when they dropped out of their lane, but that's it. These images were brought in by a Galactic News Service sprinter, loaded straight into the New Tuscany network node. Beat the cruiser by almost five hours."

Fischer whistled. "They were moving."

Carter nodded. "Indeed."

"That's one of ours," Eliwood said, pointing to the wreckage of an Albatross dropship. She was the only one in the room that hadn't served in the Alliance military. "Isn't it?"

"It is," Carter confirmed. "Destroyed during a rescue operation, launched by *Vision* to extract the local ambassador and his team. I received flash traffic from Regional Command Authority two hours ago, they're on their way here now."

"Okay," Fischer said, moving closer to the images, rubbing his beard. "So, what are we looking at here?"

Carter took a long breath. "On the surface, it's obvious the extraction went wrong. As to why—that's what we need to find out. I want to be able to brief the RCA when he gets here."

"How much time do we have?" Fischer asked.

"Two, maybe three days."

"Not a lot of time," Eliwood said.

"No," Carter agreed. "It's not."

Fischer leaned forward, reading one of the timestamps. "This image is eleven days old."

"That's right. The attack on the Embassy happened eleven days ago. The Klausmeyer building exploded four days ago. Apparently, the Embassy wasn't as newsworthy as the civilian apartment building."

"*Vision*," Fischer said, trying to place the name. "Light cruiser, right?"

"That's right." Carter tapped his link display. "Second Fleet, assigned to Sector Seventeen, according to the roster."

"Second Fleet?" Fischer's blood pounded in his ears as he made the connection.

Carter looked at him, eyebrows raised. "I know what you're thinking, and I want you to let it go right this second. He doesn't have any bearing on this investigation. *At all*."

Fischer's chest tightened, and he had to force himself to take a long, calming breath. Second Fleet fell under the command of one Admiral Marcus Young, a seasoned commander that was known to put his own ambitions ahead of anyone else's. Fischer had experienced that firsthand while serving with him aboard the ANS *Paladin*. Ironically, that was the very same assignment in which he'd met Carter, who had started him on a path to joining ASI.

"That son of a bitch just won't go away."

"Like I said, he doesn't have anything to do with this investigation. Put him out of your mind for now."

"I find it hard to believe," Fischer said. "Second Fleet is Young's baby. Nothing happens aboard any of his ships without him knowing anything and everything about it."

Carter shook his head. "Regardless, he's on his way here, and despite your personal feelings about him, I want to provide him with a full briefing when he arrives."

Fischer chewed on his lower lip. "Son of a bitch."

"He's the least of our worries right now. Finding out why the hell this mission went to shit, that's all we care about. Got it?" Carter leveled a finger at Fischer. "I know you and Young have a history. Forget about that shit right now, this isn't the time for eye poking."

Fischer raised his hands in mock surrender. "Wouldn't even think about it."

"You're a horrible liar."

"See," Eliwood said. "I keep trying to tell you. But do you listen? Noooo."

"So, what?" Fischer asked. "We interview the crew, talk to the Marines that were on the ground. Shouldn't be that hard to piece together. The longest part will be all the interviews, how many of us are you putting on the case?"

"Just you two."

Fischer coughed. "Two? Are you kidding me? There has to be —what—thirty Marines to interview, at least. That's going to take more than five days, much less five hours. Not to mention the ship's crew and officers."

"There's three."

Fischer stopped short. "What?"

"There's only three Marines. They're all pretty banged up the way I understand it. Two are in surgery right now, the female's in and out of consciousness."

"Three?" Fischer asked, still stuck on the number. "What happened to the rest of the platoon?"

"That's what we need to find out. They dropped into Calibri City, Stonemeyer's capital, early morning on 23 March. Seven days later is when these three were finally pulled out. The rest all labeled KIA."

Eliwood gasped. "All of them?"

"That's the information I got. Twelve Marines and four drop-ship pilots KIA. Plus, the Ambassador and his entire team, and an undetermined number of civilians."

"Jesus," Eliwood whispered.

"Who's the Ambassador?" Fischer asked.

Carter pushed another image onto the collection, an older, gray-haired man in a dark, high-collared suit, appeared. "Tobias Delaney. He'd been assigned to Stonemeyer for ten months. We've got a file on him, it's not very big though. All reports say he was a competent negotiator."

"Looks familiar." Then it came to him. He snapped. "Okay, now I remember this place, weren't they campaigning hard for complete independence several months back. They left the URT because of bad trade deals or something, right? This Delaney guy was pushing to get them into the Alliance."

"No idea," Carter said.

More of the memory come back to him. "Yeah, the whole

thing made it around the newsfeeds for a while. There was a big stink because no one had ever pulled out of the URT without first aligning themselves with another power."

"So, what happened?" Eliwood asked. "The Diplomatic Corps has their own ships, why didn't they just leave?"

"No one seems to know that either. The Pegasi have since suspended all unauthorized travel to and from the planet, including medical ships. The report said the Ambassador's team requested extraction, the *Vision* was the closest asset. They sent in the Marines, and things went to shit."

"And no information on why the Ambassador wanted out?" Fischer asked.

Carter shrugged. "Like I said, I got the barebones."

"Bare is right," Eliwood said.

The door opened, and Carter's assistant poked his head through. "Director Clancy is on the link for you, sir."

"Tell him I'll call him back."

"We've received multiple interview requests from the media."

"Media?" Carter barked. "How the fuck does the media know we're even involved?"

"Didn't you see the briefing, sir?" the assistant asked. "It's been playing on all the feeds. Just came in from Solomon."

"What briefing?" Carter tapped his link display, then waved a hand over the collage of images on his wall. They vanished as his hand passed over them, replaced by numerous feeds, all showing Admiral Marcus Young, standing behind a podium in his dress blacks, the stiff collar pressing into this thick neck, folds of skin almost completely concealing the red trim signifying his command. The rest of the uniform was cut to hide the man's weight. His brown hair was combed to one side, his beard neatly trimmed.

Fischer clenched his jaw, looking at the ribbons on the man's chest. While probably impressive to the casual observer, Fischer knew better. Those decorations were earned off the backs of true warriors. True patriots. Men and woman, who even on their worst day, held more honor than the man addressing the cameras.

The four golden stars on either side of the collar gleamed bright in the camera lights. Rank he hadn't as much earned as he'd stolen. And yet he wore them with obvious pride.

"The hell is this shit?" Carter stepped back, tapping his link, activating the video's sound.

Fischer's stomach turned as the man's voice came through unseen speakers.

"…and have no doubt, we will uncover the truth about this tragedy, and hold those responsible to account. I have directed the Alliance Security and Intelligence Agency to begin a complete and thorough investigation on these events, and I'm sure their work will be swift and accurate. My thoughts and prayers go out to the families of the victims and fallen soldiers, as well as the Ambassador's family. This horrific tragedy will not go unpunished. We will find those responsible, and we will make them pay. I can promise you that."

"Son of a bitch," Carter said.

"I can assure you of this," Young continued, holding up a finger. "I have my very best people on this. I am leaving this morning to give the agents on the ground all the backing my command can offer, and I'm confident that we will have more information to bring you soon."

"He has no idea what he's talking about," Eliwood said. "How the hell does he know what we'll find and what we won't."

"He doesn't," Fischer said. "He's playing up for the cameras. Besides, he knows it doesn't matter either way."

"What do you mean?"

"It's simple." Fischer shrugged. "Either we find something, or we don't. If we find something, he gets to stand in front of the cameras and tout his accomplishments like he's the one who's got results. If we don't find anything… or anything useful, he gets to put the blame squarely on our shoulders. It's a win/win for him."

"But that's bullshit," Eliwood said.

"That's how he operates," Fischer explained. "Always has. It's how he's made his career. Off the accomplishments—and failures—of everyone around him."

"Why doesn't anyone call him on it?"

"He's connected."

"Oh, come on. He can't be *that* connected."

"He is. The bastard damn-near got me booted out of the Navy."

"This is what I'm talking about," Carter said. "You can't let any of this affect the investigation. We are going to work this case like any other. I need you both on your A-game for this one, got it? It's bound to get political. We can't help that. We have to do our jobs regardless of the possible fallout."

"Fact-finding?" Eliwood asked.

"That's pretty much it. Cut and dry. What happened."

Fischer sighed, not bothering to hide his distaste for the situation. The whole thing stank. "Where do we start?"

"The Marines are being transferred to Lincoln Memorial, but I'm sure it'll be several hours before you'll get to speak with them. Your best bet now would be the *Vision* and her CO, Captain Kimball. I'm sure you'll be able to get most of what you'll need from him. He's probably not too happy right now, and that's my fault."

Fischer raised an eyebrow at his boss.

"I put the ship on Black Out status."

"Come on, boss," Fischer said. "You're killing me."

Eliwood grabbed her jacket off the chair. "If we're on the clock, we might want to get moving."

Carter nodded. "Let me know the minute you find anything I can give to Command."

"And if we don't find anything?" Fischer asked as Eliwood opened the office door.

"Find something. And Fischer..."

Fischer stopped halfway through the door. "Yeah."

"When this is over, we're going to have a long discussion about last night."

Feigning surprise, Fischer said, "I don't know what you're talking about, boss."

Carter pointed. "No surprises. Keep this thing above board. My neck's on the line just as much as yours."

"Hey, it's me," Fischer said, just before closing the door.

Carter's voice echoed out from behind it. "Exactly."

CHAPTER 5

The *Vision*
New Tuscany orbit
3 Apr 2607

"*Vision* Flight Control, this is Shuttle-927 on final, requesting clearance to dock."

Fischer leaned forward in his seat, looking past the two pilots in front of him to the warship ahead of them. He couldn't hear the response, but after a moment, the pilot nodded, and the shuttle banked to the right.

"Roger that, Control. Bay Two, confirmed. Approaching on one-seven-five." He turned, looking over his shoulder at the two agents. "We'll be on the deck in five."

Fischer gave him a thumbs up. "Thanks."

To Fischer's right, Eliwood craned her neck to look out the viewport next to her. "It's amazing that there aren't more accidents out here. Oh, shit—" She leaned away from window, then pressed her face against the plastiglass. "That was close."

Two Nemesis class fighters shot past the shuttle, falling into formation several hundred feet ahead.

"Looks like we get an escort," the pilot said.

Eliwood turned to Fischer, frowning. "Does all this security seem a little over the top to you? I mean, it just seems like it's too much."

"It does seem a little excessive," Fischer agreed, wondering if Young had anything to do with it. It certainly seemed like something he'd do, especially if it meant making life difficult for his subordinates.

"I mean, they might as well be waving a flag that says we did something, ask us about it."

"Someone obviously thinks it's bad enough to warrant the extra security. But I'm willing to bet all of this is more of a political move than anything else. They want to *look* like they're doing something. This way, there isn't any question about what's being done."

"You think Admiral Young has something to do with that?"

"Absolutely."

"You've never talked about him before," Eliwood said.

"Nothing to talk about."

"What's your beef with him then?"

"That's a long story."

Eliwood crossed her arms. "All the good ones are."

The Nemesis fighters pulled away, revealing the *Vision's* flight deck ahead. Flashing marker lights blinked around the rectangular opening and Fischer could just see the holographic plot lines overlaid against the cockpit's forward viewport.

The shuttle's engines fired, slowing the craft and a minute later, they cleared the threshold, the atmospheric forcefield flashing blue as they passed through it. The shuttle banked to the right, slowly passing over similar craft arranged in a line on the deck below. Support carts and maintenance personnel moved around the deck, busy with their assigned tasks. Only a handful stopped to consider the new arrival.

"Damn, it's pretty packed down there," the pilot said. "I don't know where the hell they expect me to park."

The cruiser's hangar bay was small compared to others Fischer had been in. A full third had been cleared off and segregated from the rest of the compartment, a single dropship sat within the cordon. A small contingent of security were arranged around it. The rest of the craft were stacked on what remained of the deck, parked almost on top of each other.

The shuttle banked again, moving away from the dropship. The co-pilot pointed at an empty spot.

"Yes, I see the spot, Control," the pilot said. "We'll be lucky if we can open the doors and not scratch the paint. Hang on back there."

The shuttle's repulser pads whined as it descended and rocked slightly as it settled on its landing struts. Fischer had his belt off before the landing sequence had finished and moved toward the hatch. Pistons hissed, and the incessant thrum from the engines whined down.

A mechanical *thunk* sounded, and the hatch unlocked, folding open. A ramp extended from the hull just behind the floor, reaching down the deck in a matter of seconds.

They were met by a man dressed in a charcoal gray Fleet utility uniform, his collar embroidered with a silver four-pointed star surrounded by three gold lines. His name and rank were displayed on a patch over his breast pocket, along with the title: Executive Officer, ANS *Vision*.

"Commander Anderson Ward," the officer said, extending a hand. "Welcome aboard the *Vision*, sir."

"Thank you, Commander. Agent Jackson Fischer. My partner Agent Eliwood."

The Commander's eyes shifted to a refueling team moving in to service the shuttle, then turned, leading them off the hangar deck. "If you'll come this way, I'll take you to see the Captain. He's expecting you."

Fischer fell into step behind the Commander, looking over his shoulder at the maintenance crew. The workers shot the agents furtive glances as they moved away from the shuttle, looking away when Fischer met their eyes.

"There a problem here?" Fischer asked, jerking a thumb at the crew.

"They're not use to having spooks on board, sir."

"We're not spooks, Commander. We're investigators. There's a difference."

"Not to them, there's not."

Eliwood leaned close. "Cheery bunch, aren't they."

"The dropship over there," Fischer said, pointing across the bay. "I'm guessing that's the bird that pulled the Marines off Stonemeyer?"

Even from a hundred yards away, the battle damage across the Albatross class dropship's fuselage was obvious. Bullet holes stitched down its length, the deck underneath was strewn with discarded gear and weapons, presumably from the rescued Marines. Fischer couldn't help but notice the bloodstains.

Ward turned, eyes shifting between Fischer and the dropship. Finally, he said, "That's right, sir. Lieutenant Powers flew that mission."

"I'll need to inspect it before I leave."

"That'll be up to the Captain," Ward said, his voice carrying the tone of finality. On a warship, the Captain was God, and no one argued with the word of God. "This way, please."

The investigators followed Ward to a hatch guarded by a pair of Marines. They wore the same charcoal gray utility uniforms as the Commander, but had black tactical vests over them. Both were armed with rifles, extra mags, comm gear, and cuffs. Pistols holstered to their legs.

A Marine with sergeant chevrons on his uniform sleeves and patch affixed to his vest, stepped forward, holding a small scanner. "Link IDs, please."

Fischer held out his hand and flicked his wrist, activating his link, connecting to the Marine's scanner. A panel appeared, displaying Fischer's face, name, and ASI credentials. After a two-tone chime, an indicator light flashed green.

Without a word, the Marine nodded and held the scanner to Eliwood. After another positive scan, he said, "You're clear for entry. Please observe all safety and security protocols while onboard. We are currently in a Level 1 Alert status. You must have a security escort with you at all times, and you are subject to search."

He stepped back and saluted Ward. "Sir."

"Carry on, Sergeant," Ward said, ducking through the hatch, leading the agents into a maze of identical corridors.

Like every other naval ship he'd ever been on, the slate gray bulkheads were utilitarian, lined with conduits, cable clusters, and access panels. On a warship, every bit of space was used, right down to the space under the crew's mattresses, usually reserved for uniforms and what little personal items they were permitted aboard.

The processed air smelled like a sterile hospital room, with none of the particulates or containments in a planetary biosphere. It brought him back to his early days in the service aboard the *Paladin*—every day a mirror image of the last. Aboard ship routine ruled. If something was a surprise, something was wrong.

They passed open shafts with ladders leading between decks and stairways along major intersections. They ducked through hatches, dodged crew hurrying between duty stations and two-man security teams, which eyed the two investigators with keen suspicion.

They made their way up three decks to one labeled "E." Two

security guards nodded to the XO as he passed, leading the investigators into the heart of the ship. The central deck on any warship was reserved for most-critical operations: engineering, vital ship functions, life support, and the command center.

The hatch to CIC was flanked by two Marine guards, each armed with a rifle. They too nodded at the XO as he passed, looking mad as hell that they'd been stuck with the duty.

"We're not going to Control then?" Fischer asked.

"The Captain is in his office, sir."

Another two turns brought them to a small alcove off the main corridor. Another pair of Marines stood guard next to a hatch marked "Captain."

"Is there always this much security onboard, Commander?" Eliwood asked.

The question wasn't completely without merit, Fischer knew, though implying lax security on any warship was a misconception. When dealing with the amount of destructive capability that these vessels could dole out, one could never go "easy" on security.

"The Captain has yet to stand down from Alert status," Ward explained. "As I'm sure you're aware, we're currently on Black Out status."

Fischer nodded. "We heard."

"We'll need to verify your clearance again," one of the Marines said, stepping forward with a hand scanner.

"The scan when we first boarded wasn't good enough?" Eliwood asked.

"Just procedure, ma'am. Sorry."

"It's fine," Eliwood said.

After running through the procedure again, the guard tapped his link. "The Fleet Intelligence officers are here to speak with you, sir."

He hesitated for a moment, listening, then nodded. "Yes, sir."

The hatch clicked, and Ward motioned for the investigators to step through, then followed as the Marines shut the door behind them.

Captain Donald Kimball sat behind a small desk, reviewing several piles of datapads. Four holoprojections lit the wall behind him, displaying maps of various ship sections. The rest of the office was filled with plaques, citations, and awards earned over a long career. The most prominent, the Protectorate's Star of Valor was centered on the bulkhead to Fischer's right, situated just above a scale model of the *Vision* that floated above a small square base on a shelf.

The Captain finished reading one pad, tapped it and set it aside, only to pick up another without looking up. His eyes darted back and forth, obviously skimming the data presented, then tapped it with a finger.

It's going to be this kind of day, is it? Fischer asked himself, watching the Captain lift another pad. The "stand and wait" routine was a tactic he was used to. Most of the Senior Commanders Fischer had met during his career utilized it in some form or another. Not having to endure that kind of behavior was one of the things Fischer most enjoyed about being out of the service.

"Engineering reports we burned through two coil rings," Kimball said, still not looking up.

Ward nodded. "Yes, sir. We're running on our secondary rings until the Black Out is lifted and Chief Potts can order replacements from Lexington."

"Understood." Kimball tossed the pad on the desk. After a second, he looked up. "That'll be all Commander."

"Aye, sir," Ward said and left without another word.

Kimball sniffed, glancing between the two agents. "I do not appreciate the Agency locking down my ship with her in desperate need of maintenance and repairs. As you can see, work does not cease. My people are professionals, Agent..."

"Fischer, sir."

"My crew understand what's expected of them and what their duty to the Navy means and I find it completely disgraceful that they're not even allowed the opportunity to contact their loved ones to let assure them they are okay. Not to mention the number of parents and wives and children I still must contact regarding their loved one not coming home."

Fischer cleared his throat. "Yes, sir. I do apologize for that, that decision was made way about my pay grade. I do understand your frustration—"

"Do you understand? I'm not sure that you do." Kimball pulled a pair of thick-framed glasses from his nose and used them as a pointer. "Let me make this crystal clear for you because I want to make completely certain you understand what's at stake here before you waste any more of my time. Not to mention my crew's. We are on the brink of war. Unless I miss my guess—which I generally do not—the Protectorate is extremely close to being caught in an all-out shooting war with the Pegasi Empire. As much as Command might think otherwise, I do not have the luxury of putting a halt on my daily ship operations at the drop of a hat, no matter what Fleet Intelligence thinks."

"I—"

"And regardless of what *you* may or may not think of me, I don't care much for what you think of me, I have an obligation to my ship and her crew, to ensure that we're ready for any engagement and my people are ready for anything that they're called to do. I don't have time to sit here and answer redundant questions.

"This mission has caused a lot of stress among my crew. They have lost, and still, they press on because the mission demands they do, but that will not last. They need time to decompress and grieve. Time they are being deprived of because someone with more planets on their shoulder than me made the decision to keep them locked down on board my ship. My men have paid the ultimate sacrifice for their world, and yet, they are relegated to boxes in the cargo hold.

"Sir," Fischer said when the Captain paused to take a breath. "Let me just say that it's not my intention to keep your people detained any longer than required. Some might not even be necessary to talk to. That being said, I do expect full cooperation from you and your crew, and if you can assure me of that, then I can promise you, we'll be off your ship as soon as we can."

Kimball set the unread pad down on his desk and leaned back in his chair. "Very well, Agent Fischer. You have ten minutes."

Fischer flicked his wrist. His link's holopanel activated and swiped through to its internal recording function. "The *Vision's* mission in Stonemeyer, what was it exactly?"

"We were three weeks into our six-week patrol in the Ulpti Corridor when the call from the Stonemeyer Embassy came in. Intelligence provided by the Embassy identified several local groups that were opposed to the idea and a few Pegasi sympathizers. But that they were experiencing increased hostile actions toward the Embassy and its staff and requested assistance."

"Did they indicate why they couldn't just leave in their Diplomatic Frigate?" Fischer asked.

"Their initial request advised that several militia groups had already attacked the Embassy and there were threats of escalated violence. The Ambassador was not prepared to move through the city without military escort. I put Lieutenant Hastings in charge of the operation."

"You only sent down one squad?"

Captain Kimball leaned forward, forearms on his desk. "Agent..."

"Fischer," he repeated.

"Agent Fischer, my men are highly trained, capable, and battle-hardened Marines. One squad was more than appropriate for the conditions and intelligence we had at the time. With the atmosphere as tense as it was, I didn't want to risk gas lighting an incident if I didn't have to."

"But it happened anyway."

Kimball glared at Fischer. "Yes."

"And this, Lieutenant Hastings?"

"By all accounts, a fine commander. I've reviewed his record, obviously. Over twenty combat drops and exemplary marks by every one of his superiors. As you might imagine, I don't have the time to get to know my men as well as I'd like."

Not that you would if you had the time, Fischer thought. "Hastings came up with the operational details?"

"That's right. A simple snatch-and-grab, nothing fancy, which is exactly why I approved the mission in the first place. Of course, in hindsight, knowing the oppositional numbers, I would never have approved it. They should've gone in with a company at full strength, local feelings be damned."

"What were their rules of engagement?"

"Standard non-engagement protocol. Fire if engaged, otherwise, no footprint. Like I said, our intelligence about the local militia forces was obviously flawed. Sergeant Thomas said they were armed with military grade weapons and gear, not a bunch of unorganized insurgents as we were led to believe."

"Who did you receive the intel from, Captain?" Eliwood asked.

"The Ambassador's team sent it along with their request for extraction. There was no reason not to believe it accurate. After the initial attack at the Embassy, my people started diving through local records, trying to get a better picture of the situation. Apparently, the militia had been causing problems for months. It's one of the reasons the Pegasi Peacekeepers had such an easy time moving in."

"Your Marines came under attack at the Embassy?" Fischer asked.

"Almost as soon as we touched down. They shot down both of our birds within the first 40 minutes. Shortly after that is when we lost contact with the extraction team. They did have the Ambassador, I know that. We had brief contact two days later, then were out of contact until we pulled them out four days ago."

"And only three were rescued?" Eliwood asked.

The Captain glared at her, jaw clenched. He shook his head. "Three fucking survivors. Three, out of twenty. And we were lucky to get them out. If it hadn't been for Lieutenant Powers, we would not have even had them."

"The dropship pilot?" Eliwood asked.

"Correct," Kimball said. "He came up with the idea that made the extraction possible and flew the mission. His operation was… not protocol, to say the least, but it worked, and we were able to get our people back. I'll be putting him in for the Star of Valor."

"I'd like to speak to him," Fischer said.

"Of course."

"I'd also like to get a look at his dropship. There's likely evidence there I'll need."

Kimball raised an eyebrow. "Evidence of what?"

"I won't know that until I inspect it."

The Captain chewed on his bottom lip for a moment, obviously considering Fischer's request. "I'll have Lieutenant Powers meet you in the hangar bay at his bird. Is there anyone else you'll want to speak with?"

"I'm not sure of that either, Captain. As we put more pieces together, I'll have a better idea."

"Yes, well, like I said before. Work aboard ship doesn't stop simply because you're here. My crew is extremely busy, so the faster you conclude your investigation, the better. Commander Ward can handle any requests you have."

"Thank you, sir."

The ship's Executive Officer was waiting for them as Fischer and Eliwood stepped out of Kimball's office. The meeting hadn't gone exactly how Fischer had imagined it in his head, but he hadn't been surprised by it either. Most warship captains were odd ducks, a result of holding the responsibility of so many souls in hand, and the billions of credits worth of equipment the ship represented.

Fischer gave the Captain a head nod as Eliwood pulled the hatch closed. "He said you'd escort us to speak with Lieutenant Powers."

Commander Ward nodded. "Follow me."

Powers stood beneath the starboard thruster nacelle of the battered Albatross Fischer had seen when they'd first arrived. Two other men, dressed in similar charcoal gray flight suits, stood near the rear cargo ramp.

"Lieutenant Powers, these ASI agents would like to speak with you," Ward said as they approached. "They have been cleared and authorized access to any and all mission documents and reports. Please accommodate them accordingly."

Fischer extended his hand, and the pilot hesitated, eyeing it with what Fischer could only guess was apprehension and perhaps a little contempt. It was never easy to talk about missions that went wrong, they were the ones you wanted to forget and never speak of again. Finally, though, Lieutenant Powers took Fischer's hand, pumping it hard.

"Yes, sir. I can do that."

Fischer motioned to Ward. "Like he said, I'm Agent Fischer, this is Agent Eliwood, we're with Alliance Security and Intel. Obviously, you know why we're here."

Powers nodded.

Fischer tapped his link. It appeared, glowing orange, around his wrist and he entered in the pilot's name and date.

"This isn't an interrogation," Fischer said, giving Ward a knowing look. "It's just an interview. I'm not looking to trip you up or catch you in a lie or anything like that. I'm just looking for the truth, that's all. I'm going to record the audio with this," he motioned to his Link, "And if you have any pertinent information on your own link, anything you think might be helpful, I'd appreciate those files as well."

"All of the mission files are stored in the bird, sir." Powers jerked a thumb at the dropship behind him.

"That's fine."

"All right," Powers said. "What do you want to know?"

"Just tell me, in your own words, what happened."

CHAPTER 6

Darkstar Six-Five
Skies above Calibri City, Stonemeyer
30 Mar 2607
Mission Time: 7days 1hrs 20mins

The whole thing was fucked from the beginning. I knew it, my copilot Inkelaar knew it, hell even Captain Kimball knew it, but there we were anyway.

It is what it is, I guess.

All things considered, our insertion was textbook. With the Albatross squawking a civilian freighter ID, we slipped past the Pegasi patrols without so much as a scan. It's not like they were looking for us, but still, if we'd've tried that in an Alliance or even Corwynn system, we wouldn't've made it a hundred kilometers.

Worked out for us though.

The coordinates for the LZ put us on the outskirts of Calibri City. It was just before dawn, and the glow from the city lights below was impressive. For a border world, Stonemeyer was a lot more developed than most others I've deployed to.

"Passive sensors up," Inkelaar said. "We should be able to see their link beacon at least. If it's on."

The flight was relatively quiet as we neared the city. The Pegasi patrols were still busy securing the area around the bombing site. Whatever caused the explosion brought down at least one building and almost another. I could see the cloud of smoke rising against the orange and pink of the early morning dawn.

"Just keep your eyes open for anything at all," I said.

We dropped below ten-thousand feet, keeping active scanners disabled. They would've lit us up like a Christmas tree otherwise. We didn't have much time to research the Stonemeyer military capabilities, and I know our sensor tech is way ahead of the Pegasi, but even if we'd seen the bastards coming, there wouldn't've been anything we could've done about it.

The Albatross is a big bitch, with a bad attitude, and she'll do what you tell her to do most of the time, but she's not built for escape and evasion, much less dogfighting. Going in without a Nemesis escort was a huge risk, but I didn't think we'd've made it any other way. Those fighters have a huge sensor footprint. There'd be no way to hide them, even from the Pegasi.

"Time to target, three minutes," Inkelaar said.

"Any sign of their beacon?"

"Negative."

"Dropping below eight thousand. Beginning orbit of target area. Start the clock."

A mission clock appeared in my helmet's HUD: ten minutes. If we hadn't heard from them by then, our orders were to drop another grav-relay and RTS. It wasn't a lot of time, but I'd worked with these guys before. They were tough, if anyone was going to make it, Hastings and his Marines would.

As we circled, a few civilian transports came close but didn't seem to notice we were military. Or at least Alliance military. They continued on course without so much as a blip.

I didn't start sweating until the mission clock dropped below two minutes.

"They should've been here by now," I said.

"Maybe they got hung up."

"Maybe."

An alert flashed on Inkelaar's screen. "Hey, shit, I got something!"

I leaned over, looking at his console. "Is it their beacon?"

He shook his head. "Not yet, but I've got one—no three—vehicles inbound from the north. They're really moving."

I pulled up the sensor images in my visor's HUD as the computer cycled through the targets, assigning each a number. The lead vehicle, a white, unmarked van, designated Tango-1 was tearing through the streets about two blocks ahead of the others, Tango-2 and Tango-3, black Peacekeeper patrol units.

The up-armored ground vehicles were a mix of SUV and truck, each with small turrets cut out of their roofs where soldiers manned small, single-barreled medium machine guns. The oversized wheels kicked up loose dirt and left a cloud of dust behind them.

"Who the hell are they chasing?" Inkelaar asked.

"I don't know," I said, hands tightening on the stick.

The Captain had been clear on one specific point: do not get shot down. Our orders were to be one-hundred percent sure it was our guys and that we could get them out without risking the loss of another bird.

The Albatross's tracking system estimated the trucks' course, extrapolating likely headings based on the terrain and their current speed. There was no doubt in my mind where they were heading. I scanned the surrounding city, my helmet's night vision painting the landscape in shades of green and black. Nothing else was moving down there at all, not for a couple kilometers in any direction.

"That's got to be them," I said. I checked our communications grid. No incoming transmissions. "Try connecting on the squad link."

"Roger."

The van passed the outer edge of the extraction zone, and I noticed the back doors were swinging open and shut as the vehicle bounced along the road. As we came around we could see the van's interior and a figure kneeling inside, flashes of light emitting from the end of the rifle in his hands.

"They're shooting at those trucks," I said.

"Darkstar Six-Five, to Darkstar ground elements, do you copy?"

The van turned a corner just as one of the trail vehicles fired its weapon. The rounds punched through the corner of a two-story brick house, sending debris and dust into the air.

"Okay." I slammed the throttle forward and dipped the nose.

"Still no beacon," Inkelaar said.

"Don't give a shit about the beacon that's got to be our guys, and we're getting them out of there." I switched to my internal ship coms. "Get ready, Chief! This is going to be a hot extract."

There was a brief buzz in my ears before the Crew Chief, Sergeant Masters, responded, "Roger that, Commander."

"Five thousand feet," Inkelaar said.

"Fangs out. Let those bastards know we're up here."

"Roger." I could practically hear his smile as his thumb flipped the safety off the controls.

The *wrrrrrrp* of the Viper III reverberated through the cabin as the Albatross's twin Gatling cannons sent a hundred rounds down range. Even above the constant thrumming of the engines, the sound of that weapon was impressive. A second later, the ground around Tango-2 erupted into plumes of earth and mortar as the 30mm rounds chewed through the street and surrounding buildings.

The truck swerved, cutting through the pillars of debris, and slammed, nose first, into a parked car on the side of the street. The patrol vehicle's rear end flipped into the air, then crashed down on its roof. Inkelaar swept the Viper over the wreck, and a second later it exploded.

Tango-3 plowed through the dissipating cloud without slowing to check on their comrades. Its turret gun spat out several more volleys at the van, seemingly oblivious to the fact that we'd just obliterated their friends. Or just didn't care.

A targeting alarm sounded as two alert panels appeared in front of me. A Pegasi assault shuttle appeared through the thick smoke rolling up from their vehicle, pulling up, away from the street, coming straight for us.

"Inkelaar!" I shouted, slamming the throttle hard and banking left.

"I see it!" Inkelaar's fingers danced over the controls. An audible hum reverberated through the cockpit as the Mark 72 launchers folded out of the fuselage. A solid tone wailed as the targeting computer locked on, and four FHE-122s blasted from their housings. They streaked through the air, trailing white smoke behind them as they curled toward the Pegasi shuttle.

The enemy shuttle veered away, pulling up hard as flares sprayed from its tail section. The first two rockets missed, lured away by the Pegasi countermeasures, but the second two found their target, ripping through the fuselage, turning the shuttle into a spiraling ball of fire.

"Target down," Inkelaar announced as additional targets appeared on the scope. "Passing three thousand. Still no beacon. I've got two more Pegasi patrol vehicles moving in from the west. If more of those show up, we're not going to be able to fight them all off, you know that, right?"

I shook my head as I lined us back up on Tango-3. "Still no comms?"

Copilot flipped a switch. "Darkstar Six-Five to Darkstar Ground Units, we are on station and ready to extract. Confirm location and status."

Static buzzed in my headphones. I gritted my teeth, watching the van swerve around another corner. Whoever was in the back was still sporadically shooting every time the doors swung open to give him a shot.

The radio crackled, interrupting the buzzing static, and a voice came over the comm. "Darkstar Six-Five, Darkstar 10, we are inbound. Request hot pickup ASAP."

"Roger, One-Zero. I pass you, Falcon."

"I— son of a bitch!"

On the ground, a building exploded just in front of the van, blanketing the vehicle in debris. The audio buzzed and wavered as interference from the blast interrupted the signal. A second later, the van emerged from the cloud and made a sharp right turn, speeding down a side street.

"Fucking Condor!" Thomas shouted over the comms. "Condor! Condor! Condor!"

A giant weight lifted from my shoulders and I pushed the throttle forward. "Copy that! Dropping below, one thousand. Chief, get that door open."

The engines screamed as I brought us around on final. The extraction location was an empty lot four blocks to the west. "Darkstar One-Zero, we'll be rails down in thirty seconds. Primary LZ is a go."

"Roger that!"

I leaned over to Inkelaar. "Let 'em have it."

Wrrrrrrp!

Rounds as big as my hand ripped through Tango-3 as it came around the last corner. Puffs of white smoke appeared on either side of the cockpit as the 122s fired, filling the air with missiles. The ordnance turned the vehicle into a mass of twisted metal. The Viper chewed through the street and surrounding buildings, decimating the landscape and creating an impromptu roadblock.

The other two trucks skidded to a stop, and several Pegasi soldiers jumped from their beds, spreading out like cockroaches, climbing over parked cars and weaving through the wreckage. Several fired wildly after the Marines, more for effect than anything, they weren't liable to hit anything from their position. Several square targeting reticles appeared on each soldier as the computer designated them hostile in turn.

"Targets identified," Inkelaar said.

"Take them out."

Wrrrrrp! Wrrrrrp!

As much as I wanted to watch the Viper obliterate those bastards, I turned my attention to the task at hand. I adjusted our flight path, aligning our descent with the designated extraction zone. The area was painted yellow, the indicators overlaid over the terrain in my HUD.

The Marine's van skidded to a stop a hundred meters away as I flared for landing, kicking up a violent torrent of wind and dust. Two Marines exited the side door, followed by another one who was practically carrying a fourth. The first two turned and fired back at the enemy.

The Viper's whirring stopped.

"Four?" Copilot said, sounding as shocked as I was. "There's only four? I don't see Hastings."

I couldn't believe it either. "Darkstar One-Zero, Darkstar 6-5, confirm location and numbers."

The voice on the other end of the comm was out of breath. "You're fucking looking at us right now!"

Two blocks behind them, another truck appeared from a side street. Target designator's flashed, and video feeds automatically zoomed in. Two figures stood behind the truck's cab, one with a rocket launcher balanced awkwardly over one shoulder, the other trying to keep his partner steady.

"Rocket!" Inkelaar said. "They're locking on!"

"Shoot!"

"I don't have a shot."

I switched over to external comms. "Marines, your seven o'clock, we do not have guns."

On the ground, one of the Marines turned. I found out later, his name was Grayson. He saw what was happening and sprinted back to the van, firing as he ran. He slid on his knees behind the van's engine block, brought up his rifle, this time sending accurate rounds downrange.

The Pegasi helper's head snapped back in a plume of red. The impact knocked him back. His hands still holding onto his partner's shoulders, pulling him back a step just as the launcher fired.

"Incoming!" Inkelaar shouted over the wail of alarms.

The rocket sliced a white trail across the orange and blue sky. It curled through the air, then veered off, slamming down several blocks away without ever finding a target.

Grayson got to his feet, sending more rounds into the cab of the truck, shattering the windshield. The figure inside jerked, and the truck started to roll forward slowly, colliding with a light pole and coming to a stop. The Marine ejected a magazine, reloading as he moved around to the other side of the van, then sent a burst into the soldier still holding the launcher.

I rotated the Albatross, presenting the open bay and ramp to the incoming Marines. The bird rocked slightly as I set her down. "Come on!"

Activating one of the onboard camera feeds, I watched Chief Masters run down the ramp and sprint across the open lot toward the band of wounded Marines. He wrapped the woman's arm around his shoulders, leaving the Sergeant free to spin and return fire with his own rifle.

A group of Pegasi soldiers appeared at the far end of the flow, weaving through several parked vehicles. Bullets twanged off our hull from various angles. After a moment, they seemed to realize one of the Marines was still by the van and shifted their fire in his direction.

One of the Marines, Wallace, ducked behind a car, popping up every few seconds to take his shots, then dropping back down. Sergeant Thomas moved back next to him, taking a knee while he swapped out magazines. He shouted something to Wallace, then stood and fired again.

Wallace darted for the ramp. He'd made it about a quarter of the way when something knocked his leg out from under him, and he went sprawling. He dropped his rifle, hands grabbing at his wound, face twisted in pain, mouth open, screaming.

Thomas fired off another burst, then moved to Wallace. He pulled him off the ground, draped an arm over his shoulder and continued toward the ramp. He jerked upright, screaming and reaching with his free hand to his back. He collapsed as Masters reached them, keeping both Marines from falling over completely. He pulled them to their feet and guided them to the ramp.

By the van, Grayson was now exchanging fire with two separate groups. Ducking behind the engine, he swapped out mags, frantically searching for his comrades.

"He's not going to be able to take them all out," Inkelaar said.

Grayson got to a knee and fired a burst into three hostiles as they emerged from an alley. One took a round in the shoulder, spinning him like a top, throwing him back into one of his allies. A second took a salvo in the chest and pelvis, dropping him where he stood. The third managed to bring his weapon up as the first fell away and spat off his own barrage.

Grayson rolled away as little plumes of earth erupted from the ground behind him.

"He might make—"

The Marine's body suddenly jerked upright. He turned, bringing his weapon around, firing as his body jerked again.

"Son of a bitch," I said.

Grayson's rounds went wide. His leg snapped out, forcing him to one knee. His mouth open in a rage-filled scream that I couldn't hear as he brought his rifle up in both hands and let off a long stream of fire. Three Pegasi troops dropped.

Then Grayson's head snapped back so hard, I knew there could only be one thing that meant.

"Fuck!" I shouted, watching as the Marine's body fell back. There wasn't anything anyone could do. I threw the throttle forward, the engines screamed, blanketing the area in a thick cloud as we lifted into the air.

CHAPTER 7

The *Vision*
New Tuscany Orbit
3 Apr 2607

Blood smeared the Albatross's deck. Bloodsoaked, filthy clothes were strewn about, as well as spent shell casings and discarded rifles. The metallic odor filled the quiet interior.

Lieutenant Powers sat on one of the folding chairs mounted on the bulkhead, face cupped in his hands. His co-pilot, David Inkelaar, was leaning against the side of the cockpit's hatch, shaking his head. Chief Masters stood a few meters away, arms folded across his chest, staring blankly at the mess on the bay floor.

"If it hadn't've been for Grayson, we probably never got out of there," Powers said, looking up at Fischer, eyes hard. "You make sure that goes in your damn report."

Fischer nodded. "I will."

"What the hell is there to investigate anyway," Chief Masters asked. "Some shitheads killed a lot of brave Marines. That's it. Story over. We need to go back and blow the hell out of them."

"Hell yeah," Inkelaar said.

"I don't disagree with you," Fischer said. He didn't elaborate, because part of him knew he couldn't, the other half didn't want to get these men spun up again. They'd been spun up when he'd first approached them, but by the end of the pilot's story, most of his steam had been run out. *Remembering the sacrifice others made so you could live will do that.*

He let a beat or three pass before continuing with his questions. "Your idea to change the dropship's transponder was brilliant."

Powers sniffed. "Can't take full credit for that one. A buddy back home used to reprogram cabs. We'd take them out joyriding all the time. Traffic nets never picked us up."

"It was a hell of a piece of flying, sounds like," Fischer said.

"It shouldn't have been."

Fischer frowned. "What do you mean?"

"I mean, I shouldn't have been there. I was slated to fly the morning of the mission and Hinners—that son of a bitch, he bumped me. Stupid son of a bitch."

"What do you mean he bumped you?"

Powers shook his head. "At the mission brief. I was next up on the rotation. We were all there, of course. The Captain was laying out the mission perimeters, the VIPs, ROEs, and assigning crews. We—" he nodded to his co-pilot "—were up for flight ops, but Hinners wanted to go. It was his last day on rotation, getting shipped back for instructor duty at FTA. Poor bastard just wanted to go on one more mission before he retired. Fuck!"

Powers punched the metal bulkhead, sending a resounding *clang* through the dropship's quiet interior.

"Everyone thought this was going to be an easy mission?" Fischer asked.

Powers rubbed his neck, clenching his jaw. "We had shit intel. Shit intel and poor planning. They went off the Ambassador's assessment and didn't think to wonder if he was wrong or not. Hell, I don't think they even took the time to verify any of it. At least the Captain nixed the whole, 'escort to the spaceport idea.'"

"What's that?"

"A lot of the mission brief was the Captain and Ambassador arguing over how exactly they were going to get the VIPs off the planet. The Ambassador wanted to use their shuttles, but that would've required travel through the city to Stonemeyer's spaceport, at least thirty kilometers away. Captain didn't like that amount of exposure. In, out." Powers glanced around as if scanning for eavesdroppers. "It's one of the first times I've actually agreed with him, to be honest."

"Don't get along?"

"It's not that we don't get along, it's just that I don't agree with the way he runs his people. He's a hard ass, I get it, but he's also an asshole."

Fischer chuckled. "I've had a few of those."

"Anyway, I couldn't tell him no. He took my spot and flew lead."

"You can't blame yourself for his death," Eliwood said.

She was trying to help, but Fischer knew that wasn't what the pilot wanted to hear. Powers's face reddened as he locked onto Eliwood with an icy stare.

"If it wasn't for me, he'd still be alive. He had a wife and kids. It should've been me down there. If I could take his place, I would."

"Maybe," Eliwood said. "But you can't. And if it wasn't for you, those three Marines lying in hospital beds wouldn't be here either. And who's to say that anyone else would've been able to pull that extraction off the way you did."

"Anyone could've done what I did."

"But they didn't." Eliwood didn't back down. "You can't focus on what someone else could've done. You have to focus on what you actually did. You saved lives, Commander. Plain and simple."

The pilot considered her, biting a fingernail, then his shoulders relaxed, and he turned his gaze back to the bloodstained deck.

"Is there anything else you can remember about the rescue?" Eliwood asked, softening her tone.

"Tactical withdrawal," Inkelaar said.

Powers snorted. "Yeah."

Fischer raised an eyebrow. "I'm sorry?"

"The Ambassador made a huge stink about it during the briefing," Inkelaar explained. "Designating the mission a 'tactical withdrawal' and not an 'evacuation' looks better on a report, I guess."

"Doesn't matter what you call it," Powers said. "The entire thing was fucked. Even the Marines didn't like it."

"How do you mean?" Fischer asked.

"Just the whole way they approached it. I thought Hastings and Thomas were going to go to blows before the Sergeant got called away. Thomas wanted to take the entire team down and smoke everyone waving the wrong flag. Hastings won out, obviously. I tell you, I liked the guy, always seemed to have a good head on his shoulders, it's a shame he didn't make it back."

"It's a shame most of them didn't make it back," Fischer said.

"I hate to say it," Powers said. "But Thomas was right. They should've taken an entire company down there."

"You said he got called away?"

"Huh?"

"Before," Fischer said. "You said Thomas and Hastings were about to go to blows before he got called away. Any idea what that was about? Had to be something important to leave a high profile briefing like that."

"Oh, I have no idea. Sorry." Powers held both hands out,

palms up. "Aside from dropping them off and picking them up, I really don't have much interaction with them. You know how Marines are."

Fischer laughed. "Very true."

"Are they going to make it?"

"Honestly," Fischer said. "I have no idea. I hope so."

"Me too."

Fischer held his hand out. "I appreciate your time, Lieutenant Powers."

"Don't know if anything I had to say was useful, but…"

"It was very helpful, thank you."

Fischer released his grip on the pilot's hand, but Powers squeezed, holding him in place.

"Do me a favor, Agent Fischer."

"Name it."

"You find out why this whole thing went to shit. Find out who killed Hinners, okay? He deserves some payback."

Fischer held the man's gaze for a long moment, then nodded. "I will."

CHAPTER 8

Haroldson Memorial Hospital,
Regional Naval Medical Facility
New Tuscany
3 Apr 2607

"... Darkstar Six-Three is down! Repeat Darkstar Six-Three is down!"

Gunfire echoed in behind every word transmitted between the Marines at the air units as the battle progressed. According to the time readout on Fischer's display, they were barely an hour into the mission, and his blood was already boiling.

Eliwood grimaced as a Marine screamed. "They're getting torn apart."

Fischer nodded. "For an underfunded, civilian militia, they certainly appear to be well armed and capable. I'd be interested to know how the hell they managed to take out an Albatross? Much less two. Those things are like flying fortresses."

"Contact right," a Marine shouted. *"Look, they're moving in the heavy!"*

"Rocket incoming! Get down!"

The recording turned to static, sound warbled and fuzzy. After several seconds, the feed returned to normal as the Marines continued their fight.

"Command, Darkstar Actual, did you copy my request for support?"

"Darkstar Actual, Vision Command, backup response units are being prepped for extraction."

"Vision do you copy? Shit, I've lost contact with Command. Darkstar Actual to all Darkstar Elements, rally on me."

The shuttle banked to the right. Fischer caught a glimpse of Haroldson Memorial outside the window and switched off the recording. The tall, white and tan building was situated in downtown Blue Lake, surrounded by manicured lawns and several landing platforms. It was the more extensive medical facility on the planet, shared by the military and civilian populations alike, and because of that, their budget was vast.

And it shows, Fischer thought, eyeing the grounds.

"Oh, that's just great," Eliwood said, craning her head to look out of the small window next to her. "How the hell did they get here so fast?"

A team of security officers held their ground between a line of reporters and their floating cameras and the hospital's main entrance. Beyond the reporters, a crowd of at least two hundred gathered, fists pumping, holding signs both hand painted and holographic. Even without hearing them, Fischer knew what they were screaming.

"The Alliance murders!"

"Fight back!"

"Silent no more!"

Eliwood shook her head as the shuttle made a wide arc over them. "Don't those bastards ever sleep?"

Even from the air, Fischer could see the Revolution 52 emblem, a red fist against a golden triangle, projected above several of the demonstrators. Wherever they could get their message in front of as many cameras as possible, that's where they'd be. Decrying military action while simultaneously condemning the Alliance for being complicit in allowing the Pegasi Empire to thrive.

"No," Fischer said. "I don't think they do."

The shuttle touched down in front of the hospital's main entrance, and several Navy guards escorted the two investigators inside.

"Sorry for the commotion," the lead guard said as the glass sliding doors hissed closed behind them, silencing the cacophony of screams outside. He was dressed in black and gray Navy fatigues, the nameplate on his breast pocket identified him as Sergeant Preble.

"Don't worry about it, they don't bother me," Fischer told him, holding out a hand. "Agent Jackson Fischer, Alliance Intelligence."

"Sergeant Preble," the guard said, shaking his hand. "They're causing a major headache for us. Had to call in all my off-duty guys to help cover. Locking down a hospital wing isn't as easy as you'd think."

The sergeant led them through the labyrinth of corridors, making too many twists and turns for Fischer to keep track of and before long, he was lost. He made a mental note to download a copy of the hospital's floor plan to his link.

"We've got security on every entrance and a response team on standby in the basement," Preble explained. "Rumor was, Command wanted to send an entire company down here, but hospital staff wanted to keep their presence as minimal as possible. They aren't the only patients in the hospital."

"Understandable," Fischer said.

They took an elevator to the fifth floor and exited into an open level. Typical hospital. Twenty or so rooms surrounding a central nursing station. A total of eight Navy guards were positioned at various intervals, doing their best to remain invisible.

Doctors wearing white medical coats over their fatigues moved purposefully between stations, talking with nurses, checking and rechecking holo-chart information and making calls. It was the kind of organized chaos Fischer was used to seeing in emergency rooms and command and control sections on warships. Most of the people he knew working in such places functioned much better under pressure than without.

Sergeant Preble walked them to the central desk. "The investigators are here to speak with the survivors."

A nurse looked up from behind the counter, her expression filled with contempt and irritation as if Fischer and Eliwood had purposely come here to ruin her day.

"Visitors aren't allowed on the floor," the nurse said, returning to her terminal.

The Sergeant gave Fischer a knowing glance, as if to say, "Good luck" and patted him on the shoulder as he stepped out of the way. "I leave you in good hands."

The nurse continued clacking fingernails on her terminal, ignoring them, making it known that she was in charge here, not the investigators. Fischer fought back his irritation and let the woman have her moment. It wouldn't do any good to fight against it, ultimately the more he allowed her to save face and maintain her level of "superiority" the more he'd be able to get out of her later when he really needed something.

He waited a beat, then pulled his credentials, setting them gently on the counter. "We're Alliance Security, ma'am, not visitors."

She looked up from her screen, eyeing the card, comparing its picture to Fischer's face. "They aren't available at the moment."

Fischer smiled, slipping the ID back into his pocket. "Look, I'm not trying to step on anyone's toes here, but I do have my orders."

Without taking her eyes from her terminal, the nurse sighed.

"Doctor Vaughan, these *investigators* are wanting to talk to the patients." The emphasis she put on the word "investigators" made it sound like they were some two-bit local private eyes, playing at being cops.

A young woman on the far side of the nursing station, looked up from her chart, the orange hue from the display giving her olive skin a radioactive-looking tone. An Alliance Marine crest on her green scrubs peeked out from behind her white lab coat. Embroidery above the coat pocket identified her as Captain J. Vaughan. Her blonde hair wasn't precisely within regs, but medical personnel, especially doctors, weren't always held to the same standard as the rank and file.

She eyed Fischer, then said, "What can I help you with?"

Fischer extended a hand. "Agent Jackson Fischer. Thanks for—"

The doctor ignored the offered hand and continued, cutting him off mid-sentence. "I have to tell you, Agent Fischer, I'm not exactly pleased you're here. These Marines have been through quite an ordeal. They need time to recover from their injuries, some of which are extensive. Not to mention the psychological trauma they've been through."

"I completely understand," Fischer said, lowering his hand. "And, believe me, I sympathize. I'm not looking to get in anyone's way here."

"And yet, you're here anyway."

Fischer grunted, then nodded to the Marine emblem on her scrubs. "Unfortunately, I've got orders, same as you. I'm sure you can understand that. I'm just here to ask some questions. As soon as I get the answers I need, I'll be on my way."

"You will not turn my hospital into an interrogation room, is that clear?"

Fischer nodded. "Crystal."

"These Marines are still my patients," Vaughan continued. "I have final say on how long these interrogations will last. If at any point I think the patient is becoming overstimulated or needs a break, you're done. No questions. If you have a problem with that, you can take it up with Admiral Grendamier. Are we clear?"

"Like I said, I'm not trying to step on anyone's toes."

"Good."

"And for the record," Fischer added. "I'm not planning on interrogating anyone. These are strictly interviews, the interrogating I leave for criminals. Besides, I left my pulse laser and fingernail extractor back at the office."

A nurse appeared beside the doctor, wordlessly holding out a holo-chart. Vaughan took it, considered the information, then nodded. "Make sure we're changing the dressings every six hours and get the medication schedule posted."

The nurse took the chart back with a nod and disappeared down the hall.

Vaughan returned her gaze to Fischer, considering him with a sharp, unimpressed gaze. "The patient's medical information is privileged. I cannot release that information without direct orders from Medical Command, and even then, it's classified."

"Not my first rodeo, Doc." Fischer activated his link's recorder, holding his hand out, palm down.

The doctor hesitated for a moment, then pressed her thumb against the back of Fischer's hand. The Link automatically tagged the file with date, time and geo-location, adding the doctors bio-signature to the file would prevent anyone from accusing the agents of trying to falsify the data. The metadata accompanying the recording would be discoverable in court proceeding, any alteration would invalidate the information.

"The Marines," Fischer said. "You mentioned their injuries were extensive?"

"Sergeant Thomas is still in surgery, repairing some internal damage from small arms fire. Corporal Biagini is in recovery, and Private Wallace was transferred to my care just within the last hour. He has some head trauma, and his left leg required reconstruction surgery, but his other injuries weren't life-threatening."

"Will the others survive?"

"The information I've been given so far suggests they will," Vaughan said, making sure to clarify her statements. "It's doubtful you're aware, but battlefield injuries are often unpredictable. Fortunately, the *Vision's* medical staff provided exceptional treatment while en route here. I'm going to put them in for commendations."

"That's good." Fischer pursed his lips, waiting for the doctor to continue.

Beside him, Eliwood coughed. "Private Wallace?"

"Yes, of course. This way."

The Doctor led them away from the central station, toward the back of the unit.

"I bet her bedside manner is freaking spectacular," Eliwood muttered, leaning in close so no one else could hear.

"Bedside manner isn't what concerns me in a place like this," Fischer replied. "If she can save my life. I don't give two shits how rude she is while doing it."

"Good point."

The last room in the unit was flanked by two Marines. They nodded as Doctor Vaughan approached. They exchanged quiet words with Vaughan, then the corporal turned and ran the back of his hand across a security panel behind him. A red light above the door blinked out, and the blue forcefield flashed, then vanished.

"Lot of security for one Marine," Eliwood said.

Fischer nodded but said nothing.

The room was dark, and though it was obviously designed for two, Private Wallace's bed was the only one present. A soft, repetitive beep echoed throughout the otherwise silent room and the whole place smelled of hospital antiseptic and bodily waste.

The private lay on an omnifoam bed, with his eyes closed. His head was wrapped in bio-synth strips and held in place by two small padded bracers the size of Fischer's fist. Tiny lights on each flickered and pulsed, obviously sending information to the displays above. Wallace's face was bruised and covered with bandages. His leg was propped up, encased in an exo-cast, his left arm looked like it was tied to his chest with bandages.

Medical data and vitals scrolled across three holo-charts suspended above the metal headboard. Several IV lines ran from equipment clusters hung from the ceiling to Wallace, all providing the Private with various medical treatments Fischer couldn't begin to understand.

The doctor moved to the bedside, poring over the charts, then bent over her patient. "Private Wallace, it's Doctor Vaughan."

The Marine's eyes flickered, head turning to face the doctor. For a brief moment, he appeared confused, then grimaced in pain and turned away, smacking his lips and tongue together.

"Are you thirsty?" Vaughan asked.

Wallace nodded.

Vaughan tapped her link and a moment later, the nurse appeared, giving Fischer a displeased look as she stepped around him and handed the small cup to Wallace.

"Thanks." The Marine's voice came out as little more than a hoarse whisper. He took a sip, then set the cup on a small bedside table. He frowned, finally seeing Fischer and Eliwood standing near the door. "Who are you?"

Fischer opened his mouth to introduce himself, but Vaughan beat him to it.

"These two agents want to ask you some questions, you're under no obligation to answer though." She straightened, glaring at Fischer. "I've already explained to them how this works."

Wallace frowned. "Questions?"

Fischer stepped forward, offering his hand. "Jackson Fischer, Alliance Intelligence. This is my partner Agent Eliwood. We'd like to ask you some questions about what happened on Stonemeyer."

The private grimaced, though from pain or memories of the mission, Fischer wasn't sure. "Where's Sarge? Is Biagini okay?"

"They're both doing fine," Vaughan said. "Being cared for by the best."

"I need to talk to Sarge," Wallace said.

"As soon as he is available, we'll make that happen," Vaughan said.

Fischer waited as the private took a long breath, then said, "Private Wallace?"

Wallace swallowed again, grimacing, then opened his eyes.

"The mission?"

"Can I sit up?"

Fischer glanced at the doctor, who nodded.

"Bed controls: Incline forty-five degrees." The bed hummed, barely making a sound even in the near-silent room. "Better?"

He nodded.

Fischer took a breath and let it out slowly. He couldn't decide whether the private was stalling or not, but he needed to keep his patience in check here. He had no doubt the doctor would throw him out at the first sign of irritation.

He needed an olive branch.

"More water?" he asked, holding out the cup.

Wallace nodded, taking the cup. "Thanks." He took another

drink, held it in his mouth for a second, then swallowed. "What do you want to know?"

"Just what happened. Nothing more."

"Where should I start? The entire thing was a fucking disaster."

Fischer tapped his link. "Let's start at the beginning."

CHAPTER 9

Darkstar Six-Three
Calibri City, Stonemeyer
23 Mar 2607
Operation: Safe Haven
Mission Status: Classified
Mission Time: 00hrs 25mins

First thing you realize when dropping into combat in an Albatross
is, for all the size and power on the outside, you ain't got room for
shit on the inside. Especially with all our gear. And they're loud
as hell, even with headphones. I know they ain't built for comfort,
but still.

I was squeezed in between Corporal Biagini and Private
Maxwell. She wasn't bad, great at comms and electronics, had
Sarge wrapped around her little finger. Her black hair was cut
short, I mean real short like she was actually trying to be one of
the guys, a real hard-ass. I had to remind myself sometimes that
she was actually a girl. Woman I mean.

Maxwell, on the other hand, his breath smelled like tuna fish,
try sitting next to that for an hour. If I'd had breath mints, I

would've given him the entire pack. Nice enough guy, but shit, brush your teeth.

Every time the dropship banked or hit turbulence, our shoulder pads knocked into each other. Standard Marine body armor consists of black, segmented ballistic plates linked together over our charcoal gray battle uniform. The reinforced ceramic plates will hold up to multiple direct impacts and blast damage and are lightweight for increased maneuverability. A tactical vest over the body armor holds all my gear; extra magazines, comm relays, hydration pack on the back, first aid, a couple frags. A few had specialized loadouts, but most of us all carried the same gear.

Our helmets are easily the most expensive piece. Its internal computer system connects us to the Milnet and syncs with our personal links, providing real-time battle info as well as weapons status, GPS data on the other team members. That shit knows how much coffee I had for breakfast. When they issued it to me, the quartermaster told me if I broke it, I'd be paying for it for the rest of my enlistment. I don't think he was joking either.

Across from me, the new guy, Private Sheridan, was wedged between Corporal Charles and Corporal Jung. You could tell he was new too, all green around the gills and shit. Nervous as hell. Didn't talk to nobody. Just stared off into space, jaw clenched tight.

"Hey Sheridan," I shouted over the roar of the engines. "You gonna share your breakfast?"

Corporal Charles laughed and slapped Sheridan on his knee. "Don't worry. If you lose it, I hear we're having chicken surprise for lunch when we get back. Love that stuff."

Corporal Jung laughed. "Yeah, surprise, it's not chicken."

Sheridan looked like he was going to be sick.

"It's too bad we can't stay to check out the sights," Jung said, practically shouting over the roar of the engines. "I hear the

Stonemeyer market cafes have the best cuisine this side of the URT."

Beside me, Maxwell laughed. "Damn, Jung, how can you think of food at a time like this?"

"I always think of food."

Jung was one of those fitness freaks. I mean, I consider myself healthy and in shape, but Jung, she took it to a-whole-nother level. Up at zero-four every day to run five miles, without fail. Killed it in the gym. She could go toe to toe with any one of us and probably win. She could definitely put the food away though. It was always a running bet during chow, how many plates she'd clean before the chefs cut her off.

Combat drops do strange things to people. When you're in the thick of it, taking fire and shooting back, most of that is just muscle memory and adrenaline, but the ride before, that's when you do all your thinking. Most of the platoon joked and heckled each other, hell, Private Andres took a nap.

One of our snipers, Sergeant Henderson, read books. Cookbooks mostly, he was fanatical about those things. He'd earned a Ph.D. in education before joining up, so everyone called him Prof. He skipped OCS and went straight into the sniper program out of basic. Guy was smart, smarter than most of the officers I met, and probably the most accurate shooter ever produced by the Corps.

The amber light at the front of the bay blinked to red as a two-tone alarm echoed through the compartment, killing most of the conversations. Lieutenant Hastings unclipped his harness and stood, nodding to Sergeant Thomas on his way to the cockpit hatch.

"Here we go," Maxwell whispered in my ear.

Sergeant Thomas stood, grabbing hold of the yellow and black safety rail above him, swaying with the shuttle. "Alright, lock it in, people! Command needs your A-game on this one. Eyes up and heads on a swivel. I want this extraction to run by the numbers. In and out. No goddamn funny shit, you got me, Grayson?"

The rest of us laughed at the gibe. Corporal Grayson, the platoon's resident clown, saluted awkwardly from his seat near the back. "You got it, boss!"

"Remember the briefing, intel says light resistance, if any, but don't let your guard down for a minute. There's a reason they called in the Marines. Am I right?"

"Ooh-rah!" we all shouted in unison, stomping our boots on the deck.

"Time on target is twenty minutes. Round these veeps up quick and will be back on board the *Vision* in time for brunch. And someone wake up Andres, for shit's sake."

Corporal Simmons, the platoon's second sniper, jabbed an elbow into the sleeping Marine. "Hey, Andres, game time."

Andres opened his eyes, instantly alert. "Let's get some!"

"One more thing," Sergeant Thomas barked. "Keep your damn fingers off your triggers. We don't need another Pentar Province, do we, Private Ford?"

"No, Sergeant!"

Private Deerman and Corporal Grayson both glared at Ford, all humor gone from their faces. I hadn't been in the unit for that mission, but I'd heard the guys talk about it. It had been Ford's first mission, popped off a three-round burst at Deerman and Grayson's feet as they were clearing a building. Neither of them was hurt, but they'd definitely had to change their uniforms after the mission was over. Word was that Ford slipped getting out of his rack a couple days later, bruised his face up real good I hear.

Lieutenant Hastings reappeared at the front of the bay, and Sergeant Thomas stepped aside to let him address the platoon. "Don't forget your assignments. Once the VIPs are secure, I want to exfil ASAP. Maintain radio and weapons discipline. Intel indicates the rebels haven't been anywhere near the

Embassy in nine hours, but that doesn't mean they don't have spotters. The Pegasi military forces are garrisoned twenty kilometers to the north and shouldn't give us any issues. Any questions?"

There were none.

"By the numbers, understood?"

"Yes, sir!" we all shouted back.

The light above the lieutenant flashed. One of the pilots, Hinners, turned, holding up a finger. "One minute!"

Hastings nodded, repeated the warning, and immediately all the metal clasps in the compartment sang as we unclipped our harnesses and stood.

I slid the clear visor down from its slot inside the top of my helmet, locking it into place. The heads-up-display activated as soon as it was down, revealing com-signal strength, weapon status, and vitals. A tiny mission clock counted up in the top left corner, as well as GPS data for me and various mission objections. Most of the widgets I cleared, swiping at the interface on my left forearm. The tech was good and mostly useful, but a lot of the time, it just got in the way.

My LR27 carbine, the smaller version of the LF17, came free of its brackets with a tug, automatically connecting to my helmet's computer. The weapon weighed about seven pounds, great for close combat, not so much for heavier engagements, but for this babysitting job, it would do.

I pulled a magazine from a pouch on my tactical harness and slapped it in, then yanked back on the charging handle. A small bullet icon flashed on my HUD, showing my full sixty-round magazine was seated. The rifle was loaded, ready to fire.

"Thirty seconds!" Sergeant Thomas shouted.

Another alarm sounded, and all the lights in the compartment shifted to red. There was a series of mechanical *clanks* as the ramp at the back of the dropship unlocked. Air roared in, pushing against the nearest Marines and sending loose harness straps flapping.

The city outside was bathed in a mixture of amber and red lights. Rows of partially lit streets crisscrossed each other, separating a tall building rife with bright, burning neon lights and a rundown warehouse district. A kilometer or two down was a row of tenement buildings. It was early morning, local time, the roads seemed relatively empty, peaceful even.

Good sign, I thought.

The pitch of the engines changed as the dropship pitched back, flaring for landing. I grabbed the support rail above to keep my balance and craned my neck, watching the city streets give away to a gated parkland. The Alliance Embassy was set inside a perimeter of manicured parklands, complete with trees, two ponds and a stream connecting the two. I bet you could almost forget you were inside a secured compound, surrounded by plasma fencing.

I leaned forward, next to Maxwell. "Where are the guards?"

He shrugged. "Who the hell knows?"

"Maybe they're on break," Jung suggested. "Bunch of retired regular army shits, probably. Fat and lazy, working on sweet government contracts."

The engines roared as the Embassy's roof came into view underneath the dropship's ramp. We all swayed back and forth as the Albatross came to a stop, hovering over the building.

"Move, move, move!" Sergeant Thomas shouted.

Henderson and Simmons were moving to their preassigned overwatch positions before Sarge had even given the order. Thing about snipers is, they do their own thing most of the time. They don't spend too much time humping with the rest of us grunts.

The rest of the platoon filed out, hunched over, moving quickly to secure the area. My position was the northwest corner. According to the briefing, it overlooked the back of the Embassy, but it all looked the same to me, nothing but an open park with a few trees scattered here and there.

I panned my 27's optics across the grounds, looking for any sign of hostiles and saw none. There were definitely signs of a fight though, scorch marks on the grass from fires, and impact-crater-scarred areas closer in. The inner wall had been torn down in several places, and the guard shack at the entrance to the Embassy looked like it had taken at least one round from an anti-armor rocket. I craned my neck to see over the side of the roof and saw the building's exterior walls riddled with bullet holes.

"What the fuck?" I said, ducking back behind the retaining wall.

Maxwell followed me down. "What's up?"

I jerked my head to the side. "Looks like someone's been shooting at someone."

Lieutenant Hastings's icon flashed on my HUD, and his voice came through the squad channel. His voice was slightly muffled by the Albatross's engines, but his words were clear. "Darkstar Six-Three, Darkstar Actual, we are clear. Dust off and hold for extraction."

"Copy that, Darkstar. Proceeding to holding pattern. Give us a holler when you're ready for pickup. Good luck."

The roof vibrated as the bird kicked up wind and dust. It banked to the side and pulled away from the building, climbing to orbit the Embassy out of harm's way. Without running lights, the matte black fuselage all but disappeared into the night.

CHAPTER 10

Alliance Embassy
Calibri City, Stonemeyer
23 Mar 2607
Mission Time: 00hrs 32mins

As the noise from the Albatross faded, the night was eerily quiet. I'm from Montgomery, the capital—New Detroit, it's never this quiet. There's always something going on, always people awake. This place seemed like a ghost town in comparison. Even the hyperloops weren't running. I could just see their transparent tunnels snaking through the city in the distance.

"Darkstar Command, Darkstar Actual," Hastings said over the taclink. "We're on station. Castle is locked down, proceeding on mission."

"Roger that, Actual," the comms operator aboard *Vision* responded. *"We've still had no contact with King."*

"Copy that. We'll advise when principle is in hand. Darkstar Actual clear."

"Where the hell are the Embassy guys?" Maxwell whispered.

I shook my head. "Hell if I know."

I watched as Sergeant Thomas and Lieutenant Hastings approached the building access on the far side of the roof. Thomas pulled on the door, locked.

"Biagini," Thomas said. "Bypass."

The Corporal kept low, leaving her position near the southwest corner and taking a knee by the door. She pulled a datapad from a pouch at the small of her back and tied into the door's security panel.

While she worked, Jung knelt next to a black case in the middle of the roof, popping the tabs on each side. She flipped back the lid and pulled out her own datapad, then tapped several switches inside the case. "Drones up in fifteen seconds."

"Looks like the Embassy's primary electrical systems are offline," Biagini said, her fingers dancing over her pad. "Secondary systems have all been locked down and rerouted to the emergency bunker. The security systems are still intact, though."

"Can you break it?" Thomas asked.

The door clicked open. "Already broken."

"Charles, Sheridan, you're up." Sergeant Thomas waved them over as Biagini backed out of the way, sliding her pad back into its pouch.

Corporal Charles nudged the door open with a boot, his rifle up and ready. He swept the barrel light into the stairwell, taking careful steps inside. He disappeared through the door, and a second later, his voice came over the comm. "Clear."

"Charlie Team, you have rear security," Hastings said over the comm. "Henderson, Simmons, you two set?"

Prof's deep voice answered. "We're set."

The Lieutenant nodded. "Let's move out."

"All right, Alpha and Bravo, let's go. Clear and move. Watch your muzzle discipline."

The stairwell was dark, lit only by flashing amber emergency lights at every landing. My HUD compensated for the lowlight conditions, but the strobing effect was playing havoc with its adaptive capabilities. The visor kept wanting to alternate between night vision and standard. I split the difference and activated my infrared, eliminating the constant back and forth. My view became a kaleidoscope of color. My team registered as orange and yellow, the surrounding building hues of black and purple.

"Emergency Bunker is on sub-level two," Biagini said over the taclink. "Can't get there from this stairwell, we'll have to cross the lobby."

On the way to ground level, we passed several locked doors, each one stenciled with numbers indicating their level. The power shut down had tripped the emergency lockdown procedures.

Corporal Charles called for a halt as he and Sheridan reached the door to bottommost level. I stopped on the landing above, taking a knee and training my rifle on the top of the door. Biagini moved forward, again tapping into the door's security system.

"Ready," she said, waiting to pop the lock.

"Hold up," Jung said. She'd taken a knee on the landing above me, operating one of her drones. A high-pitched thrumming flew over me, and I glanced up to see the little silver orb hovering in front of her.

"What'd'ya got, Corporal?" Sergeant Thomas asked.

"Picking up heat signatures," Jung said. "Four bodies, east side of the lobby."

Blue and white lines drew themselves through the air before the drone, creating a basic wireframe image of the next room. Human figures, outlined in red, crouched behind what looked like a security desk, each holding a rifle. Targeting information appeared on my HUD, giving me distance-to-target and aim-point suggestions.

"Embassy security?"

She shook her head. "Can't tell."

"What I wouldn't give to have a Ramsey launcher right about

now," I muttered to Maxwell. Cover or not, the anti-personnel rocket would turn any ambush into so much dust and ash. The Brass had opted for sending us in light this mission. That meant no heavy weapons and only limited bang. Great decision on their part.

"Biagini, check the Embassy's security database for the challenge procedures. See if you can find today's words."

"Roger that, sir," Biagini said, fingers already working.

Every detached unit had standard security procedures in place to prevent outside agencies from accessing secured facilities or programs during emergency events. Challenge codes were changed weekly and were usually kept in secure offline systems so the enemy couldn't steal them.

After a minute of searching, Biagini looked up from her pad. "Got 'em. Relaying now."

The words appeared on everyone's HUD simultaneously. Better the entire platoon gets them, and everyone sees the same thing than to try and pass them along by mouth. Inevitably, someone always screws that up.

"Charles?" Hasting asked.

"Ready, sir," Charles replied, pressing himself against the wall on the opening side of the door.

Biagini tapped her pad and the door unlocked. Charles shoved it open and shouted, "Chancellor!"

The word echoed through the large room beyond, and a moment later, someone returned the challenge. "Gangbusters."

Biagini nodded to Hastings.

"Alliance Marines," Hastings shouted. "Identify yourselves."

"Security Chief Fallon, Alliance Diplomatic Corps. You guys the extraction team?"

"That's right. Where's the Ambassador?"

"Emergency bunker, sir. We've had a hell of a time last couple of days."

"I can imagine. We're going to come out now. Keep your weapons down, alright?"

"Roger that, sir."

Charles was through the door first. Despite Hastings's commands to the security detail, he kept his weapon up and ready. Sheridan and the rest of us followed.

The lobby was just like any other high-class building I'd ever been in. High ceilings, marble floors, fake plants, the works. An empty security desk sat near the back of the room, facing a sizable all-glass entryway on the opposite side. Hundreds of spiderweb cracks covered the windows from bullet impacts.

"Clear!" Charles advised from the far side.

"Clear!" Sheridan seconded.

A man wearing a black tactical vest over a button-up, long-sleeve shirt and black dress pants stood up from behind the security desk. It looked like he hadn't showered in days. The look of exhaustion mixed with relief covered his face. His rifle hung across his chest, barrel down.

Hastings and Thomas met Fallon in the center of the chamber. The Lieutenant motioned to the blood stains on the guard's shirt. "You okay?"

"Huh?" Fallon frowned, looking down. "Oh, it's not my blood, sir."

"Where's the rest of your team?" Hastings asked.

Three men joined Fallon, each sharing the same look of exhaustion and relief as their leader. They all wore similar suits and tac-vests, armed with rifles.

"This is my team, sir. I lost five two days ago, and two more were injured yesterday. They're with the Ambassador and his staff in the bunker."

Hastings frowned, giving Thomas a knowing look. The Sergeant nodded and moved away, motioning for Ford, Charles,

Fallon, and Sheridan. They moved off to the side of the lobby, speaking in hushed tones.

"The information we received from Ambassador Delaney indicated the hostiles had backed down and there hadn't been an attack in several days," Hastings said.

Fallon shook his head. "Fought them for six hours yesterday before they finally disengaged. Not really sure why to be honest with you. Haven't seen them since."

Maxwell nudged me. "This is bad."

"Yeah," I said.

"Looks like you put up a hell of a fight," Hastings told Fallon.

"Yes, sir." Fallon sniffed, rubbing his chin with the back of his hand. "Not hard enough for some, though."

"I'm sorry for your loss, Chief."

"Thank you, sir."

"Can you get us to the Ambassador? The quicker we get to him the quicker we can get out of here."

Fallon nodded. "Roger that, sir. It's this way."

We left Sheridan, Trenton, and Ford in the lobby and followed the security team to the north stairwell. Fallon accessed the security panel with the back of his hand, and the door popped open. The staircase led us down two levels to a tight corridor of gray concrete walls and unfinished light fixtures. Supply crates lined one side of the passage, marked as food, water, and medical supplies.

He stopped at a massive eight-foot steel door at the end of the corridor, ran his link over the pad, then bent down so a retinal scanner could scan his eye. A mechanical *clank* echoed, and the blast door swung open.

A security guard, sitting awkwardly on a supply crate just inside the door, greeted us, his rifle leveled but shaking. The man's eyes widened at the sight of Fallon, our platoon of Marines behind him.

"Holy shit, Fallon," he said. "They did come."

Fallon patted the air, making a downward motion with one hand. "Easy, Chris."

He seemed to realize he was still pointing his weapon and shook himself. "Sorry about that."

"Not a problem," Hastings said, stepping forward. His rifle hung down across his chest, hand resting on the grip. He nodded at the man's bandaged leg. "You okay?"

"Took a round yesterday, clean through. Hurts like a bitch, sir."

Hastings laughed. "I'll bet. Trenton, have a look."

"Roger that, sir," one of our platoon's medics said, moving forward, pulling his pack from his shoulders. He knelt down beside the wounded guard and went to work.

The bunker's entrance was a small ten-by-ten-foot space, filled with similar crates from the corridor. A cluster of black cases sealed with red tape and marked SECURE MATERIALS – DIPLOMATIC CORPS sat near the back corner. Empty bottles of water, discarded food wrappers, and other trash littered the floor, and the reek of body odor hung thick in the air.

I turned my nose up at the smell and activated my helmet's air circulation system. It didn't help.

"What's going on out there?" A gruff voice from a room farther in called.

A low, arched passage led into the bunker proper, leading off the front room to the left. Fallon jerked his head at the passageway, indicating for the Marines to follow.

"It's the Marines, Mr. Ambassador," Fallon said, ducking his head as he entered.

Hastings and Thomas followed. I stepped around Trenton as he pulled off a bloodsoaked bandage and grimaced at the security guard's wound. Whoever had treated him had done a piss poor job of it. Trenton cursed, tossing the bandages aside and rummaging through his kit.

The Ambassador stood at the far end of a rectangular table. Several aids sat on crates along the edges of the room, and another guard lay on the ground, head propped up on a rolled up jacket.

The Lieutenant saluted. "Ambassador Delaney, I'm Lieutenant Hastings, Alliance Marines. We're here to extract you and your staff to—"

"Where in the fuck have you people been?" the Ambassador barked, slamming a hand against the table.

"Sir, I—"

Ambassador Delaney threw up his hands, ignoring the Lieutenant. "We've been cut off here for days. I sent my withdrawal request through the network four days ago. Why the hell did it take you so long to get here?"

Hastings cleared his throat. "I'm sorry, sir. I don't have an answer for you."

"Don't have an answer? What the fuck is this? Aren't you the military? You don't know what took so long?"

"Unfortunately, sir, that information is above my pay grade. We are here now, however, and our orders are to extract you and your staff. Are you prepared to evacuate, sir?"

Hastings looked like he was going to lose it. Even through his visor, I could see his face reddening. As his fingers flexed around his rifle, the Ambassador ranted away and I knew he was thinking the exact same thing I was: listen here, you arrogant fuck, do you want a ride or not? That's what I would've said.

Sarge, on the other hand, showed no sign of frustration or anger. He just stood there, listening quietly until Delaney was done. Thomas was one of those NCOs that nothing bothers them. Put Sarge in the middle of a battlefield, explosions and shit going off all around him, and he'd be quietly sipping his coffee like he didn't have a care in the world.

"Prepared to evacuate? Are you fucking kidding me? We've been up under constant assault for the last four days. Yesterday was…" the Ambassador glanced down at the wounded guard on the floor, shaking his head. "Fuck, yes we're prepared to evacuate, Sergeant."

"Lieutenant," Hastings corrected. "My orders are to get you and your staff out of here, sir. If you'll gather your—"

"Listen, Sergeant," Ambassador Delaney said, cutting him off again. He motioned to several of the sealed Diplomatic Corps cases stacked around the bunker. "I have a lot of sensitive materials here that can't be allowed to fall into enemy hands. They will need to be loaded up before I can officially declare the Embassy clear."

Maxwell leaned close. "Asshole's got another thing coming, he thinks I'm gonna carry a bunch of cases up all those stairs."

I snorted. "No shit."

Ambassador Delaney folded up the datapad he'd been working on, shoved it in a bag, then slung the bag over one shoulder. "I'm definitely going to have words with your commander about this, Sergeant. Unacceptable, the military response to this situation. Ridiculous." He pointed to Hastings, moving around the table. "I know some very high-ranking people, Sergeant. Do you understand what that means?"

"I don't, sir," Hastings said, stepping back, allowing Delaney to move past.

"Of course, you don't." The Ambassador continued out of the bunker, forcing the rest of us to step out of the way. At the blast door, he stopped, turning and throwing up his hands. "Well, what the hell are we waiting for?"

Corporal Henderson's icon flashed on my HUD, his voice

came low over the taclink. *"Heads up, I've got movement. Contacts approaching from the west. I count twenty at least."*

"Are they hostile?" Hastings asked.

The Ambassador frowned. "What did you say?"

Hastings ignored him.

"If I was a betting man?" Henderson replied. *"They all just appeared out of nowhere. Stand by, they're approaching the outer security perimeter. Yeah, you might want to expedite, sir."*

"Copy that," Hastings said. "We need to evac now."

"What's happening?" Delaney asked.

Sergeant Thomas was already motioning people out of the bunker. "Let's go!"

Hastings stepped back, allowing the Embassy staff to pass him. "Darkstar Flight, Darkstar Actual. We have the package. We're moving to extraction point. Be advised, possible hostiles are approaching our location from the west."

The pilot's voice warbled slightly, the dropship's engines thrumming in the background. *"Roger that, Actual. Beginning out descent. Time on station, three minutes."*

"Three minutes," Hastings repeated.

"Now, wait just a minute," the Ambassador said. He motioned to the sealed Diplomatic Corps cases. "We can't leave these here."

"Corporal Charles?"

Charles stepped forward, rifle slung across his chest, both hands resting on the stock. "Yes, sir?" He was slightly overweight, but considering his specialty, certain allowances were made. *Those demo guys are crazy.*

"Take care of it."

The Corporal nodded, shrugging off his pack and pulling out several red cylinders. He twisted a small dial on the top of each, then tossed them near the clusters of cases.

The Ambassador turned, moving back into the bunker. "What... now wait a minute... I don't—"

Hastings put a hand on the man's chest. "Sir, it's time to leave. We have our orders. We have possible hostiles approaching, we don't have time for these—"

"But we can't just leave—"

Henderson's icon flashed. *"Actual, Overwatch, marking contacts as hostile, they're passing the outer perimeter and taking up attack positions. I've got several moving up the guardhouse."*

"We need to move, now," Hastings told Thomas, pointing.

"Roger!" Thomas started shoving the slower staff members forward. "Come on, let's go! Now!"

Over the taclink, Hastings said, "Lobby team, eyes up, hostile contacts inbound."

Sheridan's voice was shaky. *"Darkstar Two-Two, roger that. We don't see anything."*

"Oh, they're there," Henderson said, his voice calm. *"And they're armed. Several are loaded down with heavy packs—my guess would be explosives."*

"Come on," I said, slapping Maxwell's shoulder pad. I turned, heading for the stairs, leading the staff back to the lobby. Mission brief said the birds would land right out front. From my spot on the roof, it hadn't looked like they'd managed to breach the Embassy's inner wall, that would at least provide us some cover while we loaded up.

Several distant gunshots echoed in the distance as we reached the top of the stairs.

Private Sheridan's icon flashed on my HUD and the taclink buzzed. "Darkstar Actual, Darkstar-Two-Two, contact west! Contact west!"

CHAPTER 11

Alliance Embassy
Calibri City, Stonemeyer
23 Mar 2607
Mission Time: 00hrs 47mins

"Darkstar Six-Three to all Darkstar Elements, be advised, I've got eyes on multiple hostile contacts encroaching on the extraction point."

I took a knee at the end of the corridor as multiple red dots appeared on the small map on my HUD. Tac data from the inbound Albatross fed the net with targeting information, giving us exact locations of the enemy contacts.

Rifle fire echoed through the night.

"I still don't see them!" Sheridan shouted over the taclink.

A three-meter-high, stone wall, topped with plasma wire, surrounded the Embassy's inner courtyard. The only way through was the double gate shack a hundred meters in front of the lobby entrance, on the other side of a large parking area littered with several ground transports.

The gunfire was sporadic, but with every second or third shot, a plume of glass dust erupted from the wall of windows at the front of the lobby.

"Actual, Overwatch, several contacts are now actively engaging our position," Henderson said. His voice was still calm, even with the muted gunshots in the background, but there was an added sense of urgency to his words. He wanted a green light.

"Engage hostile contacts as they appear," Hastings ordered.

"Engaging."

Behind me, the rest of the team and the Embassy staff stacked up in the corridor. Hastings moved forward, squeezing through the tightly packed bodies to get to the front of the line.

"Darkstar Command, Darkstar Actual, we have hostile contact. I say again, we are under attack. A significant force has engaged us from the west. Request additional air support. Do you copy?"

There was a brief silence over the taclink, interrupted by bursts of fire from outside. Plumes of glass sprayed through the air as rounds tore through the lobby's entryway.

"Command copies," the operator said, his voice strained. *"Continue on mission."*

Hastings and Thomas exchanged looks. Even through their visors, I could see the confusion on their faces.

"Command, Actual, acknowledge. We are under attack," Hastings repeated.

"Acknowledge, Darkstar Actual. Hostile contact at plus forty-seven minutes. Continue with extraction. Additional support units are not available at this time."

"You've got to be fucking kidding me," Maxwell said next to me.

"Roger that, Command. Proceeding on mission," Hastings said through clenched teeth.

"Fire in the hole," Charles shouted.

The floor vibrated under me as the charges in the bunker went off with a *whoomp*. A few seconds later, a thin cloud of dust rolled out of the stairwell entrance. It hung there like a goddamned ghost.

The Ambassador stood red-faced, mouth open, shaking his head. "I…I—"

A fresh salvo crashed through, sending fragments spraying. Sheridan rose up from behind the security desk and fired off a burst. My helmet's noise-canceling headphones dampened much of the sound, but the Embassy staff behind me weren't so lucky. A few screamed at the sudden blasts, all slapped hands over their ears and ducked for cover.

"We need to secure the LZ," Hastings said, leaning around the corner, as hostile return fire continued to chew through the window. "Charlie Team, north side. Bravo Team, south side. Alpha, you've got the lot. Ford, drop me some smoke!"

"Roger that," Ford replied over the taclink, already moving, pulling a fist-sized M81 smoker from a pouch on his side. He pulled the safety then cocked his arm back to throw.

Everything slowed down.

A plume of glass blew out from the window ten meters in front of Ford. The bullet smacked into his shoulder, spinning him like a top. His hand released the grenade halfway through his throw, sending the canister twirling almost straight up. It bounced off the ceiling, then fell back, rolling across the floor. A second later it popped, expelling thick, gray smoke.

The Embassy staff kept on screaming. I get it, the whole thing was fucked up. But them screaming didn't make it any easier.

Two more rounds took Ford in the back and hip, knocking him off his feet. He landed on his chest, faceplate bouncing off the marble floor, visor cracking.

"Ford!" I yelled, watching red alert icons flash across my HUD.

He was still for a moment, just lying there. Then I saw his

head turn and I let out a held breath. His suit's medical diagnostic system relayed injury data through the platoon's taclink. His shoulder pads had deflected the first round, but the bullet to his back cracked the plate, and the round to his hip shattered bone.

"Son of a bitch!" Thomas yelled. "Give me suppressing fire on that fucking entrance, now. Charles, make me an exit!"

"Roger!"

Maxwell got to his feet beside me. I felt a hand slap me between the shoulder blades. "Go!"

The smoke was so thick in the lobby I couldn't see a damn thing without my infrared on. Maxwell and I moved out of the corridor, keeping close to the wall. I brought my LR27 up, pulling the stock into my shoulder and flipping the safety off with my thumb in the same motion. The rifle's optical system immediately linked with my HUD, tagging available targets.

Blips appeared, partially hidden behind vehicles parked on the north end. Two hostiles, moving through the Embassy's main gate, cutting south across the parking lot. Just as I got my optics on target, the man's head snapped forward, a red mist hanging in the air. I didn't know which sniper had taken the shot but hitting a target on the move like that from any distance is no easy task. The man's momentum carried him forward until gravity won out and he dropped like a rag doll.

His companion ducked, moving to the dead man's side and rolling him over.

Bad move, I thought, squeezing the trigger. My three-round burst took the man in the chest, throwing him back. He landed on the pavement a meter from his companion, unmoving.

Beside me, Maxwell fired, sending a volley of fire into one of the parked vehicles—a damn nice gravbike. Fucking shame.

At the corner of my vision, I saw Corporal Charles reaching the entrance. He slapped three charges on the glass in rapid succession, then moved back to our position.

"Fire in the hole!" He slapped his trigger, and we all looked away.

I felt it as the blast wave knocked against me. The explosion sent shards of glass and twisted metal flying across the parking lot, creating a gaping hole in the wall of windows.

"Go! Go! Go!" Sergeant Thomas yelled.

I was on my feet and moving, hopping through the opening and sprinting for the closest vehicle I could see. I grunted, slamming against the trunk, then turned and brought my rifle up, firing at a group just coming through the gate. Two dropped, one taking rounds in the leg, the other in the chest. As I adjusted fire to a third target, Maxwell drew up beside me, adding his firepower to mine.

Behind us, the rest of the platoon spilled out of the Embassy's lobby, spreading through the lot to cover their assigned positions. Hastings and Thomas scrambled to control the staffers as they followed. Delaney ignored them, running with his hands over his head—like that would do any good against bullets—and dropped down beside Maxwell.

Trenton, Bravo Team's medic, and Sheridan grabbed Ford, half dragging him from the lobby to a van beside the car I was behind. Blood streamed down his leg armor, glistening in the amber parking lot's lights. Pain covered Ford's face, teeth clenched hard as Trenton worked on him.

"Goddamn it," Delaney shouted, shoving Maxwell away. "Get out there and do something! Shoot them! Kill them!"

"Sir, please," Maxwell said, pushing the Ambassador's arms away. "Stay down."

A bullet zipped past my helmet, so close I could hear the whistle, even with headphones. I ducked, dropping to my chest and rolling behind the vehicle's back wheel. My view beneath the vehicle's underbelly wasn't great, but I caught sight of two targets moving between cars. I sent several bursts down range, missing the attackers and chewing through a red delivery drone at the far end of the lot.

Corporal Grayson's icon flashed on my HUD. "Frag out!"

An explosion tore through a car twenty-five meters away, sending it ass over teakettle. The blast launched two of the attackers away, throwing them into the air. A chorus of angry shouts erupted from the line as more insurgents moved to replace their fallen comrades.

"That's right," I said, finding another target. My rifle bucked, and my three-round burst took the bastard right in the chest, knocking him on his back. "Come and get some!"

"*We need to get Ford out of here,*" Trent advised over the taclink.

"*Acknowledged,*" Hastings replied.

Warning icons flashed on my HUD as the platoon's taclink identified sixteen more targets moving through the destroyed Embassy gate. They spread out through the lot, shouting and firing almost at random. To my left, one charged, arm coming forward. A small, black orb left his hand right before a barrage of bullets slammed into him.

"Grenade!" I shouted, scrambling back on my hands and knees, trying to see where it was heading.

It bounced on the pavement, then rolled to a stop centimeters from the vehicle Ford, Sheridan, and Trenton were behind. Someone shouted, trying to warn them, but they were already moving, Sheridan at his shoulders, Trenton at his feet.

The explosion lifted the car, sending flame and shrapnel spraying in all directions. I just barely got my head down as a piece bounced off the quarter-panel, missing my helmet by about a finger. The blast knocked both Marines off their feet.

Sheridan lost his grip on Ford's shoulders as he was thrown back, and bounced across the pavement. Trenton's head snapped forward, his momentum carrying him forward several steps before he fell, chest and helmet smacking against the ground. He didn't get up. Medical warnings, transmitted from Trenton's armor, flashed across my HUD, warning the platoon that his vitals were extremely low.

Sheridan rolled to his side, fumbling with his rifle. He tried getting his feet under him, but they'd turned to jelly.

"Get down!" I yelled, waving a hand at him, trying to get his attention. I pushed myself off the ground and ran to him, sliding on my knees as gunfire zipped past. I held him steady, trying to get a look at him.

Through his visor, I could see his eyes had an unfocused, dazed look. He blinked, finally noticing me. "I…"

"You okay?"

He shook himself. "I think—"

A blast of a window from above cut him off, and the ground rumbled. I looked up just in time to see one of the dropships fly by, its matte-black hull illuminated by the street lights.

"Ahah!" I shouted, pumping a fist. "Albatross inbound!"

CHAPTER 12

Alliance Embassy
Calibri City, Stonemeyer
23 Mar 2607
Mission Time: 00hrs 58mins

BRRRRRRRRRRP!

I laughed again as the Albatross's Viper III cannon split the air with 30mm anti-personnel projectiles at seven thousand rounds a minute. It chewed through vehicles, pavement and humans alike, sparing none. Thousands of tiny plumes of debris sprayed up, marking the weapons path of destruction, zigzagging through the enemy line.

Three tried to run as their cover was sliced in half, only to be cut down mid-stride. Dust and debris were stained red from all the blood.

I pulled Sheridan behind the smoldering wreck of the car. To my right, Maxwell got to a knee and then pointed at the Albatross. "That's right shitheads, you don't mess with air—"

His body jerked back, cutting his battle cry short. His rifle fell from his hand, and he bounced against the pavement. The back of his helmet smacked against the ground and he lay still.

"*Max*!" I raced to his side, dropping my own rifle as I knelt beside him. "Shit, shit, shit!"

A bullet had torn through his tactical vest and his chest armor. I could already see blood bubbling up through the hole, and him gasping for air behind his visor as med warnings flashed across mine.

"Medic!" I shouted, hitting his visor release and sliding it back. A mask of pain and fear covered his face as he struggled to breathe.

"I don't..." he murmured, hands coming up and feeling his chest.

"Don't move," I told him. "It's going to be okay. It's going to be fine."

He tried to sit up and grimaced in pain.

Biagini appeared next to us, pushing her rifle around to her back, and inspecting Maxwell's wound. "Goddamn it. Grayson! Here, get his battle rig off."

We stripped his tactical vest off, tossing it aside before working on his battle armor. Two clips on each shoulder and two more under his arms popped open, and the front plate pulled free. Underneath, Max's charcoal uniform was growing black as it soaked with blood.

"Son of a bitch," Biagini said, shaking her head. "*Grayson*!"

The Albatross made a second pass overhead, blasting us with exhaust. We leaned over Maxwell's body, protecting it from the jet wash and dust as the Viper III howled.

A second later, Corporal Grayson appeared, heaving his pack off his back. I scooted out of the way as he dropped down, already unwrapping a bandage roll. "Oh, shit, Max, that ain't nothin' but a scratch."

He laid two of the white strips of cloth across Maxwell's chest and pulled a six-inch injector from his pack. He popped the cap and jammed it down. Maxwell groaned, hands coming up to push Grayson away.

"Hold him," the medic said, tossing the injector away. After a few seconds, Maxwell stopped squirming, his breaths becoming slow and even.

Grayson ripped open a pouch of sealant, and squeezed the green gel into the wound cavity. It took two more pouches to cover the area completely, the gel turning blue as it worked to clean the wound.

"He gonna be okay?" I asked.

"The gel will stop the bleeding," Grayson said, closing his pack. Behind his visor, I could see his eyes reading information on his HUD, medical data from the taclink.

"Hostile contacts are retreating, sir," Henderson advised of the taclink. *"They're moving back toward the outer perimeter wall."*

"Roger that," Hastings said. *"Darkstar Flights, Darkstar Actual, extraction point is clear, confirm."*

"Darkstar Six-Four confirms. Inbound for extraction."

"Six-Three inbound," the over pilot said.

Near the middle of the lot, Hastings got to his feet, keeping low. "Get the civilians ready to load up!"

The first Albatross dropped out of the early morning sky, coming in so fast it almost looked like it would crash right into the ground. It flared at the last minute, blasting the ground with jet wash from its engines and arresting its descent. It hovered for just a moment, then settled onto its landing gear, back cargo ramp folding down.

Charlie Team waved the civilians forward, ushering them into the safety of the Albatross hold. At the base of the ramp, Deerman spun suddenly, as if seeing something out of the corner of his eye and brought his rifle up. An insurgent had appeared by the

Embassy's gatehouse, firing at the fleeing staffers. A burst from Deerman's rifle dropped him where he stood.

The second dropship appeared just to the south of our position, flaring just like the first one had, then touching down, engines screaming.

"Move out!" Sergeant Thomas shouted.

Biagini got to her feet, helping Grayson with Maxwell. "Don't just stand there, Private! Get your weapon and go to work. We're not out of this yet."

"Roger that!" I pulled my 27 around in front of me, already searching for targets.

Deerman's icon flashed. "No, get back, stop!"

I turned in time to see him holding up his hands, waving the last group of staffers back. An explosion ripped through the pavement barely a meter away from him, throwing him sideways. Two of the Embassy guards were knocked back, slamming into the Ambassador behind them.

Sergeant Thomas stopped halfway to the bird, turning back and waving at me. "Wallace, Sheridan, on me!"

Sheridan ran past me, almost as if he hadn't just heard the orders. To my right, Corporal Charles and Corporal Jung were unleashing constant streams of fire into the guard house.

Hastings joined Thomas and me, pulling one of the guards, Fallon, to his feet. The Ambassador coughed, trying to push the other guard off his legs. Thomas checked the guard, then looked up at Hastings, shaking his head.

"Get him off of me!" Ambassador Delaney shouted, trying to pull his legs free.

Hastings and Fallon helped the Ambassador to his feet. Hastings pointed at the dropship closest to us. "Get to the bird!" He turned to the first dropship. "Six-Four, we can get the rest, dust off and clear."

The last two members of Charlie team, Andres and Brent, ran

up the ramp. It started closing before they'd reached the bay and the Albatross lifted into the air.

"Overwatch, Actual," Hastings said as we headed for the ramp. "Stay put, we'll pick up on the way out."

"Roger," Henderson answered.

Biagini and Grayson had just reached the dropship, moving awkwardly to get Maxwell up the ramp. Charles and Jung broke contact and ran for the Albatross, Charles grabbed Maxwell by the waist and helped the other two carry him inside.

"Wallace," Sergeant Thomas said, pointing. "Help, Trenton."

I turned, seeing the medic helping Ford across the lot. I ran to his side and draped Ford's opposite arm over my shoulders. He groaned, eyes half-open, a thin line of blood running from his mouth over his chin and onto his shattered armor. "Come on!"

We were almost to the ramp when I saw Trenton's head snap back in the corner of my vision. Glass from his visor exploded out. I groaned, clenching my teeth under the added weight as I strained to keep Ford from falling as well.

The medic landed on his back, helmet smacking against the concrete. I knew immediately he was gone. His face was nothing more than a mass of blood and gore.

"Shit!" I yelled, adjusting Ford's weight over my shoulders. "I need help!"

Corporal Charles appeared at the base of the ramp, taking Ford's other arm. "Let's go!"

As we charged up the ramp, Fallon passed us up, joining Jung at the base, covering our retreat. We set Ford down as soon as we'd crossed the threshold, then turned and helped Hastings get Trent up the ramp.

At the front of the bay, the Ambassador waved his arms frantically. "What the hell are we doing? We need to leave now!"

"Jung, Fallon, in!" Sergeant Thomas shouted.

Jung fired off another volley, then got to her feet and ran up the ramp. Fallon followed, ejecting an empty magazine and slapping in a new one.

"That's it!" Thomas shouted over the taclink. "Wheels up!"

The sudden motion of the bird lifting almost knocked me off balance. I reached up, grabbing hold of the handrail above and watched as the Ambassador attempted to mimic my actions, and failed. He toppled over, landing on one of the seats in front of him.

The ground fell away outside the open hatch, rotating as the Albatross banked left. The *brrrrrrrrrrp* of the Viper III reverberated through the bay as we gained altitude. We passed over the Embassy, slowing slightly. Whoever the pilot was, he was an ace. He positioned the ramp just over the roof, allowing Henderson to jump on, sniper rifle in hand.

"Where's Simmons?" Hastings asked, shouting.

Henderson passed the Lieutenant, heading for the front of the bay. "He's gone."

Jung slapped the ramp control, and a mechanical thrumming echoed around us.

"Ground units, clear!" Hastings said over the taclink. *"Get us out of here."*

"Roger that," the pilot responded, and the ramp closed sealing us off from the outside world.

"Command, Actual, we are rails-up. Package is secure."

"Actual, Command, we copy package secure."

I dropped down next to Maxwell as the Albatross turned away from the Embassy. "How's he doing, Doc?"

Gray popped another cap off an injector with his thumb before jamming it into Maxwell's chest. "He's going to be just fine."

The tone of his voice and hard face told me otherwise. Maxwell grimaced as the medic worked. Blood soaked Maxwell's uniform, and most of the color had left his skin.

"Damn it," Grayson said, ripping open another sealant pouch with his teeth.

Maxwell looked up at me, reaching out for my hand. I took it and squeezed. "You're going to be all right, Max. Doc's going to patch you up."

Even as I said it, I didn't believe it. Grayson squeezed more sealant out, pressing it deep into the wound with his fingers.

"I don't..." Maxwell's words trailed off, his eyes falling away as his head went limp.

"Max!" I pumped his hand. "Max, open your eyes! Stay with me. Stay with me, Max!"

He went boneless, slumping to the deck.

"Fuck!" Grayson shouted, tearing open his bag.

"*Max!*"

An alarm sounded. Red lights flashed. I looked toward the open cockpit hatch, seeing the horizon beyond rotate as the Albatross banked hard to the right.

"We're being painted!" the pilot shouted. "Two tracks, eleven o'clock low!"

I put my hand out, pushing against the seat, holding my position as Maxwell and everything else that wasn't tied down shifted across the deck. Outside, I saw bright yellow flashes through the porthole windows along the side of the fuselage, flares spreading out from their housings under the Albatross's wings.

"Incoming!" the pilot shouted. "Hold on—"

The Albatross banked to the left, throwing everything to the other side of the compartment, knocking most of us off balance. The Ambassador reached for the overhead rail and missed again, this time smacking his face against the bulkhead.

A sudden rush of wind accompanied a deafening sound as all the portholes on the right side of the Albatross blew out. I collided with Charles, and both of us hit the bulkhead. Sparks erupted from panels along the ceiling.

I pulled myself out from under Charles, using the seat to keep me from falling back again as the dropship tilted to the right.

"What the f—"

Another explosion cut me off, tearing through several sections of fuselage across from me. Multiple panels ripped free, exposing more of the compartment to the outside air. Wind whipped through the bay. It was disorienting, debris everywhere.

"We're hit! We're hit!" the pilot shouted over the taclink. *"Darkstar Command, Darkstar Six-Three, we are going down. I say again, we are going down!"*

CHAPTER 13

Haroldson Memorial Hospital,
Regional Naval Medical Facility
New Tuscany
3 Apr 2607

A two-tone alarm chimed as one of the monitor's above Wallace's bed flashed. The private grimaced, adjusting his position on the bed. He groaned, fumbling with the small self-dosing control in his hand. He thumbed the red button and let out a long breath, his body visibly relaxing.

"All right, that's enough," Doctor Vaughan said, reaching up and tapping the flashing panel.

Wallace took a steadying breath. "I'm okay."

Vaughan shook her head. "We're done." She gave Fischer a hard look, almost as if she was looking for him to challenge her. "He needs rest."

For a brief moment, Fischer considered it but decided this wasn't a battle he wanted to fight. He suppressed a sigh, and clenched his jaw. The recording ended with a tap on his link. "We can come back. Sounds like you've been through quite an ordeal."

Wallace shook his head. "That's not even the half of it, man. Fuck." He took another deep breath, grunting. He turned to the Doctor. "Can I talk to Sarge?"

"Sorry," Vaughan said, shaking her head.

Fischer hesitated for a moment, then put a hand on the private's arm. "I appreciate your time, Private. If it's all right, I'd like to come back tomorrow and continue, if you're feeling up to it."

Wallace nodded. "Sure."

"Doc," Fischer said, nodding to the door. "Can I have a moment."

Vaughan assured Wallace she'd be back and followed the agents into the hall. After pushing the door shut, she led them out of earshot of the guard. She produced her pad and started typing. "Yes?"

"The other two Marines, you mentioned one was in recovery?"

"Corporal Biagini. That's right. She's in a segregated unit upstairs."

"We're going to need to talk to her," Fischer said, deciding to take a more direct approach.

She didn't respond.

"Is there an issue?" Fischer asked. "I thought you said she was in recovery."

"That's right, she is…" she trailed off, eyes searching for anyone listening in. Fischer followed her gaze and caught two of the nurses looking away just as he met their eyes.

"Follow me."

She led them to a secured lift, which took them up three levels, opening to a small anteroom. Large red letters across the double doors outside the elevator read: RESTRICTED AREA – AUTHORIZED PERSONNEL ONLY. Printed in smaller, black letters underneath read: For Entry Contact Hospital Command Staff.

They stepped off the lift, and Vaughan turned, waiting as the doors closed behind them. Fischer held his breath, anticipating her attack before it came. But when the Doctor spoke, he was surprised at her soft, almost sympathetic tone.

"Listen, I'm not blind to what's going on here. I caught the feeds this morning but didn't realize exactly how messed up the whole thing was until you started talking with the Corporal. I'm sorry if I came off as a bitch earlier, I'm extremely protective of my patients, I hope you understand."

"No need to apologize. We completely understand," Fischer said.

"I know you need answers, I get it. But I just need to impress upon you the significance of what Corporal Biagini has been through."

Fischer frowned. "Meaning?"

"Meaning, that on top of enduring several days of captivity, beatings, and torture. She was also raped. Repeatedly."

Fischer's stomach twisted. Dealing with sexual assault victims was one of the worst aspects of his job. It was one of the reasons he'd transferred from Persons Crimes Division to Property. Even with nations cracking down heavily on human trafficking, it was still one of the most profitable black-market industries in the galaxy.

He shook his head as disturbing images flashed through his mind.

"Her physical condition is going to improve, there's no doubt about that, but mentally…" Vaughan trailed off, pursing her lips and taking a lengthy breath. "To be honest, I'm not sure you'll get much out of her, Agents. She never spoke to *Vision*'s medical staff, and she's barely speaking to our therapy consultants."

"At the risk of sounding like a heartless bastard," Fischer said. "We have to try."

Vaughan nodded. "Fine, just don't press her. There're a lot of things going in her head right now that she hasn't—or can't—process."

"I understand."

The Doctor considered Fischer, then Eliwood, then turned and swiped her link across the security panel by the secured double doors. She led them down a long windowless corridor, around a corner toward a single door flanked by two armed Marines.

"Is that why you've isolated her?" Eliwood asked.

Vaughan turned slightly but continued down the hall. "She's been through an awful trauma. We're keeping her separated from the general hospital staff and patients."

One of the Marines nodded as they approached, unlocking the door with the swipe of his hand. Inside, the ward was dark and quiet. A single nurse sat at a small station to the left. She stood as they entered, waiting until the doors were shut and locked before giving Vaughan her report. "She's awake and stable, but her memory is still spotty."

Vaughan led them to a room marked REC11. The glass door was shut, the view blocked by a curtain on the other side. She paused, scrolling through the information on her chart, then hesitated before activating the security pad. "Remember, she's been through a lot."

"Got it."

Corporal Biagini was just a head sticking up out of thick off-white blankets. That same sound, soft, rhythmic beeping emanated from one of the monitors above her head. The rest were dark.

Her scalp was bandaged, face swollen, discolored and deformed by bruises and fractured bones. As Fischer drew closer, he could see the neck brace holding her head stable. She only managed to open one eye as the trio approached the bed. Her chest rose and fell in rapid cadence as her eyes flicked between the doctor and agents like she was trying to decide which was the more significant threat.

"It's okay, Corporal. It's Doctor Vaughan. You're okay. You're safe. These people are from Alliance Intelligence. They wanted to know if they could speak with you for a moment."

Fischer was still having trouble connecting this version of Vaughan with the one that had greeted them barely an hour before. It was like after hearing what Private Wallace had to say, her opinion of what Fischer was doing had drastically changed and he was more than a little curious as to why that was.

He smiled, keeping his voice soft. "My name's Jackson Fischer, ma'am, I know you've been through something horrible, but I'd like to ask you some questions… if that's okay."

She licked her lips and swallowed, grimacing in pain. When she spoke, her voice was hoarse and raspy. "Questions?"

"I'd like to talk with you about what happened during your mission. I know you've been through a lot, and I don't want to put you through any more than you've already been through."

"Questions…" She winced, trying to face Fischer, but the brace held her neck still. Her eyes fluttered as she spoke. "Where is he?"

Fischer then exchanged confused looks with Eliwood, then leaned in. "Where is who? Private Wallace and Sergeant Thomas are here, they're safe."

She grimaced, turning away, gritted her teeth. "No. It's not right."

"What's not right? Who are you looking for?"

"Can't," she said, shaking her head. "Orders."

"She's been incoherent like this ever since they brought her in. The report I received from *Vision*'s doctors is more of the same."

Fischer ignored the doctor. "What orders, Corporal?"

"Left... him," she said. She groaned, eyes closing as she leaned forward.

Vaughan put a hand on Biagini's shoulder, gently pushing her back down. "Easy. You're okay."

Tears welled in the corporal's eyes as her head touched the pillow. "No. No."

"Can you tell us anything you remember about the mission?" Fischer asked, hoping to push through the clutter. Sometimes all it took was getting a person to start talking, then most questions would typically answer themselves.

Biagini wiped away her tears with the back of her hand. "We left..."

"I know you lost Marines," Fischer said. "I'm trying to figure out why. I want to bring whoever's responsible for that to justice. I want to get you justice."

She locked eyes with him, teeth still clenched. "Orders."

Fischer nodded. "That's right. Orders. And mine are to figure out why your mission went to shit. Can you help me? What happened to you? Why did they hurt you?"

She groaned again and turned away as more tears ran down the side of her face. Her fists tightened around the sheets, twisting the fabric tight as her entire body seemed to react to Fischer's words.

Fischer turned to Vaughan.

"I told you, she's been through significant trauma. The events of the last week are likely fragmented, or worst case, completely blocked out. The mind can only cope with so much, after a certain point, it simply starts deleting things."

Fischer straightened, knowing it probably wouldn't do any good to press right now. Biagini's fists kept loosening and tightening on the sheets and tears continued to stream down her face. She stared off into space, eyes filled with terror and pain, and

Fischer realized he might not want to know what the Marine was re-living at this particular point in time.

"All right," he said, backing away. "Let's g—"

Biagini's hand shot out, grabbing Fischer's wrist. He winced, trying to twist away as she pulled him close. Her grip was like iron. Their eyes met and for that moment, the pain and horror had left them, replaced by rage and hate.

"They lied," Biagini said. "They lied to us."

Fischer stopped trying to free himself. "Who? Who lied to you? What did they lie to you about? The mission? What?"

She stared at him, face tight, eyes unblinking. "The mission..." Her jaw moved like she was grinding her teeth. "It was a lie."

Fischer took a breath, centering himself. "It's okay, Corporal. You're safe, the mission's over. No one's going to hurt you anymore. Tell me, who lied? What did they lie about?"

Biagini eyed the Doctor as if looking for approval. Vaughan nodded. "It's okay."

The Corporal tried to turn away, but the neck brace held her in place. She grimaced, closed her eyes, and sobbed, her hand still holding Fischer's wrist. He felt her body shake and felt an overwhelming urge to embrace her, to comfort her somehow, but also knew that probably wasn't what the Marine wanted right now.

Eliwood put a hand on Fischer's arm. She leaned in close, speaking so only he could hear. "Let's not push any further."

Fischer held up a finger. "Corporal, why did the extraction fail?"

Slowly, Biagini opened her eyes, her face a mask of grave determination. "It wasn't an extraction. It was an assassination."

CHAPTER 14

Alliance Security and Intelligence,
Regional Headquarters
New Tuscany
3 Apr 2607

"Before you say anything," Division Chief Carter said, holding up a hand as Fischer and Eliwood entered his office. "This thing is on the brink of spinning out of control."

Carter sat behind his desk, datapads in both hands. Images and videos hung on the wall behind him, replaying newsfeeds and pictures from the surface. The news cycle had been showing recordings of the burning buildings and first responders pulling children out of the rubble.

Fischer shook his head. Even if he could tell them how brave Marines were suffering at this very moment, he knew no one would care. They needed their pound of flesh, and right now, they were the easiest ones to blame. They couldn't defend themselves.

Carter shook his head, tossing the pads down onto his desk. "I mean, I've seen missions go to shit before, but I don't think I've ever seen this kind of shitstorm. Not that I can think of."

Eliwood dropped into the seat next to Fischer, crossing her legs. "Oh, this one's pretty fucked. There's no doubt about that."

"What'd you find out?"

Fischer went through the story Private Wallace had relayed to them so far, ending on the words Biagini had said.

He'd replayed her words over and over in his mind as they'd left the hospital. That she'd gone through such a trauma compromised her testimony—any defense attorney worth their salt would be able to use her dissociative state to crush anything she said. He'd been through enough cases to know that the criminal cases weren't won on facts.

They weren't in a court of law right now though, and Fischer didn't have to deal with some overpriced piece of shit trying to unravel his every word. He didn't have to worry about guilt or innocence, not right now at least. Fischer was after the facts.

The Corporal's words might not mean anything, they could've just been the ramblings of a broken Marine trying desperately to process everything that's happened to her. But they could also mean everything, and Fischer needed to know which.

"It just keeps getting better and better," Carter said, shaking his head. "Listen, this is bad. We need to keep a lid on this for as long as we can. What's this Doctor Vaughan like? Can we trust her?"

Fischer nodded. "I think so."

Carter pounced. "Don't think so, Fish. I hate that phrase. We deal in absolutes here, not assumptions. Especially with this." He motioned to the holoimages behind him.

"We can trust her," Eliwood said.

"Good. We're going to feel the pressure on this one, without a doubt. We need to make sure we do this by the numbers."

"We'll go back and try to get more out of Wallace tomorrow," Fischer said.

Eliwood snorted. "Didn't you think the guy came off as a little arrogant? Half the time he was talking I wanted to punch him in the face."

Fischer shrugged. "He's a Marine. That's their whole thing, isn't it? Being arrogant?"

"I guess."

"Regardless of what Wallace says, we need to find a way to get Biagini talking," Carter said. "She's obviously got something to say. Get her isolated, see if that helps."

"She's pretty messed up, Boss," Eliwood said. "Lot's of incoherent stuff. On top of being raped multiple times, who else knows what they did to her over there. I say we send the Navy out there right now and kick the shit out of those bastards."

Carter shook his head. "The Alliance isn't going to go to war over one Marine being raped. It's harsh, and it sucks, but it's the truth. There's a lot more going on than just Stonemeyer. Right now, let's just focus on getting the information. Command will use it as they see fit."

"Or they won't," Eliwood countered.

Carter raised a hand at her, indicating he understood her point.

"She kept saying something about their orders," Fischer said. "You think you can reach out and get an official copy from Command? Those might be helpful."

Carter made a note on his pad. "I've requested a list of transmissions made to and from the *Vision* during their time on station, including the Dispatch Packet from Second Fleet. Not sure if it'll come to anything, but somehow the media got ahold of this information, and I don't think it was simply good reporting."

Eliwood uncrossed her legs, leaning forward. "You think there's a leak on the *Vision*?"

"Leak is a fairly strong word," Carter said, wincing slightly. "Might not want to call it that."

"Captain Kimball said they went dark as soon as they left," she said. "Probably won't find a lot."

"Maybe not. But if I don't look, I won't find anything."

"The biggest question I have," Fischer said, "is what did she mean by assassination?"

Carter groaned. "Don't even get that brain spinning on that, Fish."

"I'm serious. I mean, come on, we all know there are countless direct action missions going on around the galaxy every day. The way I hear it, MARSOC can't keep up with the tempo despite their crazy recruiting numbers."

The Marine Special Operations Command enlisted the best of the best from the ranks of the regular Marine combat force, utilizing them in multiple operations and taskings. The term "shadow ops" was thrown around a lot throughout the rank and file, even though higher up the chain, that moniker was strictly prohibited. MARSOC's operations were usually classified as Ultra Top Secret, their operational capabilities known only to those within the Command.

Carter pointed at Fischer, glaring. "No. Not a chance. We're not MARSOC. Not unless we absolutely have to. The amount of red tape and bureaucratic shit I'd have to go through to get read into one of those is definitely not worth the hassle."

"And you'd only get the redacted version anyway," Eliwood said.

"Exactly."

"I'm not suggesting that at all," Fischer said. "Obviously, MARSOC didn't have anything do to with Stonemeyer. Otherwise, we probably wouldn't be here right now. Matter of fact, I can pretty much guarantee you we wouldn't be here. But Biagini's statement still stands. If they were sent there to kill someone, their orders will be open to review."

"Who would send an entire platoon of Marines into theater to assassinate one person?" Carter asked, sounding unconvinced. "Besides, have you ever heard of an assassination operation combined with an extraction? You haven't, because it's not done. There are far too many variables to consider, not to mention putting a sitting ambassador in harm's way. No way anyone would green light that kind of operation. No way."

"Then why would she say it?" Fischer asked.

"She's crazy," Carter retorted. "She's hopped up on meds; her brain is scrambled, PTSD, hell, it could be delusional thoughts from a TBI—traumatic brain injury. Who knows? I'm interested in why the mission failed. Obviously, the Stonemeyer Militia were better equipped than our original intelligence estimates suggested."

Eliwood sniffed. "What's Campbell say about that?"

"He maintains that everything they've seen suggests that the militia shouldn't have had that level of capability. Especially something that would bring down an Albatross class dropship."

"Pegasi intervention maybe?" Fischer offered.

"Could be," Carter answered. "I wouldn't put anything past those fanatics."

"So, there are two things we need to be looking into then," Fischer said, moving around Carter's desk to consider the images displayed across the wall. "One, what exactly happened during the mission and how the militia got their hands on the weapons in the first place."

"No," Carter said. "The mission is the investigation. Focus on that. If the weapons come up, then we'll follow them. But right now, they're secondary. Have Campbell pull all the intel on the militia. The background information might be useful."

"You really don't think the Pegasi had anything to do with it?" Eliwood asked. "I mean, they're always looking for ways to start shit with us. It's like their whole schtick. They're making a lot of waves in the URT right now."

"Like I said," Carter said. "It could be. I'm not ruling it out at all, though it would make my job a hell of a lot easier if it wasn't."

Eliwood frowned. "How so?"

"Because if it is, the possibility of this thing exploding into a full-on intergalactic incident is high. If that happens, it'll be more than just a trade embargo or a slap on the wrist to the Stonemeyer government. We're talking full-scale regional conflict."

"War," Fischer suggested.

Carter shook his head. "I don't even want to think about that."

Fischer's link chimed. "All right, I've got damage control detail with my wife tonight. Taking her to Del Monico."

Eliwood laughed, motioning to Carter. "See, you're not the only one upset about the Feringer deal."

Fischer glared at her. "Thanks."

"No one's said anything about it to me," Carter said. "I'm hoping this Stonemeyer mess has overshadowed it enough, that by the time we get it wrapped up, everyone will have forgotten about it. For both our sakes."

Fischer stopped at the door, hand on the knob. "I'll call you in the morning."

Eliwood waved a dismissive hand at him. "Handle your business. Try the Cowboy, I hear it's the best steak this side of the galaxy."

CHAPTER 15

Del Monico's Fine Dining
New Tuscany
3 Apr 2607

For once in his life, Jackson Fischer was glad of the crowds. It was far less likely Carissa would kill him in a room full of witnesses. Of course, "less likely" wasn't quite the same as "wouldn't." A fact he kept at the forefront of his mind as he ordered another bourbon, his second, and the main course had yet to arrive.

"Maddie pushed another kid in daycare today," Carissa said, taking a sip of her wine. The waiter had assured her the Corwynn Red was their most popular selection, which Fischer decided probably meant it was their most expensive selection. He didn't want to see the bill.

"I don't understand what's going on with her lately," Fischer said.

"Maybe she's taking after her Daddy."

Fischer started to respond, then stopped. Carissa's return stare wasn't angry, not exactly, it wasn't even mean-spirited, it was merely her way of saying, she was right, and he knew it.

She brushed a strand of strawberry blonde hair from her face, tucking it behind her ear. She was five years younger than Fischer, but he'd never allowed himself to think of himself as superior to her in any way. In fact, most days it was reversed. It was hard for Carissa to separate herself from her fast-paced executive day, then come home and slow down for family life.

At twenty-six, Carissa had practically sprinted up the corporate ladder, bypassing her more-senior colleagues. Her parents owned one of the largest textile exports on Corwynn, and those connections gave her unique advantages to make a lot of money for her employers.

Historically, the planet of Corwynn had been a difficult market to break into for many Alliance companies. The conservative population there verged on isolationism and were fanatical about their privacy and security laws. But the large temperate and tropical zones on the planet allowed for a substantial agricultural market in multiple specialties. The silk produced on their central continent of Astera accounted for almost forty-eight percent of their GDP and had made a lot of people extremely wealthy, including Carissa's family.

At work, she used that position to her advantage every chance she got, making moves that both impressed and infuriated her co-workers. But she never brought it home. And never once pulled the "I make more money than you, I get to make the rules card" Fischer had seen other business execs pull on their significant others. Most of the time, he was grateful for that, but often he wondered if she was simply coddling him.

Either way, he sipped his forty-seven-credit bourbon, a beverage he wouldn't have been able to afford on his meager ASI salary and savored the smooth burn as he worked the liquid around his mouth.

Finally, he said, "I'm sorry."

Carissa raised an eyebrow. "Sorry? For what?"

Fischer could tell by her tone that she knew very well what he was about to say but he knew she was going to make him say every word. "I'm sorry I didn't tell you about the Op. It was kind of last minute, I needed to move fast and—"

"No." Carissa set her glass down on the table. "That's not it."

"Listen, babe, I know you don't like Tensley, but—"

"That's not it either."

Fischer frowned, mind racing, trying to decide what his wife wanted him to say.

Why can't you just tell me what you want me to say, instead of making me feel like a grade school student being scolded in front of the class?

He opened his mouth to respond but stopped as two servers approached the table. He leaned back, allowing a thin woman dressed in a solid black suit and white tie, to set his plate down in front of him. An older, gray haired man lowered Carissa's plate at the same time. They took a step back as a third man appeared.

"For the lady, tonight we have Del Raycan Angelfish with a solomon lemon cream sauce, with our very own Blue Lake sea cucumber," Gregor, the senior server said, hands clasped in front of his waist. His white suit and black tie contrasted the rest of the staff, a symbol of his position in the restaurant's hierarchy. He would not be responsible for serving food in his attire. "And for the gentleman, a local New Tuscan Rib Eye, with just a hint of our special seasoning and cooked a perfect medium."

He bowed slightly to Carissa, smiling. "The chef sends his regrets to the lady that he was unable to present your course this evening. As you can see, we are quite busy tonight."

Carissa smiled waving a hand dismissively. "Oh, it's fine Gregor, I completely understand. Please, give Riccardo my best, the food looks lovely."

Gregor bowed again, this time lowering his head. "The lady is very kind. Please, enjoy."

The junior servers bowed together, then turned and followed Gregor, leaving Fischer and his wife in silence. Wisps of steam rolled over his steak, bringing an almost irresistible smell to his nostrils. Fischer refused to even consider how much the food cost.

Carissa bit in first, slowly chewing, closing her eyes to savor the taste as Fischer went to work on his. The cut was perfectly aged, medium rare, and so tender he almost didn't need a knife to slice it. The outside was crusted slightly, but the inside was warm and juicy. He had to force himself not to groan as he enjoyed the meat's exquisite flavor.

They ate in silence for a time, enjoying the meal. As he chewed, Fischer scanned the surrounding patrons, something, even here among New Tuscany's elite and privileged, he couldn't stop himself from doing.

"Always know who and what's around you," his instructors had drilled into him daily during his ASI training. There is no excuse for allowing anyone, no matter who they are, to get within ten meters of you without you knowing.

Granted, much of that instruction had come during the field operations portion of the training and generally speaking, Fischer worked in an office, but the instructors had done their jobs well, and now, the process was second nature to him. Like a faucet he couldn't turn off.

The majority of the patrons never even looked up from their tables, all either focused on their food or their company. Glasses clinked together, silverware scrapped against ivory plates, murmurs of conversation filtered around the dining room, punctuated with laughter and clapping. Most of the guests were high-level executives, though Fischer had noticed a handful of local politicians here tonight who showed no irritation at the constant interruptions for handshakes and greetings.

Fischer took another bite, chewing as his gaze fell on the oval-shaped bar positioned in the middle of the restaurant. It sat atop a glass floor underneath which was an expansive fish tank, containing hundreds of varieties of colorful fish. He wondered if the food his wife was eating at this moment had been taken right from that tank.

Probably not, he thought. *Hopefully not.*

The guests at the bar conversed in groups of twos and threes, some watching the series of sporting events on holodisplays above. The team of bartenders never stopped moving, bouncing back and forth between guests with practiced efficiency, not allowing anyone to wait more than a few seconds until they were served. They tossed bottles between them, pouring and mixing as though it were as simple as breathing.

As Fischer's gaze swept across the area, he froze, meeting the eyes of a man seated at the far side of the bar, looking at Fischer through a collection of expensive looking liquor bottles. Almost immediately, the man averted his gaze, bringing an almost full glass of amber liquid to his lips, taking an abrupt sip. Fischer let his gaze linger. It could've been just a coincidence, two people gazing across the restaurant and just happening to make eye contact at the same time.

Maybe he's embarrassed, Fischer thought. *Maybe he thought he knew me and realized at the last minute he'd been wrong.* Fischer had done that before, it always left him feeling uncomfortable and stupid. But there was something about how the man sat there, something about how he'd positioned himself that kept the alarm bells ringing at the back of Fischer's mind.

"You okay?"

His wife's words brought him back to the table. "Huh?"

"For a second there, you looked like something was wrong."

Fischer shook himself, taking another bite of steak. "No, sorry, I'm fine. Thought I saw someone I knew."

"You know, Maddie needs you, right? I need you?"

Fischer almost choked. "What?"

"We need you, Jackson," Carissa repeated, setting her fork down on her plate. "If something were to happen to you…"

"Babe…" Fischer said, realizing she hadn't finished with their conversation.

She shook her head. "No, it's true. I don't know what we'd do if something happened to you. I thought that when you took this job, it was going to get you out of operations. That was the deal, right?"

Fischer suppressed a sigh. "It has, honey."

"Then what was that last night?"

"Like I said, it was a last minute thing. We had intel we had to move on and—"

"Don't you have teams for that kind of thing?" Carissa asked, cutting him off.

"Yes, but—"

"Then why weren't they the ones dodging bullets? Why was it you?"

"There wasn't time."

"Bullshit," Carissa hissed.

Fischer flinched at his wife's uncharacteristic language. She took a long breath, calming herself, then said, "I'm sorry."

"It's okay."

"I just don't want you taking those risks. Honestly, you don't need to."

They'd had the conversation several times before, and in Fischer's experience, the best course of action from this point was to agree and move on. Arguing with her about the nature of his job, or that there would be times when he didn't have a choice and putting himself in harm's way was simply a necessary evil, wouldn't end well.

"You're right," he said, and without knowing why, his eyes

flicked back to the man at the bar. Again, his eyes seemed fixated on Fischer, and again, he immediately looked away. "I'm sorry."

Not a coincidence then, Fischer thought.

He kept his eyes on the man, waiting for him to look again. He took another sip of his beer, keeping his gaze focused on one of the holodisplays above the bar.

"I love you very much, Jackson Fischer."

He looked back, finding himself swimming in her beautiful blue eyes, eyes filled with so much love and compassion, he didn't understand it most of the time, and he smiled. He reached across the table, putting his hand over hers. "I love you, too."

He lifted her hand and leaned across to kiss it. Carissa smiled at him, shaking her hand. "Not fair."

Fischer couldn't help the grin forming at the corners of his mouth. "What'd I do?"

"You know what you did." She pulled her hand away, picking up her fork and taking another bite of fish.

Fischer watched her chew for a second, then took another sip of bourbon. As the smooth, rich liquid rolled over his tongue, he glanced back toward the man at the bar. He was still watching the holodisplay. Absently, Fischer rubbed the pistol under his arm with the inside of his elbow, reassuring himself the weapon was there if he needed it.

"The Stonemeyer thing was all over the feeds today," Carissa said. "Seems like a pretty messed up deal."

"It is. Only three survivors and they're all pretty banged up."

"What happened?"

Fischer sliced another piece of meat, shaking his head. "Not sure yet. It's not going to be an easy process though, I can tell you that. I'm pretty sure one of the Marines is embellishing his story a bit, one was still in surgery and the other... well, she's really messed up. I doubt I'll get anything useful out of her. She's going to have a long road ahead of her, that's for sure."

"So, what, the Pegasi peacekeeping operation isn't so peaceful, huh?"

"Is it ever?" Fischer asked. "Actually, right now, it doesn't look like they're involved with the attacks. Not directly anyway. Right now, it just looks like local militia not happy with the Alliance presence in their system. But who knows? Hopefully tomorrow I'll be able to get more out of them."

In one last effort to prove coincidence or not, Fischer glanced at the man at the bar, and for a third time, the man's eyes were locked on. This time, the man slid off his seat as he looked away, leaving the bar area, heading for the exit.

Fischer followed him with his eyes, watching as he weaved around tables and the staff. Halfway to the exit, the man's head turned, eyes coming up in Fischer's direction. When they did, Fischer knew for certain that this man had been watching him.

"Alright," he said, setting this fork down and pushing back his chair.

"What is it?" Carissa asked, looking up, worried.

"Nothing, I'll be right back."

The man seemed to notice Fischer standing, and hurried his pace through the restaurant, disappearing through the large, ornamental glass doors at the front of the building.

Gregor appeared in Fischer's path, smiling, hands clasps in front of his chest. "Is there something I can do for the gentleman?"

"No, sorry. Thanks, Gregor." Fischer stepped around the server, never taking his eyes off the entrance.

He pushed through the doors, stepping out onto the street. One of the black-suited doormen stepped back, looking slightly disturbed by Fischer's sudden exit.

The doorman wasn't the only one. Several waiting patrons jumped, whispering to their friends, all eyeing Fischer with a mixture of irritation and amusement. He froze, hand inside his jacket, fingers wrapped around the grip of his pistol, but didn't draw.

The doorman stepped close, speaking in low tones, as he if was embarrassed for Fischer and wanted to take steps to save face for his guest. "May I call a conveyance for you, sir?"

"No," Fischer said, too harshly than he'd wanted. He glanced north, scanning across the throngs of people hustling along both sides of the street, then turned south.

The night air was warm, filled with the sounds of traffic and people walking up and down the street. Floating orbs illuminated the pavement at ground level, almost made irrelevant by the multitude of colorful holoboards and images that seemed to take up every inch of spare space on the surrounding buildings.

There was no sign of the man from the bar. He was gone.

Fischer felt a hand touch his arm and turned to see Carissa's concerned face.

"What is it?" she asked, her tone carrying none of the harshness it'd held previously. She sounded genuinely concerned. "What happened?"

Fischer released his pistol and put his arm around his wife. "I really don't know."

CHAPTER 16

Alliance Security and Intelligence,
Regional Headquarters
New Tuscany
4 Apr 2607

Eliwood looked up from her desk as Fischer entered their office, nodding at him as he tossed his leather coat over the back of his chair. Her hair was pulled back in a tight ponytail, sleeves rolled to her elbow, collar undone. Two paper cups sat empty on the desk next to her, containing only small traces of the coffee she'd devoured. She held a third cup in one hand, half-full of the dark liquid.

Multiple holopanels floated above the desk in front of her. Some displaying still images of the man he'd seen at the restaurant the night before, others were playing vid-streams from area security cameras and traffic surveillance.

"Find anything?" Fischer asked.

She leaned back in her chair, taking a sip from her cup. She grimaced, immediately leaning forward and spitting the coffee back into her cup. "Ugh." She pushed the cup away from her, smacking her tongue against her lips.

Eliwood pushed her chair back, forcing Fischer to step to the side.

Fischer rubbed at his beard, concealing his smile. "Been here a while, huh?"

She stopped at the door, glaring at him. "Someone's got to save your ass around here. You want a cup?"

"Sure."

Eliwood disappeared around the hall, and Fischer turned back to the holodisplays. He focused on the top-left panel, spread his fingers and expanded the display. A short tap sent it to the beginning. The entrance of Del Monico's was positioned at the left of the screen, the playback's current positioning capturing some of the street leading away from the restaurant. The doorman was helping the next guest in line, nodding his head enthusiastically while jotting notes on his datapad.

After a few seconds, the doors slammed open as the man ran out of the restaurant and took off at a sprint, north. Fischer muttered a curse under his breath as he watched the figure disappear into the crowd and not five seconds later, he stepped through the doors, scanning the street.

He swiped a finger along the panel, rewinding the footage, pausing it just as the man exited the building. He spread his fingers again, zooming in on the man's face. It took the computer a second to enhance and render the image, but after it was finished, Fischer was looking at a clear view of the man's face, as if he was standing right in front of him.

"Computer's still chewing on facial recognition," Eliwood said. She held out a cup, and he took it, careful not to spill.

"How long has it been working?"

"Bout an hour."

Fischer held the cup close, blowing tiny ripples in the

steaming coffee. He reached up and swiped the still image, reverting it back to the original size and starting the recording again. "How long have you been here?"

"Couple hours. Wanted to get an early start. Figured it was going to be a long day. Carissa doing okay?" Eliwood nodded to the display where Fischer's wife was just stepping up next to him, putting a hand on his arm.

"She's fine."

"Liar."

Fischer covered his smile by sipping on the coffee.

"You think he's one of Feringer's guys?" Eliwood asked, sliding down into her chair.

"No idea. Maybe he thought I was someone else."

"Okay. Who?"

"Your guess is as good as mine."

Eliwood chuckled and sipped at her coffee. "Tracked him a couple of blocks to an unregistered gravcar. Whoever he is, he's definitely not an amateur."

"Why do you say that?"

She tapped another display, bringing the panel into the forefront. The video feed played automatically. The orbital drone traffic cam followed the man as far as its coverage allowed. The view switched to another ODT, then showed the man climbing into a plain four-door. Within seconds, it lifted into the air, merging with traffic and vanished.

"Followed it on ODT as long as I could. But you know those things. Spotty. No transponder either," Eliwood said. "Completely masked his escape. I scrubbed all the feeds in the area, no joy. No record of his departure anywhere in the transit network logs."

Fischer took a sip of his coffee then said, "Not many people would have the resources to manage that."

"Right. And Feringer's contacts don't seem that bright. I

mean, they're a fairly low level operation, right? They don't have the contacts for something like this."

"Maybe we underestimated them."

Eliwood lifted her cup, index finger pointing. "You... you underestimated them."

Fischer sniffed. "I—"

A shadow fell across the doorway, and both turned as Carter entered. "Anything?"

Fischer shook his head.

"He's good," Eliwood said. "Whoever he is."

"You don't think it could've just been a coincidence?" Carter asked. "Lots of high-profile people were at Del Monicos last night, including some Alliance senators. Is it possible he just recognized you as ASI? Maybe he thought you were there, blowing his cover or something."

"I don't know, Boss," Fischer said. "He seemed to be looking right at me. I didn't really get the impression he was watching anyone else."

"I'm sure facial recognition will ping him," Eliwood said. "For some reason, it's just taking longer than normal."

"You going to hit the hospital again?"

Fischer leaned back against the office wall, folding his arms across his chest. "Thomas should be in recovery by now. Wallace should be up to continue. I'm worried about Biagini. She's really messed up."

"Yeah, well, getting tortured and raped would probably do that to anyone," Eliwood said.

"No disagreement from me there," Fischer said. "I think it's more than that though. Especially with her whole assassination comment and the repeated mentions about orders. Something happened down there. Something she doesn't want to talk about."

"Maybe this will help," Carter said, pulling a pad from inside his briefcase. "Campbell pulled some strings inside the Diplomatic Corps and pulled the Embassy shipping records. Lots of incoming shipments marked eyes-only. He says most of the inventory is redacted, but his contact says that's pretty standard for the DC."

Fischer took the pad and started scrolling through the data. "Redacted huh? What does the DC have to redact? Pens and paper? The occasional high-dollar banquet?"

"Lot of people to bribe, cajole, and swindle out there," Eliwood said.

"Hey, they're making better lives for everyone," Fischer said, mocking the Corps official line.

Eliwood rolled her eyes. "Sure they are."

Most of the data on the pad was incomplete or entirely redacted. The more Fischer scrolled through the data, the more apparent it became that the pad would probably be useless.

He held it up. "Sure is a whole lot of nothing here."

Carter nodded. "Go through it anyway. I want to be able to tell command we did everything we could and looked at every piece of information available when this thing is ready to present."

"Speaking of," Fischer said, tossing the pad onto the desk. "Any luck on the comm logs?"

"Got shot down almost immediately."

"That Kimball asshole is a real dick," Eliwood said.

"True," Fischer said. "But he's following procedure. In his position, I'd probably handle it the exact same way. He's covering his ass is all."

"Agreed," Carter said. "I was just hoping I'd be able to bypass all the red tape involved with going through Regional Command Authority."

"Red tape, bureaucratic bullshit kills investigations," Eliwood said.

"Truer words were never spoken," Carter acknowledged. "I have a feeling, though, that once the shit starts flying and the calls for action against Stonemeyer and the Pegasi start rolling, the red tape will shrivel up fairly quickly."

Fischer motioned to the wall of images to his left. "We don't even know the Pegasi had anything to do with this. Aside from the clean up afterward, we haven't seen any evidence to the contrary."

"Doesn't matter," Carter said. "You know how the masses will look at it. Especially with everything they're doing out in the URT right now. Either they assisted with, or were complicit in the attack, it doesn't matter. Either way, the spin is the same. Hold on."

Carter frowned, tapping this link. "Yes?" Fischer couldn't hear the conversation, but by the look on his boss's face, whatever it was, he wasn't pleased. "We'll be right there."

Eliwood stood, obviously picking up on their boss's change in demeanor. "What's up, Boss?"

"Sergeant Thomas. He's missing."

CHAPTER 17

Haroldson Memorial Hospital,
Regional Naval Medical Facility
New Tuscany
4 Apr 2607

Fischer turned away from the empty bed, shaking his head. "I still don't understand how the hell he could've just walked out of here. You had security on his room, right?"

Sergeant Preble, Doctor Vaughan, and two other Marines stood near the entrance to the room, all sharing the same perplexed expression.

"And wasn't he still recovering from surgery?" Eliwood added from the far side of the bed.

"The surgery was just a final repair to some internal injuries," Vaughan said. She stood with her hands in her coat pockets. "He was in and out of recovery in less than two hours and transferred down here shortly after."

Eliwood walked her fingers across an imaginary line in front of her. "And then he just waltzed right on out, without so much as a 'Can I get your jacket, sir?'"

"That's not what they were stationed here for," Sergeant Preble said. "My men were stationed here to keep people from getting into the rooms, not for keeping the patients in them."

"And the sight of a man right out of surgery in a hospital gown didn't trigger any kind of red flag?" Eliwood asked.

The Sergeant's cheeks flushed. "Now, just a minute—"

Fischer raised a hand. "All right. No one is accusing you, or your men, of doing anything wrong, Sergeant. Were you able to track him on CCTV?"

"All the way to the elevator."

"The elevator?" Fischer frowned. "What do you mean? Don't you have coverage through the entire complex."

Preble nodded. "That's right, we do. But the system received some interference around the same time your man here was making his great escape. He had help."

Fischer and Eliwood exchanged glances. She raised an eyebrow at him. "Seems to be a trend."

No shit, Fischer thought.

"But that doesn't explain why he would leave in the first place," Doctor Vaughan said. "It doesn't make any sense. He was receiving the best medical treatment the Alliance could provide. Sure, the surgery was relatively minor, but still. Unless he's got a considerable pain tolerance or he gets his hands on some good drugs, he's going to be in a lot of pain."

"And the others?" Fischer asked.

Vaughan shrugged. "They're both where we left them. Corporal Biagini has been in and out of consciousness all night, but she's slowly progressing. Private Wallace is still immobilized, but other than that, he's recovering very well."

"We're going to need to talk to both of them again," Fischer told her.

"Private Wallace shouldn't be a problem," Vaughan said. "The Corporal though, she really does need a substantial amount of time. Like I said yesterday, her trauma is only partly physical, and mental injuries sometimes can take months, even years to heal. If at all. Some of the worst kinds of injuries are the ones you can't see."

"Can you give us a minute please?" Fischer asked motioning to the door.

Vaughan and Preble both hesitated, but finally turned and left, closing the door behind them.

Fischer sighed. "I just don't get it."

"What?" Eliwood asked. "That the guy bounced, or that someone helped him, or that someone has the connections to hack the hospital's security protocols and conceal his escape?"

"Yes."

"You think it's a military thing? They'd certainly have the power to mess with the system? Thomas is a lifer, he doesn't have anything else but the Marines. He's not going to do anything without orders. There's got to be someone pulling strings for him."

"But the question is still 'why?' No one knows what happened during the mission. He hadn't been accused of anything, hell, until today, I hadn't considered any of the survivors as suspects of anything. Makes me wonder if the others could've gotten out of here, would they have?"

"But why?" Eliwood asked. "It doesn't make any sense. You'd think they'd want to help us get to the bottom of this thing, and help bring whoever fucked this whole operation up to justice. I mean, somebody's head's going to roll for this, right? You think Thomas thought he was on the chopping block?"

"It's possible, but if that were the case, you'd think he'd want us to hear his side of things. Vanishing in the middle of the night only makes him look guilty."

"He didn't even try to contact the other two. Just left them. Isn't their thing, never leave a Marine behind?"

Fischer nodded, scratching his beard. "Yes... yes, it is." Something Biagini had said floated into his mind. "Not leaving anyone behind..."

A half-grin formed at the side of Eliwood's mouth, as if she could see the wheels spinning inside Fischer's mind. "What is it?"

"I need to talk to Biagini again. I need to know what she meant."

Eliwood turned, leaning forward to look out of the room's only window. "Doesn't sound like Vaughan is too keen on you talking to her."

"I'll deal with that."

"What are you going to do?" She looked over her shoulder, one eyebrow raised. "Hack the security system too? Because my guess is that's the only way you're ever going to get in to talk to her."

Fischer grunted. "You're probably right."

She turned from the window, a hand to her ear. "What was that?"

Fischer rolled his eyes, heading for the door.

"No, wait. Say that again, I couldn't quite hear you."

"You heard me," Fischer said, pausing with his hand on the door handle. "Track down Thomas. Call Carter and get a team down here. I'm going to talk to Wallace and see if I can figure out just what the hell is going on."

CHAPTER 18

Darkstar Six-Three
Calibri City, Stonemeyer
23 Mar 2607
Mission Time: 01hrs 15mins

There's a feeling you get when a ship's going down that's three parts terror, one part thrill. I remember the red lights flashing, the alarms, people screaming, the Albatross shaking as it dropped out of the sky. I felt almost weightless like I was back in zero-gee training, but it wasn't anything like the serene feeling I'd had floating through the void, watching the stars blink around me. This time I felt my stomach twisting in knots and had to fight back the urge to vomit.

I grabbed the seat in front of me as the dropship lurched, throwing me sideways. The motion wrenched my hand free of the rail, and I twisted, slamming into the side of the bay. I caught a brief glance of the world spinning around us through a small window and heard the engines laboring, trying to compensate and keep us aloft.

The pilot's voice warbled over the Albatross's internal

comms. "We're going down! Darkstar Six-Three we are going down!"

The impact tossed me into the air. The world spun, becoming nothing but a blur of screaming and flailing limbs. An instant later, I slammed back down to the deck, the air rushing from my lungs. Pain erupted through my body, stars danced in my vision and blackness crept in around my peripherals.

An entire section of the fuselage ripped away, revealing a blur of buildings as the Albatross slid across the street. Metal groaned as the bird tilted, the right wing dipping toward the street. It caught a parked car with a screeching wrenching of metal, spinning the entire craft halfway around before ripping the wing completely off.

Sparks danced through the bay as several fires broke out, filling the compartment with smoke. My fingers hurt from holding on so tight as the dropship lurched and skidded down the street. My jaw ached from clenching my teeth. By the time we came to a stop, I barely had any strength left to push to my knees.

Maxwell's body had slid all the way across the bay, bumping into Ford's which also lay unmoving. Ford's head was cocked sideways, his eyes open, staring at nothing, and even from across the bay, I knew he was gone.

Hastings pushed himself up on all fours, coughing through a broken visor. Even in the darkness of the bay, I could see blood running down his face.

He pushed himself to his feet and yelled, "Clear the bird! Everybody off, now!"

The ringing in my head made it hard to concentrate. I pulled myself to my feet, reaching for my rifle but found nothing. I spun, searching, scanning a deck cluttered with bodies and smeared with blood.

"Wallace!" Biagini yelled, stepping over Maxwell's corpse. "What the hell are you doing? Get moving!"

"Can't find my weapon!"

"For fuck's sake." She turned and shoved Ford's body aside, revealing a weapon. It wasn't mine, I could tell by the gray serial stenciled on the butt, but I took it anyway and tanked out the magazine, checking the load.

"Come on!" she yelled again, stepping over Ford and past me.

"Help! My God, someone help!" The Ambassador sat with his back against the forward bulkhead, trying to push a body off his legs. Maxwell's body.

Hastings knelt down and eased my friend's corpse off Ambassador Delaney and pointed toward the opening ramp. "We need to leave now, sir!" He met my eyes and pointed. "Wallace, check the cockpit."

"Roger that, sir," I said. I still felt like the world was rocking around me as I made my way through the bay, stepping around loose crates and over the dead. A panel above the seats next to me flew open in a shower of sparks. I jumped, ducking away as the colorful fountain filled the air.

The cockpit's hatch hung open, attached to the frame by only the top hinge, swaying back and forth like a flag in some summer breeze. Inside, multiple display panels flickered. Sparks popped and snapped. A series of cracks stretched through the windshield, along which jagged pieces were missing. Smoke from fire inside the control panels billowed through the openings as if sucked out by a vacuum.

"Hey," I said, leaning forward between the two pilot seats. "You all right? We gotta—"

The sight of the co-pilot to my left cut me off. His head hung forward, body still strapped into his seat, arms hanging loosely at his sides. The visor on his flight helmet was shattered, and bright red blood poured out through the sawtoothed openings. I craned my head down and saw a large piece of glass sticking out of the middle of his face.

Fuck, I thought, almost throwing up.

I almost jumped out of my skin, turning to see the pilot's head slowly come off his chest. His hands came up in front of him, grasping for something but finding nothing. It almost looked like he was trying to find the flight controls.

"You're alive!" I said, not really believing what I was seeing.

I flipped up the man's visor. Blood streamed down from his face, pooling in part of his canvas jumpsuit. His head swayed back and forth, and his eyes couldn't seem to focus, almost like he was drunk.

"Hey, you okay?" I asked, dropping to a knee beside him.

He opened his mouth to speak, but the only sound his lips made was a wet gurgle as he spat blood. His body twitched as he struggled to find the controls, hands grasping at air.

I reached for the harness release on his chest. "It's going to be okay, man. We're getting the fuck out of here."

"…Going… down…" he wheezed.

"We're already down, buddy," I said. "Come on, help me out he—"

Glass shattered and something smacked into the pilot's head, slamming him into the headrest. I fell back as a spray of blood and gore covered everything, including me.

"Fuck me!" I shouted, eyes locked on the sea of blood.

Another bullet smashed through the windshield, then another, spraying glass, clattering into the bulkhead. A few more *thunked* into the pilot's chest, his limp body jerking with every impact.

"*Contact right!*" Thomas shouted over the taclink.

Outside gunfire erupted all around the downed dropship. I sat there, almost frozen, looking at the dead pilot, thinking how close I'd come to taking those bullets instead of him.

An explosion outside rocked the Albatross, knocking me back into the co-pilot's seat. There was a flash of red and orange outside the cockpit's window, then a cloud of thick black smoke rolled past.

A chaotic stream of communication filled the taclink as I pulled myself out of the cockpit. The bay was empty, save for Maxwell and Ford's dead bodies left lying unceremoniously on the deck. Even through my helmet, I could smell the thick odor of blood and death.

My gaze lingered on Maxwell's body. I wanted to help him. I had this overwhelming compulsion to pick him up and carry him out with me, thinking somehow I could still save him. But there was no coming back from that. Instead, I picked my way through the bay and out onto the streets of Calibri City.

The Albatross had crashed right in the middle of a four-lane street, surrounded by a few tall office buildings and apartments. What traffic had been on the road, had come to a screeching halt, cars, trucks, bikes, vans, all hovering a meter or two above the choppy pavement in both directions. Some of the people seemed oblivious to the firefight going on around them, throwing their hands in the air, honking horns as if we'd just ruined their morning commute.

The dropship's remaining engine changed pitch every few seconds, from spinning up to winding down. I swear, I thought the thing was going to explode right there and take us all out.

I found Jung and Biagini crouched behind a small four-door car. Jung was desperately trying to get a drone into the air, and Biagini was taking potshots at an enemy I couldn't see.

"Where are they?" I asked, taking a knee next to her.

She fired off another burst. "Fuck if I know. Just keep shooting."

Hasting's voice came over the taclink. *"Darkstar Six-Four, Darkstar Actual, Six-Three is down. Repeat, Six-three is down, request evac immediately!"*

"Actual, Six-Four, I've got multiple waves of hostiles

encroaching on your position, the area's too hot for an extraction."

"Is he fucking kidding," I shouted over another one of Biagini's volleys.

She shook her head. "Fucking pilots."

"Six-Four, Actual, we need air support now, over. We are pinned down and outnumbered.

A stray bullet zipped past my helmet, so close I feel it. "Son of a bitch!" I brought my 27 into my shoulder and fired back, aiming at nothing.

Biagini laughed. "That's the spirit!"

"Wallace!" Sergeant Thomas shouted, but it wasn't over the taclink. I turned, seeing Thomas, the Lieutenant, Fallon, and the Ambassador kneeling behind a flatbed delivery truck, parked in an alley right off the main street.

"Yeah, Staff Sergeant?"

He pointed to the Ambassador. "Stay with him. Don't let him out of your sight."

I dropped down beside Thomas and looked over Delaney. For all his shit talking back at the Embassy, the guy looked scared out of his mind. A thin stream of blood trickled down the side of his face. His suit was disheveled, shirt untucked. His eyes flicked and darted around, and his body flinched at every shot.

"I can't stay here," he said, pulling at Fallon's arm. The Embassy guard was practically holding the Ambassador down, keeping him from running off and getting himself shot and killed. "Do something Sergeant! Get me the fuck out of here! I can't stay here! I have to go!"

I put a hand out. "Please, sir. You have to calm down. It's not going to—"

"I don't have to calm shit!" he shouted back, cutting me off. "Do you know who the hell I am? I'm Senior Ambassador Tobias

Delaney, ranking Alliance official in this entire region! I order you to get me out of here! Do you hear me, Sergeant?"

He was looking at Hastings, but the Lieutenant was ignoring him. "Six-Four, do you copy? We need those guns now!"

"Actual, Six-Four, we copy," the pilot answered, his voice clipped and hard. *"We are inbound. Mark your position, over."*

We're the big flaming pile of shit in the middle of the road, I thought.

Thomas turned. "Biagini, Grayson, IR flares now!"

"Roger!" Biagini shouted, pushing her rifle around behind her and dropping behind the trunk of the car. She pulled a six-inch cylinder from a point on her vest, slapped the button on top with her palm and tossed it into the street. You couldn't see the infrared strobe with the naked eye, but our HUDs could pick them up no problem, and they'd light up the street like a Christmas tree for the dropship. "IR's up!"

A second later, Grayson advised the same.

"Darkstar Actual, this is Vision Actual, report status, Lieutenant. What is your situation?"

I shared a confused look with Sergeant Thomas. What the hell was the Captain doing on the air?

Hastings seemed confused as well, hesitating slightly before answering. *"Vision* Actual, Darkstar Actual. Sir, Six-Three is down. We are under heavy enemy fire and are pinned down. We need immediate reinforcement now, sir."

"Do you have King?"

Hastings looked at Delaney. "Roger that, sir."

"What is it?" the Ambassador asked. He pointed to Hasting's helmet. "Who's that? Is that the Captain? I need to speak with him."

He tried to get up, but Fallon pushed him back down. "Stay down, sir! Please."

"Darkstar Actual, we are working on extraction protocols now. Stand by."

"Stand by my ass," Sergeant Thomas muttered.

"Darkstar Six-Four to Darkstar ground elements, I have your position marked, we're starting out attack run now. Sit tight."

I leaned out of the alley, looking up the street back toward the Embassy. The horizon had turned light blue with just the barest hint to orange behind the silhouette of the city. My HUD tagged multiple hostile targets in the distance, moving up between cars and out of alleyways.

"Where the fuck did they all come from?" I asked to no one in particular.

"Jung!" Hastings shouted. The Corporal looked his direction, and he continued, no waiting for her to respond. "I need a map."

"Roger!" She pulled one of her recon bots from its case on the ground next to her, thumbed the activation switch and tossed it over.

A series of lights came to life as the little orb spun through the air. It's internal gravdrive kicked on, slowing its flight and bringing it to a hover a meter from the Lieutenant's face. Blue lines traced themselves through the air as the bot's interface materialized and Hastings went to work.

He used both hands to manipulate the map, rotating it and zooming in on several different locations.

"What the fuck are you doing, Sergeant?" Delaney demanded, slapping Fallon's arm away. "Recall that dropship and have them pick us up!"

Hastings didn't look away from the map, continuing to work his way through the city as he said, "The dropship can't set down, the LZ is too hot. We're going to have to clear the area of hostiles or move to a secondary extraction point."

"Secondary! Get that damn ship on the ground right now!"

The Ambassador jabbed a finger downward. "That is your job! I order you—"

"Sir, please," Fallon said, practically begging the guy to sit and be still.

I really wanted to reach out and punch the asshole right in the face. That would've shut him up.

"Six-Four to ground units, here comes the pain. Keep your heads down."

The Albatross appeared out of the night sky as if materializing from nothing. It banked hard around a building behind us, lining up on the street, its engines screaming. Its nose dipped, and it charged forward, the Vipers on both sides spinning up. The Wrath of God was about to reach out and touch someone.

The Viper III lit up the street around them, sending hundreds of rounds down range in an instant. The brrrrrrrrrrrrp rumbled in my chest as the Albatross passed overhead, the cannon's completely annihilating everything in its path. A car exploded, cut in half by the stream of bullets. The blast sent both halves twirling into the air. The front half crashed into another vehicle, shoving it into a line of militia, sending them running. The back half landed in the street, spinning like a top on one corner before crashing down in a flaming mess.

"That's right, run you motherfuckers!" I shouted, jumping to my feet.

The rest of the platoon joined in the celebration, cheering and pounding their fists in the air as the Vipers chewed through cars, pavement, and people like a hot knife through butter.

The Albatross flared suddenly, nose coming up as its engines screamed. A rocket shot up from the ground, trailing a thin column of white smoke. It sliced through the air, coming within feet of the dropship's nose. The Albatross lifted away, turning to bring the Viper to bear on the enemy position.

"Six-Four to ground elements, be advised there is an air-to-

ground rocket emplacement one hundred and twenty meters north of your position. They're tucked in pretty good, can't get a bead."

A red diamond flashed on Hastings's holomap as the Milnet received the Albatross's targeting data, indicating the location of the rocket emplacement.

"Why don't they just land?" Delaney shouted. "Sergeant, I order you to tell them to land right now!"

"If we can take out that position and push them back another block, it may give the bird enough time," Sergeant Thomas said, pointing at the map. "Take this alley here, they'll never see us coming."

Hastings nodded. "Make it happen."

Thomas immediately turned, making for the street. "Henderson, Biagini, Wallace, on me!"

CHAPTER 19

Calibri City, Stonemeyer
23 Mar 2607
Mission Time: 01hrs 32mins

The only enemy fighter we encountered as we moved through the alley had been pissing. He'd been just standing there, his back to us as he drew a thin stream onto the wall like there wasn't a gun battle going on right around the corner.

Henderson didn't even give him the dignity of finishing before he shot him. Put a bullet through the back of his skull while he was standing there, holding his dick. Damn, I mean, what a way to go...

We kept low as we emerged from the alley, coming up behind a row of parked cars. The main enemy force was between us and the rest of the team, completely unaware that we'd managed to infiltrate their lines.

Another rocket shot out, arcing through the early morning sky after the retreating Albatross. A stream of flares erupted from the dropship's spine, briefly illuminating the dark buildings with brilliant yellow light before slamming into a building ten meters short of the Albatross. The explosion sent fire and concrete down, raining destruction on the street below.

I ducked as something plinked off my helmet.

"Left," Thomas said, keeping his voice low, using the taclink even though we were right next to him.

We followed him another block, occasionally catching sight of attacking militia, shouting as they weaved their way down the street toward the downed dropship and the rest of the unit. Their endless stream of curses was punctuated by occasional small arms fire seemingly aimed at nothing at all.

"Sarge, look out," Henderson said, stepping forward and pulling on Sergeant Thomas's shoulder, forcing him to a knee.

"What the hell?" Thomas shouted.

A burst of fire echoed from down the street and bullets chewed through the building just behind where Thomas had been standing. Henderson stepped past him without saying a word, and brought up his sniper rifle. It didn't even seem like he took any time at all to aim, almost immediately pulling the trigger. The rifle bucked slightly but made virtually no sound. As the barrel came level again he fired a second shot, then a third.

When the target was down, Henderson lowered the rifle, keeping it at low-ready across his chest, barrel down. "Good to go." The calm in his voice was disconcerting. Everything about the sniper's demeanor suggested this whole thing was nothing more than a walk in the park for him.

Thomas got to his feet, keeping low. "Thanks."

Henderson nodded.

None of the enemy even seemed to notice the exchange. If they had, they'd only seen their friend drop, and maybe guessed it was from the team at the dropship. Just a stray bullet. Shitty luck, right?

We caught sight of the enemy position half a block later. I don't know how the hell they set up a fighting position so fast, but they'd managed to put a couple of cars on their sides and had tucked themselves back beneath a sizable concrete overhang, making it impossible for the Viper to reach them from the air.

Two men stood at the back of one of the cars, working on reloading their shoulder-fired rocket, but from the look of it, the bastards couldn't seem to agree on who was to reload the weapon, or who was going to fire the next round. Two more crouched behind the overturned cars, watching for the enemy and failing miserably.

They all wore mismatched dark clothing. Nothing that resembled a uniform of any kind. The one holding the rocket didn't even have a shirt on, just black pants that looked like they were a couple sizes too small. He had a rifle slung over one shoulder that kept sliding off, slowing his reloading process.

I leaned down just enough to see over the car, resting my rifle on the roof. Henderson dropped to his belly, quickly assuming a comfortable firing position. Biagini took a knee at the front of the car, putting her rifle on the hood and pulling it into her shoulder.

"Shirtless," Henderson said, his voice low.

"Right side," Biagini said.

I nodded. "Left."

I heard the Albatross's engines behind us. Over my shoulder I saw it coming back down the street, getting ready for another attack run.

"Dropship's coming back," I said.

The militiaman seemed to recognize it as well, moving to get into a better firing position, still working on reloading the launcher. His partner finally managed to get the round loaded into the back of the weapon, holding out both arms and shaking his head as the other hefted it onto one shoulder. He moved up between the two overturned cars, took a knee and aimed.

"On three," Henderson said. "One."

I centered my 27's optical sights on my target and took a

steadying breath. It probably wasn't necessary to take all four out simultaneously, we had enough firepower among the four of us, but this way it was done and over with and we minimized exposing ourselves this far away from our main force.

"Two"

My finger slid from the frame down to the trigger, pressing against it, feeling the pressure.

"Three." The cough of Henderson's rifle punctuated his command.

I squeezed my trigger. My 27 barked once and jerked. My target shook as the bullet slammed into his chest.

I just barely saw the red cloud of blood and gore as Shirtless's face exploded. Reflexively, the man's hands let go of the launcher. The launcher tipped, then fell to the ground, bouncing away from his still standing body. It was like his body didn't know its head was completely missing. Finally, the headless corpse rocked and fell back.

A fountain of blood sprayed Shirtless's partner as he shuffled back a step, horrified at his friend's falling corpse. He had enough time to fumble with his rifle's sling before Henderson's second round caught him in the side of the head.

"Clear," Henderson said. "Two down."

"One down," I said.

"One down," Biagini echoed.

Thomas slapped Henderson on the shoulder as the sniper got up. "Nice work. Come on."

Sarge led us across the street to where the four militia fighters lay dead and kicked the headless corpse. "Take two Motrin and call me in the mornin', fucker." He turned away, and his icon appeared on my HUD. "*Darkstar One, to Air, enemy position pacified. Skies are clear.*"

"*Roger that, One,*" the pilot said. "*Much obliged.*"

"Don't mention it, just hurry up and pick us up will you?"

"Copy that, One. Inbound."

Henderson bent down next to the headless corpse, examining the launcher. "The hell?"

I looked over his shoulder. "What's up, Prof?"

The sniper turned the weapon over, shaking his head. "This thing looks like an SFLR. It's been painted over, but..." He pulled his tac-knife out and scratched at the chassis, chipping off a streak of gray paint. "Yeah, it's definitely Alliance."

"What the hell did you say?" Thomas said, squatting down beside him.

I saw it too. As Henderson worked his knife, a series of letters and numbers appeared, weapon designators for an Alliance Military Shoulder Fired Light Rocket System.

"How in the fuck did they get their hands on our weapons?" I asked.

"Grab it," Thomas said, standing.

Henderson helped me sling it over my shoulder. It took a second to adjust to the added weight, but I managed to get it balanced and nodded. "Good to go."

"Come on," Thomas said, nodding to the dropship as it cut through another group of militia. "Let's get—"

The rocket appeared without any warning, this time blasting down from the roof of a tall tenement building above the Albatross. The dropship barely had enough time to launch flares before the rocket slammed into the tail, exploding in a brilliant fireball.

"Fuck!" I yelled.

The dropship spun to one side, trailing smoke and flame in its wake. The Viper cannon continued to fire, tearing through everything in its path even as the ship dropped out of the air. The Albatross's nose slammed into an office building, smashing through glass and steel, crumpling the dropship's cockpit like a tin can. Metal groaned as the fuselage buckled, folding up on itself.

Another explosion ripped through the dropship's frame, turning the entire aircraft into one huge fireball. It rolled down the side of the building, spitting fire and debris as whole sections were ripped free. It crashed down hard, sending waves of smoke and flame rolling away in all directions, and a third explosion turned the remaining remains into so much slag.

"Son of a bitch," Biagini said, getting to her feet.

Hastings's icon appeared on my HUD, his voice strained over the taclink. *"Command, Actual, Darkstar Six-Four is down! I say again, Six-Four is down!"*

"Move!" Thomas shouted, already running.

I sprinted after him, mind racing at what had just happened. Half our team had just been wiped out, and the rest of us were now trapped in the middle of this God-forsaken city.

We were totally fucked.

Calibri City, Stonemeyer
23 Mar 2607
Mission Time: 01hrs 47mins

I could hear those militia bastards cheering and shouting as we raced back through the alley toward the rest of the unit. I wanted to step out and blast every single last one of the sons of bitches. I couldn't get the image of the flaming dropship rolling down the side of that building out of my mind. My friends burning alive with no escape.

The launcher bounced on my back as we ran, clinking against my armor. I'd carried one before in boot. It was just the inert launcher, not one with a high-explosive armor piercing round locked inside. It was definitely an Alliance SFLR, but I couldn't shake the thought of the thing just randomly firing and incinerating my face.

We came out of the alley, emerging back onto the main street where the rest of our team engaged the militia. I still couldn't figure out why they weren't attacking through the alleyways like the one we'd just used to flank their entire unit, it didn't make any sense. Then again, these weren't trained warriors either. Tactical battlefield thinking probably wasn't part of their recruiting posters.

Lieutenant Hastings had been going back and forth with Command over the taclink, requesting an additional bird for evac, but it didn't sound like Captain Kimball was having any of it.

"...*too many unknown variables*," Command was saying as we rejoined the others. "*We need you to designate a secure, secondary LZ before we can commit another bird. It's just too hot down there, right now.*"

Sheridan, Grayson, and Fallon were all taking turns laying down suppression as Jung and Charles worked on establishing some kind of defensive position. The Ambassador was still hunkered down in the alley, complaining about the military always fucking shit up. I prayed for a stray round to take him right in the throat.

"Wallace, Biagini, do something useful!" Thomas shouted, motioning to where the others were shooting. "Henderson?"

The sniper was already moving away, heading for higher ground. He gave Sarge a dismissive wave without so much as looking back. Thomas shook his head but didn't correct him. Instead, he moved next to Hastings and awaited instructions.

"*Command,*" Hastings said over the taclink. "*I don't know where the hell you want us to go!*"

"*Actual, Command, stand by, we are coming up with a—*"

The taclink connection terminated, Command's icon vanishing from my display as if the Battlenet had just dropped offline. The link icon flashed, indicating it was trying to reconnect but wasn't receiving a signal.

"I've lost my Net connection," I said, turning and tapping my helmet. Sarge waved acknowledgment as several others called out similar circumstances.

A few seconds later, Sarge yelled, "Switch to squadlink!"

I tapped the command into the panel on my suit's forearm, shaking my head. "What is going on?"

Beside me, Sheridan squatted down. "Where the hell did the Net go? They can't just take it out, can they?"

"Not a chance," Biagini said over the SL.

I leaned over the car's roof and fired off two bursts. The group of militia in my sights ducked, then one lurched, head snapping back as his body became stiff as a board. It hadn't been my shot. Must've been Henderson.

"Yeah, well," I said. "I hate to break it to you, Corporal, but they did."

"*All right, people,*" Hastings said, his transmission coming through our platoon's short-range transmitter. "*We've lost contact with Command through the Milnet. We'll stay on SL until Vision can reestablish the network.*"

Several rounds zipped around me, but at that point, I wasn't even fazed.

"How the hell did they do that?" Sheridan asked. "They'd need to take out our repeater buoys and everything."

"Come on, man, we got killing needs done!" I said, watching as a militiaman began cutting across the road ahead, large automatic rifle in his hand. "Hold up, he's got a 17," I shouted, leveling my sights.

"Impossible," Sheridan said.

I sent a burst into the man's chest, knocking him back, off his feet, and sending the weapon spinning through the air.

"You're fucking seeing things, Wallace," Biagini said.

"Like hell," I told her, finding the weapon on the pavement with my optics and zooming in. "That's definitely a 17. I'm looking at it plain as day. Right there, behind that orange car, a meter away from the dead guy."

It took a second for Biagini to find the spot, then she leaned back from her sights and gave me a confused look. Her eyes flicked to the painted launcher on my back. "What the hell is going on here?"

"I was right, yeah?"

She nodded. "Yeah."

"What the hell does that mean?" Sheridan asked.

"We can't just stay here!" Delaney's panicked shout echoed across the street. "Do something, Sergeant! Tell them to pick us up! They have to!"

"He's right you know," I said, popping off another burst.

"What's that?" Sheridan asked.

"We can't stay here. No way we can keep them all back until evac gets here. *If* they get here."

Sheridan fired off a burst, then turned. "You don't think they'll come get us?"

Biagini answered before I could respond. "Of course, they'll come get us. But it's kind of hard to call for a ride when you don't have a phone."

She had a point.

"*Jung, Grayson, Biagini,*" Thomas barked over the SL. "*We need wheels.*"

Biagini shot me a knowing glance. "Looks like Sarge read your mind."

I shrugged. "Great minds, right?"

She headed off behind us, joining the other two. The rest of us continued to exchange fire with the militia. They'd slowed their advance considerably, but I wasn't sure why. I knew they outnumbered us at least three to one. They could've easily overrun us. Not to mention the heavy firepower they wielded.

Thomas's icon flashed on my HUD. "All right, rally up! Taxi's here! Move, move, move!"

I slapped Sheridan on the shoulder and pushed off the car. On the other side of the still-smoking Albatross, the SUVs sat idling, doors open. I laughed. The last one was actually a cab, painted yellow and red.

"Load up!" Hastings ordered, pushing the Ambassador into the second car. He pointed to the Albatross. "Charles, clean it up!"

"Roger that, sir!" Charles answered.

He got to have all the fun.

"I love road trips," I said, heading for the first car.

"Stop pushing me, Sergeant! I can—ow!" Delany complained.

I pulled off the launcher and put an elbow through the back window, shattering the glass. I wedged the weapon in between the clutter of clothes and random items in the cargo compartment, then climbed into the passenger seat and slammed the door shut. "Wouldn't it be horrible if that smug motherfucker had an accident on the way?"

In the driver's seat, Jung laughed. "No doubt."

Henderson slid in behind Jung. "He doesn't stop calling Hastings 'sergeant,' might have to take care of the problem before then."

It was a tight fit. Charles climbed in behind me, and I could feel the vehicle sag under our combined weight. Our armor wasn't designed to ride in regular passenger cars and I began to feel very claustrophobic as Jung pulled away.

"Where we heading?" she asked.

I keyed my squadlink. "Where we are heading, Sar—"

A barrage of bullet's sparked off the SUV's A-pillar, shattering my window. The glass sprayed over the interior, clinking against our armor. Behind me, Charles's LR27 barked out shots as I struggled to get mine up and on target.

"*Go!*" I shouted, firing off a dozen rounds.

"*West,*" Sergeant Thomas said over the SL. "*Go west! After four blocks turn left and go south!*"

Jung slammed the accelerator down hard. Tires spun, and the

rear end shifted back and forth, then the vehicle sprang forward, speeding away.

"Fire in the hole," Charles muttered.

I craned my neck and watched through the side mirror as the wrecked dropship exploded in a brilliant fireball. Streamers of flame and smoke shot in all directions as Charles's charges turned the aircraft into slag.

I sat with my 27 between my legs, barrel down, rocking side to side as the SUV rocketed down the road. My shoulder pad kept bumping into the door frame. We sped through a mass of vehicles, simply abandoned right there in the middle of the road and got a bunch of angry glares from onlookers watching from the side of the road.

Pink clouds dotted the pale blue sky ahead. We were supposed to be done and gone before the sun had even started thinking about coming up. Might have been a pretty sight—had we not been getting shot at. I'd never seen a Stonemeyer sunrise.

"There," Thomas said. *"Turn there."*

Jung angled our vehicle through traffic, around several cars stopped right in the middle of the intersection, then turned south. After another couple blocks, we turned back west, merging with traffic.

"Slow down," Henderson said.

"What are you crazy?" I asked, twisting back to look at him. "They're trying to kill us back there."

He nodded. "Back there, yes. Not up here. Don't want to draw attention to ourselves by tearing through the city like a bunch of fleeing criminals. Just keep it slightly above the limit. Don't get pinned in."

"Okay, but what do I do with that?" Jung asked, nodding to a row of approaching emergency vehicles, coming at us from the opposite direction, lights flashing.

"Just wait," Henderson said, putting a hand on Jung's shoulder. "Slow down and pull to the side a little. Give them plenty of room."

"Shit shit shit," Jung chanted, following Henderson's directions.

I held my breath as the vehicles approached, a couple police followed by two fire trucks and an ambulance. I could see the faces of the people inside, all of which were intently focused on the road. They didn't look military at all, and not at all like the militia forces we'd fought. They genuinely looked like local first responders.

They ignored us. Passing by without giving us so much as a cursory glance. I let out my breath, shaking my head. "Fuck, that was close."

"Smooth sailing, folks," Henderson said. "Smooth sailing."

The further we got from the attack, the more normal the city started to look. Traffic began picking back up, and Jung had to be careful clearing intersections so we wouldn't get T-boned. Running a couple red lights probably wasn't going to get us too much attention with all the first responders in the area heading to the scene.

As we turned back south, I caught a glimpse of a silver shuttle banking between buildings, heading toward the crash site. It was marked Stonemeyer Defense Forces and was followed by two fighter escorts. They were old units, outdated by probably twenty years, ancient by Alliance standards. That's how it was on this rock. Hell, we were driving on wheels. Actual wheels.

"Bout time they show up," I muttered, craning my neck to watch them fly over.

"*In another block take a right and go west again,*" Thomas said.

I motioned as we neared the intersection and Jung nodded. "Got it."

After ten minutes and a few more turns, Thomas said, "Okay,

third building up on the left, should be an underground parking garage. You see it?"

Jung and I scanned ahead. I nodded pointing.

"Got it," Jung said.

We pulled through the open entrance and down a ramp, leading us into darkness. The garage was relatively empty, lit by recessed lighting panels along the ceiling. Jung followed the signs, taking us to the bottom of the garage and found spaces near the back.

I hopped out as the other two vehicles pulled up next to us. My 27 hung from its sling across my chest and I held my arms out to the side as Thomas got out of the second SUV's passenger seat. "We have reservations here or what?"

Thomas didn't seem to get the joke. The Ambassador climbed out of the vehicle behind him and immediately headed for an unmarked steel door ten meters away.

"Let's go," Thomas said, motioning everyone forward, after Ambassador Delaney.

I frowned at him but moved in to follow. "What's up, Staff Sergeant?"

He shook his head. "Some kind of safe house."

"Safe house?"

"Yeah."

Delaney tapped a complex security code into the panel next to the door, and it clicked open.

"I hope it's five-star."

CHAPTER 21

Diplomatic Corp Safe House
Calibri City, Stonemeyer
23 Mar 2607
Mission Time: 06hrs 11mins

"Look at this shit," I said, motioning to the holodisplay in the center of the safe house's main room.

A woman dressed in a ridiculous purple dress, the front cut so low it barely covered her chest, stood in front of the camera, pointing to a pillar of smoke in the distance. "… and a spokesperson for the Calibri City police department said that they'll be working the scene in conjunction with Stonemeyer Defense Forces and Pegasi Peacekeepers. Clarence Lintail, the local Pegasi Consul, said this just minutes after the fighting had ceased."

The image changed to a thin man, dressed in traditional orange and red Pegasi robes, a high, ridged collar reaching up behind his head. The whole outfit looked uncomfortable as hell.

Biagini stepped up beside me, opening a bottle of water. "Of course, the bastards are going to jump all over this."

"His Majesty, the Most High Ruler Sasidon, condemns the actions perpetrated by the Holloman Alliance and calls for their immediate surrender to local Peacekeepers so we may have a trial and bring those responsible for this tragic and horrific act to justice. But do not fear, the Most High will protect you and will continue to enrich your lives to the best of his considerable ability."

"Justice my ass," Biagini said. She moved back to the computer she'd been working on since the moment we'd arrived and went back to typing.

Grayson pointed at the computer. "You better be careful what you look at on that thing. I'm sure the local network is mined."

"You don't have to worry about that computer," Delaney said from the kitchen. He held up his datapad. "Alistair Electronics supplied our Embassy with top-of-the-line components, from the computer network to this very apartment we're in now."

I gave Fallon a questioning look, and the chief nodded. "Even if they were looking for us, they wouldn't find us here. It's shielded for scans and is covered with intrusion detectors and countermeasures."

The woman in the purple dress reappeared on the screen. "The Consul went on to say that the reckless and irresponsible actions of the Alliance military have cost the lives of many Stonemeyer citizens and put thousands more in jeopardy."

"What a crock of shit," I said, leaning back against the wall, tossing the magazine I'd been loading onto the pile with the rest.

A wide shot of the Embassy appeared, making a point to focus on the tarp-covered bodies around the gate, but not showing the hundreds or thousands of bullet holes that marked the outside of the building.

The view faded to a shot of the Albatrosses, smoke still rising from the twisted wreckage. Several investigators stood around the two dropships, pointing and discussing things the camera couldn't pick up. Stonemeyer military forces surrounded the site, augmented by heavily armed and armored Pegasi Peacekeepers. And let me tell you, they looked like peace was the fucking last thing they wanted.

Their bulky red armor shined in the afternoon sunlight. Each armor segment was trimmed in black and gold, the traditional Pegasi Black Star emblazoned on each round shoulder plate. The five-pointed star had come to be known throughout most of the URT as the Black Star of Death. Their helmets were reminiscent of something out of the Middles Ages back on Old Earth; full face armor with two small horizontal slits for the eyes, separated by a black line down the middle. Bulky body armor—that looked uncomfortable as shit, by the way—covered their chest, torso, legs, and arms. Each carried a long rifle, held at the ready across their chest, barrel down.

Yeah, I thought. *Peacekeepers my ass.*

The view changed back to the reporter. "… And our sources here on the ground tell us the numbers of casualties is still climbing, but they're refusing to release any numbers until they've had a chance to work through the entire scene, which as you can see, is extremely large and complex. The Consul did tell us just prior to our broadcast here, that the Pegasi Empire is committed to helping rebuild, and would be happy to provide any resources needed—even loans to help clean up and repair buildings and streets and personal property damaged in the attack."

"Bullshit," Biagini said. "That Emperor of theirs doesn't give a shit about these people. Most High my ass. That entire religion is fucked."

"Lots of religions have been created on a lot more ridiculous shit than that," Jung said.

"Bunch of lunatics, you ask me," Biagini said.

Fallon nodded at the display. "And when they realize that the loans come with a forty percent interest rate and obligations for citizens to serve in the Empire, they'll be locked in, and the Pegasi will own this entire planet. That's their Peacekeeper's whole damn purpose."

"And why the hell aren't they talking about the militia?" I asked. "None of this would've happened if it wasn't for them. It's like they're trying to put all the blame on us when none of it was our fault."

Fallon shook his head. "Stonemeyer's kind of a shitshow right now. I mean, they always have been, most of the frontier worlds are, but now more than usual. They're not set up with any kind of real governments, just half-ass bureaucrats that haven't had any real experience in running a planet of their own. No one wants to work together. Everyone thinks their ideas are the only feasible ideas and that no one else's will work. Yeah, it's a shit show."

"But why avoid putting the blame on the militia?" I asked. "Seems like kind of a no-brainer to me."

"They're scared. Plain and simple. The Stonemeyer Militia isn't just one organization, it's actually several. Well over fifty cells, all operating independently of each other and they don't have any rules. Nothing is off limits for them. Hence, why they've been attacking our Embassy. The local governments worried that if they push too hard, the cells will combine their efforts and take them all out."

"Would that happen?" Jung asked.

Fallon shrugged. "It's possible. But that possibility makes the whole thing with the Pegasi even more delicate."

"Why do they even care?" I asked. "Seems like the whole thing is beyond them."

"They don't," Fallon answered. "For one thing, they just want the land and revenue. For another, there's an entire market of cheap labor here."

Biagini looked up from her computer. "You mean slaves?"

"Not quite. More like indentured servants. There's a few

hundred thousand homeless people on Stonemeyer. All of them lost their jobs when the planetary leaders decided to leave the URT and lost all the mutual aid contracts. That's where most of the militia comes from.

"So why not ask the Alliance for help?"

"That's the thing," Fallon said. "They don't want any outside assistance. They don't want anyone seeing them as a lesser entity. They want to be on the same playing field as the Alliance, as the Pegasi, even some of the bigger independents like Corwynn and the Nine. Most of the URT is like that. So, if they reach out and ask for help, they're admitting to everyone that they're on a different playing field and they can't do that.

"And there are some here that want the Pegasi to annex the planet. A lot of people like the stability and security that represents."

"Slavery, you mean," Jung said. She held up her hand as Fallon opened his mouth to argue. "Look, I know what you're probably going to say, but my parents were killed when the Pegasi invaded Tosh-Marin, so don't try and sell me any bullshit about the upsides to Pegasi annexation. There's nothing peaceful about it."

"I'm sorry," Fallon said. "Wasn't trying to say that at all. I was just going to say that some people would rather have something in place to provide them with security, jobs, housing, all of that, the Empire provides."

"At what cost though?" Jung asked.

"That's stupid," I said. "If they want security, why not deal with the Alliance instead? At least we're not going to invade your shit."

Fallon sniffed, shaking his head. "You got me, man, I just work here. Some of it doesn't make any sense to me. Like I said, Stonemeyer's been a shitstorm for a long time. Lots of different parties vying for control. They were damn near on the verge of civil war when the Pegasi showed up. And now that they're here, if the Stonemeyer government admits to having civil issues with local insurgents, it reinforces the Pegasi's reasons for being here. 'Peacekeeping.'" Fallon held up air quotes at the last word.

"Convenient," I said.

"I'm telling you, that's what they do," Fallon said. "They look for vulnerable worlds and then pounce. Annexation is the majority of what the Empire does to grow and feed its people. I'm actually surprised they haven't commandeered the feeds to spin it their way."

"Fucking lunatics," Biagini repeated.

"So, what's the militia's endgame?" I asked.

"Independence," Fallon said. "Always has been."

"They're doing a bang-up job so far," I said.

"No one ever said they were doing it the right way."

"Going to need another box of rounds," Jung said, setting another refilled magazine on the table.

"Gotcha," Fallon said, holding out another box.

I pushed the final round into the place and set the magazine I'd been loading on top of Jung's. "This is a pretty legit setup, by the way. Whose idea was this place, anyway?"

Fallon looked up from cleaning his rifle, a half-grin on his face. "Mine actually."

I chuckled. "No shit?"

"Did ten years in the Marines before I got out to do this. Slightly better pay, a lot less bullshit."

"You got that right," Biagini said.

"This not standard for the Corps?" I asked.

"Hell no," Fallon said. "Hell, even the extra security on the Embassy isn't normal. They hired me on to do some security consulting. Stonemeyer is one of the furthest deployed embassies the Corps has, not to mention the obvious political strife they were going through, they wanted to make sure the staff was protected. It took a little bit of convincing, but once I had it, stockpiling it was no problem at all. The Corps has more money than they know what to do with." He shrugged. "The Diplomatic Corps anyway, when I was in the Marines, they had trouble paying for enough socks for everyone."

"Still accurate," Biagini said.

"So, where's Stonemeyer's Defense Force in all this?" Jung asked. "They just sitting around with their thumbs up their asses, waiting for these terrorist fucks to attack foreign embassies?"

"They're around," Fallon said. "But like everything else about this place, organized and capable aren't a big part of their doctrine."

"The militia *are not* terrorists," Delaney barked, from the other room. He never looked up from his datapad. "They are just struggling to survive like everyone else out here. However, misguided their actions may be."

I couldn't believe what I was hearing and for a moment forgot about bearing and rank. "Are you fucking serious? We just lost half our fucking team out there, and you don't want me to call them terrorists?"

"Excuse me?" Delaney's face flushed red.

Hastings cleared his throat. "Alright, enough talk for now. Lock it up and get the work done."

I bit my lip and shook my head. My fingers went to work loading another magazine, my eyes bore laser holes into the Ambassador's face. He stared back, cheeks flushed, but his expression suggested he wasn't quite sure about continuing the exchange.

At her terminal behind me, Biagini said, "Now that's interesting."

Hastings stepped around the Ambassador, moving up behind Biagini. "You have something, Corporal?"

She tapped the keys for another second before answering. "Well,

I've wasted a lot of fucking time on this damn network, I can tell you that. Their network is shit, even for being an indie world. Took me an hour just to figure out the base code the network's running on."

"Can you reestablish comms?"

We'd been out of communication with *Vision* for almost five hours. Not even the safe house's secure terminal had been able to break through the interference. It was hard to tell whether it was just us that couldn't get a signal off, or if the entire planet had been isolated.

Biagini shook her head. "The local network has a shit-ton of restrictions on communications, and that includes simple personal messages to large data dumps, everything's locked down. From what I can tell, even the local net is regulated right down to personal connections. Outgoing calls, even to the orbitals, requires specific licenses only issued by the government. But it looks like even those have been suspended."

"Seems like a pretty extreme way to go about containing the backlash from this thing," Hastings said. "I mean, eventually it's going to get out. When we get back to *Vision* and depart the system, the Alliance is going to know everything."

"The Alliance." The Ambassador practically spat the words. "That bunch of self-absorbed bureaucrats couldn't pass effective legislation if it slapped them in the face."

Hello Kettle, I'm Pot, I thought.

"I don't think it's the local government, LT," Biagini said. "Most of these restrictions are new, looks like most of them were put in place about six months ago."

"When the Pegasi showed up," Fallon added.

"First step in occupation," Hastings said. "Suppress communication."

"Yes, this history lesson has been so enlightening," Delaney said. "Had you simply asked, I could've have told you all this and saved you hours of trouble, Sergeant. The only reason we managed to get a signal out is because of our burst transmitter in orbit, which of course, they've obviously taken out."

Hastings's nostrils flared, and I could see his jaw muscles flexing.

"The real question here," Delaney said, looking completely unconvinced, "is what do you think you could possibly do that hundreds of the tech-heads haven't been able to since the start of the occupation?"

Biagini looked over her displays, glaring at the Ambassador, fire in her eyes. I'd seen that look exactly one time before, right before she'd gone apeshit on a couple of drunk Navy techs on *Vision*. It hadn't been pretty. She'd doled out several cuts and bruises during the fight and had barely received so much as a scratch in return.

She took a long breath before speaking again, turning her gaze back to her computer. "When I couldn't tap the network for outgoing calls, I figured there had to be nodes still hardwired into the system for the calls to be allowed to go through. Most of the current nodes are kept in secure government relay stations around the city, firewalled from outside interference. But I managed to find some of the old nodes left over from when the colony first landed."

"Old nodes?" Hastings asked, leaning over her shoulder, looking at her display.

"Exactly. Most of the time when new colonies are set up, they don't have the infrastructure to support a global data network right away, so they install these comm relay nodes to boost the signal. Now, the network's been upgraded a lot over the years, right? same as any world, but most of the time the outdated nodes aren't dismantled, they're left as backups should the new ones fail or drop offline or whatever, Communications and power are the two most redundant systems on any world. Especially out here in the indie systems."

"Can you tap into one of the old nodes?"

Biagini shook her head. "No. I'd have to navigate the existing network for that, and as soon as I do, whoever is monitoring the system will pick up the intrusion and lock it down."

"So, we're no better off," Delaney said, throwing up his hands. "An amazing history lesson. Thank you. We're still stuck down here with no way to call for help. That's just great."

"But," Biagini growled, not taking her eyes off her display. "If we could *get* to one, I could probably physically tap in. Might be able to hot-wire a signal and get a message to *Vision*."

"Awful lot of maybes there," Delaney said. "If this is how you let your Marines operate, Sergeant, it's no wonder this whole thing went to shit."

"It's Lieutenant!" Biagini shouted, slamming her fist on the table.

Delaney jumped back, crying out in surprise. His face twisted into a mask of terror and anticipation. I'll be honest I was silently cheering for her to jump right over that table and kick his ass. I'd've paid good money for that shit.

Hastings held up a hand. "That's enough. Respectfully, sir, I am Lieutenant, and I'm the commander of this *military* operation, not you. You have no authority here. So, you can either keep your mouth closed and let us do our jobs, or I can have Corporal Grayson here give you a sedative until we get off this damn rock. Which would you prefer?"

I almost laughed. I had to cover my smile as the Ambassador stood in shock at the Lieutenant's words. His cheeks turned bright red again as his mouth opened and closed, as if trying to formulate a response but nothing was coming out. My guess is no one had ever spoken to him like that in his life, not even his parents, which was probably why he'd turned out to be such as asshole.

When Delaney didn't respond, Hastings turned back to Biagini. "You think you can tap the node with your equipment?"

"One hundred percent."

"If *Vision* is still up there," Jung said.

"She's up there," Hastings said.

The Ambassador shook his head. "What do you mean' *if?'* You think your warship left? They can't leave! They can't just leave us down he—"

"*Sir*!" Hastings shouted, pointing a finger. He held it there for a few seconds, then pointed to one of the chairs in the kitchen. "Sit down and shut up!"

The Ambassador didn't even hesitate, immediately moving to take the closest chair and sitting without a word. Hastings glared at Jung, who shrugged, wincing.

"Can you locate one of those nodes?"

"Already done," Biagini said. "Jung can I borrow one of your drones."

Jung tossed the magazine she'd been filling and reached for her kit. A few seconds later one of her small orb-shaped recon drones was floating into the air above Biagini's terminal. The Corporal tapped a few more commands, and the drone flashed, creating a topographical map of the city.

"This is us," Biagini said, pointing to the flashing blue triangle. She pointed to an orange triangle. "This is the comm node, about seven kilometers to the northeast. Looks like the entire complex was shut down ten years ago for building repairs, and it never opened back up. But it's still got power."

Hastings took a minute, scanning the room, obviously considering our next course of action. I felt a little bit of anticipation about the idea. Don't get me wrong, I believed her, but still. Heading off into the open when everyone and their brother was out searching for you wasn't exactly my idea of a good idea.

"We'll wait until dark, then hit it."

Calibri City, Stonemeyer
23 Mar 2607
Mission Time: 17hrs 11mins

Without our ballistic gear, the ride to the comm node was actually pretty comfortable. Granted, I'd've preferred having my armor and helmet, but even knowing what I know now, I think it was the right call to leave it behind. If we were spotted, it'd be a hell of a lot easier to disappear into the city if we didn't stick out like sore thumbs in all our gear.

We'd kept our tacvests and most of our battle kit, that stuff, at least, could be easily concealed, but I couldn't help but feel almost naked without having my Milnet connection and HUD. We'd pulled our taclink gear out of the helmets—they're designed for use either way—and worked our way through the streets, dodging police patrols and military shuttles we knew were searching for us.

The comm node was right where Biagini said it would be. The seven-story structure was missing several exterior walls, and sections of the finished levels were nothing more than steel frames and concrete pillars. A four-meter-high fence, topped with plasma wire surrounded the complex, but it'd been cut through many times over. It was obvious that people came and went from the place and weren't even bothered.

That was good for us.

We left the vehicles in a small lot behind a warehouse a block away. Charles, Grayson, Jung, and Fallon stayed behind with the Ambassador and the rest of us made our way through a dark alley, stopping at the edge of the complex to survey the site.

"Looks empty," Thomas said.

Hastings nodded. "Jung?"

"*Drones are up, sir. Initiating building scans now.*"

"Henderson?"

There was a moment of silence before the sniper answered. When he did, it sounded like he was slightly out of breath and irritated that he had to stop and answer the question. "I'm almost there."

Hastings turned to Biagini. "How's it looking?"

"Looks like a few squatters on the third and fourth levels, southwest corner. We can avoid them though if we stay to the north stairwell." She swiped her fingers over the pad, checking every level in turn. "The node's on level six."

"Any security?"

"As far as I can tell, the only power going into the complex is to keep the node running on standby power."

"All right," Hastings said. "Move fast and smooth. All the targets in there are soft, do not engage unless you absolutely have to, and even then, I doubt they're armed. If you can do it without gunfire, do it. Minimal footprint. If we can get in and out of here without anyone being the wiser, let's aim for that."

"Wallace, you have point."

I nodded. "Roger."

"Stay sharp," Thomas said. "Heads on a swivel."

Hastings brought up his rifle. "Let's move out."

I pulled my 27 into my shoulder, took a breath, then led the team out of the alley. I swept my optics side to side as I crossed to the fence, stopping next to one of the many openings cut into the chain-link, and pulled it back for the others to slip through.

A makeshift, homeless camp that was more like a small city within a city had grown up on the other side of the fence. Shipping containers brought in from who-knows-where surrounded the building along with tarps and tents of all shapes and sizes. Fires burned throughout the encampment, throwing dancing shadows in every direction. The first couple camps we passed were empty, turned into a mixture of storage and trash heaps, though I couldn't tell the difference.

Back home on Montgomery, New Detroit has a massive homeless population. They've practically taken over the entire city. After the meltdown of 2190, everything basically went to shit. People lost everything, from business execs to the barista at Galactic Brew. The entire planet took a hit. This place wasn't to that level, yet, but it was well on its way.

I noticed several groups off to our left, all standing around fires, talking amongst themselves, none of which even so much as looked in our direction. In my experience, the people that lived in places like this paid little attention to anyone else, mostly keeping to themselves and protecting what little they had from other homeless. Most of them were usually high on whatever, and none of them would give a shit about us or what we were doing there as long as we weren't bothering them.

I motioned to the others and pointed two fingers at my eyes. Biagini, who was on my three nodded and relayed the signal down the line.

All of the windows on ground level had been knocked out—probably years ago—the remnants scattered over the floor, along with trash, shit, and piss. The place smelled horrendous. Honestly,

I don't know how people actually live in places like this. My stomach turned as I stepped through one of the open window frames, working my way across the lobby to the northern stairwell.

"How we looking, Henderson?" Hastings asked as he started up the stairs.

"*Aside from the couple groups of civies, everything's clear,*" Henderson responded on the squadlink. "*So far, no one's even twitched.*"

"Roger. Jung?"

"*You're clear all the way to six, LT.*"

"Good."

The sixth floor was almost entirely empty, save for the piles of trash everywhere and scattered desks and chairs, relics of when the relay station had been operational. The node itself was behind a locked door in a small room dead center. It took Biagini all of about four seconds to bypass the locking system, and she was through and examining the old hardware inside.

Racks of electrical equipment lined the walls of the small closet. A lot of the casings were marked with a stylized "A" and the words "Alistair Communications" stenciled underneath.

"Wallace, Sheridan, overwatch. Pick a side," Thomas said, pointing to the north and south windows.

I moved south, staying back away from the glass, looking out over the city. Several blocks away I could see a definite line where the old, rundown part of the city met the new, updated, lived-in part. The streetlights and buildings glowed yellow in the night. Neon adverts flashed, but unlike the nicer planets, these all flickered and were missing sections.

It was a peaceful night, considering.

Air traffic was light. I only saw a few shuttles and transports moving over the city and wondered if that was because of us. Wouldn't've surprised me. Shutting down air traffic was a smart move, kept us from getting off world. A Stonemeyer defense shuttle slowed and hovered above the street several blocks away, I could see the SDF shield in the glow of the building lights below. A spotlight blinked on and swept over the ground below. It moved back and forth for several seconds, before switching off and the shuttle continued on.

They're looking for us, I thought.

"Alright, good," Biagini said, her voice echoing across the empty space. "It's pretty much like I thought. These nodes are old TH33 models, about a hundred years out of date." She tapped the casing of one. "Alistair still makes these things, though. Sell like hotcakes out here."

"Do we have comms?" Hastings asked.

"Just a sec... shit." Her fingers danced across her pad, and the flashing red dot on the node's control panel turned a steady green. "We're in. It's a low-frequency audio connection. No data, but we're in."

"Can you hail *Vision*?"

"I can call whoever you want."

"Do it," Hastings ordered.

She tapped a few more commands then nodded. "You should be good to go."

Hastings tapped his link. *"Darkstar Command, Darkstar Actual, come in. Darkstar Command, do you copy?"*

After several seconds with no response, Biagini checked her pad. "It's working, sir. We're online."

Hastings sent the broadcast. No response.

They really did leave, I thought, my stomach turning.

Hastings and Thomas exchanged worried looks, obviously thinking the same thing. If *Vision* was gone, that meant we'd all be stuck here on the shitty world, being hunted like wild animals. Eventually, the bastards would catch up with us. The only questions were whether we'd be tried in a Stonemeyer court or Pegasi.

In the latter, no matter what our defense, we'd be found guilty and executed, there wasn't any doubt about that.

The taclink bud in my ear crackled briefly. *"Darkstar Actual, this is Command, we copy you. It's good to hear from you. The Captain is on his way to control. Stand-by."*

"Stand by?" Hastings asked. "Command, we need evac now."

"I'm sorry, Actual, Captain's orders."

"The fuck is he talking about?" I muttered to no one in particular. What was the problem? They could set an Albatross right down on top of this homeless city, and no one would ever know. Hell, no one would even care.

Several minutes of silence later, Captain Kimball's voice came over the taclink. *"Command Actual, where the hell have you been? Report mission status now."*

"Yes, sir," Hastings said. "I believe our communication buoys were taken out by the hostiles and the local network is locked out for all transmissions. We need immediate evac, sir. I can send you our—"

"How in the fuck did the extraction turn into a bloodbath, Lieutenant? You were supposed to be in and out, clean and no fuss. Instead, I've got a hundred dead civilians, millions of dollars in property damage, and a Pegasi Consul so far up my ass when he talks my lips move."

"Sir, I... what do you mean civilians?"

"All the reports coming out of Stonemeyer's news agencies are pretty clear that you engaged a crowd of peaceful demonstrators outside the Embassy, crashed your birds when the Stonemeyer authorities attempted to detain them and killed several Pegasi Peacekeepers in the process."

Hastings stared dumbfounded at Sergeant Thomas, who shared the Lieutenant's expression.

"What a load of shit!"

Thomas held out a hand to silence me and shook his head, eyes locked on Hastings. "This is bad."

"Sir, I don't know what the reports are saying, but that is absolutely not the case. We were engaged by a well-armed hostile force which shot our birds out of the sky during the extraction. They were definitely not civilians."

"*I've got a lot of reports that say otherwise, Lieutenant.*"

"Well, those reports are fucking wrong, sir. I've got a lot of dead and injured Marines that say different."

"*Do you still have King?*"

The son of a bitch didn't give two shits about us. All he was concerned about was getting the Ambassador. Part of me couldn't believe what I was hearing, the other half, the half that knew what most ranking officers were like, knew better. Kimball didn't care about us. His only concern was how his report was going to look when he sent it up the chain. The people don't matter at all; it's only the mission.

"*Actual, are you still there?*"

Hastings shook his head. "Yes. Yes, sir. I'm still here."

"*Do you have King?*" Kimball repeated.

"Yes, we do. We need air to get him out."

"*The Stonemeyer government and Pegasi Consul have denounced this whole operation as an act of war against the Sovereign Independent World of Stonemeyer and the Pegasi Empire. They've ordered us to maintain a five-hundred thousand kilometer orbit and are limiting all inbound traffic to commercial and non-Alliance traffic.*"

"They shot at us first!" Biagini blurted out.

Hastings nodded, holding up a hand. I could hear the irritation start to rise in Hasting's voice. "Sir, we came under heavy fire from a heavily armed and well-trained and organized military force. They'd already attacked the Embassy on several occasions before we arrived and were returning to finish the job. Those are facts. Undisputed."

"*But the government is disputing them, Lieutenant. And by Interstellar Law, I cannot breach air space without evidence to the contrary or an Executive Order from Regional Command Authority.*"

"I've already told you—"

"*Your word is not evidence, Lieutenant,*" Kimball barked cutting him off. "*I can tell you the reports of you using the Vipers to mow down civilians is being pumped non-stop through the feeds. They've produced hundreds of eyewitnesses.*"

I'd left the window, moving over close to the others. "Get the fuck out of here."

"They're fucking lying," Biagini said.

Sergeant Thomas shook his head. "Son of a bitch is sweeping us under the rug."

"They *were* armed, sir," Hastings said, jaw clenched. "They had enough firepower to bring down two fully functional Albatross dropships. How could civilians do that? They are spreading lies about what happened, sir."

"*Then prove it! Upload your mission data. Give me something I can use.*"

Hastings looked at Biagini, who grimaced. "Sorry, sir, I told you, audio only. There's no way to get data through here. I can tell you this, we won't last long down here, the entire planet is looking for us."

"*And there is absolutely no way for me to get a bird to you, Lieutenant. No way. The Pegasi cruiser,* Silent Resurgence, *has gone to high alert and deployed its ready fighters to patrol all approach lanes to the planet. Even if I wanted to get a dropship there, I wouldn't be able to.*"

"Captain, we have King with us right now," Hastings said, almost pleading. "The Terrace Accords specifically state—"

"The Accords don't apply if we've already taken hostile action against the planet, Lieutenant."

"My people were dying, sir."

"And I believe you," Kimball finally said. And for the first time during the entire conversation, I thought I heard some sympathy in his voice. *"Unfortunately, you can't prove it, and everything else says otherwise."*

"We have the data, sir. We just need to get off the planet to get it to you."

"Lieutenant, what is it that you are not comprehending? There is no air. There is no extract. We have been shut down. Do you understand?"

Hastings's nostrils flared, veins pushing through his neck as he ground his teeth. "What are your orders?"

"For now, sit tight. We are still waiting on orders from RCA. Once we have those in hand, we'll know how to proceed."

"Sit tight?" Biagini asked. She started to say more, but Hastings held up a hand.

"Sir, our taclink is inoperable. We don't have active comms. We are currently tapping into an old network node, but we won't be able to stay here. Once we leave, I'm not sure when we'll be able to re-establish comms."

"Smoke signals?" I suggested. Sergeant Thomas glared at me.

Biagini worked her fingers over the pad, then took a knee in front of the open node panels, examining the internal components. "I might be able to set up a shotbox, but it'll be tricky."

"No choice, Lieutenant. You're going to have to sit tight until we can work out a plan."

"Sir, I... standby one," Hastings muted his link. "What are you talking about, Corporal?"

"A shotbox, sir. Basically, a burst transmitter routed through the node, connected to my taclink computer. Local networks would pick it up pretty quick and could trace it, so we probably wouldn't get but a few transmissions before they could pinpoint our location, but it would give us a few shouts at least."

"And you have the components to set it up?"

She considered the circuitry again and nodded. "Yeah, I think so. We'd have to leave it offline until we were ready to use it." She pointed to the ceiling. "They wouldn't be able to call us, but we could call them. It'd give us, one, maybe two connections."

"Do it." Hastings keyed his link. "Alright, Command, we might have a communication option, but it's extremely limited. We'll only get a few transmissions before it becomes a liability."

"*Understood, Lieutenant*," Kimball said. "*We'll continue to work the issue from our end*."

Jung's voice came over the comm, quiet and tense. "*Actual, Two Bravo, I'm picking up some movement. A couple of vehicles just stopped two blocks north of our position and several unknown targets dismounted. Moving drones in for a better look*."

"Copy that, Two-Bravo, are they hostile?"

"*I'm not sure, sir*."

"*They're armed*," Henderson said. "*I've got twenty militia closing from the east*."

"How in the fuck did they find us?" Sergeant Thomas asked, moving to the window. "Eyes up, everyone, we've got incoming."

I followed Sarge to the window, desperation wishing I still had my HUD. The Milnet connection with Henderson's targeting scopes and Jung's drones would've shown me exactly where they were and how many. I felt blind. Not to mention being without my armor made me feel naked.

I strained my eyes, trying to see what the others saw, but it was all just shadows. I pulled my 27 into my shoulder, panning the optic around, using its infrared filter to see, but they must not have been close enough. The only movement I could see was the homeless, still blissfully unaware of our presence.

"*What's your situation, Lieutenant?*" Kimball asked.

"Standby, sir," Hastings said, leaning through the door frame. "How much time do you need?"

"I don't know," Biagini said. "Five minutes?"

"We don't have five minutes," Sergeant Thomas said.

"Do what you can," Hastings said, then keyed his taclink. "Actual to Command, we've got hostiles moving in, our position is compromised. We'll recontact when we can. Actual out."

Before Kimball could argue, Biagini cut the link.

"What can I do to help?" Hastings asked.

"I need time to get a few components free," Biagini said, frantically disconnecting wires and pulling parts free of their housings. "I can put it together on the move."

"Contact north!" Grayson shouted over the SL, gunfire echoing in the background.

"We need to move," Hastings said. "Now."

CHAPTER 23

Shanty Town
Calibri City, Stonemeyer
23 Mar 2607
Mission Time: 17hrs 36mins

"*Contact east,*" Henderson said. "*I've got six on scopes.*"

"Engage as necessary," Hastings said. "Don't let the bastards flank us."

I took the steps three, sometimes five at a time, rushing to the ground. Gunshots echoed in the distance. I hit the ground floor running and slid to a stop next to one of the shattered windows.

Outside, the homeless were scattering, knocking over fire cans, shouting, tearing down tents, and trying to collect their worthless shit. Some guy was struggling to push a cart full of what looked like trash, around piles of identical trash, and dodging people trying to salvage their own trash.

I didn't see any sign of the attackers in the chaos but knew they were out there. I could hear them.

"*Target down,*" Henderson said over the squadlink, his voice calm and collected. I swear the guy was more at peace with killing people than I was eating pizza.

Biagini appeared next to me, then Sarge and Hastings and Sheridan. Thomas took in the situation and shook his head. "Too many unknowns."

I nodded.

"Darkstar Actual, Two-Bravo, we've got more contacts approaching from the northwest," Jung said.

"Understood, Two-Bravo," Hastings said. "We are coming to you. Sit tight."

Hastings tapped me on the shoulder. "Let's go."

I nodded and stepped through the open window. Ever fiber in my body told me to sprint through the camp, charge through as fast as I could and get to the other side. But somewhere in the back of my mind, I knew that was wrong. I broke into a jog, making sure I scanned all the approaches as I led the team through the homeless maze.

Slow is smooth, and smooth is fast.

"Actual, Eyeball," Henderson said. *"You've got a group moving on the camp to your left."*

I slowed, immediately bringing my weapon up. Shots rang out, echoing through the night. I could see the flashes over a row of tents, followed by pained screams and curses. A homeless woman charged out from between two of the tents, terror etched on her face. A burst of gunfire came from behind the tents, flashes showing brief shadows on the thin fabric walls.

The woman's body arched back, her scream cut short as her body collapsed. Her arms seemed to fold up under her as she fell, dead before she hit the ground.

I fired without actually having a target, sending bursts through the tent, tearing through the walls and snapping poles. I didn't hear anyone scream or go down, they probably just ducked out of the way. I fired a couple more bursts for effect and quickly moved past, stepping over the corpse.

Beyond the row, I stopped at the edge of a large shipping container, covering the rest of the team as they moved past the tents. The doors on both ends had been removed, clothes hung from lines strung across the interior, and several sleeping bags covered the floor. It was practically a luxury hotel to these people.

"Move!" Thomas shouted, not stopping to admire the accommodations. He led the group into a small clearing, suddenly turning to the left and firing. "Get to the fence!"

Biagini and Hastings moved past him as he dropped to a knee, continuing to fire sporadically at an enemy I couldn't see. I almost bumped into Sheridan, who'd paused at the edge of the container.

I pushed him. "Sheridan, what the fuck are you doing? Go!"

He stumbled forward, moving into a jog after a few steps and I followed, rifle trained in the direction Sarge was shooting. Thirty meters away, a small pack of militiamen was moving through a cluster of wrecked cars long since stripped over anything of any value.

Sarge fired again, taking one in the shoulder, throwing him into his companion, knocking both of them to the ground. A third stepped out from the back of one of the wrecks, bringing his rifle up.

Should've already had it up, I thought centering my optics and squeezing the trigger. The short burst slammed into the guy's chest, catching him mid-step, having only brought his weapon up halfway. He doubled over, collapsing to the ground without a sound.

I slapped Sarge's shoulder. "Go!"

Still on one knee, he fired over another burst, then ejected an empty magazine as he stood. He slammed another one in, then ducked through the fence flap Hastings held open.

"Prof, get to the trucks!" Hastings shouted as we headed into the alley.

"Already moving."

"Wallace, rear security," Sarge shouted as we ran through the alley.

"Roger!" I slowed, turning to clear the area behind us.

Rear security sucks. Especially when you're trying to move quickly. You have to really pay attention to what your feet are doing. Otherwise, you run the risk of tripping over yourself when you're checking your six. Saw a few guys fall in basic, knocking over teammates, dropping their weapons, breaking gear.

Back in the homeless camp, a handful of the contained fires had spilled over, immediately setting everything in reach ablaze.

Figures moved in all directions, but I couldn't tell if they were the enemy or just homeless shits escaping the fire. Twice I leveled on someone entering the alley, only to realize it was just a filthy, rag-wearing vagrant, scared shitless because of the chaos surrounding them.

Someone stepped out from the right side of the alley. Backlit by the fire, I couldn't see much other than a dark outline. Walking backward, I brought my carbine up, squinting through the optics for a better picture. I saw the rifle in his hand, but just before I squeezed the trigger, his head exploded and he collapsed to the side.

I froze, both waiting for another target to appear and wondering who'd shot him. A moment later, another figure rounded the corner. A hand shot up, fingers spread.

"Friendly," Henderson said. He'd slung his sniper rifle over one shoulder, holding his silenced pistol in the other hand, barrel down.

I let out a sigh of relief, shaking my head. "What the hell, Prof?"

He grinned, slapping my shoulder as he passed. "Somebody's gotta take care of your rookie ass."

Shouts from Grayson and Fallon echoed down the alley ahead, punctuated by gunfire and cursing. When Prof and I reached the lot, the rest of the team was already engaged, moving for cover behind waist-high containers and our vehicles.

The convoy was tucked behind a series of loading docks, partially concealed by stacks of empty container boxes. The enemy had effectively cut off one of the two ways out of the loading area, spilling out from a drive between two squat warehouses, taking up positions behind identical containers and a few loading trucks parked across the lot.

Grayson darted between stacks, moving to the far side of the vehicles, firing as he went.

"Two more," Grayson shouted. "One o'clock!"

"Get to the trucks," Hastings said. "We need to leave now!"

Near the last vehicle, Corporal Charles knelt next to the rear tire, sending rounds down range. He emptied his magazine, stripped it, got to his feet, and made for the driver's door while slapping in a fresh mag. Sheridan ran around the front, pausing to lie across the hood and shoot. A couple militiamen dropped as they stepped out from one of the loading trucks, and Sheridan continued around to the passenger side.

Biagini pointed at the Ambassador. "Get in!"

Delaney frowned, looking between trucks. "But... but this isn't my..."

"*Move!*" Biagini yelled, shoving the Ambassador forward into the back seat. Without hesitating, she climbed in behind him.

"Wallace!" Jung shouted, opening the driver's door to the second vehicle.

I sprinted over, watching out of the corner of my eye as Henderson smashed out the back window of the last vehicle and rolled into the rear cargo compartment. Fallon slid into the back-seat next to me as Jung climbed behind the wheel.

"This isn't a fucking cargo ship!" Jung said, looking over her shoulder.

"Just go!" I shouted, turning to prop my rifle on the back of the seat. The SUV was still small, but without my armor, at least I could move around and not feel like I was trapped in a moving coffin with wheels.

The Lieutenant, Grayson, Fallon, and Thomas all piled into the first car.

"*We're rolling,*" Hastings said over the SL.

The SUV vibrated as the engine turned over. Jung slammed it into gear, and we lurched forward, tires screeching. I fell side-ways as she swerved around something in the road, knocking Fallon into the door.

"Shit! Easy, Jung!" I shouted, pushing myself upright again. Outside of basic, I didn't expect that many of us had a ton of experience driving anything without repulsers.

"Just shut up and hold on!"

I pressed my boots against the back of the front seat, using it as leverage against the rocking of the SUV. I wouldn't be able to take precision shots, but I could put lead downrange, and right now that was all that mattered.

Behind us, the last SUV swerved around a pile of containers, the same one Jung had just dodged. Biagini had smashed out her window and was holding her rifle one-handed outside, firing back at the enemy. I could just see Prof sitting in the back, firing his pistol.

"*Contact front!*" Thomas advised over the SL.

Ahead, Grayson veered hard right, pulling out onto the street. The vehicle leaned over, and for a second I thought it was going to roll. Tires screeched as the SUV swerved, righting itself and raced away. Red flashes illuminated the backseat as Hastings fired, blowing out the rear glass.

"Hold on!" Jung shouted as we burst out of the alley.

Fallon's window exploded, sending glass shards spraying through the cab. He screamed, falling away from the window, grabbing his face, blood pouring through his fingers. I pushed him down, lifting my rifle over him and firing back. The shots blasted my ears in the confined space. I could barely see what I was shooting at.

"I can't see!" Fallon screamed. "Fuck, I can't see!"

The SUV leaned over as Jung turned to follow Grayson. I pushed against the top of the door, holding myself upright. My chest pressed against the back of Fallon's head as I struggled to get my rifle back in line.

"Stay down!"

I turned, leaning against the seatback and fired through the back window. I couldn't tell if I was hitting anything, but I kept firing regardless.

"I think my eye's gone!" Fallon shouted. "It's gone!" Blood streamed through his fingers, covering his uniform and tacvest. It was everywhere, on the seats, on the floor, on me.

I fired again, and my rifle went dry. I ejected the mag, sending it flying into the cargo area behind the seat and reached for a fresh one. My fingers found only empty pouches.

"I need a mag!" I shouted, turning to Jung.

She swerved around a car on the street, and quickly pulled one from her pouch, handing it back over her shoulder without saying a word.

I slapped it in and turned just as the last vehicle shot out of the alley behind us. It came out a little too hot, the passenger side wheels lifting off the pavement at the apex of its turn. It sideswiped a row of parked cars, sending sparks and glass flying, then finally corrected, rocking as it accelerated after us.

I held fire, watching as the muzzle flashes from their rifles illuminated the cab. Something above them caught my eye, and my blood went cold. "Incoming!"

The rocket streaked toward us, its ass end glowing orange and trailing a line of white smoke. It arched down and slammed into a parked car several meters behind their SUV, exploding in a brilliant fireball and spray of twisted steel.

"Shit!" Jung shouted.

Jung swerved around another car, throwing me against the door. I almost lost my grip on my 27, managing to snatch it out of the air before it went flying. "Take it easy!" I yelled, pushing myself upright again.

"Easy my ass!" Jung shot back, jerking the car the other way.

Another rocket shot through the night sky. Then another.

I craned my neck, watching as the first one veered off, slamming into a storefront, shattering the glass entryway and exploding seconds later. The blast wave rocked the last car, spraying it with smoke and shrapnel.

"Where the fuck are these guys coming from?" I shouted. I was just trying to hold on now, there wasn't anything to shoot at. I couldn't see anything but the blur of the buildings and the cars around us.

"Trucks!" Prof said, over the SL. "They've got trucks! Oh, shit!"

Everything seemed to happen in slow motion then. I saw the rocket a second before it slammed into the ground, just behind the last SUV. The explosion threw the rear end into the air, sending chunks of concrete, smoke and dust flying. The SUV went sailing, flipping end over end until finally crashing down on its front end, steel crumpling, glass shattering.

"Wait!" I shouted, slapping Jung's shoulder. "We have to go back!"

"Are you fucking crazy?"

"Look!" I pointed.

She glanced back over her shoulder, eyes widening at the sight of the wrecked SUV, smoke billowing from the engine. She pounded the brakes, tires screeching. Beside me, Fallon fell forward into the back of the driver's seat, screaming, hands still covering his bleeding face.

"Shit!" Jung shouted, slapping the steering wheel.

I keyed my squadlink. "Two-Delta, to Actual, vehicle down! Biagini's truck has been hit!"

Ahead of us, the first SUV screeched to a stop as well, and I saw Hastings jump out of the back. He walked several steps away, his rifle slung across his chest, barrel down, hand on the grip. "Son of a bitch!"

I got out, eyes locked on the wreck, waiting for someone to crawl out. I looked at Jung. "We gotta go get them!"

One of the militia trucks appeared through the smoke, swerving to a stop between it and us. I ducked low, bringing my rifle up, moving to the back of the SUV. The driver's door opened and a man wearing ripped jeans and a red shirt jumped out. He held a rifle by its barrel, and only when his feet hit the pavement did he look up and realize we were still there. His excited expression changed to panic as he tried to get his rifle up.

"Too fucking late, asshole!" I fired. The rounds hit center-mass, knocking him back into the truck, then he collapsed to the ground.

The back door opened, and another militiaman jumped out, but this one was ready, firing on his way out. He was shouting something I couldn't understand, reaching for his friend with one hand while squeezing off shots with the other.

I ducked back as bullets zipped by me. "Come on!" I yelled to Jung. "We need to help them!"

"Wait!" She shouted back.

"What the hell are we waiting for?"

She was still in the driver's seat, twisted backward. She pointed. "Look!"

Another truck appeared through the smoke, stopping just in front of the first. Another group of militia jumped out, immediately taking cover behind the trucks and engaging us with small arms. Bullets zinged off the SUV's frame and chewed into the street and buildings around us.

Through the gap between the two trucks, I saw several swarm our last SUV, smashing out the remaining windows and yanking open doors.

They pulled Sheridan out first. I could see him struggling, but it was four against one, and they were winning. Biagini came out next, her body limp, I couldn't tell if she was still alive. Neither Henderson nor Charles put up a fight, both unconscious or dead, their bodies hauled roughly into the back of the trucks. Delaney put up a little bit of a fight, but not much. It only took two of them to get him loaded.

"Lieutenant!" I shouted.

Another truck appeared, coming to a stop next to the second. A lone figure stood just behind the cab, behind what looked like a medium-sized auto-cannon mounted in the bed. He was already bringing it online before the truck had stopped.

"Fuck!" I dove back into the SUV. "*Go! Go! Hit it!*"

I got my rifle over the seat and started spraying as Jung hit the accelerator. I didn't aim. Spray and pray as they say. I just wanted to get as many rounds as I could downrange, hoping one or two of them would slow the gunner enough for us to get away.

We'd only gone 10 meters when the auto-cannon opened up. Its slow, methodical thump, thump, thump, cut through the night air as it sent 20mm rounds rocketing toward us. Plumes of dust and bits of concrete spat up behind us, the volley chewing a path of destruction.

"Hold on!" Jung shouted, just before swerving hard right.

I groaned, holding onto the seatback, trying not to fall on Fallon, who'd stopped screaming and was now just groaning with every bump and jolt.

Something hit my leg. I reached down absently, thinking it was one of the empty magazines I'd tossed, but pulled up a data-pad. I frowned, turning it over in my hand. It looked like any old pad, but the backside was embossed with the planet and stars of the Diplomatic Corps. The Corps motto, "Bringing the galaxy closer," was stenciled underneath.

"Son of a bitch," I said, tossing it aside, turning my attention back to the wrecked SUV, growing smaller as we sped away.

I felt a pit growing in my stomach. We'd just done something that no Marine should ever do: we'd left Marines behind.

CHAPTER 24

Haroldson Memorial Hospital,
Regional Naval Medical Facility
New Tuscany
4 Apr 2607

"It wasn't your fault," Eliwood said, her tone soft and under-standing.

Fischer raised an eyebrow at her. Emotion wasn't something Eliwood let into her life lightly, and never in front of anyone outside her circle. Unless, of course, it was sarcasm, that she exuded in abundance. She was sitting at the head of the bed, leaning in close, listening intently to everything Wallace had been saying.

She was right though, Fischer knew, but he also knew it didn't matter. Wallace was a Marine, and unless he'd died with his friends, he'd failed them by not going back to get them. No amount of logical reasoning would change his mind on that point.

"I should've gone back for them. Should've saved them." He turned away, staring off into nothing. "Maybe if we had..."

"If you had what?" Fischer prompted.

Wallace shook his head as if clearing his thoughts.

"If you would've gone after them, you would've been captured too," Eliwood said. "You did everything you could."

Wallace turned to her, determination on his face. For a moment, it looked like he was going to argue. His lips parted to speak, then his entire demeanor changed, almost as if he'd finally been hit by the realization that there hadn't been anything he could've done. He bowed his head, sighing. "Maybe you're right."

Fischer let the moment hang for a beat, allowing the Marine to work through his internal demons. He'd seen it before. These were some of the most critical parts of any interview, the time when the subject realized they don't have anything left to lose and finally starts spilling everything.

"It's just," Wallace started. He sighed again, grinding his teeth.

"What?" Eliwood asked.

When Wallace didn't answer, Fischer moved on, wanting to keep Wallace talking, not lamenting on his failures. "What happened after the comm station? Where did you go?"

"Back to the safe house. Took us a while to get there, had to switch vehicles because ours were so beat up. Those fucking Pegasi Peacekeepers were everywhere. They owned the streets. But they never came knocking. I guess it's kind of unreasonable to think they could knock on every single door in the city."

"No doubt," Fischer agreed. He took a breath, trying to formulate how he wanted to ask the next question. "But you found Biagini?"

"What?" Wallace asked.

"I mean, she's here, right? You had to have found her after they took her. What happened there?"

Wallace chewed on his bottom lip, obviously considering his answer. "That's right."

Fischer frowned. "How'd that happen?"

Wallace sniffed and rubbed his nose with the back of his hand. "It was kind of by accident really. We picked up Sheridan's emergency beacon. Led us right to them. They were in pretty bad shape. How's Biagini doing?"

"Better," Eliwood said. "But she's got a long road ahead of her."

"I should've killed those motherfuckers for what they did," Wallace said, through gritted teeth. "Every. Last. One."

"So, you found Sheridan and Biagini," Fischer said. "What about the rest of them?"

"Dead."

"What happened—"

Fischer's link chimed, the priority call interrupting his recording. He frowned, reading the ID panel glowing over the back of his hand. "Fischer."

"*Go secure*," Carter said.

Fischer tapped the link twice, and his call transferred to his implant. "Go ahead."

"*We found Thomas.*" He was in a hurry from the sound of his breathing. "*Get your asses to HyperTrans Blue Lake now.*"

"What's there?"

"*Thomas. But he's not going to be there for long.*"

Fischer straightened. "We're on our way." He terminated the call.

Eliwood stood. "What's up?"

Fischer pointed a finger at Wallace. "We'll be back, don't go anywhere."

Wallace scoffed, holding out both hands, IV lines and monitor wires attached to both. "Where the hell am I going to go?"

In the gravcar, Fischer hadn't even secured his harness, and their pilot was lifting off. Fischer rocked in the seat, putting out an arm to steady himself as the pilot gunned it.

Across the compartment, facing him, Eliwood was securing her own straps. "Why didn't you tell him?"

Fischer pulled his harness tight. "Tell him what?"

"That Thomas was missing, and we found him."

"Doesn't need to know. I want him to think everyone is safe and sound and there's absolutely nothing to worry about. I don't want anything to taint the story he's telling us. Well, any more than it already is."

"You think he's lying?"

"No, not entirely, but he's definitely embellishing some parts."

Eliwood cocked her head to one side. "How do you know? What'd he say?"

"It wasn't really what he said, so much as how he said it." Fischer shrugged, then groaned as the shuttle banked hard to the right. "I don't know, just a feeling I have. Usually, I get a good read on people. He just comes off as a little arrogant."

"Yeah, I said that."

"Yup. And you were spot on."

Eliwood turned, watching through the window as the shuttle raced over the city. "So, tell me, what the hell is this Thomas guy's deal? Where the hell is he going?"

"Your guess is as good as mine," Fischer said. "Could be he's mind-fucked like Biagini and doesn't know how to handle it. I've heard of it happening before. Marines get into some crazy shit, and it messes with their minds. PTSD is no joke."

"You think something bad happened out there? Something they don't want to talk about?"

"I don't know. The operation going south is bad enough, but I don't think that alone would warrant the feeling I'm getting off Wallace. We need to get Biagini talking, and hopefully, she can corroborate Wallace's story. Maybe even fill in the parts he's leaving out."

"What if she doesn't? What if something did happen out there and that's why Thomas is running. Maybe Wallace is lying to cover it up."

"I don't know," Fischer said. "That's kind of a stretch. What could possibly be that bad?"

Eliwood shrugged.

"We'll be on the ground in five minutes, Agents," the pilot said, leaning around the edge of this chair.

"Thanks." Fischer rubbed at his beard. "Wallace was right about one thing for sure."

"What's that?"

"This whole thing is one big cluster of a shitshow."

Eliwood laughed. "That's cause you're on the case. If it was anyone else, none of this shit would be happening. Face it, you're a shit-magnet, Fish. No other way to put it."

"I don't try to be."

"Doesn't matter. You are."

Fischer's link chimed. The holodisplay told him Carter was calling again. He patched in Eliwood and answered. "We're almost there."

"I've got a tactical team en route, they'll be on the ground in about eight. Thomas is moving through Terminal 5 but hasn't made it to security yet. Looks like he found some new clothes: black pants, brown jacket."

"How the hell did he get there?" Eliwood asked.

"Cab dropped him off. We're getting the local cops to detain and process it."

"Should be able to backtrack his route then," Fischer said.

"Okay, great," Eliwood said. "But it doesn't explain where the hell he's going?"

New Tuscany's hyperloop system was one of the most extensive in the Alliance, consisting of thousands of kilometers of transit tubes crisscrossing the planet. For the most part, transport wasn't regulated, and cost very little, but because of the size of the terminal in Blue Lake City, HyperTrans had set up a local security force to keep things under control.

"There's a total of seventeen cabs leaving in the next hour," Carter said. "The majority of which are making transfer stops and then making return trips to Blue Lake."

"He could be going anywhere." Fischer groaned again as the shuttle banked hard.

"On the deck in thirty seconds," the pilot called back over his shoulder.

"I don't know why this guy thinks he needs to run," Carter said. "But we need to figure out why. There's obviously a reason. A court-martial for AWOL is serious."

"We'll bring him back," Fischer said.

Eliwood leaned forward. "And I'll make sure he does it without burning down the terminal."

"Let me know when you have him."

Carter terminated the connection as the shuttle's engines flared. Fischer white-knuckled the restraints, the sudden increase in power pushing him against the straps. The shuttle lurched as it settled onto its landing struts and Fischer decided he'd much rather be on his gravbike.

Both agents had their straps off before the pilot signaled the all clear and were waiting at the hatch when it unlocked and folded open. Fischer started down before it touched the ground, hopping off as several terminal security guards approached.

He flashed his credentials. "Agent Fischer, Agent Eliwood, ASI. You were told we were coming?"

The lead guard nodded, extending her hand. "Constable Seville. We've got a cart waiting."

Fischer raised an eyebrow. "A cart?"

Seville motioned to a waiting gravcart several meters away. The small vehicle had two forward facing benches and one facing the rear. It floated on thrumming gravpads, rippling the air underneath it.

"Fastest way through the terminals," Seville said, already moving toward it.

"For shit's sake," Fischer grumbled, following reluctantly. He clenched his teeth as the cart sped through the wide-open concourse, fingers wrapped securely around the seat's support handle by his thigh. Seville sat behind the wheel, shouting and waving at groups milling around, barely missing some.

"Where's the tactical team?" Fischer asked through still-clenched teeth.

"They're standing by in one of our shuttles, just in case he gets through security and manages to get on the transport capsules," Seville said, swerving around a corner into a wide, new corridor.

"Can't we just close down security?" Eliwood asked. "It's just one Marine."

Seville laughed. "Are you kidding? Do you know how much money goes through HyperTrans every minute? We're talking billions every hour. The only time the terminals have ever been shut down was when they had a hauler crash into one of the tubes, it was closed just long enough to clear the debris and re-seal it."

Eliwood chuckled. "So much for caring about public safety."

"Safety? Agent, the only thing these people care about is the money. Everything else is secondary. Including lives. That's just the world we live in"

"How much farther?" Fischer asked.

"We're almost there."

They rounded another corner, entering a long, open corridor. The crowds had thinned out here, allowing them to speed through relatively freely.

"This is Seville. Go ahead," the guard said.

Fischer turned, confused until he continued a second later.

"Yeah, black pants, brown coat. He's near Gate 3. Right, we're pulling up now."

Fischer's fingers brushed against his pistol, ready to pull it free. The guard noticed his movements and shook his head. "Wait. Don't draw unless you need to. If we can take him without causing a big ruckus, it'll go better for me. You don't have to answer to the bean counters, I do."

Fischer hesitated, his fingers feeling the coarse handle of this pistol, wanting nothing more than to hold it as they made the approach. If the career Marine was willing to go AWOL, it was anyone's guess as to what else he'd be willing to do.

Please don't go sideways, Fischer prayed, stepping off the cart.

A declining floor led them from the corridor into a large, domed chamber where a number of different ramps led out to waiting passenger capsules, waiting to enter the extensive, planet-wide transit system. A ticket counter took up most of the entryway leading into the departure area where people were lined up waiting to process through. All seemed oblivious to security's arrival, and for that, Fischer was grateful.

Fischer motioned for Seville to take her people left while he and Eliwood moved right, walking carefully—not fast, but with purpose. He maneuvered through clusters of people, eyes scanning those waiting in line to enter the checkpoint.

"Got him," Fischer whispered, stopping behind a small group of waiting passengers, and nodding toward the middle of the line.

Staff Sergeant Richard Thomas rocked back and forth on his heels, obviously anxious to get through the line, head continually scanning around him, looking for threats. Fischer knew they had a matter of seconds to act before things went awry. As soon as the Marine saw them coming, it would be over.

Thomas grimaced as the line moved, favoring one side. The hood on his jacket was down now, which was smart, it meant that he was thinking somewhat clearly and didn't want to get tagged by the security network.

"He's going to see us coming," Eliwood whispered, leaning close.

Fischer shook his head, searching the room for a better approach. "Shit."

The only other option was to let him board, then take him during transit, but Fischer didn't like the idea of having to fight the Marine in a confined space like that. He was sure they'd all be on the losing end if it came to that.

Movement at the far side of the chamber caught Fischer's attention, and he cursed under his breath. Seville was already moving in, a four-man team close on her heels, making a beeline straight for Thomas. Fischer stepped out from behind the crowd, fingers tightening around his pistol's grip.

"Son of a bitch," Eliwood growled.

Seville stepped around the last person concealing her approach just as Thomas turned his direction. The security guard froze, eyes locking with the Marine and for a moment nothing happened.

Time stood still.

Fischer's heart pounded as he tried to calculate the time it would take to cross the distance and tackle Thomas. He didn't think he could make it in time, and from this angle, he didn't have a clear shot, there were too many people between him and his target, not to mention everyone serving as backdrops.

And then Thomas moved.

CHAPTER 25

HyperTrans Blue Lake
New Tuscany
4 Apr 2607

The Marine's hand slid into his jacket, and Fischer's heart sank as he realized what was about to happen. He opened his mouth to shout a warning, but it was too late.

Thomas's other hand shot out, wrapping around the neck of the nearest person in line, a woman in her twenties dressed in a red and blue pantsuit. She screamed as his arm clenched around her. She dropped her handbag and datapad, reaching up to claw at her capturer's thick, hairy arms, her eyes bulging in terror.

Thomas walked her back, moving away from Seville and her team, ensuring the woman was between them at all times. She tried to pull away, yelling at him to let her go, but her words came out as little more than hoarse whispers. He yanked her back, and she barked out a painful scream.

"Shut up!" Thomas yelled, his free arm coming up, pistol in hand. He pressed the muzzle to the woman's temple, blazing eyes locked on the security team. "Get the fuck back, or I'll kill her! I'm not fucking around."

Seville leveled her pistol. "Sir! Put the gun down! You don't want to do that."

Fischer pulled his pistol free, thumbing the safety off. *Come on, Sarge,* he thought, *just listen to her.*

Screams filled the chamber as more and more people realized what was happening around them. They scattered like cockroaches from a light, putting as much distance between themselves and the standoff as they could. One older gentleman bumped into Fischer as he fled, barely even noticing in his panic.

Thomas looked over his shoulder, saw Fischer coming and moved the gun over. "Back!"

Fischer froze but didn't move his sights. "Easy, Sergeant."

"Go fuck yourself! I'm getting out of here, period. I don't want to talk. I don't need a deal, nothing. I'm walking on one of those pods, and you're not going to do anything to stop me."

"Drop the gun!" Seville yelled.

Fischer clenched his teeth as Thomas shifted the gun back to the security team. "Get back!"

"Hey!" Fischer said, angling his pistol away, but still keeping it ready. "Listen to me. Look at me!"

Thomas kept his pistol trained on the security team but looked back at Fischer. He frowned, finally seeing Fischer for what he was. "You're not security?"

"Alliance Intel, look, I just want—"

"I ain't talking to no goddamn spook," Thomas sneered.

"I'm not a spook. I'm just an investigator. Listen, I just want to ask you a few questions, that's all."

"Fuck that. I know what you want. I know what's going on here. I'm not an idiot. I did my job. I followed my orders. I did what I was supposed to do!"

"No one's saying you didn't! Please, just put the gun down

and talk with me. We can go somewhere private. You pick. All I'm interested in is your story. I want to know what happened on Stonemeyer, that's it. That's my job."

"You don't want to know what happened there."

"Yes, I do. Why do you think I'm here?" Fischer watched the Sergeant's body language, looking for any sign that he was making a dent in his armor. Everyone had a breaking point, something that would cause them to fold and talk. That was all most people wanted anyway, a chance to have their side of the story heard. They wanted their time on stage. He didn't see any of that on Thomas's face.

"I don't give a shit why you're here. I'm not staying, and you need to back the fuck up!" He flexed his grip on the woman's neck, and she screamed, tears flowing freely down her cheeks, smearing her make up.

"P-p-please... help me," she whimpered, terrified eyes glued to Fischer, pleading every bit as much as her words.

"It's going to be okay," he told her, holding out his weak hand, palm out. "We're just going to talk."

Thomas swung the pistol back to Fischer. "I told you, I'm not fucking talking to anyone. I want a capsule, and I want it now."

"You're not going anywhere," Seville shouted. "We've got a tac team waiting outside. You're trapped."

For shit's sake, Fischer thought. He pointed at the guard. "Enough! Back up!"

Thomas shuffled back, frantically looking over his shoulder, searching for the team. "I'll kill her. I swear to God, I will!"

"Just calm down," Fischer said, projecting a calm in his voice that he didn't feel at all. "Come on, you said you were following orders, whose orders were you following?"

"Fuck off!"

"I know you were sent in for the Ambassador and the op went to shit," Fischer said. "I already know that."

"You don't know shit! That bastard Delaney got my entire team killed!"

"How? How did he get your team killed?" Fischer's mind raced. He was right there, he just needed to find the right leverage. The man was a lifer, he's spent his entire life in the Alliance Marine Corps. He was completely and totally indoctrinated. What was the one thing that he'd hold closer than anything else in his life? His mission and his men.

"Come on," Fischer continued. "Help me figure this thing out. The bravery your team showed on the battlefield was nothing less than valiant. Help me honor their memory and get to the bottom of what really happened out there."

Thomas's hardened expression softened slightly, and Fischer knew he'd done it. He'd found his in.

"I told you," Thomas said, his voice carrying slightly less anger than before. "You don't want to know what happened out there, sir."

"Yes, I do. I want to know, I need to know. Help me. Your men deserve to be honored and remembered for what they actually did, not for what some Pegasi bureaucrat says they did. I get it, orders are orders, but it's up to you to know whether or not those orders are valid. If they're illegal, you're not bound by them. You don't have to follow them."

"I don't know how to do anything else."

"Work with me."

Thomas held Fischer's gaze, obviously considering his words. After what seemed like an eternity, a look of what appeared to be resolution came over the Marine's face. Fischer felt the tension, which had been building up inside him over the last several minutes, start to fade.

"My whole life has been following orders. My life is the Corps. It's in my blood. Following orders is the only thing I know how to do. My whole life…" The Marine's eyes panned away, looking off at something in the distance. "Look at what they make you give…"

The relief Fischer had briefly felt immediately left him. The hairs on the back of his neck stood up as he realized what was happening. His stomach twisted and jaw clenched hard as every fiber of his being willed the sergeant to make another decision.

"You have a choice."

The distant expression faded from Thomas's face, replaced by hard determination. "I am a Marine. I am bound by oath and soul and blood."

"Don't do this," Fischer pleaded, finger sliding down onto the trigger.

The woman Thomas held sobbed, her legs turning to jelly under her. The Marine who'd spent an entire life building muscle and training to kill didn't even seem to notice as her legs gave out, holding her upright without any trouble at all.

"I will serve the Alliance until I die or am faithfully discharged from service. Until then, I will do my duty."

He released his hold on the woman, shoving her to the ground with one hard push. The gun shifted over in slow motion, the barrel bigger than anything Fischer had ever seen before and he didn't hesitate.

He fired.

CHAPTER 26

HyperTrans Blue Lake,
Terminal 5
New Tuscany
4 Apr 2607

Fischer leaned over, hands resting against the edge of the ticket counter, processing everything from the last hour.

Disappear or die. That had been Thomas's plan. It was a simple plan, one he'd seen countless others follow during his tenure in security, and even before. What Fischer couldn't reconcile, though, was why a career Marine would choose suicide by cop over answering questions about how his fellow Marines had died. That didn't make any sense to him.

Someone had found a jacket to cover Thomas, it didn't cover anything but the Marine's face, but still. It was something. His corpse lay face up, in a large pool of bright red blood, which fortunately had finally stopped pumping out.

It'd taken the HyperTrans security team almost ten minutes to secure the area after the shooting, calling in help from the rest of the terminal and bringing the tactical team inside to assist. What passed for their investigation team arrived and began collecting witness information and taking pictures, all while dodging Eliwood's commands to keep off the scene.

A team of four suits—and not cheap ones—arrived at the chamber's entrance, two men and two women, all looking none-to-pleased about the situation. HyperTrans executives, without a doubt, concerned about the bottom dollar and not in the senseless loss of human life. They gave the corpse a cursory glance, then all shifted their attention to Fischer like he'd done something wrong.

The woman in front, dressed in a maroon skirt that seemed a little too short to be considered proper business attire and loose blouse with a neckline that did nothing to conceal her figure, pointed at Fischer. Seville nodded, looking at Fischer over her shoulder. When she was finished, the security chief nodded again and started making her way across the chamber to Fischer.

Seville opened her mouth to speak as he neared, but Fischer beat her to it.

"They want to reopen the terminal." It was a statement, not a question.

Seville hesitated for a moment, then sighed, nodding. "Sorry."

"Not your fault. Don't worry about it."

"Like I said before, it's the money."

Eliwood jogged up. "What do the suits want? They think they're going to get into our scene they've got another thing coming."

Seville shook her head. "I don't think you'll have to worry about that."

"Fucking money moves people," Eliwood said.

Fischer nodded. "Indeed." He turned his attention back to the corpse in the center of the chamber. "You can tell them that as soon as ASI has finished processing the scene, they can reopen the terminal. Not before."

"They're not going to like that."

"To hell with what they like." Eliwood jerked her chin at the executives. "I'm sure they can afford it. I'd be willing to bet each one of those shoes is worth more than my entire yearly salary. Each shoe, not each pair. Just look at those things."

Seville raised her hands, palms up. "I had to ask."

Fischer waved a dismissive hand between them. "You're just doing your job."

"Look," Eliwood said, motioning toward the entrance.

Chief Carter appeared at the top of the ramp, passing the group of HyperTrans executives without giving them so much as a glance, eyes scanning the entire area as he entered. A team of ASI investigators followed in his wake, automatically breaking off to handle pre-assigned tasks.

Carter shook his head as he approached the trio. "What. The. Fuck?"

"You said it, boss," Eliwood said. "Son of a bitch didn't give us much of a choice though."

Carter gave Thomas's corpse a sideways glance, then looked up at the ceiling. "Video?"

Fischer and Eliwood both turned to Seville, who took a second to realize the question had been directed at her. "Uh, yes... there's cameras, sir."

"Going to need it."

"We're already working on it, sir," Seville assured him.

"The complete, unedited, feed."

Understanding registered on the security chief's face, and she nodded. "Right."

Carter turned and stepped toward Thomas's body, shaking his head, hands on his hips. "Why the hell would he do that? Doesn't make any sense."

"Kept talking about this oath and orders and serving the Alliance," Fischer said. "Not sure how all that fits here."

"Unless someone ordered him to kill himself," Eliwood suggested.

Carter held up a hand. "Let's not even go there, okay? This is bad enough. I've gone through the original intelligence and request for assistance, even the orders sent straight from Regional Command Authority. Nothing in any of these documents said anything other than extract the VIPs from a hazardous situation. Nothing. Campbell is going through the communication logs from *Vision* as we speak."

"Finally got through to the right people, eh?" Eliwood asked.

"For all the good it's going to do," Carter said. "I have a feeling it's just going to be more of the same. So far, we've uncovered exactly zero articulate fact that explains what happened other than the militia going apeshit on our guys. And for what? There had to be a reason they attacked the Embassy."

Fischer crossed his arms. "Wallace says that they attacked again after the squad made contact with the *Vision*. Somehow they tracked them through town after they escaped from the crash site."

"How the hell did they do that?" Carter asked.

"Maybe they've got a hell of a spotter network." Eliwood suggested.

Carter canted his head to the side. "But you don't believe that."

Fischer shrugged. "It does seem pretty thin."

"Everything about this case seems pretty thin," Carter said.

"Agreed."

"And besides that," Carter continued, "why survive a week on a hostile world, being hunted by a group full of fanatical sons of bitches, only to make it back home and kill yourself inside of twenty-four hours? *That's* pretty fucking thin."

"I just need more time with Wallace," Fischer said. "I'm close to cracking him."

"You think he's lying?"

"I don't know that he's lying, but he's definitely holding something back. Especially considering what happened here." Fischer nodded to Thomas's corpse. "But he's the only one that's going to be able to shed any light at all on this."

"What about the woman?" Carter asked.

Eliwood blew out a breath. "She's really messed up, boss. It's going to take her a minute."

"We don't have a minute."

She held up both hands in surrender. "Not arguing, just saying."

Carter nodded, turning back to Thomas. "So, the only one that's going to give us any insights at all is this Private Wallace."

"Until we can get to Stonemeyer itself," Fischer said. "Yes."

Carter laughed. "You can forget that. Not going to happen. Not anytime soon, anyway. If ever. The Pegasi has completely sealed off the planet to anyone even remotely resembling Alliance. Their Ambassador is screaming for heads to roll and calling for reparations."

"They want us to pay for their fuck-up?" Eliwood asked.

"That's about the gist of it."

"Unbelievable."

"Oh, I believe it," Fischer said. "I believe it one hundred percent."

Carter seemed to realize for the first time that Seville was still standing with them. She'd been silent during their discussion, lingering at the edge of the conversation.

"Security Chief Seville," Fischer said, wanting to head off any rants Carter might have against the ineffectiveness of HyperTrans security or their people. "She got us here in time to prevent Thomas from getting away."

Carter nodded at the Chief, then turned back to Fischer. "This whole thing is going south fast. We need to get a handle on it before it spins even further out of control. I'd like to have something to give somebody, instead of the whole, 'we're still investigating it' bullshit."

Fischer nodded.

"Get the woman talking," Carter continued. "We need her to corroborate what Wallace is saying. Without that, it's one man's word against an entire planet. We need her."

"Even then," Eliwood said. "It'll just be two. You think that'll make much more of a difference?"

"If we can prove that she was violated and tortured by those bastards, it will go a long way toward swinging public opinion in our favor."

Fischer ground his teeth. The idea of using the woman's horrific experience to *sway opinion* made his blood boil. This was a person, not a political pawn. What happened to her—and Private Wallace for that matter—was real. It would affect them for the rest of their careers, not to mention the rest of their lives. And here they were talking about making the masses feel better about calling out their enemies on their bullshit.

They'd known each other a long time, and Fischer knew Carter came from the same stock he did. From the very first time they'd met in that cramped interrogation room aboard the *Paladin*, he'd known the investigator was top-notch and the furthest thing from a company-man a person could be. They'd worked together for over ten years, and if there was anything Fischer could say about his mentor, it was that his focus was always on the mission.

That being the case, time in command had skewed his thinking; it wasn't Carter's fault. Fundamentally speaking, Carter was still the same hard-charging investigator he'd always been. Operationally, however, he had become indoctrinated into the "company way." As much as Fischer hated to admit it, Carter had become the very thing he'd hated all those years ago.

It was just the nature of the beast.

"We should probably make sure Wallace doesn't get wind of this," Fischer said. "Last thing we need is a paranoid witness. He's already embellishing enough as it is already."

"You think so?" Carter asked.

"Definitely."

Eliwood nodded agreement.

Carter nodded. "I'll make the call. We definitely don't need this thing going anymore sideways than it already has. Got a call just before all this from one of my contacts in Second Fleet. Young has expedited his arrival. We're running out of time."

Fischer's body tensed at the mention of the Admiral. His experiences with Admiral Young had been far from pleasant. Even after Fischer had almost single-handedly saved the Del Raycan Ambassador from an apparent Pegasi assassination attempt, the Admiral had still persisted in trying to hinder Fischer's career. For no other reason than it hadn't been Admiral Young himself who'd accomplished the feat. Young—who'd been a Captain at the time—had purposefully left Fischer's life-saving actions out of the official report, putting the success of the mission squarely on his own shoulders.

"I still don't understand why he's coming all the way out here for this," Eliwood said.

"I do," Fischer said. "He wants to be able to say he solved the mystery. He wants all the credit and accolades. He can't stand sharing the spotlight with anyone."

Carter shook his head. "Like I said before, forget about him. He's not our problem right now."

"What are you going to do about him?" Fischer motioned to Thomas's body where a group of ASI lab techs were busy setting up a cordon and bringing in their reconstruction equipment. Along with the terminals' security footage, they'd be able to recreate everything in a VR sim, allowing investigators and prosecutors alike to experience, first hand, what had happened.

"I'll get this cleaned up," Carter said, his tone finally softer than before. "You two do what you do but do it fast. We need to wrap this up before anyone else decides to punch their ticket."

CHAPTER 27

Militia Hideout
Calibri City, Stonemeyer
24 Mar 2607
Mission Time: 18hrs 7mins

I could smell something burning. My ears rang, and my head pounded. The world around me was blurry, and I remember being confused about where I was and what happened. Bits of ash fluttered through the air. I could hear the fire popping, but I couldn't see it.

I called out for someone, but it sounded like I was underwater. I saw Charles slumped over the steering wheel, eyes closed, not moving. Behind me, Delaney was picking himself up. Henderson had pinned Sheridan to the floor and was struggling to get off him in the cramped space.

I heard metal groaning and glass shattering, then I felt the hands on me. Several hands, grabbing ahold of arms, shoulders, my hair. They yanked and pulled me out, then dragged me away. I tried to fight, but against so many... I never had a chance.

More converged after they got me out, pulling the rest free

and beating them into submission before following.

"Yeah, real tough, are ya?" I shouted as they heaved me into the back of the truck behind Sheridan. "Take these ropes off, motherfuckers, then we'll see."

They laughed as the vehicles lurched and bounced, knocking us into each other and there was nothing we could do to protect ourselves. Sheridan kicked one and got a butt-stroke to the face for his troubles. Knocked him out cold.

They laughed even harder.

After a while, I stopped seeing the flashes of streetlights as we passed underneath them, and it was full dark. The buildings all started to look the same. I tried counting the seconds, trying to figure out how far we'd gone, but after a couple minutes I lost count and realized it didn't really matter anyway. They'd taken so many turns I'd never be able to navigate back to rest of the platoon, and they wouldn't have been there anyway.

The truck slowed, pulling into the back lot of an old, shitty apartment building. Trucks and cars were parked haphazardly around the lot, surrounded by small groups of militia soldiers.

They dragged us through a kitchen filled with stacks of food and supply crates. A pile of weapons took up most of the table at the side of the room and boxes of ammo covered the counters. They half-carried, half-dragged us down a flight of hard, wooden stairs, letting my back bounce against every step on the way down.

We ended up in a large room in the basement with even more supplies and weapons. By the look of things, the bastards had been stockpiling for a while. More soldiers were clustered around the large square pillars running down the center of the room, cheering and pointing as they tossed us to the ground.

I'd barely managed to get up on my knees when they descended on us again, pulling at our gear, ripping our boots and grays off.

"Hey Carn," one of the soldiers said, holding up Charles's tacvest. "Look at this!"

The soldier stopped yelling at Delaney and looked up. The Ambassador was curled up in the fetal position on the floor, trying desperately to pull away from the man's grip.

"What is it?" Carn snapped, more than a little irritated at the interruption.

"Lot of bang on this belt, boss."

Carn let go of Delaney's jacket and stepped around the rest of us, moving to where they were stripping Charles of his gear and clothes. They'd stripped us all down to our underwear, not bothering to tie us up, guess they figured the four rifles they had trained on us would do the trick. Some of them were fighting and bickering over who got what, but in the end, it was Carn that made those decisions, and even though he wasn't the head guy, everyone seemed to defer to his judgment.

Carn examined the vest for a moment, then looked down at Charles. "You the guy blew up the bunker, eh? You really did a number on that place."

He wiped the blood off his mouth with the back of his hand, glaring at Carn. "Should've used more."

One of the guards kicked him between the shoulder blades, sending him falling forward. He barely got his hands underneath him in time to stop his face from meeting the bare floor. They were on him immediately, pulling him back to his knees.

Carn moved to one of the open supply crates by the pillar behind him, shaking his head. "What is it about you Alliance fucks that you think you can come to our world and fuck with our way of life? Really kind of pisses me off." He pulled a wrench the size of his forearm out of the crate and hefted it in one hand, feeling the weight. "You know what I mean?"

"No!" I screamed, trying to get to my feet. One of the guards smacked me across the face with the butt of his rifle, dropping me to the floor. Stars dance in my vision, tongue playing at loose teeth.

"You son of a bitch!" Sheridan yelled, crawling forward to pull me back.

"Next one's for you big boy," the guard said, grinning.

Carn pointed at me with the wrench. "Hey, go easy with that one. Turk's not going to like it if you fuck up her pretty face." He took a step toward Charles, tapping his open palm with the end of the wrench. "Not going to make any friends around here with that attitude."

"Go fuck yourself," Charles growled, never taking his eyes off of Carn.

Without another word, Carn swung the wrench, connecting with the side of Charles's face with a sickening crack. The blow knocked out teeth, and sprayed blood everywhere. He collapsed, unconscious, a line of mucus and blood streaming from his open mouth.

"Awfully brave man with a big metal wrench," Henderson said, struggling against his captor, trying to get to his feet.

It took two of them to hold him back while a third stepped up and punched him in the mouth.

Henderson laughed. "That all you got?" He spat blood at them.

They took turns on him after that. One on each arm, holding him while a third worked him over, punching him again and again. The wet smacks of fist against flesh echoed around the main room. Prof held on for as long as he could, but soon they weren't holding him back, they were holding him up, and finally, they just let him drop to the floor.

"Lock 'em up!" Carn said, dumping the wrench back into the crate. "'Cept for him." He pointed at the Ambassador. "Turk's going to want to talk to him."

We heard the screams all night. Sometimes they'd ask him

questions, sometimes they'd just keep hitting him. Eventually, they took him away, upstairs to one of the rooms. Their leader, Turk, he didn't come down to the basement much.

There were times I thought I could hear Delaney screaming through the air ducts, but I kept fading in and out of consciousness, and at that point things start to get a little spotty.

The cells were little more than small closets off the main room with no windows. Sheridan and I shared a room for most of the time, I couldn't have asked for a better partner. Never once treated me like a liability, never let on that he felt sorry for me just because I was a woman. He treated me like just another Marine, and that was exactly what I needed.

After that first night, whenever they'd want to educate us, they'd take us one at a time, past the kitchen, to one of the upstairs rooms and shut the door.

They dropped me into a chair, not even bothering to tie my hands. As soon as my butt hit the seat, someone backhanded me, knocking me to the floor. Pain flared in my mouth, and I tongued my teeth, tasting blood. I was sure some of them at least were going to come out the next time someone hit me.

"Damn it, Rom!" Carn shouted from somewhere behind me. "Not the face."

"Shit, sorry, Boss. I got excited."

Hands grabbed me, lifting me back into the chair, slamming me down hard. I had trouble holding my head up straight, the room wouldn't stop spinning.

"See, not too bad," Rom said, bending over to examine my face. "Just a little bit of redness."

Carn stepped around in front of me, leaning in to consider Rom's handiwork. He shook his head, smiling. "You are pretty, aren't you?"

Even through the haze and fading consciousness I gritted my teeth and said, "Go fuck yourself."

He laughed, straightening. "Nah, I'll just wait for the left-overs. Turk gets first dibs."

At the time, I didn't understand what he meant, not until Turk showed up later. I don't even know if it was his real name. Don't really give a shit, to be honest.

"Remember," Carn said, backing away to give Rom room to work. "Not the face."

Rom nodded, stepping up, balling his fists. "Yeah, I got it."

I don't know how long they hit me, I tried doubling over to protect my chest and stomach, but they'd always pull me back. I tried to kick but hit nothing but air. My coordination was gone, my energy sapped. Even if I'd made contact, I doubt I would have done any real damage.

Rom slammed a fist into my side, sending lightning through my body as ribs cracked. I cried out, folding over and falling out of the chair. They didn't bother holding me up that time, just let me collapse to the ground, gasping for air. Every time I took a breath, pain flared in my chest.

I blew a wad of blood and spit onto the floor. The line of spittle stuck to my lip, slowing dripping out.

A pair of boots appeared in front of me. "You want this to stop, don't you?"

I tried to speak, but it just came out as a pained wheeze. I spit more blood out, then swallowed what I couldn't clear. The slimy texture of saliva and metallic taste of blood turned my stomach.

"You—" I started, cut off by a flare of pain as I took a breath. I grunted, fighting off the pain, then said, "Gonna buy me something nice after this?"

A chorus of laughter filled the room, and I felt the hands grab me again, lifting me back into the chair.

Rom shook his head. "You're one tough bitch, you know that?"

I tried to spit at him, but nothing came out.

"All you have to do is tell us where the weapons are," Carn said behind me. "Just point us in the right direction."

The effort to speak was almost not worth it. "Don't know... what you're talking... about."

Rom hit me again.

I'm not sure how long we were in there before the door opened, but when the tall, dark-haired man entered, I knew exactly who it was. His beard was trimmed short, speckled with white and gray, his matching hair was pulled back into a short ponytail. He had to be in his forties. His body had the look of someone who'd spent a lifetime in the military or doing hard labor.

Unlike the rest of them, his brown jacket, black pants, and shirt were clean and pressed, like he'd just picked them up from the laundry. He wore a pistol holstered to his hip and a bunch of medals hanging on colorful ribbons around his neck that clinked together as he walked.

Both Carn and Rom stepped back as their leader approached, not quite bowing in reverence, but definitely out of respect or fear, or both.

Turk's eyes were hard, blazing fire even just standing there, silently considering the scene. He cocked his head to the side, holding my gaze. "And how are your lessons going?"

"She ain't talkin'," Rom blurted out. He started to say something else but cut himself off at an abrupt glare from Carn.

Turk ignored the man's comments. He just stood there, looking at me with those burning eyes. I can't get those eyes out of my mind. They bore through me, almost like he was looking into my soul. But there was more to it than that. There was hate in those eyes. He hated me, and I had no idea why.

He nodded to the others then took a step back.

Four of them grabbed me, pulled me out of the dark, window-less room they kept us in, brought me to another room and threw me on a table. The back of my skull smacked against the hard surface, sending stars across my already blurry vision.

Turk appeared at the foot of the table, rolling up his sleeves. "Time to educate her on Stonemeyer politics."

I tried to fight, but there's only so much you can do against five men. The max I'd ever fought against in the arena was three, and I'd been in peak condition, not slowed by a concussion and at least of a day of almost constant beatings. That's without even considering the last time I'd had something that even passed as meal.

I pulled and kicked, but eventually, they managed to overpower me and pinned me down.

Turk cut my shorts free with a knife and had his way. The pain was incredible, but it only lasted a minute. After that, everything seemed to fade away into a land far away. Like it was happening to someone else. The only thing I saw were his eyes, glowing with rage and fury, boring into me as if my whole existence had wronged him somehow.

When he was done, everyone else got a turn.

I traced the cracks in the ceiling over and over, imagining they were roads. If I could get to them, they'd lead me home. I imagined I was floating in the ocean, lost and adrift in the middle of a vast sea of nothing. I imagined a ship would come by and I could wave and scream and shout, and they would see me and rescue me.

But no one came.

I was alive, but with every breath I took, and every moment that ticked by, I wished I wasn't.

I just wanted the nightmare to be over.

CHAPTER 28

Militia Hideout
Calibri City, Stonemeyer
26 Mar 2607
Mission Time: approx. 4days 5hrs

The cell door swung open, slamming back against the wall, cracking the gray plaster. The impact jerked me back from semi-unconsciousness as two soldiers entered, pulling Sheridan between them. They tossed him to the floor near the back of the room, laughing as he grunted in pain.

"Don't worry, sweetheart," one said on their way out. "We'll be back for you in a bit." He blew me a kiss and winked. I dreamed of crushing his skull.

The door slammed shut again, leaving us alone. They'd taken Charles shortly after they'd taken Sheridan and Henderson and he had never returned. Henderson's mouth had finally stopped bleeding, but he'd need to have massive reconstructive surgery to repair the damage they'd done to it.

I hadn't seen Delaney in a while either, hadn't heard him either for that matter. I saw him once on the second day when

Carn and Rom had been pulling him upstairs, a bag over his head. Like he could see anything anyway. All the windows were boarded up and insulated for sound. He never put up a fight, just allowed himself to be dragged wherever they wanted him.

They kept him separate from the rest of us, but I could hear them sometimes when the screams died down. Turk's voice echoed through the walls, punctuated by wet smacks and cries of pain. "Where is it? You're a liar!"

I couldn't hear what Delaney answered. Whatever he said, Turk didn't like. I'm sure it was just his usual babbling nonsense about the Alliance and just wanting to help. I'd heard him say that a hundred times and it only seemed to make Turk even angrier. Then he would go back to hitting him. Eventually, his screams turned into sobs and groans, then silence.

I saw him one other time, hanging in the middle of one of the rooms, his hands tied above his head as they sprayed him with a hose. With every breath, he blew out mouthfuls of water, and every time he opened his mouth more went in. It was a constant cycle. No matter which way he turned, he couldn't get away from the spray. They'd let off every now and then, giving him half a second here, half a second there, to catch his breath and then they'd start all over again.

Sheridan groaned, rolling to his chest, slowly getting his arms under him. I moved to help him, but a wave of agony pushed me back down. I leaned back against the wall, gritting my teeth against the pain.

Sheridan put a hand up. "Don't. I'm okay."

I blew out a pained breath, trying to avoid sitting directly on my crotch. The throbbing down there… constant, radiating waves of pain that took my breath away every time I moved, despite how much I willed the pain to go away.

"Charles isn't going to make it much longer," Sheridan said, sitting up, leaning against the wall. A combination of sweat and tears streaked his dirt and blood covered face. Blood streamed from his nose, and his left eye was swollen pretty good. He could open it, but I doubted he could see. "Saw him in the kitchen on my way up."

My heart sank. "I'm going to kill every last one of them. Every one. And I'll save Turk for last so I can take my time with him."

"There was something different about him this time," Sheridan said, sitting back against the wall. "Kept asking if I knew where the weapons were."

"What the hell do they keep talking about? What weapons?"

Sheridan touched his swollen eye and winced. "Hell if I know."

The door opened again, slamming against the wall with a resounding *crack* and two more militiamen appeared carrying Henderson. His eyes were barely open, his head bobbed as they walked him to the rear of the cell, then dropped him to the floor. The guards left without a word, slamming the door behind them.

Prof pushed himself to his elbows, licking a fresh cut upon his upper lip, then wiping it with the back of his hand.

"You okay?" Sheridan asked.

"Fine," Prof said. "thtill not thure what thothe bathtards are after. Thomething about weapons."

With his teeth gone, nothing sounded right. His deep, gruff voice didn't seem so menacing when he couldn't pronounce his letters correctly. All his "s's" sounded like "th's." Despite everything that had gone on the last couple of days, despite the Albatross crash, the death of so many of my friends, being captured and violated six ways from Sunday, it was everything I could do to not laugh when Prof spoke. A grin formed at the corner of my mouth, and I hated myself for it. There was nothing funny about this at all.

I wiped the smile away before Henderson saw and said, "They asked you about the weapons too?"

Henderson nodded.

"It doesn't make any sense," I said. "I mean besides our weapons, which they have, I don't know why they're so hard up for more. They seem to have enough."

"No shit," Sheridan said. "They've got enough weapons out there to arm twice as many guys as I've seen here. And this is only one of their cells."

"Huh?" I asked.

Sheridan shrugged. "Back at the safe house, when Delaney was telling us about it, he said there were several cells. Said they all worked independently of each other but had central leadership."

Henderson pointed at the door. "I'd be willing to bet this ith their leaderthip thell."

"I don't know," Sheridan said. "I get the impression they're taking orders from someone else."

"But what the hell?" I said, "It's not like anything they get from us is going to make any difference. What do we have? A couple LR27s and thermal grenades, big deal."

Sheridan tapped his link again. The flickering, orange light the panels emitted illuminated the room. He worked through several menus but had no luck. "That code inhibitor they flashed is good. Not getting anything on here at all."

"Even if they hadn't," I said. "I'm sure they've got this whole place shielded, just like the safe house was. And what's the range on that thing, anyway, a couple kilometers at most? I'm telling you, it's pointless to keep trying."

"It's not." His fingers danced across the holographic interface, scrolling through options and menus. "There's always a chance."

"Best thing you could do with that is to record a message to your family, let them know you love them. Maybe someone'll find it one day, and it'll get back to the Alliance."

Sheridan blew out a long breath, finally shutting the link off, plunging the room back into darkness. "You think the others made it out of here?"

"If anyone could make it back to the ship, it's Hastings."

"But they'll come looking for us, right? They're not going to just leave us down here. I mean Delaney's still here right? The whole mission was about him."

"That bastard can rot," I said.

"Haven't seen him in a while."

"Haven't heard him either," Sheridan said. "You think he's dead? Like they killed him?"

"Who gives a shit about him?" I asked. "We need to get Charles out of here."

They'd done work to all of us over the last two days, but they'd worked especially hard on Delaney and Charles. The first night they'd broken all the fingers on Charles's right hand, smashing each knuckle so he couldn't move them at all. He'd never work with explosives again. Even with surgery, I doubt they'd be able to repair that kind of damage. Maybe they could if they gave him an entirely new hand, I'd seen docs do crazy things with prosthetics.

"Bastards," Sheridan said.

There wasn't much else to say. All three of us shared the same opinion. We all wanted nothing more than to go through each and every room in this place and cut down every last one of them.

Sheridan rubbed his jaw, wincing as he touched his reddish-purple skin. "We need to get out of here."

I snorted before I could stop myself. "No shit, Captain Obvious. What was your first clue?"

"I mean it." He straightened, expression completely serious.

"I know we could do it. We just need the right opportunity. Catch them with their guards down. If I can get my hands on a gun—"

"And how are you going to do that?" I asked, not bothering to keep the skepticism out of my voice.

He put his hands out, palms to the ceiling. "I don't know, but somehow we could do it. These shitheads aren't really trained all that well. Their tactics are shit. They can't fight for shit. Put them one on one against us, we'd win every time."

"He's right," Henderson said before I could argue. "They ain't trained for thit. Their thituathional awareneth ith almost non-exiththent—fuck off." He gave Sheridan the finger.

Sheridan put a hand over his mouth, covering the smile that had formed there. "Sorry."

I couldn't fault Henderson's assessment. Aside from the ones assigned to move us from cell to cell, none of the soldiers really paid us any attention. They didn't even look up as we were hauled past. It probably wouldn't be too hard to get the drop on the first couple maybe, but after that, it'd be a different story.

"Even if we could get out hands on a gun and take out the guards, what then?" I asked. "How far are we going to get with three injured Marines that can barely walk, and one that probably can't at all? Not to mention we have no weapons and no transport?"

I didn't even bother mentioning Delaney. If push came to shove and we had an out, I had no issue at all leaving that smug son of a bitch back here. Maybe the militia would do us a favor and kill him before we got back with help.

"So we leave them here," Sheridan said.

"Not an option," I said, shaking my head. "We don't leave anyone behind."

"I'm not saying that. But you're right, we wouldn't get far at all with Charles, even Prof. I mean, how far will you make it before you have to stop?" My face flushed, eyes going hard.

Sheridan must have seen it too because he immediately started backpeddling. "I didn't mean…"

"It's fine," I told him, a little too harshly.

"He's right though," Henderson said.

I frowned. "What do you mean?"

"You're going to have to leave us behind if you plan on making it back to the rest of the unit. No other way to do it."

"We're not leaving you behind."

"Listen," Henderson said, putting up a hand, "you go back for help. Bring the rest of the thquad back and waste these bathtards, then we all get out of here. But you're not going to be able to do that if we're thlowing you down."

All the options started running through my mind, and slowly I began to see they were right. I didn't like it. Not one bit of it, but as I started playing out the scenarios, I realized they weren't wrong, no matter how much I didn't want to agree with them.

"Okay," I said. "Do you have a plan?"

CHAPTER 29

Milita Hideout
Calibri City, Stonemeyer
27 Mar 2607
Mission Time: approx. 5 days, 2 hrs

On the fourth day, they finished with me and Sheridan at the same time. We made eye contact briefly as they dragged us through the main room. My right eye was swollen shut—extra education from Turk and his crew. I remember blood and semen dripping down my legs as they dragged me back. I could see Sheridan in front of me, still on his feet, struggling to keep up as they pushed and shoved him through the main room to our cell.

They threw him in first and tossed me in after. He managed to keep his footing and was able to turn and catch me before I hit the ground.

"Aww, look at that," Turk sneered. "The long-lost lovers reunite. Hope we didn't ruin her too bad for you."

"Fuck off, asshole," Sheridan shouted, holding me up, giving me time to get my feet under me.

They slammed the door, leaving us alone. Sheridan helped me to the floor, apologizing as I grimaced.

"It's okay," I said. Even talking was painful, now. The words I formed in my head weren't the same words my lips spoke. It took awhile for the room to stop spinning, and even then, everything was spotty. The room kept threatening to fade away. Every few seconds, I'd start to nod off then jerk back awake. It always took me a few seconds to remember where I was and what was going on.

"Don't understand…" I asked as Sheridan wiped my legs with a dirty cloth. I barely felt it, like it was happening to someone else.

Sheridan shook his head. "Wish I knew. Keep asking me the same questions over and over again, and I keep telling them I don't have any fucking idea what they're talking about."

I looked past Sheridan to where Charles leaned against the wall. His head was slumped down on his chest, eyes swollen shut, face bleeding from a multitude of cuts and a broken nose. Every time he exhaled, he blew bloody bubbles from his nostrils and sent tiny specks of blood spraying over his bare chest.

His mangled hands rested on the floor on either side, and his broken leg was still wrapped tight. We'd tried to wrap his fingers, but every time we tried, he woke up and pulled away before passing out again. Blood soaked the rags we'd managed to get in place. The rest of the wounds trickled blood onto the floor. His chest rose and fell in shallow breaths, and I couldn't help but think that every one he took would be his last.

"We need to get out of here," I told Sheridan, like he didn't know already.

He nodded, then followed my gaze to Charles. "We can come back for him. We can find the Lieutenant and come back for him. Kill all these motherfuckers."

Leaving Charles was the last thing either of us wanted to do, but at the same time, I also knew we didn't have a choice. We hadn't seen Henderson since the night before when Turk had showed up around what I thought must have been midnight and dragged him away.

The room started fading again.

"Hey," Sheridan said, his face appearing in the hazy darkness, centimeters from mine. "You okay?"

My crotch throbbed, every movement sending waves of pain and nausea over me. I grimaced, sucking in a sharp breath as another searing pain shot through me. I had to lie on my side, using the wall for support. I shut my good eye against the burning, fighting back the tears that were more for anger than anything.

The darkness was so inviting. It was like a warm blanket I just wanted to wrap myself up in and go to sleep. Sleep. That's really all I needed. I could go to sleep and wake up and all of this would just have been a nightmare.

Sleep.

Something pressed on my face. I recoiled, opening my eye to see Sheridan, his expression a mixture of concern and fear. "I need you to stay awake for me, okay, Corporal? Can you do that?"

I had trouble keeping my head up. It was so heavy. "Sorry."

"It's okay. Just focus on me, all right?"

I shifted my position on the floor, trying to find the least painful position, but it didn't matter. The pain was everywhere, it didn't matter where I moved. It was always there. Flashes of agony woke me for a moment, but I immediately felt the call back to the darkness.

"He was really pissed today," I said, my voice little more than a whisper.

"Why?"

I shook my head. "Don't know. Didn't ask me anything. Just fucking started in. Did this…" I pointed to my eye.

"Heard them screaming at Delaney earlier," Sheridan said. "Kept saying he was lying and cursing him for turning something off, but I never could figure out what. I almost got the feeling they knew each other."

As he spoke, his voice became more and more distant until it wasn't much more than a muffled whisper. The darkness poured over me and I felt the blanket wrap itself around me. I knew I was going to pass out and couldn't do anything to stop it. I welcomed the darkness. Welcomed sleep.

I don't know how long I faded in and out. Could've been days. But I remember Sheridan waking me up, his face glowing orange in the dark cell. His good eye almost seemed to sparkle.

"What… what is it?"

Sheridan smiled. "They're here."

CHAPTER 30

Haroldson Memorial Hospital,
Regional Naval Medical Facility
Blue Lake City, New Tuscany
4 Apr 2607

Corporal Biagini winced, shifting on the bed. She groaned and clenched her teeth. "Sorry, it's spotty. I'm having trouble…"

Fischer raised a hand. "It's okay, take your time." *Time that we don't have*, he thought. He desperately wanted—no… needed —to know what happened next.

It'd taken her almost two hours to get as far as she had. Some of her memories of the fighting hadn't exactly matched up with Wallace's, but Fischer was willing to chalk that up to perspective. He hadn't heard anything yet that reinforced his hunch that Wallace was lying. Not yet.

Was it possible the corporal was telling the truth? Sure, but Fischer wasn't convinced.

Biagini gasped, her body tensing, and her thumb pressed down on the injector's control switch. Fischer suppressed a groan as she pushed the small red button, again and again, trying to combat the pain that must have been raging inside her.

Eliwood shook her head at him, obviously thinking the same thing he was. *There goes the rest of our questions.* He decided to press on anyway.

"The rest of the team found you? What happened then? What happened to Hastings and the rest of them?"

The Corporal held her breath for a few seconds, eyes shut, waiting for the medicine to do its work. She blew it out, her entire body visibly relaxing and she opened her eyes. A single tear ran down the side of her face.

"Hastings…" she closed her eyes again, turning away, her face contorting into a mask of pain and sadness. "The orders…"

Fischer frowned, looking at Eliwood as if to confirm he'd heard the Marine correctly. "What orders?"

"The orders…" Her head bobbed slightly, eyes fluttering.

"Corporal," Fischer said, a little more forcefully than he'd wanted. Biagini's eyes flicked open, wide with fear and confusion. "What orders?"

She broke into sobs, body spasming with everything breath. She clicked the red button again. "He tried to stop them…"

"Who tried to stop them? Stop who?" Fischer knew they were on the verge of breaking this thing all the way open if he could just get a little more information from her.

"I'm sorry," she said between sobs. "I'm so sorry."

Fischer leaned over her. "It's okay, you don't have to be—"

Eliwood put a hand on his arm, shaking her head. Fischer hesitated, then realized Biagini wasn't actually talking to him.

She clicked the button again. "God, what did we do? He saved me! He saved me! Oh, God, what have we done?"

Another click. And another.

Finally, the medicine started taking effect, and the Corporal's eyes began to flicker, slowly closing. Her body relaxed, sinking into the bed. Her eyes narrowed, head tilting to the side and she was asleep.

He glanced at Eliwood then nodded toward the door. She closed the door behind them and said, "Did you see that look on her face?"

"Hold on," Fischer said, giving the Marine guard a side-long look. They moved out of earshot.

"She's really messed up about her team being killed," Eliwood said as they stepped out of the ward. "I'd say even more so than the fact that she was repeatedly raped and beaten."

"Survivor's guilt," Fischer said. "We need to know how they died. We still haven't heard anything about that building exploding or contacting the *Vision* for the pickup, which we know they did."

"At least we know Hastings wasn't going to leave without his people. I'd just like to know how they found them."

Fischer nodded, replaying everything Biagini had just told him. "How they found Biagini and Sheridan and the others?"

"Yeah. Wallace said they picked up on their beacon, but Biagini said their links weren't working. So, how'd they track them down?"

"Alliance military links are more advanced than civilian models," Fischer explained. "You can flash the core, but the emergency locator beacon operates completely independently of the main software."

"So, they found them and then blew up some random building?" Eliwood asked. "That doesn't make much sense?"

"You think anything that's happened in the last two days has made any kind of sense?"

"Granted, but you said it yourself, there's a lot more going on here than this mission. And remember what Biagini said yesterday, that thing about the assassination? What the hell was that all about?"

"Let's see if we can find out."

Wallace's room was dark and quiet. He opened his eyes as Fischer and Eliwood stepped inside, frowning.

"Everything okay?" Wallace asked.

The confusion on the private's face gave Fischer a bit of solace. At least the gag order had been received and implemented in time. That was probably the only thing that had worked out in their favor during this whole investigation. Wallace would hear about Thomas, there wasn't any doubt about that. Fischer knew they wouldn't be able to keep the information from him for very long, someone would mention it eventually. The order prohibiting the Marines and hospital staff from discussing what had happened at the hyperloop station didn't apply to the media.

We've got a day at most, Fischer told himself. *Then all bets are off.* He wondered how the private would react when he learned about Thomas. *Probably not well.*

But for now, Fischer had time, and he would need to pull on all of his knowledge and experience to coax the rest of the information out of Wallace and tie this all together before it blew up in all of their faces.

"Fine," Fischer lied. "Had some problems with the Revolution 52 nuts is all. We got it sorted out."

Wallace chuckled. "Those crazy bastards? What are they protesting now? They find out the chicken surprise in this place isn't chicken? I'm telling you, Agent, I'm not sure what was harder to survive, Stonemeyer or the cooking in this place."

Eliwood moved to the side of the room, leaning up against the wall, crossing her arms. "I thought hospital food was supposed to be the best in the service?"

"Shit, maybe in the officers' mess," Wallace said. "But this place... bleh. You think you can sneak me in some steak or something? Maybe a decent burger? I'm fading away to nothing in this bed."

"We'll see what we can work out." Fischer said, pulling one of the plastic chairs away from the wall near the foot of the bed. He spun it around, then sat backward, resting his arms on the seatback. "Before we got called away, you were telling us about what happened after Hastings contacted the *Vision*. Rocket hit the truck —Biagini and Henderson and Sheridan, yeah? What happened after that?"

Wallace's jovial expression faded. He shook his head. "We couldn't get to them because of all the militia troops. We'd've been captured too, right? I mean, I know there wasn't anything we could've done, but it still eats at me, you know?"

"Doesn't make you feel any better about it," Fischer added.

"Fuck no, it doesn't. It kills me." He tapped his chest. "And after we found out what happened to them..." he trailed off, shaking his head. "Fuck."

"Let's talk about it. What happened?"

"I know they raped Biagini," Wallace said, jaw clenching, nostrils flaring. He stared at his hands, squeezing them together, knuckles white. "I know that. Motherfuckers."

"You said you followed Sheridan's beacon?"

"That's right. After the first day, we decided just to drive around town, searching. Hastings didn't want to leave anyone behind, and frankly, neither did the rest of us. Never leave a Marine behind. That shit's real."

Fischer nodded. "I know. So, you found them."

"Yeah."

"So, what happened?"

"We found them and made it to the safe house, laid low and waited for the bird to pick us up."

Fischer straightened. "Wait a minute. What happened to Hastings? To Sheridan? The rest of the team? They didn't make it back to the bird."

Wallace blew out a long breath, eyes darting around the room.

"They bought it at the hideout, man. What do you want me to say? Those militia bastards were tough as shit."

He's lying, Fischer realized. Wallace had been completely detailed about everything up until this point, he'd never hesitated, not once. Sure, he'd probably embellished some things along the way, but Fischer hadn't gotten the impression that he'd been lying.

Fischer quickly went back over their previous conversations, trying to pull out any hint of deception, but couldn't remember his radar ever going off. Something had changed. Something had happened that Wallace didn't want to talk about.

Finally, Fischer said, "Tell me about the hideout. How did Hastings die?"

Wallace shifted uncomfortably on his bed. "I told you, those bastards were tough. Got shot while we were clearing the hideout. I found Sheridan and Biagini in the basement, they were really messed up. Well, I mean, you've seen her. You know."

"Yeah, I know that."

Wallace shook his head. "He was a good lieutenant, you know? As far as lieutenants go, I guess. Could have been anyone, though. He went upstairs, Sarge and I went down. If we'd gone up, it could've been Thomas, or me."

"That's very true."

"Anyway, we made contact with *Vision* a couple days after that, and the rest I'm guessing you know already."

"What took so long?" Fischer asked.

"Wanted to be sure it was clear to call for retrieval. Picked up a lot of local chatter about the hideout battle. The Stonemeyer government was blaming it on rival cells within the militia, trying to paint the picture that it was falling apart. The Peace-keepers were sweeping through cells, arresting anyone even suspected of being in the militia. It was kind of a shitshow for a couple days."

Something tugged at the back of Fischer's mind—one of the

images he'd seen in Carter's office the day before. Then it hit him. "So, what caused the explosions?"

"I'm sorry?"

"The explosions," Fischer repeated, "that brought down the Klausmeyer building. All the news footage we saw showed emergency crews digging through the remains of the building. Looked like it had been blown to all to hell. What happened?"

"Uh," Wallace hesitated. "I don't..."

"And Sheridan, when did he get killed?"

"I told you…"

"You didn't say shit," Fischer said. "It had to have been right before the extraction bird picked you up because the pilot didn't say anything about Sheridan. Or about Jung for that matter. The only one that he saw was Grayson, holding off the enemy so you could board the Albatross."

The frustration that had been simmering at the back of Fischer's mind boiled over. "Your story's got some fairly big holes, Private."

Wallace put his hands up. "Hey man, I'm just telling you what I remember. I hit my head during the pickup, remember? Some of this shit is still kind of fuzzy."

"Okay, so how did Sheridan get killed?"

"Got hit when the Peacekeepers found us," Wallace said, face reddening. "Shit, man, what the fuck are you trying to say?"

"I'm not trying to say anything. I just want you to tell me the truth."

"What, you think I'm lying about this shit?"

Fischer raised both eyebrows. "I don't know, are you?"

"Fuck off, asshole. You asked me to tell you what happened, I'm telling you. Sheridan and Jung bit it before we got picked up. That's what happened. Shit." Wallace crossed his arms, looking away from Fischer's doubtful stare.

"And the explosions?"

Wallace threw up his hands. "I don't know, it was still standing when we left. Maybe those bastards blew their own shit up. You'll have to ask them."

"Oh, trust me," Fischer said. "I will."

"Whatever, man. I told you what happened. Albatross picked us up, and now we're here. If I never see that God-forsaken planet again it'll be too soon."

Fischer watched as Wallace's eyes flicked around the room, looking anywhere but at Fischer.

"There's something you're not telling me," Fischer said.

"I told you, man, that's it. That's everything. I don't know what else you want me to say. It was a shitty deal. The whole thing was completely fucked, okay? Right from the beginning."

"Two days is a lot of time for nothing to happen," Eliwood said. "You really expect us to believe you just sat around that whole time waiting to call for a bird? Why didn't you call right away?"

"Jesus Christ, are you deaf? I just said the place was crawling with cops and Peacekeepers. They were everywhere. We didn't have a choice. We had to let it quiet down, or they would have found us."

"But they did find you," Fischer corrected.

Wallace sniffed, rubbing his nose with the back of his hand. "Yeah, that's right. I guess those Peacekeepers have better tracking systems than we think, huh?"

"They tracked you down after you called *Vision* with Biagini's shotbox?" Eliwood asked.

"That's right," Wallace answered, nodding. "Came down practically on top of us. I guess they were waiting on us."

"So, after days of no contact at all, they just magically appeared out of nowhere, exactly where you were?" Fischer asked.

"Hey!" Wallace jerked upright on the bed, jabbing a finger a

Fischer. "You don't know shit, okay? You weren't there. I don't know how the hell they found us. I know we were damn lucky to get out of there when we did, I know that."

Fischer opened his mouth to argue but shut it as the door to the room slid open. Sergeant Preble leaned in, a concerned look on his face. "Excuse me, Agent Fischer, can I talk with you for a minute."

Fischer turned back to Wallace, glaring, then nodded. "Yeah."

They stepped out of the room and Eliwood slid the door shut behind him. Preble was sweating and out of breath. He put both hands on his hips, taking long deliberate breaths, trying to slow his breathing.

Fischer frowned. "What's wrong, Sergeant?"

"It's Biagini."

CHAPTER 31

Haroldson Memorial Hospital,
Regional Naval Medical Facility
Blue Lake City, New Tuscany
4 Apr 2607

"How the hell did she get out of her room?" Eliwood asked, following the security guard down the empty corridor. They were on the top floor of the hospital, passing doors marked for maintenance and equipment. "She was doped up on meds when we left her not thirty minutes ago."

"She definitely wasn't," Preble said. Knocked out one of my guards, took his security pass."

"That seems to be a trend around here," Eliwood said.

"Yeah."

"Is anyone talking to her?" Fischer asked.

Preble shook his head. "Won't speak to anyone but you."

Eliwood gave Fischer a questioning look. "She say why?"

"She did not."

Two security guards stood at the end of the corridor, watching over a nurse who squatted in front of a gray haired man propped against the wall. The old man's gray utility overalls were stained with drops of blood, and his hand pressed against his forehead. His nose and mouth were stained red from an apparent broken nose, and a gash above one eye had been recently treated.

He's alive at least, Fischer thought as they approached.

"How is he?" Preble asked.

The nurse looked up. "Fine. Some bio-syth and painkillers, and he'll be good as new."

"Didn't even see her coming," the old man said. He took his hand away from his forehead, looking at his bloodstained palm.

"I'll make sure you get the rest of the day off," Preble said.

"Hell with that, I'm retired, Sergeant. Recon, Second Marines." He pulled up his pants leg, revealing prosthetic leg, emblazoned with the Alliance Marine Corp crest. "I've had worse."

Preble smiled. "So you have."

"She say anything to you?" Fischer asked, leaning forward to read the man's name badge. "Jon."

"Who, the girl?" Jon shook his head. "Never even knew she was there until she was smashing my face against the wall. Might've just let her in, she asked nice enough. What's she in trouble for anyway?"

Fischer shook his head. "No trouble."

"Yeah," Jon said, laughing. "No trouble. That's why a whole squad of security and two ASI agents are after her? Sure, mister, whatever you say."

"Come on, it's this way." Preble led them through the open door marked, "Service Area - Authorized Personnel Only."

"You've got to be kidding," Fischer said, following Preble through the door.

Inside, a wireframe cage surrounded a steel ladder that led up to an open hatch on the ceiling. Sunlight spilled through the opening, and Fischer could see New Tuscany's cloudy blue sky. One of Preble's hospital guards held pulled the gate open as the sergeant neared.

Preble looked over his shoulder, one hand on the ladder. "What's wrong, Agent? Don't do heights?"

"It's not the heights that gets me," Fischer replied, starting up the ladder after the sergeant. "It's the sudden stop at the bottom I don't like."

Two more guards, standing on either side of the open hatch, helped the trio out onto the roof. A deep thrumming sound reverberated around them, vibrating Fischer's chest. Most of his view was blocked by huge air processing units and ductwork and clusters of cables that snaked between them.

"Where the hell's she going?" Eliwood asked as one of the guards helped her through the hatch. "Thanks."

Preble jerked his head to the side. "This way."

He led them through the maze of processors, around a fenced-in communications cluster and half a dozen more maintenance closets. Preble paused behind one of the last processing units, its gray metal casing glinting in the sunlight. "I've got fire and rescue on the way."

Corporal Biagini stood on the top of the roof's retaining wall, ten feet away from him, her bare toes curled over the edge. Her hospital gown and dark hair whipped in the warm wind. Her head was down, eyes focused on the street twenty-seven stories below.

"Fantastic," Fischer said, his words laced with sarcasm. *I'm not a negotiator, I'm an interrogator,* he thought, pulling his service weapon and handing it to Eliwood.

"Good luck," Eliwood told him.

He took a long breath, shaking his head. "Why do I always get the crazy ones?"

She smiled. "I guess it's just your sparkling personality."

"It's definitely not that."

Fischer approached her slowly, one hand out, palm up, trying to look as non-threatening as possible. His foot crunched against the loose pebble roofing, and she turned, eyes red from crying.

"Stop," she told him, pointing. "Don't come any closer."

"All right." Fischer held up both hands. "All right, relax. Listen, I'm just here to talk, that's all. You're not in any trouble."

She shook her head. "You have no idea what kind of trouble I'm in. You don't!" Her face contorted into a mixture of pain and anger as more tears welled up under her eyes. "You don't know what we did!"

"That's what I'm here to find out. Listen, whatever it is, we can work it out. Trust me. It's not worth this."

"No." Biagini shook her head. "You can't work this out. No one can." She looked up at the passing clouds as if they could provide her with some kind of comfort and sobbed. "I'm so sorry. God, we were so wrong. So wrong. I knew it. I fucking knew it, and I didn't do anything to stop him."

Fischer frowned. "Stop who? What are you talking about? Hey, it's okay, just come down from there and we'll talk about this, that's what I'm here for." He took a step forward.

She put up a hand. "*No!*"

Fischer retreated. "All right. Easy. Relax. It's going to be okay, I promise."

"It's not!" she screamed. "It's not going to be okay. He's dead! They're all dead. Hastings and Sheridan..." she broke off, sobbing. "I'm so sorry."

"I talked to Wallace," Fischer said, mind racing. "I don't know about Sheridan, but I know there wasn't anything you could've done for Hastings. What happened at that hideout wasn't your fault."

Biagini's pained expression shifted, becoming confused. She sniffed, wiping snot away from her nose with the back of her hand. "What did he say?"

Progress, Fischer thought. "That Hastings was shot when he rescued you and Sheridan. You couldn't've stopped—"

Biagini laughed. "Wallace is such an asshole. We were stupid to listen to Thomas. I knew the orders were bullshit. I knew they were wrong. I knew it. And I did nothing."

There's the orders again. "What orders? Whose orders? To extract the Ambassador?"

Biagini shook her head. "I told you, Agent Fischer. It wasn't an extraction at all."

"You said it was an assassination. Who were you there to kill?"

Biagini opened her mouth to answer, then looked away, more tears welling in her eyes. "I love the Corps, Agent Fischer. All I've ever wanted to be was an Alliance Marine. Ever since I was a little girl, I wanted to wear the uniform. My parents hated the idea. Said I'd have to sell my soul to the Corps and I'd never get it back." She shook her head. She held her arms out, motioning all around her. "They were right. Look what they make you give."

"Whatever happened, you can make it right. We can work together and fix this. We can."

Her face darkened. "Can you bring back Hastings? Can you bring back Sheridan?"

"I—"

"No! They're gone. They're gone, and it's my fault." She broke into sobs again. "Sheridan saved me. Brought me back from the abyss and I betrayed him. I left him there. I let him die. It's my fault! You can't fix that!"

"I know you're hurting. I know your heart is breaking for your friends, I've been there, trust me. Let me help you. It doesn't have to end like this. You've served the Corps with honor, Corporal. Tell me what happened."

"Honor." Biagini shook her head. "I lost that on Stonemeyer.

The only one of us with any left was Sheridan. Look what it got him."

"What happened to him? What happened to Sheridan?"

She hung her head, her body gyrating as she wept. "I can't."

"Yes, you can."

"Please," Biagini said, taking a breath, steadying herself. "Forgive me."

She turned and stepped off the ledge.

Haroldson Memorial Hospital,
Regional Naval Medical Facility
Blue Lake City, New Tuscany
4 Apr 2207

"No!" Fischer shouted as he reached the ledge and watched helplessly as Biagini plummeted to the pavement. It was almost graceful, as if she was gliding through the air. She abruptly smacked into the ground. Fischer turned away, grateful he hadn't been able to hear her body breaking. He leaned back against the wall, sliding down to his butt, rubbing his beard with both hands.

He closed his eyes and tilted his face up to the sun. "Son of a bitch."

"What the hell?" Eliwood leaned over the waist-high retaining wall. She stared down at Biagini's body, shaking her head, then straightened. "Did any of that make any sense to you? Cause it didn't to me."

Fischer took a long breath. "She blames herself for Sheridan and Hastings dying. Maybe even the rest of her team, too."

"Survivor's guilt? Wished she could trade places with them. That they'd've lived and not her."

"I don't know," Fischer said, his voice soft, unsure. "I think it's more than that."

It had to be more than that. She'd seemed convinced that they'd done something wrong, but that they'd had no other choice. Fischer didn't like where this was going. Not at all.

"You don't think she killed them or anything like that, do you? Cause I didn't get that vibe at all."

"No," Fischer said, shaking his head. "But it was how she said the thing about the orders, and that she knew they were wrong."

"That's the second time she mentioned the orders."

"At least," Fischer agreed.

Sirens echoed up from the street as two security cars, and an ambulance pulled up next to the corporal's body. Fischer stood and looked over, watching as the medics went to work, kneeling in the pool of blood surrounding Biagini's corpse.

Eliwood looked away. "What about their orders?"

"Exactly. What about their orders? As far as we can tell, their orders were to extricate a sitting Ambassador from his Embassy, right? That's it, nothing more. It doesn't make any sense. When I mentioned Hastings getting killed, she looked at me like I was crazy. She laughed like she knew something I didn't. She said 'You don't know what we did.' Who's 'we?' The squad? What'd they do?"

"They got their asses kicked," Eliwood said. "Sometimes crazy shit happens in battle, right? You said it yourself."

"She said 'the Corps makes you give up your soul.'"

"Huh?"

"When I asked her about the orders, she said she'd sold her soul to the Corps."

"Okay, and? What's their slogan? Bound by oath, soul, and blood? That's exactly what Thomas said, right before…"

Fischer nodded, rubbing his chin, feeling the coarse hairs tickle his fingers. "She was about to tell me something about those orders. I could see it in her eyes. She wanted to tell me."

"Why didn't she?"

"Right. Why didn't she?"

Eliwood was silent for a moment, considering. "Because someone ordered her not to?"

"Life in the Corps revolves around following orders. That's a Marine's whole purpose: to follow orders, even orders they don't agree with. What could've been so important that two decorated Marines would rather die than talk about what happened on that mission?"

"Only one more person that can tell us."

Fischer nodded. "Problem is he's lying."

"Who, Wallace? But why though?"

"That's the million-credit question, isn't it?"

"You think anything that he said was legit?"

Fischer shrugged. "I don't know. The longer he went, the deeper it got. He definitely got mixed up there at the end, especially about Hastings and Sheridan dying. I think he realized it too."

"You think Biagini and him are following the same orders?"

"Let's go ask him."

Sergeant Preble stepped up as Fischer pushed off the retaining wall. He held up and hand, stopping them. "I'm sorry, Agent Fischer, I can't let you do that."

Fischer frowned. "What do you mean? Can't let me do what?"

The sergeant pursed his lips, inhaling through his nose and glancing down at his boots. The expression on his face told Fischer everything he needed to know. They were getting shut down. He felt his face start to flush before the Sergeant finished speaking.

"I can't let you back in there."

"The hell you can't," Eliwood said, taking a step forward. "This is an official investigation, and Wallace is our only witness. You don't have any jurisdiction or authority to keep us from him."

"This is our case, Sergeant Preble," Fischer said, trying to keep the frustration out of his voice.

"Not anymore it's not." He tapped his link, bringing up a screen and showing it to Fischer. "Orders from RCA. Access to Private Wallace's room has been restricted to authorized medical staff only. No one else. That order came straight from the top."

"That's bullshit," Eliwood said, leaning forward to read the document."

"Who issued these orders, Sergeant?" Fischer asked.

Eliwood read off the name before Preble could respond. "Admiral Marcus Young."

Fischer's teeth clenched together. *Of course, it's Young,* he thought, the vein in his neck pulsing. He jabbed a thumb behind him. "Does he know about *this*? Does he know that our witnesses are quickly going away?"

"I don't know, sir."

"He damn well needs to." Fischer moved to step past the sergeant.

Preble cleared his throat. "I've also been instructed to escort you from the building, sir."

Fischer shook his head. "Unbelievable."

"I'm sorry, sir," Preble said. "It's not my call."

"It's not your fault."

"I'm just following—"

"I know," Fischer said, cutting him off. "You're just following orders."

CHAPTER 33

Alliance Security and Intelligence,
Regional Headquarters
New Tuscany
4 Apr 2607

Carter stood as Fischer stepped through his office door, hands up as if warding off an attack. "Listen, before you start, I'm not happy about this either."

"What the fuck is all this about, Boss?" Fischer blurted out. His anger had only grown during their trip from the hospital. "Young has no authority over our investigation, who the hell does he think he is restricting access to our only surviving witness?"

Carter shook his head. "Listen, the orders came from way above me. I don't know, I'm out of the loop on this one. All I know is Command has classified everything about the Stone-meyer Incident Ultra Top Secret. As of twenty-two minutes ago, RCA has full authority over the investigation, and we've all been issued gag orders."

"You're fucking kidding me?" Eliwood said. "They can't do that."

"They can," Carter said, "and they have. They've also requested all your files and recording from your interviews."

"Did you tell them where they could put their request?" Fischer asked, putting both hands on the chair back in front of him. "I mean, what the hell, Dan?"

"I don't know. I really don't. I'm sorry. I argued against it, but my say holds about this much weight upstairs." He held up his hand, thumb and forefinger barely touching.

"This is such bullshit," Eliwood said, leaning back against the window sill, crossing her arms.

"I don't disagree with you," Carter said.

"Honestly, Boss, have you ever seen anything like this?" Eliwood asked. "I mean, really? Shutting down an entire investigation like this, as high profile as it is? Especially when there are so many questions we haven't found answers to yet."

"I want to find out what happened too. I do. But all of this is happening on levels that I've never seen, and behind doors I don't want to open. The impression I got when they told me was, 'Forget about Stonemeyer and your career will be fine.'"

"Oh, for shit's sake, Dan, you know this is bullshit," Fischer said.

"Yeah," Carter agreed. "It's bullshit. But there's nothing we can do about it. Nothing at all. Period. We just have to let it go."

"I can't do that, Boss. You know I can't," Fischer said. "Something happened on Stonemeyer. Something bad. Something that someone doesn't want getting out. I mean look at this footage."

Fischer moved around the deck, pointing to one of the video playbacks floating among hundreds of others against the wall. He tapped the image, bringing it to the forefront then spread his hands apart, enlarging the image.

"Fischer…" Carter started.

Fischer held up a finger. "Just give me a second."

Finally, he found what he was looking for and brought a second image up next to the first. He enlarged this one as well and stepped back. "Look at this."

Carter stepped around Fischer, considering the two images. "Yeah, okay?"

Fischer turned to his partner. "Do you see it?"

Eliwood moved around the desk, canting her head to the side and squinting at the flickering images. After a moment, her eyes went wide. "Holy shit."

"Exactly."

Carter held his hands out. "Okay, what's the secret. Enlighten me."

Fischer pointed to the first image. "This is the Klausmeyer building, right? The one that was supposedly destroyed by our guys during the fighting, right? The explosion brought down the entire building and almost this one here."

"Yeah, that's bad."

Fischer held up a finger. "Right. And what's this say right here?" He pointed to a line of text at the bottom of the second image.

Carter leaned forward and read the text aloud. "Suspected militia stronghold destroyed in the fighting." He straightened, shaking his head. "You're going to have to spell it out for me."

Fischer moved back to where he'd been standing behind the chair, returning his hands to the backrest. "Wallace said they went straight from the hideout to the safe house, then to the extraction point. He didn't say anything about blowing up half a city block."

"Maybe he just hadn't gotten there yet."

Fischer shook his head. "Not a chance. The rest of his story is packed full of little details that normal people wouldn't remember. This," Fischer pointed at the first image, "he wouldn't've left this out unless there was a reason."

"That's a pretty big hole," Carter said.

"Yeah, well, the guy ain't that smart," Eliwood said.

"He was confused about when Sheridan died, and Biagini laughed at me when I told her about Hastings. Said Wallace was an asshole. I'd say those are two pretty big questions we need to answer."

Carter twisted his wrist, activating his link. The orange holodisplay blinked into existence, rotating into position above his forearm and wrist. He tapped several keys. "It doesn't matter."

One by one the images on the wall vanished, blinking away in a flash of holographic light.

"It does matter, damn it." Fischer picked the chair up an inch and slammed it back down. "It matters because good Marines died out there and we owe it to them to figure out why. We owe it to them to make sure their sacrifice wasn't for nothing."

"Fish…"

Fischer ignored him. "And I want to know what happened that was so bad, two Marines have killed themselves, and another has been put on lockdown, and the only people that seem to give a shit about finding out what exactly happened during that mission are being shut out of the case."

"I'm sorry, Jackson. I really am. But there's nothing you or I or anyone can do about it. It's out of our hands now. Command will finish the investigation and make the report to the President. That's it. Forward your information on and purge the files."

"This isn't right."

"Right or wrong don't matter, Fischer. It's just how things work sometimes. When you're talking big things like this, there's too many players and factors to truly consider. Hell, I'm glad it's out of our hands. It's a lot less stress out of our schedule. I can tell you that."

Fischer's blood boiled inside his arteries, it pounded in his ears. This wasn't the first time Marcus Young had tried to derail his career, but he knew damn well it was going to be the last. This case felt different for some reason. There was obviously more at stake than usual, that was obvious, but on a personal level, Fischer felt like he owed something to the Marines that didn't come home. He owned them his honor.

They fought with bravery and valor, and he would make sure whoever was behind this disaster would get precisely what they deserved.

"It matters, Dan," Fischer said.

"Go home," Carter said, tapping his link. The display rotated around his arm and disappeared. "Take a couple of days with Carissa and come back with your head clear. This isn't the end of the world. Trust me, there are bound to be more bullshit cases in the future, that I can promise you."

CHAPTER 34

Fischer's Apartment
Blue Lake City, New Tuscany
6 Apr 2607

Fischer's link chimed at six o'clock the next morning. He rolled over, opening one eye and immediately regretted it. The orange light from the caller display on his wrist was blinding in the darkness. His head still pounded from the night before, squinting he looked past the link display to the half-empty glass of Star Cask 51 sitting on his bedside table.

"You going to get that?" Carissa asked, rolling away from him and pulling the covers with her.

He licked his lips and tried to blink the sleep from his eyes. Aniyah Eliwood's name glowed red against the transparent pale orange display, a notation next to the ID indicated she'd already called three times.

He groaned and tapped the command for audio only. "Do you have any idea what time it is?"

"Jackson, where the hell have you been?"

"Been sleeping. What do you want?"

"Shhhh," Carissa chided, throwing a pillow at him.

"Get up," Eliwood said. "You're going to want to hear this."

"Hold on." Fischer took a deep breath and rolled out of bed. He sat on the edge for a moment, waiting until the room stopped spinning and pounding between his ears subsided. When the room stabilized, he groaned, rubbing at his temple and squeezing his eyes against the waves of nausea threatening to double him over.

"Fish," Eliwood's voice seemed like a distant thing, and he wasn't quite sure if it was real.

His body swayed slightly, every part of him screaming to lay back down and go to sleep. Sleep would fix everything. If he could get past the throbbing pain.

"Fischer!"

Behind him, Carissa rolled over, pushing him with a foot. "Get up. And be quiet. Don't you dare wake up the baby."

Slowly, Fischer opened his eyes. The fuzziness was starting to clear. He swallowed and pushed himself off the bed, keeping one hand on the mattress as he stumbled through the darkness.

In the kitchen, he leaned back against the counter and closed his eyes again. "What is it?"

"Open your door."

"What?"

"Come open your damn door."

Fischer opened his eyes, finally processing what she'd said. "The door?" He moved across to the living room, swiped his link over the lock and pulled open the door.

Eliwood looked like she hadn't slept in days. Her hair was tied back into a messy bun, and there were dark circles under her eyes. "Wallace is dead."

Fischer's eyes snapped open, his head instantly clearing, mind becoming alert. "What? How?"

"Sometime last night. Docs are saying there were complications from surgery and there wasn't anything they could do for him."

"Vaughan said that?"

She shook her head. "No, another one. Can't remember his name."

"Wait, complications from surgery? Vaughan didn't tell us anything about another surgery, he was fine."

A thought immediately began forming at the back of Fischer's mind, a thought he didn't want to entertain at all. No, it couldn't be. No one would be that stupid, not after what had happened with Biagini and Thomas. Murder?

No way, Fischer told himself. *Not a chance.*

The deaths of the two Marines had only been covered for a day in Blue Lake City's news feeds. And even that was a stretch. Both were mentioned and then dismissed, forgotten about in the shadow of major entertainers making birth announcements or political candidates running for office in next year's election cycle or another crazy Revolution 52 nut, staging a protest at the Pegasi Embassy and being forcibly removed.

ASI had barely been mentioned in the HyperTrans terminal shoot-out. The events had been reduced to a depressed Marine whose tragic experiences and traumatic brain injuries had caused him to crack. A doctor Fischer hadn't heard of from Haroldson Memorial had even confirmed the reports, though capped it by saying any other information is being restricted until the next of kin could be notified.

Biagini had received less time. Her final moments—which had been caught on video by a passing cab driver—had been reduced to two lines of dialogue. "Sadly, an Alliance Marine committed suicide today, jumping from the top of Haroldson Memorial Hospital, the Blue Lake City's premier medical treatment facility for all veterans. No details are being released at this time, but our thoughts and prayers go out to the family in this time of grief." And then it was back to sports scores and the weather.

The lives of two Marines that swore to protect the Alliance at all costs, summed up by fifteen seconds of airtime.

"Fish?"

Fischer shook himself. "Sorry. I just…"

"You think it's bullshit, right?"

"Of course, it's bullshit," Fischer said loudly, then quieted, remembering Maddie was sleeping. "The guy was perfectly healthy two days ago. Well, relatively speaking, I guess. But no way knocking on death's door."

"You think someone—"

"Don't say it. Don't even think it. Forget a can of worms, that's opening the entire case." Fischer retrieved a glass from the cabinet, filled it with water from the tap and chugged it.

"You look awful," Eliwood said.

Fischer emptied the glass and poured another one. "You're no spring chicken yourself."

"There's something else."

"What?" Fischer asked.

"I finished going through *Vision's* comm logs, and—"

"What the hell do you mean you were going through the logs? We turned everything over to the RCA."

"Yeah, we did."

"Did you purge it?"

"Well," Eliwood drew the word out.

"Woody?"

"Of course, I purged it. Like I told the asshole from Fleet, sometimes it takes a little while. The Agency computers are shit."

"Jesus, Woody." Despite his concern, a smile began to form at the corners of his mouth.

"What can I say? I hate unfinished business. You can't trust those military shits with anything these days. Not very thorough."

Fischer shook his head. "You get caught with that shit, it's your ass. You know that, right?"

"No way anyone's ever going to find that file. My brother's in broadcast tech, remember? He knows all the tricks to keep information hidden from people you don't want to see it."

"These are not the kinds of people you want to be messing around with, Aniyah. If Wallace really was..." he trailed off. Even he didn't want to say it.

"I know, I know. But listen, according to the logs, *Vision* received two separate data packets from Second Fleet Command during the same data dump, two milliseconds apart. One went straight to the CIC, the other to a private account and was automatically deleted from the ship's main core."

"Deleted?" Fischer hesitated, the glass of water centimeters from his lips.

"It gets better. The first packet was the Stonemeyer mission instructions, orders to extract Delaney and get him back to Alliance space. The second was an encrypted video transmission from your buddy Young to none other than Sergeant Thomas."

Fury flared inside Fischer, flushing out the remains of his hangover. His hand gripped tight on the glass, knuckles going white. Blood pounded in his ears. Jaw clenched, he said, "Son of a bitch."

"You're going to shatter that thing."

"Shit," Fischer said, barely hearing her.

"I did some quick checking, something I probably should've checked at the very beginning but didn't. Young and Thomas are related. Second cousins, to be precise."

Fischer slammed the glass down on the counter, sending water splashing all over. He winced at the sound and held his breath for several moments, listening for any signs of life from the two bedrooms.

He let out a long sigh. "Do we know what was in the video?"

Eliwood shook her head. "No. The data was purged as soon as Thomas viewed it. Literally, the second the file ended, it erased itself from *Vision's* servers. I have to tell you, Fish, it takes a lot of skill to bypass those systems. A hell of a lot. We're talking top-grade military encryption and programming. That file probably cost more to generate and send than the entire production cost of a Nemesis class fighter. He definitely wasn't sending a 'come home soon' card."

The fact that Young knew more about the events on Stone-meyer than he was letting on didn't actually surprise Fischer. In fact, it would've surprised him more to know there had been a conspiracy surrounding Stonemeyer mission and the Admiral hadn't been involved. But if Young was behind the failure of the mission, that meant he was also involved in the tragic events here on New Tuscany. Fischer knew Marcus Young was capable of many things, but murder? That seemed too much of a stretch even for him.

"You think those were the other orders Biagini talked about?"

Fischer nodded. "I'd stake my career on it. The question now is, what did those orders say and how do we prove it? There's no way to pull that data from *Vision's* backup servers?"

"The file never even made it to the backups," Eliwood said. "I'm telling you Fish, that is some pretty damn high-level shit. I mean, I've only heard rumors of that kind of 'smart-file' from big firms like Gigatron or Alistair or places like that. I mean, sure they exist, but like I said, they're expensive as hell. That kind of stuff is usually kept for Black Ops type shit, you know? Not for something like this?"

"Well, obviously something was important enough for Young to send one to Thomas. And you're right, knowing Young, he definitely wasn't sending greeting cards. I doubt he's ever done anything that sentimental in his life, not even to his kids. That message is the key. We need to find out what was on it."

"Good luck," Eliwood said. "There's only one person in the entire galaxy that knows what was in that file, and he sure as shit isn't going to share with us."

"There's got to be fragments left right?" Fischer asked. It was a long shot, and he knew it, but what did they have left?

"Even if some traces of the file were still left in *Vision's* core, we start poking around in there, and it's going to send up red flags all over the place. We've been locked out of the case, remember? We don't have the authority to just barge in and demand access to their servers. Not to mention we'd probably be arrested."

Something triggered in the back of Fischer's mind. "Wait a minute. What did you just say?"

"That we'd get arrested? I'm mean, probably not right? But they wouldn't be happy."

Fischer shook his head, mind racing. "No, about the companies that had the smart-file tech. What did you say?"

"What, Gigatron and Alistair? They're two of the biggest tech companies in the galaxy. Gigatron has several Alliance contracts for JumpLane drive technology, and Alistair Holdings owns more shit than God."

"Alistair. Wasn't that who Delaney said provided all the signal countermeasures at the Embassy's safe house?"

"I hope you're not suggesting, what I think you're suggesting," Eliwood said. "Jackson, that's crazy. Are you saying that one of the biggest companies in the history of mankind, is involved with one single mission on a worthless, third class planet on the edge of nowhere? Come on. Those folks still drive cars with wheels. Alistair's got bigger fish to fry, don't you think? And it doesn't explain Young's involvement either."

"It explains how he sent that second set of orders to Thomas."

"No, it doesn't. You're projecting. We don't have any idea what that message said. Do I think the whole thing's shady as hell? Hell yeah, I do. We can't even connect them to the Embassy or militia because it's all hearsay. Hearsay from dead people, I might add."

"But what if it is all about him?" Fischer asked. "What if this whole thing is about Delaney? He'd been pushing for the Stonemeyer annexation for months, right? A lot of people could stand to lose a lot of money on that deal. Or make money, for that matter. If he was the driving force behind that deal and someone didn't want to see it happen…"

"That's insane, Fischer."

"Biagini said it was an assassination, not an extraction. She mentioned another set of mysterious orders and that she knew they were wrong. What if that second set of orders were instructions to kill the Ambassador?"

Eliwood shook her head. "Not a chance. Besides, listen to this." She opened her link and began swiping through screens.

"What?"

"You know our lab guys started processiing Biagini's body before Second Fleet showed up and yanked us, yeah?"

"Yeah."

"Well, I've got an ex on the lab team, we… uh… still talk. He said that when he processed Thomas's link, it'd been wiped, like completely. No positional data, no nothing. Complete refresh and restore. I don't know about Wallace's, but I'm sure it'll be the same."

"Okay?"

"Biagini's link wasn't completely wiped. He was able to clone the core before the Navy guys booted them out of the lab, and he managed to bring the data with him."

"You're kidding? He could be charged with treason for that!"

Eliwood shook her head. "This was timestamped 29 March 2607, 1905hrs Standard. That's 0605hrs Calibri City time.'"

"The morning they were finally extracted," Fischer said.

She tapped her link, and a reverberating ambient hum began,

the sound quality was muffled somewhat, but there was no doubt in Fischer's mind who was speaking.

"...*for what they did*," Private Wallace said. "*Just wish we could've killed more of the bastards before we left.*"

There was silence for a couple seconds, then footsteps and movement. Someone cried out, almost like they'd been startled. There was a bang, and someone grunted in pain.

"*Sheridan, no!*" Biagini screamed.

"*Get the hell off me, man! What are you doing?*" Wallace shouted.

The struggle turned into fighting, shouts and curses accompanied by loud metal bangs like they were throwing each other into something.

Fischer frowned. "What is that? They're in a shuttle or something?"

"Keep listening," Eliwood told him.

"*You son of a bitch! I knew it!*" Sergeant Thomas shouted.

A gunshot went off, and someone gasped in pain.

"*No!*" Biagini screamed again.

The fighting continued for another few seconds until Thomas's voice yelled, "Lying bastard!" More fighting, then what sounded like doors slamming open and brakes squealing.

"They're in a car?" Fischer raised an eyebrow at Eliwood.

"I think that's the van that Powers, the dropship pilot, described."

Fischer nodded, remembering.

"*That son of a bitch!*" Thomas yelled again, then the sound of more gunshots rang out.

More horns blared.

"*Did you get him?*" Wallace asked.

After a pause, Thomas said, "*Yeah, I got him.*"

"*You sure? If he...*"

"*He won't. He's done.*"

Wallace didn't sound convinced. *"We should go back and make sure."*

"There's no time. Hit that thing and let's get the hell out of here."

"Right. In three, two…"

The recording stopped.

"What the hell was that?" Fischer asked.

"Sounds like Sheridan and the rest of them had a difference of opinion about something," Eliwood said.

"Difference of opinion?" Fischer repeated. "Sounds like they shot him for it. Play it again." Fischer leaned closer as the recording repeated, listening to everything with his investigator ears. "Sheridan was trying to stop them from blowing that building up."

Eliwood raised an eyebrow at him. "You think?"

"Listen. Play it again, listen to what they're saying."

She started it a third time. After it finished, Fischer pointed at her bright display. "There, at the end, Thomas tells Wallace to 'hit it.' Then he counts down, like someone would when detonating an explosive. You heard the struggle, sounded like Sheridan was trying to take something from Wallace, I'd be willing to be he was trying to get that detonator."

"That's really thin, Jackson. Like, really super thin."

Fischer shrugged. "It fits."

"And they shot him for it? That seems kind of…"

"Fucked up?" Fischer asked.

Eliwood nodded.

"The whole operation was fucked up. From the very start. What if Sheridan survived? What if he's still alive? He can fill in all the missing pieces."

"It doesn't matter even if he is, Fish," Eliwood said. "We're off the case. There isn't anything we can do. If Young's behind this whole thing, we can't go to the military. If it is true, and we keep chasing after it, we'll end of just like Biagini or Wallace or Thomas, or worse."

"I need to go there."

"What—to Stonemeyer? You're crazy. Carter will never sign off on that. You're *off* the case, remember? Not to mention they've locked down the entire system to all Alliance spacecraft. Even if you managed to get to the system, you wouldn't be able to get anywhere close to the planet."

"Carter doesn't have to know anything. Gives him plausible deniability."

"Fish, they're not just going to let you in. What are you going to do, show up and flash your credentials? 'Yes, hello, I'm Agent Fischer, I'm just following up on an investigation that I'm no longer a part of.'"

"Getting there won't be an issue. Once I'm there, I'll figure it out. If he's alive, I'll have his beacon to search for."

"And if he's dead?"

"Then I'll have more pieces to pick up."

"Wait a minute," Eliwood said, her face telling Fischer she'd finally put together what he'd said. "You're not saying…"

"Yep."

CHAPTER 35

The Doris
High Orbit Approach, Stonemeyer
10 Apr 2607

Fischer smiled as he ducked through the hatch, onto the *Doris's* bridge, hearing his friend argue with someone over the ship's comm.

"What the hell is all this Rancil? Of course I have my clearance papers, but you're killing me with these transit fees."

Fischer stopped behind the pilot's flight couch, watching the pilot's fingers dance over the holodisplay in front of him. The transparent screens wrapped around the front half of his station. Jones gave Fischer a grin, flashing his overly-white teeth. His bright, almost crystal blue eyes glowing in the flickering orange and blue light of the display.

"Everything all right?" Fischer asked.

Jones put a hand up to his mouth and whispered, "We're good, old friend of mine. It's fine."

A speaker on the bulkhead just above Fischer's head buzzed and crackled. The male voice that followed came through with a slight mechanical edge. Whether caused by the *Doris's* aging systems or cheap replacement parts, or both, Fischer didn't know. In either case, it didn't seem to bother Jones in the slightest.

"Clearance and transit fees are all part of the package, my friend, you know that. Sign of the times, man. Sign of the times."

"What do you think this is, amateur hour?" Jones said. "I must've made this trip a hundred times. Never been hounded this hard."

"Come on, Jonesy, don't break my balls, man. I don't make the rules. We're all trying to get used to this whole new process ourselves. Deviations from the transit schedules are hard to get approved. That was true even without our new friends. What can I say? Protocols are protocols."

The bite in the man's words gave Fischer the impression that he didn't care for the new Pegasi "help" any more than he cared about the new protocols. Fischer wondered if the two additional warships in high orbit hovering above the elliptical plane, giving them an overview of the system, were part of those new protocols. The three Apostle class cruisers dwarfed everything else in the system, despite only massing a quarter of the tonnage of Alliance cruisers.

Compared to an Alliance world like New Tuscany where billions of people lived and conducted business from all over the galaxy, and thousands of ships came and went all the time, the JumpLanes around Stonemeyer looked almost barren. Fischer craned his neck to see the sensor panel on Jones's display. The computer had identified just over a thousand ships, either parked in orbit or in the process of transiting to the Emergence Point.

"Still robbery," Jones said. He gave a slight shake of his head to Fisher and mouthed, "We're fine."

The man on the other end laughed. *"Robbery? I'm doing you a favor here, not the other way around. Do you know how hard it is to push this through?"*

"And it's deeply appreciated. I don't know what I'd do if these things go bad. You ever smell a rotten patari nut, Rancil? Whew, disgusting! One time I smelled them, that was enough."

"Can't stand 'em."

"You and me both, buddy."

A small panel appeared in the middle of Jones's display. He tapped it, then gave it a backhand swipe, removing it from the view. "All right, we're good now?"

There was a slight pause on the other end, then, *"Oh yeah, we're good."*

Jones shook his head. "Robbery, I tell ya."

Rancil laughed. *"Keep your head on a swivel, brother. Peace-keepers out here don't play. You guys get caught down there, and they trace it back to me..."* He trailed off, but his meaning was clear.

"You're good, man. Have I ever done you wrong?"

Loomis looked over his shoulder. "Well, there was—"

"Tat, tat, tat," Jones said, holding up a hand.

"Just do me a favor, Jones, don't get me fired—or worse—over some damn nuts, all right? In and out, right?"

"Hey man, I'm here for you."

"Uh-huh. Traffic control, clear."

The connection terminated, and Tensley leaned back in his couch, craning his head around the edge of his display. "Input from the peanut gallery is not required or appreciated."

Greg Loomistripoli sat in the forward couch, the top of the seatback came up to the deck Fischer stood on. He eyed them both around the backrest. "I was just sayin'..."

"Don't 'just say,'" Jones told him. "Keep your *just sayin'* to yourself."

"Yeah, yeah."

"There, see, what'd I tell ya?" Jones asked Fischer. "You want to apologize now or later?"

Fischer chuckled, putting a hand on the metal rail under Jones's elevated seat. "We're not done yet."

"Ha! Well, you still owe me two thousand."

Fischer coughed, eye bulging. "Two thousand?"

Jones waved at the display. "You heard the man. New protocols, what can I say?"

"Bribes you mean."

"Potato, potahto."

Fischer shook his head. If Carissa didn't kill him for just coming out here, she would when she saw their credit account. He wondered if he pulled this off, how open Carter would be to compensating him? *Not a chance,* he thought, dismissing the idea immediately.

In the grand scheme of things, two thousand credits wasn't much, especially as far as illegal transit fees went. He'd heard of some operators paying upwards of ten to one hundred thousand credits to skip the required customs screening and enforcement process. But those amounts weren't commonplace, and definitely not this close to the URT. The Rim Territories weren't as rich as the more established worlds, but what they lacked in credits and resources they made up for in freedom and space.

As the *Doris* dipped toward the planet, he felt the pull of the drives flaring to life, pushing them past the planet's outer beacon. Stonemeyer itself was unremarkable. Just another colonized world with fertile land and deep oceans. The main continent, just above the equator, was dotted with cloud cover, thickening closer to the coast.

"Looks like storms are moving in, boss," Loomis said, pointing.

"Great," Fischer said, still trying to work out how he was going to spin the expense to his wife. Falling on his sword might well be the best option.

Jones tapped a few commands into his console, a smile still plastered on his face. "Hey, it could be worse."

"Worse? How the hell could it be worse?"

"Could've been arrested. Hell, those Emperor-worshiping shits could've just blown us out of the void. Heard of them doing that before, you know?"

Fischer forgot about the credits for a moment. "Wait, what?"

"Yeah," Jones replied, shrugging. "Sometimes they just pull the ol' shoot first, ask questions later. Course, most of the time, there ain't anyone left to give the answers, but still."

"And you didn't think that was pertinent to share before we made the transaction? Or that you needed creds for bribes? That would've been a nice tidbit of information to have."

Jones raised an eyebrow at him. "Would that've stopped you?"

Fischer opened his mouth, ready to continue his rant, then paused, sighing. He knew better than to argue, and besides, his friend was right. "No."

"See."

Fischer shook his head. "Two thousand…"

Jones laughed. "Relax. We got this. No problem."

"No problem?" Fischer repeated, unconvinced. "No problem until we're getting shot at."

"That rarely ever happens… most of the time."

An alert chime sounded, and a panel appeared.

"Ah, see." Jones pointed. "I told you. No problem."

Fischer leaned over to read the message and shook his head. They'd received priority approach vectors for Calibri City, giving them clearance to land.

At least it was money well spent, Fischer thought.

"So," Jones said, adjusting course, "you really think Young is behind all of this?"

Fischer sighed. Over the last four days, he'd done little else besides consider that possibility. He didn't like the Admiral, in fact, he'd go as far as saying that he flat out hated the man, but this? He couldn't quite put it together. Young had already attained more rank than Fischer would've ever guessed possible, and there wasn't any sign of him slowing down. Rumor was he was up for a Central Fleet Command within the next year, and that would be the final stepping stone to Fleet Admiral.

What in the galaxy would a man in his position have to gain from causing a mission as simple as this to fail? What would anyone have to gain for that matter?

"I really don't know," Fischer said. "Most of the evidence I have is extremely circumstantial. Do I personally think he is? Yes. But how do I prove it? That's the question."

"And what if you do?"

"What do you mean?"

"I mean, what do you do if you prove it?" Jones said. "You just going to walk back into the office and blast it everywhere? You said they shut you down and booted you all off the case, right? Why do you think that is?"

"I—"

Jones continued, cutting Fischer off. "And if you're right, and Young is behind this, he's not the only one. He's a powerful guy, sure, but one guy couldn't have pulled this off alone. And by the way, what exactly did he pull off? Blowing up a shithole apartment building, raiding a worthless insurgent cell? Everything you've told me so far doesn't really add up to much."

Fischer opened his mouth to argue, but Jones held up a hand. "I know you don't like the guy. Hell, I can't stand him either. But a guy like that isn't just going to risk his whole career for a world in the middle of nowhere that no one cares about. And if he's working with someone, who's he working with? And why?"

Fischer shook his head. "That's the question, isn't it? It's why we came all the way out here."

"No, it's the reason *you* came all the way out here. I came out here for…" Jones trailed off, looking to the ceiling for answers. "Huh, come to think of it, I don't really know why we're out here."

"Seeing the sights?" Loomis suggested.

Jones shook his head. "This shithole? No thanks."

"Your loyalty and devotion to a friend?" Fischer asked, grinning.

"No, that's not it." Jones snapped his fingers. "Credits! No, that's not it, either. And it's not because I owe you anything. As a matter of fact, I think you're in the hole to me already."

"Must be for the action, then," Fischer said.

Jones shook his head. "I'm a sucker for punishment."

Twenty minutes later they were gliding over the city, descending toward one of the elevated hyperloop tubes that zigzagged around blocks of high-rises. The office towers and apartment buildings weren't anything compared to the skyscrapers on any of the Alliance worlds. Then again, Stonemeyer was a relatively new world.

Rain pounded against the *Doris's* main viewport, water streaking up the large, clear panels. A dark blanket of clouds, stretching to the horizon, gave the entire scene a distinctly ominous foreboding and Fischer hoped it wasn't a sign of things to come.

They weaved through a pair of partially completed towers. Each had hundreds of car-sized construction bots buzzing around the exposed steel frames, welding, cutting, and bolting. With modern techniques, building large structures like these would take weeks, but the cost was substantial. Fischer couldn't help but wonder how Stonemeyer managed to finance all of this.

"Lots of bike traffic," Fischer said, watching the small gravbikes zip through the city.

"Cheap transport," Jones said. "That's the name of the game

out here, man, and the cheaper, the better. You can buy a gravbike for a quarter of the cost of a standard flyer. Those and regular wheeled ground cars are normal out here."

"Makes sense."

Local security patrols queried them as they passed through the city, registering their clearance data from traffic central, and continuing on without giving them any grief.

Jones waved a dismissive hand at two single-seater patrol shuttles as they dipped away, heading back downtown. "What a joke."

"What's that?"

"Didn't you get a look at the drives those things were sporting?" Jones asked, giving Fischer an unconvinced frown.

Fischer shook his head.

Jones snorted. "AL29 Bravos. Little shits barely put out enough power to heat seats. Wouldn't be able to catch me even if they wanted to. Ha! You sure did pick a winner coming here."

"How about we try not to test the theory."

Jones held up a finger. "Not a theory my friend. *Doris* might look dated, but she'll hold her own, trust me."

"Uh huh."

"Hey, if I remember correctly, it was your fault the last time we were in a shitty spot, and it hasn't even been a week."

"It's been eight days," Fischer corrected, crossing his arms. "And technically it wasn't my fault."

"Well, who's fault—Hey!" Jones ducked in his chair as two Pegasi fighters zipped by overhead, their jet-wash rocking the small frigate. The gray-and-black hulls almost disappeared in the rain as they flew away. Jones fought the controls for a moment, adjusting their course and pulling them out of the turbulence. "Sons of bitches."

Fischer watched as the fighters banked left, looking like they were turning around for another pass. He blew out a relieved breath when they leveled out, heading away from them, out across the city. Clearance or no, if the Pegasi military discovered he was on the planet no amount of bribery would make it better. Lying and paying off a government official was one thing, but once they found out who he was and who he worked for, he wouldn't have to imagine the pain and torture Biagini and the rest had gone through. Pegasi Peacekeepers weren't exactly known for their delicate ways.

"You know where you want to start looking?" Jones asked.

"Yeah."

Jones leaned around his display. "Hey, why don't you do something useful down there and kick on the tac-array?"

Loomis grunted and tapped a holographic button. An audible hum reverberated through the cockpit as one of the frigate's sensor clusters folded out of its recess on the hull just below Fischer's feet.

Fischer activated his link and the main panel rotated into position over his forearm. He accessed the frigate's sensor network with a swipe of his finger, and a secondary panel appeared, informing him that the unit was receiving.

It was a long shot, he knew. The chances of locating the Marine was low, but it was the only thing he had. It'd be a one in a million shot if the *Doris's* sensors picked them up at all. But, long shot or no, if he didn't try, he wouldn't know.

"Anything?" Jones asked.

Fischer sighed and swiped the panel closed. "Probably just out of range."

"Or there might not be anything to find at all," Loomis said.

"Won't know if I don't look."

"I know, I'm just saying."

Jones brought up a map of the city. Numerous landmarks, imported through the local transit net, appeared at various locations. This included several no-fly zones marked in red. The pilot motioned to the map. "Buyer's choice."

Fischer considered the information on his link. The data Eliwood had copied from the Agency's servers before purging it glowed back at him. Allowing anyone other than Agency personnel access to classified information, especially anything this sensitive, was punishable by life in prison. He'd already broken several regulations, not to mention laws, just by coming out here. Sharing ultra-secret information with the only person in the galaxy that could help him solve this mystery was the least of his problems. He swiped a finger and sent the data from his link to the frigate's computer.

The map overlaid the data from Fischer's link, a location five kilometers east of one of the no-fly zones flashed green. A small text panel hovered over the map, indicating it was the location where the final extraction had taken place.

"Bingo," Fischer said, downloading the coordinates back into his link.

"Find what you're looking for?" Jones asked.

"Hope so. You think you can let me off right around this area here?" Fischer pointed to an empty lot to the north of the restricted area.

Jones consulted his displays, zooming in and panning around. "Probably. Look, I know we're already out here, so you're going to go anyway, but what exactly do you think you're going to find down there? Everybody's dead."

Fischer closed his link. "Answers."

CHAPTER 36

Four Kilometers East of Extraction Zone
Calibri City, Stonemeyer
10 Apr 2607

The blast from *Doris's* engines blew Fischer's hood back, exposing his face and head to the rain and torrent of wind. Water kicked up by the frigate's down blast drenched him. He turned away, raising an arm to protect his face as the ship rose into the air. He spat grit from his lips and wiped the wetness from his face.

"Thanks for that," he growled, pulling his hood back into place.

"You're welcome," Jones answered, his voice barely audible over the jet-wash, but Fischer could hear the smile and knew his friend was just exacting some jovial punishment for dragging him all the way out here.

The truth was, they owed each other. They'd been trading favors back and forth ever since they'd first met when Jones had been a pilot on the verge of being discharged from the Navy. It had been by chance, by sheer luck that together, they stopped a battle that would have ended in many lives lost, including their own.

"Don't go far," Fischer said.

"I'm just a call away, brother."

The rhythmic beating of raindrops against his jacket drowned out most of the city noise around him. Occasionally, a gravcar would pass overhead, or a siren would wail in the distance. Ground cars—which most of them on this startup planet were—moved up and down the roads, but it was by no means bumper to bumper traffic.

No one gave him a second look as he crisscrossed streets and alleys, making his way toward the restricted area, following the directions on his link. He kept his pace casual, keeping his profile low, being a complete foreigner to this place.

A dump truck rumbled down the road, its bucket filled with large chunks of broken concrete and twisted steel. It turned a corner and disappeared. Another one appeared a few moments later, heading in the opposite direction, its bucket empty.

Least I know I'm heading in the right direction, Fischer told himself, flipping his hood back into place and setting out into the rain again.

The Stonemeyer police had cordoned off the area for blocks around the Klausmeyer building, not allowing anyone but relief workers and vehicles past the barricades. The devastation seemed orders of magnitude larger than what he'd seen on the newsfeeds.

The surrounding buildings had taken substantial damage in the blast. Whole sections of the closer buildings had been cut out, replaced by temporary structural supports. Orange electro-fence had been set up around the worst of it, keeping even the repair crews clear while scores of drones worked.

Three giant cranes had been set up in the street, holding aerial platforms aloft, allowing repair crews easy access to the damaged higher levels. Aside from the drones, the entire operation was extremely primitive, with none of the advanced counter-grav equipment that would have been utilized on a Core world. In the Rim, it was all about cost-effectiveness. These ground vehicles could to the job of their more advanced brothers but cost about a third of the price. Not to mention a substantially lower operating cost.

Fischer's link chimed, the holopanel showing Jones was calling. "What's wrong?"

"Nothing, man. I just wanted to make sure everything was all right down there."

"Everything's fine. It's pretty quiet actually."

"You find anything yet?"

Fischer frowned, slightly concerned at the nervous tension in his friend's voice. "Just got here. You okay?"

"I know, I know, yeah, I'm good. I just keep seeing these damn Pegasi patrols, and they're giving me a bad case of get-the-hell-out-of-here, know what I mean?"

Fischer's eyes fell on the Peacekeeper squad on the other side of the barricades. The soldiers' blood-red armor glistened in the rain, the black horizontal eye slits on the otherwise featureless helmet seemed to see everything. Their bulky armor looked like overkill for a security detail, but unlike some Alliance Marines he'd seen standing post, these Peacekeepers looked ready for anything. They held their weapons across their chest, barrels down, ready to level and fire on anyone.

"Yeah, I know what you mean."

Fischer flicked his wrist, rotating his comm panel out of the way. He swiped through a few menus before finding the one he wanted. The Marine taclink frequency was encrypted and broadcast on specific Alliance frequencies known only by the personnel using the system. Fortunately for Fischer, that information had been included in the initial data dump and was one of the things Eliwood had included in her download.

Military links were considerably more powerful than the standard civilian model, with more advanced features, range, and capabilities. The military unit also provided a unique emergency beacon that could lead medical teams straight to the patient, bypassing the need for someone to physically direct the crews, allowing them to remain focused on the fight.

It took a moment for the search program to initialize, but then it was sweeping the buildings across a three-block area, looking for anything with an Alliance beacon. The raindrops passed through the display without affecting the graphical interface, and Fischer watched as the link scanned.

Nothing.

He swiped back to his map of the city, tracing the route he'd taken to get here, then looking for where the dropship had picked the survivors up on their last day. He tapped in the next route and started off, ducking into an alley, heading away from the scene. Several homeless people looked up from underneath makeshift shelters as he passed but ultimately paid him no mind. Keeping to themselves and ignoring strangers was just part of their daily life here.

As he moved further east, the homeless population seemed to increase as the quality of structures declined. Wallace's description of the camp surrounding the comm station came to mind, and Fischer wondered how big of a homeless problem Stonemeyer actually had. No wonder people were challenging the government.

For a brief instant, he wondered if the Pegasi's interference here might actually be a good thing, but he immediately dismissed the idea. The Empire never did anything out of any kind of moral obligation or sympathy for their fellow man. It was all about land and power.

And apparently, it doesn't matter how bad the land is, Fischer thought, passing a family huddled around a small fire. A boy, dressed in a dirty, oversized shirt, looked at him and smiled through a tangle of long, messy hair. He sighed and looked away, forcing himself to ignore the pull on his soul. How could anyone raise their child in a place like this? The thought of Maddie sleeping on the streets, with nothing but the clothes on her little back and only a hope of food, turned his stomach.

"Enriching lives my ass," Fischer muttered, hearing the Pegasi Consul's speech in his mind.

He paused at the end of one of the alleys, keeping to the shadows as two local police cars shot by, lights flashing, sirens blaring. No one else seemed to even notice.

He waited for traffic to clear, then jogged across the street, cutting between two squat rectangular warehouses.

Taking in the growing number of homeless, he shook his head, wondering if they'd ever have the opportunity to get out of this place and actually do something with their lives. Odds were against it though. And from what he could tell, the ruling class of the world didn't care. None of the information he'd seen had even remotely addressed the homeless issue, which was obviously more than a small portion of the population. So, either they didn't realize it was as bad as it was, or they were willfully ignorant.

Either way, Fischer thought. *They don't have any right governing these—*

His link chimed, stopping him in his tracks. His eyes flicked down as a panel appeared over the city map. His heart pounded in his chest. He took a breath and held it, waiting for the unit to dismiss the reading as a glitch. A moment later, another panel appeared, flashing confirmation. Fischer read the message three times.

MARINE BEACON 48B-48204-SHER LOCATED.

"Holy shit."

CHAPTER 37

Warehouse District
Calibri City, Stonemeyer
10 Apr 2607

Fischer stared down at his link, watching as raindrops fell through the glowing holodisplay, waiting for the unit to correct itself and say the signal was some kind of a glitch. Data panels appeared, giving him vital signs, direction, and distance. A red crosshair flashed on his map, indicating a position to the west.

"Think I found something," he said over the link.

There was a slight pause, then, *"What you got, Boss?"*

"Alliance signal, very weak, couple klicks west of here. I'm going to check it out."

"You serious? What kind of signal?"

"Looks like it's a Marine Transponder."

"You think it's still attached?"

"Only one way to find out."

The ground under his feet rumbled as a shadow passed over. He looked up and saw the belly of a Pegasi troop transport floating over the rooftops.

"You are advised to report to the Population Processing Center in your district for residential assignment and census." A loud female voice boomed over the blocks of homeless. *"We are here to help you through these trying times and enrich your lives."*

"Go back to your own shithole planet!" a man on an overturned bucket shouted from underneath the edge of an orange tarp. By the look of his setup, he'd been there quite some time.

Fischer turned and moved away, then told Jones, "Sending you the coordinates now but don't move in yet. Those Peacekeepers see you move in again, they're going to know something's up."

It took another ten minutes to navigate the camps which had spread from alleys and sidewalks to fill the streets, leaving no room for ground traffic to flow. Whole blocks were sectioned off, hundreds of people milling about, kids running and playing, elderly sitting, talking about the good old days. On more than one occasion, Fischer heard someone curse the Pegasi, and lament on how things had been bad before they'd arrived, but they were worse now.

The rain had slowed to a drizzle by the time he reached the signal. The old building in front of him had obviously been abandoned years ago. The windows had long since been boarded up, the boards themselves covered with colorful graffiti. Most of the new art was inundated with anti-Pegasi sentiment. One had even drawn the helmet of a Peacekeeper, marked over with a do not enter sign.

Fischer tapped his link and waited as it scanned the building. A moment later, the birds-eye view morphed into a 3D rendering of the structure. The layout wasn't perfect, but it gave him a starting point. The signal icon flashed on the fifth floor, northeast corner.

Fischer hesitated, considering the possibility that this very well could be a trap, that someone had hijacked Sheridan's link and were using it to draw others in. It'd been done before; he'd seen several reports about the Pegasi luring in additional victims after their initial attacks.

It's possible, he thought, chewing his lip. But *it's not probable.*

"How you doin' down there, Fish?" Jones asked in Fischer's ear.

"I'm close," Fischer said, scanning the area, looking for anyone that might be following him. That was always probable.

"Best way to pull you out there is to pull a Roya Vosar. No other way around it."

Fischer eyed the top of the building, frowning. Not only was the building probably half a century old, it obviously hadn't been maintained in at least ten years. Anything more than a stiff breeze was liable to knock the thing over. "Not sure if that's a good idea."

"Course it's not a good idea," Jones said. Fischer could hear the laughter in his voice. *"But it's the only one we got. Isn't another place to set her down otherwise. Especially if we gotta pull out hot."*

Fischer sighed. There wasn't any point arguing. Maybe it wouldn't come to that. "All right, hold tight, I'm going to check it out."

"Roger that."

Fischer started up the stairs, stepping around and over piles of trash and clothes. The building's double doors had been removed, replaced with thick plywood meant to keep intruders out. Both boards were attached to the frame by one or two nails, both hanging open, allowing him to duck through without even having to move them.

Once inside, Fischer drew his pistol, keeping it pointed at the ground. The building's entryway was dimly lit by thin streams of light spilling in through cracks in the boarded-up windows. He pulled a palm-sized flashlight from his pocket and clicked it on. A small path had been worn through the dirt and debris that filled the rest of the space, leading from the front entrance to a hallway near the back of the building.

His footsteps echoed across a concrete floor as he followed the path bringing him to a graffiti-covered door held open with rope and stone blocks. Inside, a stairwell led down to the building's basement and up to the higher floors.

He brought his pistol up to chest level, holding his light out with the other hand, and started up.

The doors to every level were propped open in some way or another, revealing long corridors that stretched into darkness. On the third floor, Fischer thought he saw light coming from one of the rooms and heard the thrum of a generator but didn't stop to investigate. If the signal upstairs turned out to be nothing, he could always check it out on his way back down.

Fischer paused on the fifth-floor landing. Unlike the rest of the doors which had been open, this one was closed. Well, mostly closed, he realized. It hung open about an inch from the frame.

He stepped close, eyes scanning the edges and corners for any sign of trip wires or alarms. He put his ear close to the opening and held his breath, listening for movement on the other side. He thought he heard another generator, but the noise it produced drowned out anything else.

The door moved when he pressed on it, creaking on old hinges. Fischer winced as the sound echoed through the stairwell. The corridor on the other side was cleaner than the others had been.

Relatively, Fischer thought, stepping over a cluster of white trash bags, stacked next to the doorway.

His light cut through the darkness, illuminating several closed doors. Near the end of the corridor, a thin sliver of light shone through a partially opened doorway. Cables on the ground connected that room to the one directly across the hall.

He tried all the doors in turn as he passed, most were locked. On one, the handle came off in his hand, the knob on the other end of the door clattering to the floor. Fischer froze, eyes shooting up and down the corridor, hoping the noise went unnoticed.

When no one appeared, he continued on, the incessant thrumming of the generator increasing as he made his way. He stopped a meter away from the open door, considering the cables laid across the floor, between the door rooms. The chances of anyone being in the room with the banging generator was slim, but in a place like this, it wasn't outside the realm of possibility.

He pushed the left door open and peered around the edge. The generator sat near two open windows in the main room, vibrating as it ran. The space around it had been cleared to prevent anything from accidentally catching on fire. The stench of exhaust filled the air as he moved through the apartment, clearing the single bedroom in the back, filled with nothing but old clothes and more trash bags.

Back in the corridor, he stopped at the door across the hall and listened, not that he was liable to hear anything over the generator. After a few minutes of just standing there, waiting for something to happen, he adjusted his grip on his pistol, slid the light back into his pocket, and pushed the door open.

CHAPTER 38

Abandoned Tenements
Calibri City, Stonemeyer
10 Apr 2607

The door groaned as Fischer pushed it open. His pistol was ready, and his heart pounded in his ears. Inside, to the right, a man was in the process of pushing himself off a small couch. He paused as Fischer stepped in, eyes bulging at the sight of the pistol.

He was older, in his seventies at least. His thin gray hair was cut short, his matching beard unkempt and scraggly. His dark brown skin was weathered by years of hard work. A torn, green t-shirt hung loosely over his frame, his gray sweatpants worn thin. His socks were filthy, the big toe on one foot sticking through a hole in the fabric. He stared back at Fischer with old, tired eyes, waiting.

Fischer held a finger to his lips. "Don't move. Don't scream. Do you understand?"

Slowly, the old man nodded, never taking his eyes off Fischer's pistol.

"Anyone else here?"

The man hesitated for a moment as if trying to decide whether or not to answer.

"It'll be better for you if you answer truthfully."

Finally, the man nodded.

"Where?"

He pointed to the closed bedroom door across from him, to Fischer's left. Fischer cleared the rest of the space with his eyes, keeping the gun trained on the old man. Fischer was sure he could take him without any difficulty, but sometimes old men were scrappy.

The small kitchen nook behind the door was empty, as was the bathroom beside it. Fischer let the door close quietly behind him.

"Who's back there?"

The man pointed again. "No danger."

Fischer's face scrunched, trying to decide what the man's angle was. "Are they friendly?"

The man nodded.

"Are you friendly?"

The man nodded again.

"Prove it," Fischer said, stepping away from the door and motioning at the bedroom with his pistol. "Open it. Keep your hands up. Don't do anything stupid."

The man got to his feet and moved slowly to the door. "No danger."

"Slowly," Fischer warned, sliding his finger to the trigger.

The man twisted the handle and pushed, letting it swing in. He stayed in the main room and backed away, motioning inside. "No danger," he said again.

Fischer inched forward, peering into the room as the door swung open.

A single mattress lay on the floor in the center of the room, on top of which lay a man dressed in a torn, charcoal gray, Marine uniform, unbuttoned. His eyes were closed. His head was dressed with gauze, as well as his upper left arm and left leg. His boots and socks had been removed, leaving bare feet exposed. A wide bandage wrapped his chest, covering him from his armpits to just about his belly button. It was stained in several places.

"Holy shit," Fischer said, stepping up to the door.

Several bottles of water lay empty beside the mattress, as well as discarded food wrappers and a bucket they'd been using as a toilet. A candle burned on a small table in the corner beside several sealed packages of bandages and medical supplies.

Fischer's link chimed as it connected to the only other unit in the room and a panel appeared, displaying Allen Sheridan's name, rank, and unit identifier. A second panel rotated into view, showing Fischer the man's vitals.

"Is he alive?" Fischer asked.

The man nodded. "Alive."

"Stay there." The man nodded again, and Fischer stepped into the bedroom. "Private Sheridan?"

The man opened his eyes, searching the room for a moment, then went wide when they fell on Fischer. He propped himself up on his elbows, eyes darting around looking to see if anyone else was in the room. "Rashi?"

"Your friend's fine," Fischer said, lowering his pistol.

"Who are you?"

"Jackson Fischer, I'm with Alliance Security and Intel. I'm going to get you out of here."

Sheridan frowned. "How'd you find me?"

"Traced your link ID." Fischer tapped his link's display. "Can you walk?"

Sheridan sat up, grunting with obvious pain or effort, or both. "Leg's pretty messed up, but I'll manage."

"How bad?"

"Pretty sure the bone's shattered. "He blew out a pained breath. "I don't understand. How did you even get here? Pegasi shut the whole planet down to all Alliance craft. Rashi and I saw it on the feed the other day."

"Long story."

Sheridan leaned to the side, looking around Fischer. "Where's the rest of the team?"

Fischer raised an eyebrow. "Team?"

"Yeah, the rescue team."

"You're looking at it."

"What do you mean? You're it? You're the only one they sent? Where's the Marine S&R team? The dropships? The Nemesis escorts?"

Fischer laughed. "It's just me. And no one sent me, I came on my own."

Sheridan frowned. "I don't understand."

"Like I said, it's a long story. The short of it is, everyone back home thinks you're dead. Thought it myself until your friend here opened this door."

"Did anyone make it out?"

"Three. Thomas, Biagini, and Wallace."

Sheridan's face darkened. He spoke through clenched teeth. "Motherfuckers. What happened to Grayson? They kill him too?"

This time it was Fischer's turn to frown. "Did who kill him?"

"Thomas!" Sheridan blurted. He grimaced at the sudden movement, clutching at his chest and groaning. "Son of a bitch. Did he do it himself or did he want to spread the wealth around a little bit and make one of his lapdogs do it?"

"Lapdogs?" Fischer questioned.

"Biagini and Wallace! He had them wrapped so tight around his finger... I thought Grayson would eventually see past his bull-shit. I guess not."

"Grayson was killed during the extraction. Shot by militia soldiers."

"Son of a bitch," Sheridan growled. "So what bullshit are they spewing out now? I guess they said I died in the bunker, right? That everyone died at the bunker?"

"They didn't mention a bunker."

"Oh right, the *orders*. Course they didn't say anything about that."

Movement at the corner of Fischer's vision caught his attention. The old man held out two bottles of water. "Water, please?"

Fischer watched him, eyes narrowed.

"Rashi's okay, man," Sheridan said. "Who do you think's been taking care of me this whole time?"

"No danger," Rashi said again, nodding.

"He doesn't speak a lot of English, but he tries. Not exactly sure what his native language is."

Fischer accepted the bottle, then stepped back, giving the man room to pass. He gave the second bottle to Sheridan, then proceeded to check the Private's bandages one by one. Sheridan winced and leaned away as Rashi prodded one of the many stains on his chest bandage.

"Easy."

"No pain?"

"Yes, a lot of pain."

"You water." Rashi pushed the bottle closer to Sheridan's lips, practically shoving it in the Marine's mouth.

Sheridan groaned, clenching his teeth. "His bedside manner leaves much to be desired."

Fischer tapped his connection to Jones. "Where are you?"

"Oh, you know, I figured I hit the spa. I haven't had my nails done in years. My toes were starting to look a little rough."

"We're ready for pickup."

"We?"

Fischer glanced at Sheridan. "We."

"Rashi comes too," Sheridan said.

"I don't—"

"He comes," Sheridan said, cutting Fischer off. "If he stays there and the Pegasi learn he helped me, they'll kill him. I'm not willing to have his death on my conscience. Are you?"

Fischer thought about the request. Returning with the Marine would go a long way to lessen the backlash from his illegal trip out here. Might even spare him his job. The old man, though, that was a different story. He could claim asylum sure, but Fischer could just see the Pegasi spinning it to make it look like he'd kidnapped the old man. Not that anyone outside this room even knew or cared who Rashi was.

In the end, it probably wouldn't matter anyway. If either the Stonemeyer Council or the Pegasi Empire found out an Alliance Security and Intelligence agent had disregarded the embargo and illegally entered their territory, there would be hell to pay.

Finally, Fischer said, "Fine. He comes. But we have to leave now. Where you at, Jones?"

"Five minutes out. But you guys better be ready, I've been getting pinged pretty damn hard the last couple of minutes. They're definitely getting curious."

Fischer held out a hand to Sheridan. "Come on, let's go home."

The Marine took his hand, and with Rashi's assistance, Fischer pulled him to his feet. Sheridan grunted, keeping all of his weight on his right leg. Both Fischer and Rashi took an arm, pulling it over their shoulders, keeping the Marine between them.

Sheridan grunted. "We won't make it long on the street. There have been Peacekeeper patrols everywhere.

Rashi nodded emphatically. "Danger."

Fischer was first through the door, going slow and helping Sheridan walk, one-footed, across the main room. "We're not going to the street."

Fischer paused a few steps from the front door and Rashi carefully extricated himself from Sheridan's opposite arm to pull the door open. He kicked a heavy plastic case in front of it, propping it open, then returned and pulled the Marine's arm back around his shoulders.

The sound of the thrumming generator reverberated across the hallway. They made slow progress through the hall, Rashi was doing more harm than good. He almost tripped three times on their way to the stairwell, threatening to pull all three of them down with him.

By the time they reached the stairs much of the color had faded from Sheridan's face. Beads of sweat rolled down his face.

"You good?" Fischer asked.

Sheridan groaned, speaking through clenched teeth. "Hundred percent."

"*Fish?*" *Jones asked through Fischer's link.*

"Almost there."

"*I think—Oh, shit!*"

"Jones? What's wrong?" Fischer looked up at the ceiling, listening. The distant roar of engines permeated through the old building's solid concrete walls. "Jones?"

The building shook, knocking dust off the walls and ceiling. A series of impact tremors vibrated the floor, a *whoomp whoomp whoomp* shuddered down from somewhere above them.

"Jones?"

"*One moment, please,*" Jones said, voice stressed and clipped. "*Some nice people wanted to come and have a conversation.*"

"Shit," Fischer said, glancing back down the corridor.

"What's wrong?" Sheridan asked.

"We're blown." He turned to Rashi. "You got him?"

The old man hesitated for a moment, then nodded. "Yes."

Fischer leaned Sheridan back against the wall and moved to the nearest door. Locked.

"Come on." He took a step back and kicked out hard. The door swung open with a crack, revealing a room filled with the same white trash bags that had filled every other space on this level.

Fischer picked his way through the piles of bags, as more auto-cannon fire echoed through the open windows at the opposite end of the room. Sirens blared up from somewhere, but he couldn't see the patrols yet. On the street below, throngs of people were picking up their meager belongs, trying desperately to evacuate the area before the shooting started.

"*Loomis shoot that son of a bitch!*" Jones shouted.

The *Doris's* co-pilot wasn't connected through their link, but Fischer could hear his voice in the background. "*I can't hit nothin' when you're flying like a crazy shit.*"

"*All right, well I'll just let us get shot then. That'll be fun, won't it?*" More cannon shots rang out, and Jones grunted. "*Shit, that was close. Loomis!*"

"*I got it!*"

Fischer looked up just as the *Doris* shot out from the edge of the building, banking hard to the right, its rear guns sending blasts of orange and red streaking through the air. The frigate disappeared above the opposite row of buildings a second later, just before two Pegasi fighters appeared, cannons on the edge of each of their forward-swept wings blazing.

"*Better get out of there, Fish. Looks like the locals are trying to get in on the action.*"

As the sounds of the fighter engines faded, the sirens grew louder.

"Shit." Fischer left the window, returning to the other two men. "We gotta go."

"No up?" Rashi asked, pointing with his free hand.

Fischer shook his head, pulling Sheridan's arm over his shoulder. "No. We go down. To the street."

Rashi nodded. "Street. Yes."

"Come on."

CHAPTER 39

Warehouse District
Calibri City, Stonemeyer
10 Apr 2607

"Watch it," Fischer said, dropping to a knee behind a wrecked car left abandoned on the side of the street. Sheridan groaned as Rashi helped him down.

Two police gravbikes rounded the corner ahead, blue and yellow emergency lights reflecting off the wet streets and surrounding buildings. They flared briefly before touching down on the street, kicking up spouts of water and bits of trash. The homeless folks scattered, ducking into alleys, or flat-out sprinting away in either direction. The two officers dressed in black uniforms climbed off their bikes pulling stun-sticks from their belts and arcing them.

A few men ran past Fischer and company's hiding spot, trying to get to the front of the crowd to throw rocks and whatever else they could find. The officers ducked behind their bikes, returning their stun-sticks to their belts, and pulling short barreled rifles from racks on the side of the bikes.

"By order of the Council, you are all to disperse. These blocks are now closed to any and all unauthorized personnel. Disperse now. Anyone remaining will be detained."

"Go to hell!" one man yelled.

Another man stepped forward to throw something, and a muted pop rang out. Something slammed into the man's chest, knocking him back. The crowd around him scattered as he rolled across the pavement. The man came to a stop on his chest and slowly pushed himself off the ground.

Non-lethal, interesting, Fischer thought, inching closer to the front of the abandoned wreck.

"Stand down!" the police announcer said. There was a pop and another man dropped, this one spinning like a top after being hit in the shoulder.

"This is going to be fun," Sheridan said.

"We need to get to those bikes," Fischer said. He locked eyes with Rashi. "Can you handle him?"

The old man looked confused, as if trying to process what Fischer had said, then he nodded. "Can handle."

Fischer drew his pistol from its holster under his arm and watched as another group of homeless scattered. "Stay low."

He moved in a crouch, darting between wrecks and through makeshift tents and under low hanging canopies. Behind him, Rashi and Sheridan struggled to keep up, having to pause several times to catch their breath or adjust their grips on each other. The people around them barely even noticed as they cut through their "homes," moving to clear paths as they watched their friends continue to hound the officers.

Fischer felt a tinge of sympathy for the two men as they ducked and fired, then ducked and fired again. They were only really carrying out orders. He doubted they had any real malice in their hearts toward these people. After all, who were they hurting? From what he'd seen, absolutely no one at all. There was no doubt, at all, in his mind that this was because he had come here, and Jackson Fischer didn't take that lightly.

He paused behind an orange tarp hung in the air by a thin rope stretched between two eight-foot poles. The poles holding it up bent severely, threatening to snap in half under the next gust of wind.

They were about fifty meters from the first two officers, both of whom were now standing behind their bikes as their backup arrived, hovering low over the crowds, using their bikes to push the people back. The nearest officer had removed his helmet and was taking steady, well-aimed shots at the crowd, laughing between each pull of the trigger. His partner had crouched down behind his bike, shouting into his link, asking for more reinforcements.

The gravbikes appeared to be standard law enforcement design with upgraded thrusters and enhanced power cores. Technically, they were built with a maximum of two passenger's in mind, but Fischer knew it'd be able to handle three without an issue.

I can take out the first one before his partner even realizes I'm there, Fischer thought, scanning the street between them. He'd have to weave through a few piles of junk and several tents, but he could do it, and the obstructions would help cover his approach —not to mention the angry crowd a hundred meters behind him.

He turned to Sheridan, holding out his pistol by the barrel, handle toward the Marine. "I'm not trying to sound like a dick, but can you handle this?"

Sheridan laughed, taking the weapon. "Yeah, I'm good."

"Good, cause I'm about to do something very stupid." He turned back to the officers, trying desperately to control his breathing. "Just make sure none of Rashi's friends there try and take advantage, okay?"

Sheridan frowned. "Okay? What are you—"

Fischer pushed off with a grunt, running hard through the forest of junk and tents. He hopped over an extinguished fire pit, then ducked under a blue support rope holding a tarp aloft.

Don't look, don't look, don't look, Fischer thought, trying to project his thoughts on the officers, mentally willing them not to see him.

With ten meters to go, Fischer rounded the final tent. He was running at full speed now, boots splashing through shallow puddles, hood flapping behind him, rain pounding against his face. Halfway to the first bike, the officer noticed him, looking up from his rifle, confused, almost shocked that someone had managed to get so close without him noticing.

He opened his mouth to shout, twisting his body to bring the rifle around, as Fischer jumped forward, driving both feet into the man's chest, knocking him back. The officer lost his hold on the rifle as he flipped, finally managing to bark out a pained cry as the weapon spun away, clattering across the wet pavement.

Fischer landed on his back, pain flaring through his body like lightning. Gritting his teeth, he pushed the pain away, rolling to his hands and knees, then pushed himself up. The second officer was on his feet now, pulling his stun-stick from its clip on his belt.

"You son of a—"

Fischer dropped down, lashing out with a spin kick, catching the man at the ankles, knocking his feet out from under him. The officer fell back into his bike, knocking it over. He scrambled to his feet as Fischer did, bringing the stun-stick around for a sideways blow. Fischer brought his boot up, kicking the man's wrist, knocking the weapon from the officer's hand. He stepped forward, and drove a fist into the man's stomach, then another.

As the officer stumbled back, grasping at his stomach, Fischer reached for the helmet. He swung it hard, connecting with the side of the officer's helmet before he could get his hands up to defend himself, cracking the visor. The officer grunted and dropped to the ground.

A spark of electricity shot through the air, smacking into Fischer's side. He cried out, dropping to one knee as pain radiated through his body. He caught himself on the second bike, pushing himself up as the second officer came on, shouting. He swung the stun-stick down, cracking against Fischer's raised forearm. Lightning flashed like fire eating through his skin, raced down his arm.

Still holding the officer's helmet in his other hand, he let out a wordless scream, pushing back against the agony, twisting to smash it into the man's face. The officer grunted, leaning back at the waist, dodging the helmet by an inch. The swing threw Fischer off balance, his momentum carrying him sideways as the officer came back with another jab of the stun-stick.

Fischer's scream was abruptly cut off as electricity arced through his body, causing his muscles to seize all at once, locking him up. The effect only lasted for a few seconds, though, as his momentum carried him away from the weapon. He regained enough control over his limbs to get his hands under him so he wouldn't smack face first into the pavement. He rolled to his side as the shadow of the officer came after him.

The officer stepping over him, stun-stick raised. "Son of a b—"

There was a flash of movement as someone crashed into the officer, tackling him to the ground. Getting to an elbow, Fischer saw Rashi smack the stun-stick away, and unleash a flurry of punches into the officer's face and head. Stars danced in Fischer's vision as he struggled to rise. The officer heaved upward, thrusting his hips high, knocking Rashi off and rolling to his knees.

Rashi cried out as he hit the pavement, landing on top of the first officer, who still hadn't moved. Fischer roared, charging forward, driving his shoulder into the officer's kidney. The officer's head hit the ground with a wet smack, leaving a bloody smear along the pavement as he slid several centimeters, then didn't move again.

Breathing heavily, Fischer got to his knees, eyes locked on the bloody stain. "Goddamn it."

Fischer stood and helped Rashi to his feet, then moved to the gravbike, inspecting the controls. "Good, still unlocked."

"You're not seriously expecting all of us to ride on that, are you?" Sheridan asked, hobbling up, using a metal pipe as a crutch.

"No ride," Rashi said, shaking his head.

"What?" Fischer asked, swinging a leg over. "It's not like we have much of a choice."

"Do you even know how to ride one of those things?"

Fischer patted the hard alloy housing. "Got one just like it back home."

Sheridan raised an eyebrow. "Just like it?"

"Close enough."

On the ground, the first officer rustled, groaning inside his helmet.

"Come on," Fischer said. "We don't have a lot of time."

Rashi helped Sheridan climb on behind Fischer, then took a step back considering both men.

The Marine groaned as Rashi positioned his foot on the rest. "Son of a bitch, that hurts. Come on Rashi, there's room." Sheridan pressed forward into Fischer's back.

The old man shook his head. "No ride."

Fischer toggled the throttle controls, giving the counter-grav pads power. They kicked up a swirl of wind around the bike and sent ripples through the pooling water underneath.

"Wait," Sheridan said. "Rashi, please."

The old man smiled. "You go. Rashi stay." He pointed to the

building they'd come from. "Rashi home. I like. Marine, you take care, yes?"

"Rashi…"

Rashi bowed, then turned and jogged away, weaving through the maze of tents and piles of junk.

"Hold on," Fischer said and gunned the throttle.

CHAPTER 40

Skies above Calibri City
Stonemeyer
10 Apr 2607

"*You did what*?" Jones shouted.

Wind howled in Fischer's ears as he rocketed between two apartment buildings. Even yelling, he barely heard himself. "I got a bike! Where are you?"

"*What the hell did he say, Loomis? Did you hear that? Sounded like he said he got a bike!*"

"Son of a—" Fischer dropped his nose down, letting off on the throttle, flying under a lumbering transport barge that appeared out of nowhere. He rolled right, avoiding a passenger cab, then gunned the throttle.

"You're going to get us killed!" Sheridan yelled, his grip tightening around Fischer's waist.

"It's fine!" Fischer said, bringing them back level. He spared a look over his shoulder. Three police bikes dipped below the barge, and another corkscrewed over it, all four with lights flashing and sirens blaring. "We're fine... ish."

Sheridan followed Fischer's gaze and shook his head. "You're not going to lose them. Radio's faster than we are."

"Jones, where the hell are you?"

"*Just taking in the sights. Chatting up the locals, the usual. Seems like a nice place.*"

"Jones!"

"I*'m coming, keep your pants on. You're not the only one with friends right now. Loomis can't shoot to save his life. Absolutely worthless. Yes, I'm talking about you. Well, then shoot something then*!"

Ahead of them, small puffs of dust and bits of concrete sprayed from an exterior wall, tracing a line across the front of the tenement building. It took a second for Fischer's mind to process what he was seeing, and by the time he realized what it was, it was nearly too late.

Sheridan also made the connection. "They're shooting at us!"

They were approaching a large four-way intersection filled with ground traffic and pedestrians. Fischer made a snap decision and rolled the bike hard right, almost putting it on its side. It slid through the air, counter-grav pads thrumming as they compensated for the maneuver. They came within centimeters of smashing into a four-story office building with large glass windows spanning its height from ground to roof. The bike leveled out, skimming over the windows, shattering them as Fischer gunned the throttle again.

"*Are you trying to kill us*?" Sheridan yelled, pressing his entire body into Fischer's back.

Fischer pulled away from the building, leveling out as they shot forward. He glanced down at his link, trying to read the map.

"Look out!" Sheridan's hand came up in front of Fischer, pointing.

Another police bike had just dropped out of the sky ahead, lights reflecting off the glass buildings on either side of it. Fischer jerked the controls, rolling left, missing the officer by barely a meter. He glanced behind him, watching as the bike's rider got turned around.

"What the hell was that?" Sheridan asked.

Fischer shook his head. "Not sure." He looked down at his map again, glancing between it and the landscape ahead. One of the transparent hyperloop tubes appeared on his right, the massive support columns dwarfing the small warehouses surrounding it. It continued straight ahead for a number of blocks, running parallel to the road.

"Jones, you see me?" Fischer asked.

"*Hold on,*" Jones said. "*Loomis, for shit's sake, do something useful, please! I don't care, if we don't get out of here, it's going to be the least of our problems. Fish, what's that? Yeah, I got you?*"

"You see that hypertube?"

After a moment, Jones answered, "*Yeah, I see it.*"

"There's a large transfer station a few blocks ahead, you think you can get there?"

"*Can I get there? The hell do you think this is, the first day of flight school?*"

"Step on it."

More shots zipped through the air around Fischer. He heard them this time, which meant they were getting closer. He glanced behind him and counted at least four police units.

They're really pissed off, he thought. He weaved the bike left then back right again, not wanting to give them a stable target to hit. Plumes of smoke erupted from the building to his right, spitting bits of debris into the air.

"You got a plan for that?" Sheridan shouted, patting Fischer's shoulder then pointing above them.

Two Pegasi assault shuttles dropped out of the low-hanging, dark clouds, in tight formation. They raced along ahead of

Fischer, banking left to pull in front of them, trying to cut off their escape.

A voice boomed through the air. *"You are under arrest. Stand down now, or we will be forced to fire upon you."*

"Too late for that, asshole," Sheridan shouted back.

Desperately, Fischer scanned the street ahead for an escape, glancing at his map, but there wasn't anywhere to go. The turret on the side of the shuttle began rotating back, bringing the twin-barreled auto-cannon to bear.

"Last warning! By order of the Emperor, land, or we will shoot."

"To hell with this," Sheridan said, raising his hand in front of Fischer again. This time holding the pistol Fischer had given him. He fired, hand jerking slightly at the recoil, but even one-handed, the Marine controlled the weapon as if it was just another extension of his body.

The nearest shuttle exploded. A fireball erupted from its portside engine, ripping through the wing and into the fuselage. The blast threw the craft into a spin, shearing off the wing completely. It rolled into its companion, both hulls smashing and crumbling together as they careened into the side of a glass-walled building.

The second shuttle exploded, sending pieces of both spinning into the air. Flaming debris trailed black smoke through the air as they rolled across the surface of the wall, shattering glass and snapping steel support pillars.

"Shit!" Fischer shouted, jerking the controls to avoid a spinning piece of burning fuselage. He shot through a thick column of smoke and felt heat from the fire as they passed the falling wreckage.

The shuttles crashed into the street as one large, mangled wreck, exploding again as the drive ruptured. Even half a block ahead of the explosion, Fischer felt the blast. He glanced behind him and saw the fireball curling into the air, and debris smashing into the surrounding buildings.

"What the hell was that?" Sheridan asked.

"I don't—"

"*Heads up, boys! Daddy's home.*"

A shadow passed over them and the deep thrumming of the *Doris's* engines reverberated through the air. The frigate flared, pulling up directly in front of Fischer's bike, the back-cargo entrance open. Loomis stood at the top of the ramp, one hand holding onto a support rail above him, the other waving Fischer inside.

"*You're not going to get a signed invitation,*" Jones said.

Fischer gunned the throttle, pushing the bike through the opening, then set the bike down hard. Sparks erupted under the bike as it slid across the cargo bay's metal deck, spinning to the right.

"We're in!" Fischer shouted, holding on as the bike spun one-hundred-and-eighty degrees before crashing into one of the several large cargo containers secured to the deck. The impact knocked both men from the bike, sending them toppling to the deck.

Fischer landed on his side. He rolled another meter before righting himself and getting to his knees.

A mechanical whine sounded through the bay as the ramp closed. Sparks erupted off the end of the ramp, and several rounds zipped past Fischer, striking the containers behind him. He ducked, as Loomis yelled, "Get down!"

The frigate's engine boomed, and Fischer slid back across the deck along with the bike and Sheridan. The Marine screamed in pain as he rolled over his destroyed leg, then suddenly went silent, going limp as he passed out. His body slid like a rag doll behind the gravbike, smacking into the closing cargo ramp. The front of the bike crashed into the ramp just to the left of Sheridan's unconscious body.

"You might want to buckle up back there!" Jones shouted.

Fischer managed to get a hold of one of the containers and got his feet under him. He stood, using the container as leverage, and muttered. "Thanks for the warning."

Carefully, Fischer made his way to the unconscious Marine, kneeling down beside him. Loomis appeared next to him. "He okay?"

Fischer nodded. "He's alive. Need to get him to a rack though."

"He can use mine," Loomis said, wrapping his arms around Sheridan's legs as Fischer looped his hands under the Marine's shoulders and across his chest. "One, two, three."

Fischer grunted, lifting the Marine off the deck. Sheridan's eyes snapped open, and he let out an ear-splitting scream, reaching for his injured leg.

"Sorry, buddy," Loomis said, adjusting his grip, trying to get the least amount of pressure on his leg as possible.

"Son of a bitch," Sheridan said, sucking in a sharp breath.

"It's going to be okay," Fischer reassured him as they reached the stairs. "We're going to get you home."

CHAPTER 41

The Doris
JumpLane 0781 - in Transit
10 Apr 2607

Sheridan blew out a long, relieved breath as the injector hissed, pushing pain inhibitors into the Marine's body. "Holy shit."

"Better?" Fischer asked, setting the injector on the small fold-out tray next to the bed. The bed itself wasn't much more than a tray; a flat two-meter slab of steel alloy with a mattress that folded off the bulkhead.

The little cabin didn't have much room for anything else. It was more like a closet than anything. Slightly bigger than the quarters Fischer had occupied during his service in the Navy, but not by much. He sat on an overturned crate next to the bed.

"Much." Sheridan adjusted his position on the bed, laying his head back on the pillow, visibly relieved.

They hadn't bothered to unwrap his wounded leg. They'd all decided there was nothing they could do for it other than re-bandage it, and that wouldn't do much. None of them had any real medical knowledge, and the general consensus was they were just as likely to do more damage than actually do any good. It wasn't like they'd be able to repair it with painkillers and gauze.

"You know," Sheridan said. "Before you showed up today, I'd pretty much decided I wasn't ever getting off that rock. Rashi was a good guy and all, but there wasn't any way in hell he was going to save me. Ow!"

Loomis winced, pausing halfway through wrapping the Marine's arm. "Sorry."

Sheridan blew out another breath. "It's all right."

Fischer stood, giving Loomis more room to work. "We were lucky. Plain and simple. A million things could've gone wrong down there. Hell, they could've gone wrong before I even got here, and they did. At least now we can start to put everything right. This whole thing has really kicked off a shitstorm."

"This whole thing was a shitstorm to begin with. Even before we got here. I mean, who the hell cares about some shithole planet in the middle of nowhere anyway?"

"It's halfway between the Alliance and the Empire," Fischer said. "Makes it strategically important, if nothing else."

Sheridan laughed. "Strategically important. What a bunch of shit. If it was really that important, they would've sent more than just us. They would have sent a battlegroup and not just a light cruiser. I mean seriously, what the hell was Command thinking? I've never met Admiral Hunter, but everything I've ever heard about the man suggests that he's one hell of a leader and commander."

"I've met him," Fisher said, nodding. "He's as smart as they come."

"Then explain to me why this op went as south as it did." Sheridan propped himself up on an elbow, face reddening. "Explain to me why all my friends are dead! And I'm not talking about this mission, I know whose fault that is. I'm talking about this whole damn thing. You've seen the city. You've seen the conditions here. That's damn near the entire place—everything I saw anyway. What possible use could the Alliance have for a place like this?"

"Your guess is as good as mine," Fischer said, regretting that he didn't have any real answers. "I've got my guesses, but there's a lot of holes, I was hoping you'd be able to fill some of them in for me. Trust me, I want the people responsible for this cluster to burn just as much as you do."

Sheridan's eye twitched. "All due respect. No, sir. You don't."

Fischer held the Marine's gaze for a moment. A fire burned behind those tired eyes, a fire with the potential to set the entire system ablaze. He'd seen it before, and if left alone, the fire would consume him, eat the Marine alive from the inside. There wasn't any reasoning with it. His only hope was to guide it in the right direction.

Finally, Fischer nodded. "You're right."

"You said Thomas and Wallace…" Sheridan cut himself off, sucking in a breath as Loomis finished clipping the dressing. "They made it back?"

"And Biagini," Fischer corrected. "But…" He sighed.

Sheridan frowned. "But?"

"Look, there's not an easy way to say this, but they're dead. All three of them."

"I don't understand, I thought they made it back home?"

Fischer nodded. "They did."

"How?"

"Biagini killed herself after—"

"No way," Sheridan said, cutting him off. "That's a mistake. There's no way she'd do that. Not after everything she'd been through. No way!"

"I'm sorry, but she did. She jumped off the top of the hospital where she was being treated."

"Jumped or pushed?"

Fischer sighed. "I watched her jump."

Sheridan's face darkened. "The fuck do you mean, you watched her? Why didn't you save her, help her?"

"Wasn't anything I could do. I tried to talk her down, tried to reason with her, but…" Fischer shook his head as the image of Biagini standing on the ledge replayed in his mind. His stomach turned as he watched her fall. "I'm sorry."

Sheridan stared at him for a long moment before finally looking away, clenching his jaw muscles. "She was the reason any of us made it out of there."

Fischer stayed silent, watching as the Marine worked through his own thoughts on what had happened. If Wallace had been telling the truth about what had happened at the militia stronghold, Sheridan and Biagini would've been through a lot together. That would've created a bond stronger than most.

After a few moments, Sheridan's expression seemed to shift from pain and anguish back to anger. His eyes hardened again, and he turned back to Fischer. "What happened to Wallace and Thomas?"

"Wallace was murdered," Fischer answered. "I can't prove it, but I know he was. And Thomas…"

"What?"

Fischer swallowed hard, seeing the Sergeant's body jerk as his bullets slammed home. "I killed him."

Sheridan lay there in silence for several moments, then finally, nodded. "They got what they deserved then."

"What happened?"

"You want the long version or the short version?"

"That depends."

"On?"

"On how much of Wallace's story was true or not."

Sheridan chuckled, shaking his head. "I'd have a hard time believing anything that came out of that guy's mouth. Everything he ever told us sounded like bullshit to me. Course, like you said, I couldn't ever prove it. He talked a lot of shit, but once it came time to grab your nuts and go to work, he curled up like a scared puppy."

"That's kind of the impression I got, too."

"Hell, even on the way down in the Albatross, before the mission had ever really started, he was talking shit. Talking about taking names and kicking ass, real stupid stuff, right? Like who the hell says that kind of shit anymore?"

"Some people just like to hear themselves talk."

"No one more than Wallace. Every day in the barracks he'd have some new story about how he beat the Navy guys at something, or when he was in training, he had the record for this or that. Most of the stuff he said no one could ever find any record of at all, and after a while we just let him talk. In one ear and out the other, right?"

Fischer nodded.

"So, yeah, he talked shit all the way to the point when we first engaged the militia outside the Embassy. I remember Ford going down first. I'll be honest, I wasn't ready for that. I can still see everything like it was in slow motion. Fuck, I saw his hand cock back, going to throw that grenade and—*bam*—everything just kind of exploded around him and the next thing I see was Ford spinning around. He must have taken another round at some point before we made it to the bird. There wasn't anything we could do. Chest wound like that..." Sheridan trailed off, shaking his head.

"Trent got hit next. Shit, he never had a chance. Took a round right through the visor. He was dead before he hit the ground."

"Wallace said he carried Ford and Trent onto the bird."

Sheridan shook his head. "That son of a bitch didn't do anything but help himself. Hid under a car most of that initial fight, curled into a ball, yelling that he was taking fire and couldn't move. I carried Ford in, then went back for Trent.

Wallace was screaming for the pilot to takeoff. Wanted to leave before the rest of the team was even on board. Wallace was no Marine. He was a coward."

"And the birds were shot down?"

"Yeah." Sheridan looked away. He rubbed his nose with the back of a finger. "We lost a lot of good people, sir. A lot of good people."

"You don't have to call me sir."

"Sorry."

"Don't have to be sorry, either."

Sheridan chuckled, then nodded. "Those militia bastards really had our number. "Intel guys really fucked us there. No offense."

Fischer put up a hand. "None taken."

"I mean, how do you miss that kind of capability? It's not like they were hiding it. Fallon said they'd been steadily increasing their attacks for several days before we even got there."

"Right, okay, did Fallon or Delaney ever say what set them off? I know they were anti-establishment, anti-government, right? Wanted to take over the government, set up their own little kingdom."

"Who the hell knows what those bastards wanted," Sheridan said. "You want my opinion, I think they just wanted something to shoot at. The cause didn't matter. I know they were against the Pegasi occupation. I know that."

"So, one thing I still haven't been able to put together," Fischer said. "Why did the militia have such a hard-on for the Ambassador?"

Sheridan chuckled. "They left that part out too, huh? Figures. Delaney was the whole reason that operation went to shit. For an ambassador, he really didn't understand the people he was working with. Like my dad always used to tell me, don't ever piss off the guy with the bigger gun. It'll never work out in your favor."

"Makes sense."

"And you want to know the most ironic part about the whole thing?" Sheridan asked.

"That's why I'm here."

Sheridan shook his head. "That bastard gave them the bigger guns."

CHAPTER 42

Suspected Militia Stronghold
Calibri City, Stonemeyer
28 Mar 2607
Mission Time: 6days 20hrs 40mins

I woke to the sound of gunshots in the distance. I reached out and shook Biagini's foot. "Hey, wake up."

"Huh?" Her faced twisted in pain and she propped herself up on her elbow. "What's that?"

"Somebody's shooting."

I moved to the door and pressed my ear against the cold steel. I could hear the soldiers on the other side scrambling to get their gear, shouting at each other, asking who was shooting at who. No one seemed to know.

I heard Rom's voice. "They're coming for their friends!"

"What'd he say?" Biagini asked.

I held up a finger. "Hold on."

"There! There! Look out! They're coming down!"

More shots. Someone's painful scream was cut off abruptly by a burst of gunfire. Footsteps pounding outside, kicking over some of the crates. More gunshots.

"One down."

I froze, looking at Biagini, eyes wide. I knew that voice. "That's Thomas."

There was more commotion, then the sound of someone kicking a door, shouting "Clear" a second later.

A single shot rang out.

"Get down!"

"That's Wallace," Biagini said.

I pounded on the door with my fist. "Sarge! Wallace! In here."

"Get back," Wallace said from the other side. The door exploded inward, and Wallace came in, rifle up.

I threw my hands up. "It's us, it's us, don't shoot!"

Wallace lowered his rifle, his eyes sweeping over Biagini and me, then falling to Charles in the corner. "Holy shit."

The Corporal's broken body lay face down, but one of his mangled hands lay on the floor behind him, fingers snapped and bent in awkward, unnatural positions. Blood had continued to seep through the makeshift bandage we'd made for his leg and had started pooling underneath him.

"Basement's clear," Wallace said, shaking his head. "We found them, Lieutenant."

Sergeant Thomas stepped into the room behind him. "Bastards. Grayson, get your ass down here." He knelt in front of Biagini. "You look like shit, Corporal."

Biagini coughed a half-chuckle, grimacing in pain. "I've had better days."

"Can you walk?"

"Not very well."

Thomas nodded. "We're going to get you out of here."

Wallace put his hand out for me and pulled me to my feet. He cocked his head at my swollen right eye. "Can you see out of that thing?"

"Good enough to outshoot you."

He grinned. "We'll see about that."

Grayson appeared in the doorway, wincing at my black eye. "Geez, Sheridan, what happened? You insult the guy's mom or something?"

"Said she couldn't cook for shit," I answered.

The medic stepped around me, pulling his kit off his shoulders. He took a knee next to Biagini. "How you feeling, Corporal?"

"Like I look."

"We'll get you fixed up."

Hastings and Jung appeared next. Our little cell was filling up quick. He nodded at me. "Sheridan."

"LT, good to see you. Did you find Henderson?"

Hastings flared his nostrils, sighing, then nodded. "We found him."

"Son of bitches beat him to death, looks like," Jung growled. Then she saw Charles. "Oh no." She moved around the edge of the cell and knelt next to him. "How?"

I rubbed some fresh blood off my lip. "Sometime last night. Didn't even realize 'til this morning."

She scooted back half a step when she saw his hands. "What the hell did they do to him? Jesus Christ."

I shook my head. "They were definitely pissed about something. Far as I could tell, it had something to do with our weapons, but I only caught bits and pieces of their conversations. They didn't talk much down here. How'd you find us, sir?"

Hastings tapped the back of his hand. "Your beacon. Once we got within range, it was easy."

"I'm surprised it was still transmitting. They flashed an inhibitor code on our links as soon as they got us here."

Jung looked up from caressing Charles's broken fingers. "Beacons are specifically shielded against that kind of stuff. They operate on a completely different system than the comms."

"Finally, the Marines did something right," Wallace said.

"Can you clear them?" I asked, holding my hand out.

She pulled a small datapad from a pouch on her vest, tapped a few commands and nodded. "Done."

My link's display flickered to life over my wrist, all the options previously locked out coming back online. It automatically re-synced with the team's squadlink. "Great, thanks."

"Where's the Ambassador?" Hastings asked.

"Screw that guy," Wallace said, letting his rifle hang across his chest, draping his arms over the butt.

"Not sure, sir," I said. "Turk—their leader—took him with a couple other guys a few hours ago, right after Henderson stopped screaming. Heard them talking about a map."

"A map to where?" Hastings asked.

"To whatever they were looking for, I guess. It's been quiet around here ever since."

"Maybe that computer upstairs will give us something," Jung said, standing.

Hastings nodded. "Let's check it out. Grayson, how's she doing?"

"She'll live, sir. I'm giving her a bunch of antibiotics and painkillers though, she's going to be pretty out of it."

"I need everyone I can get, Corporal."

Grayson looked over his shoulder, eyes hard. "Sir, we're lucky we're not carrying her out in a body bag."

Hastings hesitated for a moment, then said, "Make her as comfortable as you can."

Grayson turned back to Biagini without another word, pulling items from his kit and quietly discussing his process with her.

"Wallace, stay with them," Hastings said. "Sergeant Thomas, Jung, Sheridan, with me."

We followed him upstairs to one of Turk's private rooms. I'd passed it several times before, on my way to the education room, but I'd never actually been inside. The cell leader's room was sparse, containing a single bed along one wall and a computer terminal along another. A mass of holopanels floated on the wall above the main terminal.

"Can you work it?" Hastings asked as Jung stepped around him, surveying the unit.

She sat down and started tapping on the keys. Icons flashed and additional panels appeared as she worked. "Just a standard network interface, sir. Nothing too fancy. Looks like a couple of the systems have lockouts established, but I think I can bypass. Biagini would probably have an easier time, though."

"Do what you can."

"Yeah, I'm bringing up the last program they had running, looks like a map of the city."

A top-down map of Calibri City appeared on one of the holo-displays above Jung, marked with several indicator icons. Jung scanned over the data on a panel in front of her then leaned back, looking up at the map.

She pointed to one of the markers. "That's us. That's the Embassy over there."

Hastings pointed to another marker twenty-five kilometers to the north of the Embassy. "What's that?"

"Hmmm," Jung consulted the panel in front of her again. "Not sure."

"Wait a minute," Thomas said, leaning over Jung's back. She glared at him as he pushed on her shoulder. He didn't seem to notice her irritation, circling the space around the marking with his finger. "I've seen this area before."

"Where?"

"That tablet that Grayson found. Delaney's tablet." He keyed his squadlink. "Grayson get up here."

A minute later the medic appeared in the doorway. "Yeah, Staff Sergeant?"

"You still have that tablet you found?"

Grayson frowned. "The Diplo Corps one?"

"Right."

"Yeah, got it right here."

"Bring up the map of that other safe house you found."

"One sec, I've got to power it up again. Didn't want to kill the battery if we needed it later." It took a few moments for the pad to boot, then Grayson started swiping through the menus. "Yeah, right here. According to the geo-tag, it's the Embassy's secondary safe house." He turned the pad around, showing us all the map. The location was an exact match for the unmarked icon on Turk's map. "But what the hell do these guys want with that?"

"I still don't understand why you'd need two," Jung said. "I mean if the first one went tits-up, wouldn't you just cut your losses and leave?"

"It's always good to have a backup," Hastings says.

"Might be a good spot to lay low for a while," Thomas suggested. "Stay under the radar for a couple days before calling for extraction."

Hastings nodded. "Maybe."

"Uh, Lieutenant," Jung said, pointing to the holo-map above her. Another marker icon had appeared, flashing red next to the hideout's icon. "Something's happened."

Hastings leaned over her shoulder, considering the map. "What do you got, Corporal?"

"A new marker just appeared, sir."

"What's it indicate?"

"I think that's us, sir." She pointed to the tablet. "More to the point, it's that."

"The hell you talking about?" Grayson leaned forward, squinting at the map.

"Look. See here? This is the hideout building we're in. That's where we parked and came through that service entrance. Here's the back lot. That's us."

"How do you know it's the pad?" I asked, leaning over Grayson's shoulder at the small device. There wasn't anything special about it, just looked like a regular datapad.

"Shut it off," Jung said.

Grayson nodded. "Right." He powered the device down, and we all crowded around the display. A few seconds later the marker vanished.

"What the hell?" Thomas said.

"So, what, they were tracking Delaney?" Grayson said.

"Looks that way," Jung said.

"That explains how they were able to track us," Hastings said. "Practically brought them right down on us at the comm station. I didn't think it was just using the relay. Didn't make a whole lot of sense."

"But why didn't they just attack us at the safe house?" I asked. We'd stayed there over a day; they'd have plenty of time to track us down.

"It's because it was shielded."

We all turned to see Biagini standing in the doorway, leaning on the frame. Wallace stood behind her, positioned ready to catch her if she fell. Her face bruised, half-naked body covered with dirt and patches of dried blood, her hair matted with sweat and grime.

Grayson handed the pad to Thomas and moved to steady her, glaring at Wallace. "Jesus, I told you to keep her still."

Wallace held his hands out. "Are you kidding me, have you met B?"

Biagini grimaced as Grayson helped her to the bed. It creaked as she sat down. She sucked in a painful breath through her nose and shook her head. "Shit."

"You okay?" Grayson asked.

"Ugh, fine." She sat still for a minute, eyes closed, obviously concentrating on her breathing. "I'm fine."

Hastings kept his gaze on her for a moment, then turned back to the map. He dipped his chin slightly, eyes locked on the icon marking the second safe house. "You think that's where they went?"

It took me a second to realize he was speaking to me. "Yes, sir. Heard them say if he was lying, they'd come back and kill us all in front of him."

"Lying about what?" Jung asked.

Hastings gave me a sidelong look, eyebrow raised. "Any ideas?"

"Sorry, sir," I said. "But I know they were very interested in finding that place."

"And weapons," Biagini added from the behind us.

We all turned to her.

"Weapons?" Hastings asked.

She inhaled. "Turk was obsessed about finding more weapons. I heard him mention it a couple of times."

I nodded. "That's right. Asked about them constantly."

"Our weapons?" Hastings asked. "Why the hell would he be interested in those?"

"That's what we thought too," I said. "But the bastard was convinced we knew where they were. I guess where you guys were. Not sure why he was so hard up for Delaney."

"Not to mention that they already had them," Grayson added. Everyone paused, looking at the private, still standing in the doorway. He held his hands out. "What? Don't you remember the rockets? That launcher we found during the exfil, it was Alliance tech, remember? That's how they shot down the dropships."

"That's right, I found it," Wallace said.

I rolled my eyes.

"What? I did."

"It doesn't matter who found it," I said.

"Sure as hell does."

"Enough." Hastings held up a hand. "If they already had access to Alliance weapons, the question becomes why do they need more and where did they get them from?"

"We need to destroy them," Thomas blurted out, then added, "Sir."

"Destroy them?" Hastings asked. He pointed to the icon on the map. "We don't even know if that's what this is. It could be anything. It could be another safe house. It could be nothing."

"Sir, if there's a possibility that these bastards are in possession of stolen Alliance equipment, we need to stop them, whatever their plans are." Thomas rubbed the back of his neck. "And if that's where they took the Ambassador…"

Slowly, Hastings nodded. "Delaney is still the mission."

"That son of a bitch?" Wallace blurted out. "What the hell do we care what those bastards do to him? How many times has he almost got us killed now?" He pointed at the pad Thomas held. "She said it, if they were tracking him, he brought them down on us every time."

"I doubt he was aware of the tracker," Hastings said. "From what they've said, he didn't seem very agreeable to give them any information."

"Maybe not at first, but it sure looks like he did eventually." Wallace hesitated, then added, "Sir."

"We should kill them all," Thomas said. "If we manage to get Delaney back, then it's a bonus."

Wallace slapped the stock of his 27. "Agreed."

I glanced between Wallace and Thomas. They'd both always kind of had a rough side and didn't always fall strictly in-line with

Marine regulations, but I'd never seen either of them on the verge of breaking their bearing over something like this. It was border-line insubordination, if not simply disrespectful.

"The Ambassador is not a bonus," Hastings corrected, giving both of them reproachful looks. "The Ambassador is the mission. I'm still not one-hundred percent sure weapons have anything to do with this, but it's not outside the realm of possibilities."

"Sir, if they have Alliance weapons, we need to get them back," Thomas said.

"That's a very big 'if,' Sergeant. I'm not going to make critical decisions based on 'ifs.'"

"Sir, I—"

Hastings held up a hand. "*If* there are weapons there," he nodded to the map, "then we'll deal with them at that time. For now, however, that is our only intel suggesting a location for the Ambassador. And since this entire damn thing is about him, we go to find him."

CHAPTER 43

Calibri City, Stonemeyer
28 Mar 2607
Mission Time: 6days 22hrs 4mins

I couldn't believe it'd been a week already, but then again, so much had happened, it felt like we'd been there a lifetime. I looked around the van's windowless interior, at the faces of my fellow Marines, everyone exhausted, but everyone ready to fight. We'd lost half our team since dropping in, and the mission wasn't finished yet.

I couldn't help but think whether the whole thing was worth it or not. Watching Biagini groan as we made our way through the sparse traffic, wincing every time Jung made a swift lane change, I was leaning toward the latter. All of this for one man. The math just didn't seem right to me.

The metal floor didn't look that comfortable, but it was easier for her to lie down than sit. The rest of us sat on the benches on either side of the van's interior, almost like we were back on the dropship, descending to the Embassy just as we'd done six days before. A lifetime ago.

The van's windowless walls eliminated the risk of being seen, but every time I heard a police siren, my heart skipped a beat.

"We're clear," Jung said from the driver's seat. I saw the flashing lights of a police car pass us, continuing down the road until it disappeared in traffic.

"Take your next left," Grayson said from the passenger seat. He leaned around his seat. "We'll be there in five, LT."

"Roger," Hastings said. "You going to be okay?" He motioned to my swollen eye.

I stretched my face, forcing my eyelid to open. Aside from the constant, dull throbbing, I could see just fine. "Good to go, LT."

He nodded. "You're with Biagini. Wait in the van until we're clear, then come up."

"I can fight," Biagini grunted, sitting up. She grimaced, her breath catching in her throat.

I had to admit, the same thought was running through my mind as well, but I kept my mouth shut. Now was not the time to argue over ops plans. I had to trust the Lieutenant, and he had to trust that I'd protect Biagini and their backs.

Hastings shook his head. "We need rear security, and you got the duty. Don't like it, take it up with your recruiter."

Biagini looked like she was going to argue, then a smile spread across his cracked lips. "Roger that, sir."

"Jung, Grayson, you two have point, Wallace you're last man in the column. Standard clear, room by room. Don't shoot unless you're sure of your target. The Ambassador's in there, we don't want to shoot him by accident."

Wallace slapped the bolt forward on his rifle. "Or do we?"

"Cut that shit out, Wallace," Thomas growled, pointing a knife-hand at him.

Hastings glared at him. "Stay on mission. We're almost done. We do this thing, and we're that much closer to going home. Got it?"

Wallace nodded. "Yes, sir."

"We all on the same page?" Hastings asked, looking at each one of us in turn. We all nodded. "Good. Let's finish this."

"Two minutes," Grayson said. He leaned over to Jung, saying something I couldn't hear, pointing ahead. She nodded.

I pulled the bolt back on my rifle, confirming for the tenth time there was a bullet seated in the chamber, then let it snap forward. Images of sending an entire magazine worth of bullets into Turk's lifeless corpse flashed through my mind as my heart pounded with anticipation.

Time for some payback, I thought, scooting forward to the edge of my seat. Through the van's windshield, I saw a few tall buildings a few blocks ahead. "Which one is it?"

Grayson pointed. "Klausmeyer Building, six up on the left. That brick one, see?"

The eight-story tenement building looked outdated compared to the others around it but was definitely in better repair than most of the rest of the city. I spotted two of the militia vans parked on the street in front of the building's entrance, both facing us. Two figures dressed in plain clothes stood on the sidewalk beside them wearing long coats, obviously concealing their weapons.

I pointed. "Two out front."

Hastings moved up between the two front seats, squatting on the balls of his feet. "Sheridan get on that door."

"Roger that, sir." I moved around Thomas, grabbing hold of the sliding panel door and tensing to yank it open.

"You got the shot?" Hastings asked Grayson as the medic lifted his 27, pulling it into his shoulder. It was risky shooting through windshields, impact glass could send the rounds glancing off in random directions, completely missing your intended target.

Grayson thumbed his safety off with a click. "I got this."

"Drive straight at them," Hastings told Jung, pointing. She nodded.

Through a gap between Hastings and Grayson's seat, I could see the two sentries. One was taking a long pull on a cigarette, the other scanning up and down the street. He did a double take on our van as we approached, and even from a block away, I could see the recognition in his face. He tapped his partner on the shoulder and pointed. With the cigarette still in his mouth, the first sentry stepped forward, his arms out to either side as if asking, "What the hell are you doing here?"

"Now," Hastings said.

Jung pushed the pedal to the floor, and the van's engine roared. She steered across the street, cutting off traffic to a chorus of angry horns and squealing brakes. The expression on the sentry's face turned from irritated confusion to shocked disbelief. The cigarette fell from his lips, and he reached for his rifle, slung inside his jacket.

Grayson fired. The gun blast rang in my ears and glass sprayed out as multiple rounds pierced the windshield. The smoker's head snapped back a half-second before another round took him in the shoulder, spinning him back, exposing the second soldier. He managed to get his rifle out, but never got it up to fire. Grayson's bullets stitched across his chest, knocking him back onto the sidewalk.

Jung kept the pedal down, sending the van bouncing over the curb. It lurched again as the tires rolled over the first man's corpse, then brakes squealed, bringing us to a stop at the base of the stairs.

"Go! Go! Go!" Hastings shouted.

I already had the door open. Thomas and Wallace were out first, followed closely by Hastings. Grayson bailed out of his seat, falling into line as I hopped out to check the second sentry.

Jung knelt next to the one she'd run over. "One down."

"Two down," I said, checking the second. I moved to the base of the stairs, training my sights on the door as the team moved up.

Wallace didn't hesitate, booting the double doors as soon as he'd reached them. They swung up, banging against the walls behind them and he charged in, rifle up.

He snapped off two rounds. "Tango down!"

"Move!" Hastings shouted, bringing up the rear, taking the stairs two at a time.

I watched as the team disappeared into the building, then moved back to the van, standing by the open side door. "You okay?"

Biagini sat with her back against the far bench, rifle draped across her lap. She looked far from okay, but it was the only thing that came to mind. "Fine. Just wish I wasn't stuck here."

I turned back toward the building, scanning up the brick wall, checking each window in turn. "Roger that."

"Moving to two," Grayson said.

"Watch, watch! Left side!" Thomas shouted through the squadlink, gunshots echoing in the background. "Thomas, Wallace, down."

"Roger," Thomas answered.

A high-pitched scream cut through the chatter.

"Jung's hit!" Wallace said.

"Grayson!" Hastings shouted.

I turned to Biagini, her stone-faced, frustrated expression mirrored my own. We should've been up there fighting, not sitting here on our asses, watching two dead guys. She pushed herself to the edge of the van, grunting. She got her feet on the sidewalk and pulled herself upright, using the van's door frame as leverage.

"Whoa," I said, stepping forward to help. "What are you doing?"

"This is stupid. I can fight. We need to be up there."

"But—"

She ignored me, pushing past me, limping for the stairs. "You got my back or what?"

"Second floor, clear!" Hastings said.

I hesitated for a moment, almost not believing what I was seeing. She paused at the base of the stairs, leaning one hip against the railing. "You coming? Or you got something better to do?" Without waiting for an answer, she turned and started up the stairs.

"Shit." I followed her through the building's entrance, into a dark hallway.

Shouts and screams and gunfire bounced off the ceiling above us. We stepped around a dead soldier, laid out on his back, eyes open in surprise, blood pooling underneath him. The rooms on the level had already been cleared, their doors hanging partly open, but still, I checked them anyway.

Complacency kills.

We passed a bank of elevators on the left, marked with caution tape and a sign warning people that they were out of service. At the back of the hall, we came to a small storage and mechanical room on our right, and an open door leading into the stairwell on the left.

More gunshots rang out, some coming from below us, some coming from above.

"Which way?" I asked Biagini.

She shook her head. "Doesn't matter. Pick one."

"He's going down!" Grayson shouted, his voice reverberating through the SL.

Gunshots echoed down through the stairwell, I could see the muzzle flash two landings up. "Grayson, who's coming down?"

"Hostile, got past me. He's—"

Tat-tat! Tat-tat!

A soldier appeared on the landing above, bounding the stairs as the bullets pierced the wall behind him. I shifted aim and fired, putting a four-round burst into this chest. The impact of the bullets and his downward momentum flipped him backward, spinning him three-hundred and sixty degrees to land on his stomach. His body slid face-first down the stairs, coming to a rest on the floor a meter from my feet.

I stared down at the corpse, breath coming in rapid gasps. "Holy shit."

"*LT, behind you!*" Grayson shouted. *Tat! Tat! Tat!*

I heard several more shots reverberating up through the floor, then Wallace's voice came over the squadlink. "*Basement's clear.*"

"*Moving,*" Hastings said. Boots pounded on bare floors above, and a minute later he added, "*Third floor, clear.*"

"*Coming up,*" Thomas advised, coming up the stairs a second later with Wallace in tow.

"What the hell are you two doing in here?" Thomas asked, pausing at the base of the stairs.

"Helping," I said, immediately feeling childish for saying it.

"Hold here." He pointed to the floor. "Don't let anyone down there."

Frowning, I thought that was kind of a strange request, considering I would've done that anyway. I wasn't checking IDs at a gate after all. Instead of arguing, I nodded. "Roger that, Staff Sergeant."

They cleared the remaining floors, all of which were empty. Then Hastings came over the SL and told us all to meet on the second floor.

Biagini and I exchanged a look, and I knew we were both thinking the exact same thing.

Jung.

CHAPTER 44

Calibri City, Stonemeyer
29 Mar 2607
Mission Time: 6days 20hrs 11mins

Corporal Jung looked peaceful, lying in a pool of her own blood. She'd taken a burst straight through the chest. The bullets had torn through her tacvest and punched several holes out through her back. She'd been dead before the last one passed through. I'm surprised she'd even had time to scream out.

"Son of a bitch," Hastings said, kneeling beside her. He ran his hand over her face, closing her eyes then sat back, shaking his head. "She was a hell of a fighter."

I looked down the hallway and saw the body of a dead militia soldier lying facedown, blood splattered on the wall above his corpse. Stepping closer to him, I saw it was Turk and kicked his foot hard, knocking it into the wall. "You deserved worse, you son of a bitch."

"Where's Delaney?" Biagini asked, leaning against the wall at Jung's feet.

"Dead," Wallace said, deadpan. He jerked ahead to the stairwell behind him. "In the basement."

"That's it then," I said. "We can get out of here now. Call the *Vision* to come get us, right?"

"No," Thomas said, "we can't."

Hastings stood. "What it is, Sergeant?"

"Delaney's not the only thing we found down there."

The stairwell brought us to the small side of a long rectangular room, lit by panels in the ceiling. My breath caught in my throat as we stepped into the large open space, my eyes not believing what I was seeing.

"Son of a bitch," Grayson said. "I thought this was a safe house."

"Well, I guess, now we know why those assholes were so hard up to get Delaney to talk," Wallace said, letting his rifle hang across his chest, sliding his hands into his pants pockets. "Damn that's a lot of shit."

Spread out before us, filling almost every inch of space, were large, rugged plastic containers marked DIPLOMATIC CORPS PROPERTY. Several of the closed ones were opened, and it was plain they were far from confidential papers or gifts for foreign dignitaries.

Wallace stopped at the first open container and lifted the short-barreled rifle from its holding brackets. "I didn't think anyone outside of MARSOC had access to these things."

The weapon was a modified version of our own LR27 rifle, with a shortened barrel and stock, upgraded optics and link-sync capabilities. The type of weapon used exclusively by operators in Marine Special Operations Command. I'd met a couple of them after basic, they're some badass operators, and I'd be willing to bet if they knew someone was selling their treasured weapons to a bunch of militia soldiers in the outskirts of the United Rim Territories, someone would be pissed.

I moved down the line of crates. All of the labels read like they belonged to the Diplomatic Corps, but every single one of them was filled with Alliance military weapons.

At the end of one of the rows, I found Delaney. The Ambassador was lying face down, a puddle of blood beneath his head. Someone had put a bullet into the back of his skull and left him there. It looked like it'd happened fairly recently too, the blood still seeped from the wound, glistening in the pale white light from the ceiling.

"Look at this," Grayson said, holding up a yellow and red arm-sized rocket—ammunition for the Ramsey launcher like we'd found on the soldiers after being shot down.

Hastings took the rocket, looking it over. "Well, this explains how they took out the dropships."

"But it doesn't explain how they got them here," Biagini said, leaning back on the edge of one of the containers.

"So, what are we talking about here?" Grayson asked, shutting the lid on rocket containers. "The Diplomatic Corps was bringing in weapons and arming the militia? How does that even make any sense."

I remembered something I'd heard Turk say and snapped my fingers. "That's what he was pissed about." Everyone turned to me. "Turk, I mean. He kept blaming Delaney for not following through on his end of the bargain. Kept saying he owed much more than they'd received."

"So, what, Delaney had a change of heart after he'd already made a deal with the devil?" Grayson asked.

"We don't know anything," Thomas said.

Grayson shot an exasperated look and sat down on one of the sealed crates. "Don't know anything? How do you explain all of this? How else could this stuff have got here?"

"The bigger question is what are we going to do with it now?" Biagini asked.

"What do you mean?" I asked.

"We can't just leave it here, right? I mean we have to do something with it."

"We collect it as evidence," Hastings said. "We record everything and secure the location as best as we can. We report everything to Command as soon as we get back. We can disable the weapons before we leave, so they can't be used and hide them in place."

"We can't do that," Thomas said.

Hastings turned to face the Sergeant. "What did you say?"

Thomas propped his arms on the buttstock of his rifle, hanging across his chest, barrel pointed to the floor. "I said we can't do that, sir. We can't report this to Command."

"And would you like to explain to me why?"

"Orders, sir."

Grayson and I exchanged a confused glance.

Hastings frowned, cocking his head to the side. "Orders? Unless I missed something, there was no reference to any illegal Alliance ordnance in our mission brief, Sergeant."

"These orders were sent through different channels, sir. But I can assure you they are valid."

"What are you talking about? Whose orders?"

"Admiral Young, sir. Second Fleet Commander."

"I know who Admiral Young is," Hastings snapped. "Why was I not made aware of these orders before now? And why is the Admiral issuing you orders outside of the chain of command?"

"I'm sorry, sir, my orders were strictly need-to-know, classified above Top Secret." Thomas spoke with the air of someone who had the best hand at the poker table, not like just another enlisted ground-pounder talking back to his commander.

"Need-to-know?" Hastings stepped toward Thomas, hands out to the side. "How in the hell does the unit commander not fall into that category? The Admiral has no right issuing orders to an NCO that contradict those given to his superiors. What were those orders, Sergeant?"

"The Admiral can do what he wants, sir," Thomas shot back. "He's an admiral. He gives orders, I comply. It's as simple as that. His instructions were to keep anything that would bring a bad light on the Alliance under wraps. Destroy the evidence and keep silent."

"A gag-order?" I asked. "He's ordering us to keep quiet about this?" Slowly, I tapped my link, activating the recording mode.

Thomas ignored me. "My orders plainly state: any and all projects, materials, or persons that might bring dishonor to the Alliance and/or its departments were to be rendered safe, eliminated, or destroyed."

"Materials or persons?" Hastings repeated. "Are you saying he ordered you to kill those involved?"

"Yes."

Hastings turned, walking away from Thomas, shaking his head. "Young doesn't have that kind of authority. He can't authorize direct actions on non-military targets. Only the President can do that."

I looked over at Delaney's corpse. My original thought was that he'd been put down by one of the militia soldiers, maybe even Turk himself, but now, looking at the fresh pool of blood draining into a grate in the middle of the floor, I entertained a different, more horrifying thought. I looked from the Ambassador to Sergeant Thomas. His eyes meeting mine and my blood ran cold as I saw the truth there. He'd killed the Ambassador.

"What the hell do you think was going on here, Lieutenant?" Thomas asked. "This isn't some diplomat running a small side business, trying to make some extra scratch on the back end. This was a legitimate backroom arms deal. These things don't happen without a lot of backing from the top. Details that those officials would rather not have seen the light of day."

"You're talking about black-bag kind of shit," Grayson said. "I've heard about shit like that. Scary stuff."

"Black-bag or not, it doesn't give anyone—much less Admiral Young—the authority to issue those kinds of orders."

"I'd like to see you tell that to the Admiral, sir." Thomas sneered, crossing his arms. "Way I see it, he issued a lawful order, one that protects the sovereignty of the Alliance. One I'm going to follow to the letter. We need to destroy every trace of these weapons. Every trace of this operation."

"There's some charges back here, Sarge," Grayson suggested, jerking a thumb at a row of crates near the back of the room.

Hastings put up a hand. "Negative. Stand down, Corporal. We aren't destroying anything."

"Sir, I've just told you what my orders are," Thomas said. "We can't leave this stuff here like this. We have to destroy it."

"Your orders are not my orders, Sergeant. And they definitely are not legitimate. They did not come through proper channels, nor did they originate from an authority able to issue them."

It was Thomas's turn to step forward. "Sir, you're saying you're disobeying the Admiral's orders?"

Hastings pointed at Thomas, his eyes hard. "I'm following the last *lawful* orders I received, which was to preserve all life and material that I could from the Embassy and its personnel." He motioned to the containers full of weapons around him. "And while I doubt these containers are on any official registry, they are marked Diplomatic Corps. But independent of that, they are clearly evidence of a crime perpetrated by some, if not all of the Embassy personnel here on Stonemeyer, a fact I'm sure will need to be investigated long after we've departed this city. Our job in that respect is to preserve the evidence so that it might be collected by the proper authorities. That is basic military law. Chapter one. Page one. Those are the orders and instructions I'm following, Sergeant. If the Admiral has a problem with that, he can tell me about it when we're back on station."

"I can't let you do that, sir."

Everyone froze, the tension in the room palpable. I looked from Hastings to Thomas and back again, stunned, not wanting to believe what I'd just heard.

Hastings turned back to Thomas, eyes blazing. "Excuse me?"

The Sergeant stood firm. "My orders are clear, sir. I cannot allow this, whatever it is, to leave this room, much less this planet."

Grayson hopped off the crate he'd been sitting on. "Sarge, come on."

"Sergeant, I've already explained to you that those instructions are not valid. They violate the MCJ and were not properly disseminated. Not only are they not valid, but by law, we are prohibited from destroying evidence of any kind. Period."

"And I don't agree with your assessment, Lieutenant. My orders, given to me directly from Second Fleet Command, supersede any previous instruction, including yours."

I couldn't believe what was happening. The two men looked like they were on the verge of going to blows. Here we were stuck on a hostile world, in the middle of a shitstorm, having lost the majority of our team, and they wanted to argue over the legitimacy of orders?

"They supersede nothing," Hastings said. "They are invalidated, unlawful orders that directly conflict with the MIM and I, or anyone else, am not bound by them. Neither are you."

Thomas shook his head. "I am, sir. And so are you." He drew his pistol, leveling it at Hastings's head.

"Are you fucking kidding me?" Grayson shouted.

"Staff Sergeant," I said, "put the gun down. What are you doing?"

The Lieutenant's expression never changed. "Sergeant

Thomas, you are in violation of the Military Code of Justice, Articles 1.2 and 3.206f: disobeying a superior officer and aggravated assault with a firearm. You will lower your pistol now and relinquish your weapons. You are under arrest."

"I'm not violating anything," Thomas growled. "I'm following my orders. You will stand down and step aside so we can carry them out appropriately. Once all this is over, then you can argue with Young over the legitimacy of these orders."

I stepped up beside Hastings. "Sir, I—"

The Lieutenant put his hand up. "Sergeant Thomas, under the authority given to me by the rank and military regulations, I am placing you under arrest. You will relinquish your weapons and surrender now, or you will be charged with treason."

"Treason?" Thomas sneered. "You're the only one going to be charged with treason. You're the one disobeying orders here, Lieutenant, not me. Grayson, Sheridan, take the LT into custody."

Grayson and I looked at each other, neither one of us making a move. He shared my worried and confused expression, and I could tell he didn't want to comply just as much as I didn't.

"The Lieutenant is wrong!" Thomas shouted, looking at each one of us in turn. "We have orders in hand, and he wants to just throw them out the window. Arrest him!"

"The only one in the wrong here is you, Sergeant," Hastings said, his voice cold and steady. "I'll only say this one more time. Lower your weapon and surren—"

The gunshot rang in my ears like thunder and everything around me slowed down. Beside me, Hastings stumbled as his head snapped back, a red hole in the center of his forehead. He fell back without a word, skull cracking against the bare, concrete floor. He lay on his back, unmoving, open eyes staring blankly up at the ceiling.

"What the fuck?" Grayson shouted, dropping to a knee beside Hastings. There wasn't anything he could do.

"Holy shit!" Biagini said, backing away.

I did the only thing that came to mind, I drew my pistol. "Drop it!"

Thomas shifted the barrel toward me. "You don't want to do this, son."

My voice cracked. "Put the fucking gun down right now, Sarge! Or I swear to—"

"Or what?" Thomas shouted cutting me off. "You'll shoot me?"

I'd earned the handgun marksmanship ribbon in basic, the only one in my unit. Garnered an almost perfect score and some pretty decent accolades from the range master on my trigger control and weapon handling skills. But standing here, looking down the sights at one of my teammates, who was, in turn, pointing his weapon back at me, I couldn't keep my hands from shaking.

"You... you fucking shot him," I said, still not wanting to believe it. "You killed him."

"Treason on the battlefield is punishable by death, even summary execution if the actions are deemed harmful to the unit still in theater. *That's* also in the MCJ."

Biagini limped forward, wincing. "Sheridan, put it down. Now is not the time."

"There won't be another time," Thomas barked. "Everything that's happened here today—this entire goddamn mission—is classified. None of you will utter a word about what you've seen during this operation. *Those* are your orders."

"How can we not talk about this?" Grayson said, looking up from Hastings's corpse, his hands red with the Lieutenant's blood. "People are going to want to know how Hastings died."

"And the Ambassador," I added, not lowering my gun. "Was he dead before you got here or after?"

"I killed him," Thomas said, almost as an afterthought. "And I quote: 'Sanction with extreme prejudice. Prevent any and all details about the Embassy's involvement with the militia at all costs. These orders countermand and supersede any instructions to the contrary.' You want to argue about legitimacy? Those orders seem extremely fucking clear to me."

There was a click behind me. "Put the gun down, Sheridan."

I turned slightly, trying to keep Thomas in view. Out of the corner of my eye, I saw Wallace standing there, his pistol leveled at the back of my head.

"As far as the rest of the galaxy is concerned," Thomas said, "Hastings died under enemy fire. He died a hero, along with every other Marine we've lost on this God-forsaken rock."

"We lie?" Grayson asked.

"We follow orders," Thomas countered.

Biagini raised a hand, her eyes pleading. "Sheridan, please."

"He's wrong," I said. "Can't you all see that?"

"Can't be wrong if he's following orders," Wallace said.

"Yes," I said. "He can."

"Put the gun away, son," Thomas said, his voice more relaxed, calming. "It's a shitty situation all around."

"A shitty situation? You just killed two men in cold blood! How the fuck can you say it's just 'a shitty situation?'"

"You're upset, I get it, but don't let your anger shield you from the truth. My orders come from the second highest Naval authority in the fleet. Those are the orders that we must follow, no matter how much we don't like them."

"So we just kill anyone that doesn't agree with them?"

"Do you think I wanted to shoot Hastings? I would've much rather he just simply follow his orders. Had he done that, he'd still be alive. Unfortunately, we don't have the luxury to debate these things here and now. This operation is sensitive enough as it is. Now, I'm not going to tell you again." He adjusted his grip on the pistol. "Put your fucking gun down."

I felt something hard press against the back of my skull, Wallace's pistol. "Do it, Sheridan."

I stared at Thomas. Blood pounded in my ears. My stomach turned and my skin burned. Hatred, unlike anything I'd ever felt before, boiled up from somewhere deep inside. In that moment, I wanted nothing more than to put a round through the bastard's face, put him down just like he'd put down Hastings. I wanted to watch his blood spread out on the floor and fill every little crack as the life flowed out of him.

But I didn't pull the trigger. If I fired, one or both of them would fire, and I'd be dead right along with them, and then no one would ever know what happened here. No one would know how this coward had killed one of the best men I'd ever known. I swallowed hard, moving my finger off the trigger and onto the metal frame. I blew out a long, frustrated breath, my arms and hands shaking as I slowly lowered my pistol. My knees felt like they were going to give out.

Wallace kept his pistol pressed against my skin while prying mine from my fingers. "Easy, man."

"I don't believe this shit." I stood, frozen in place, staring down the barrel of Thomas's pistol, waiting for a flash, wondering if I'd feel it or not. My gaze dropped to Hastings's body, and I tasted bile at the back of my throat.

"You didn't have to do that," I said. "You didn't have to kill him."

"Disobeying orders in the face of the enemy—"

"Don't give me that bullshit," I said, cutting him off. "He *was* following orders. The orders he received. No one else received anything different. No one but you has seen anything other than what we were briefed. Where are they? You have a copy of them stashed away somewhere? How do we even know you're telling the truth?"

Thomas lowered his pistol. I felt Wallace behind me still and knew his weapon was still pointed at my skull. "I don't care if you believe me, Sheridan, but I *am* telling the truth. Our orders are to clean up this mess no matter what. It's a shitty job. It's not what we signed up for, but it's the hand we got dealt. Now, are you with us or not?"

"Am I with you?" The magnitude of what he was saying hit me like a gut punch and I realized if I didn't say the right thing he was going to kill me right here and now. No questions asked. No second chances. I could see it in his eyes. He felt no remorse for killing Hastings and would probably feel even less if it came to putting a bullet in my head as well.

I looked down at the Lieutenant's corpse, my shoulders slumped as remorse and helplessness washed over me. There wasn't anything I could do to save him, but I could remember him. I looked up at Thomas, looked into those evil, dark eyes and made a silent promise: people would know the truth about what happened here today. No matter the cost.

Behind me, Wallace stepped closer. "Well?"

"I'm with you." The fact that I even had to say the words enraged me. That I was standing here, making a deal for my life with the people that were supposed to be my brothers in arms, cut me to the core. I looked over my shoulder, the barrel of Wallace's pistol centimeters from my face. "Now back the fuck away from me."

He hesitated, then finally lowered the pistol. "Good answer."

It was the only answer I could've given. I stepped away from both of them, moving toward Hastings. "Either of you ever points a gun at me again, and I'll kill you."

"Let's go right now then," Wallace said, stepping forward.

"No." Thomas holstered his pistol and put a hand on Wallace's chest. "He said he's with us. That's good enough for me. We've got work to do."

CHAPTER 45

Calibri City, Stonemeyer
30 Mar 2607
Mission Time: 7 days 1hr 3mins

"*The Bird is in-bound, Sergeant, ETA fourteen minutes*," Captain Kimball said, his voice tiny and mechanical through the shotbox Biagini had built.

I pulled myself up into the back of the van behind Wallace, then turned to help Biagini. She sat on the floor, leaning back against the bench, her face twisted up in pain.

"Ready to get the hell out of this place," Wallace said, smiling.

I ignored him. I just wanted to get away from them. I sat on the bench near the door, as far away as I could get from them. It was becoming harder and harder to hide my rage and I knew sooner or later, I'd slip, and they'd see it.

We'd spent all night setting the charges, making sure every single piece of ordnance in that basement would be vaporized. I spent the entire time sweating bullets. None of us were the experts with explosives Charles had been, and I couldn't help thinking the charges were going to go off at the worst possible moment and vaporize us all right along with the weapons.

I left my link recorder active, picking up everything. Every conversation, every question, every order. I'd almost thrown up when Thomas ordered me and Wallace to move Hastings's body. I forced myself to do it, dragging him across the floor, trying to ignore his blood smearing a trail behind him.

"Good," Sarge said after we'd moved him to the side. "I didn't want to have to step over him all night."

You should've thought about that before you put a bullet between his eyes, I thought, glaring at him. I wanted to scream at him. Wanted to scream at them all. I couldn't believe we were all just going along with it, like Sarge hadn't just shot the Lieutenant in cold blood right in front of us. Every time Thomas spoke, I felt my blood boil. A couple times, Grayson reached out and touched my arm, somehow aware of how close I was to lashing out.

They hadn't given me my gun back. I'm pretty sure they were thinking the same thing I was thinking: once I had a gun in my hand I was going to make some changes to the squad's chain of command.

Grayson got behind the wheel and Thomas climbed into the passenger seat next to him. He leaned back, holding out the detonator for Wallace. "Here."

Wallace took the controller in both hands, grinning like a kid on Christmas. "Oh, hell yes."

"Just wait until we're outside the blast area to set it off. It's going to be one hell of a bang."

"You're right it is. You ready for this Sheridan? This shit's going to be badass."

I ignored him.

The van's engine rumbled, and Grayson pulled away from the curb. Biagini winced as we rolled onto the street.

I reached down and put a hand on her boot. "It's going to be okay. We're almost out of here."

She nodded.

"I hope *Vision* nukes this place from orbit," Wallace said. He held out the detonator. "This is a good start though." He laughed.

The urge to reach out and snatch it from him was almost over-whelming. I could smash the thing pieces and there'd be nothing else they could do. The bird was already on its way down. They wouldn't be able to go back and reset everything. The only problem was I'd probably get killed in the process. I ran the possibilities through my mind as we drove away, in the end, the result was always the same. But then another thought occurred to me.

Was my life worth the truth? The only answer I could come up with was "yes." It had to be. Because I was the only person in the galaxy who could preserve the truth. Hastings, Charles, Henderson, Jung, Maxwell, Trent, Ford, Brent, Deerman, Andres, Simmons—all of them deserved to have their stories told, not to be left to rot on some backwater planet with only a golden star and a form letter citation read at their funeral. They all deserved more than that. Better than that.

"What are you looking at?" Wallace asked, eyebrows knitting together.

His words brought me back to the van, and I realized I was still staring at the remote. I turned away. "Nothing."

Wallace held the remote out, smiling. "What? You want to push the button?"

My chest tightened, fear mixed with anger. I wondered if he, or Sergeant Thomas for that matter, had considered what I planned to do once we got off-world. If they did, I was a dead man anyway. There wasn't any other way around it. They'd have to kill me to preserve their story.

I looked at him out of the corner of my eye. "No, I'm good."

"Come on. Don't you like blowing shit up? I thought you wanted to be this super-secret spec operator, right? Wasn't it you that said you wanted to get into MARSOC? Well, this is the shit you're going to be doing. Or didn't you think about that?"

"I've thought about it plenty," I said without looking at him, trying to mask my contempt.

"Well then?"

"I said I'm good."

"Eh, let him be," Thomas said from the front of the van. "He just needs time to think about his future. Isn't that right, Sheridan?"

I wondered whether he was talking about my desire to join special ops, or simply surviving the next twenty minutes. I didn't know, but I'd put money on the latter. The arrogance of both of them disgusted me.

"Just let him be," Biagini said, her voice weak. She waved a hand through the air, grimacing in pain. "Just everyone shut it, okay?"

Wallace snickered. "Whatever you say, Corporal."

"She's right," Grayson said. "We all need to focus on getting out of here. He turned and looked at Sergeant Thomas. "Complacency kills, right?"

"That's right," Thomas said. He leaned over his seat's armrest, looking back at Wallace. "Do it."

A wide grin spread across Wallace's face as he adjusted his grip on the detonator. "God, I wish I could see this thing go off."

Thomas laughed. "A little bit of revenge. Feels good in the morning, doesn't it? Put a hurting on them for what they did. Just wish we could've killed more of the bastards before we left."

As I watched Wallace's fingers move around the remote, every muscle in my body tensed. Part of my mind screamed at me to stay put, to survive and tell the story, but without any evidence, what would it matter? With nothing to back up my story, the chances of anybody believing me over the rest of them was slim to none.

I put my hands on the floor and caught Biagini's gaze just before I pushed off. Her face was filled with pain and fear. She shook her head at me, as if she knew what I was planning. She mouthed, "No."

In one fluid motion, I pushed off the bench and launched myself at Wallace, hands reaching for the remote. Wallace cried out, pulling it toward him, trying to shield it from my attack as if it were a baby he was protecting from a predator. My fingers wrapped around his, and I could feel the hard edges of the remote as I slammed my shoulder into his sternum.

"Sheridan, no!" Biagini screamed.

"Get the hell off me, man!" Wallace screamed. "What are you doing?"

Wallace twisted away. He pushed himself up, driving his own shoulder into me and pushing me back, they dropped back to the seat and kicked, slamming his boot into my stomach. The blow knocked me into the side of the van. The back of my head cracked against the hard metal and stars danced in my vision.

"You son of a bitch," Thomas yelled. "I knew it!"

A loud bang echoed around the van and pain flared in my side like I'd been punched in the kidney. I gasped dropping to one knee.

"*No!*" Biagini screamed again.

Wallace charged forward again, punching. A hazy cloud of confusion began to form in my mind. Pain burned in my side and needles attacked my eyes.

You need to do something or he's going to kill you, I told myself.

Agony rippled through me as Wallace's fists pummeled my face. I got my hands up and ducked away from his attacks. I managed to wrap one of my arms around his wrist and I twisted and yanked down hard, pulling him off balance. My knee connected with his chin and I felt his teeth smash together. He went limp in my arms.

Before I could even recover, something crashed into me from the side, launching me toward the back of the van. My feet tripped over Biagini's legs and I slammed down hard onto the floor.

"Lying bastard!" Thomas screamed.

I scrambled to my feet, turning just in time to see his boot flash through the air. The world burned white as it connected with my chin, knocking me back into the door. The impact snapped the latch and both doors flew open. A moment later, I was airborne.

I seemed to hang there for an eternity, watching as Thomas stopped in the open doorway, a hand on the ceiling. I hit hard, landing on my ass and immediately flipping backward. The back of my skull slammed against the street, sending blinding pain through my head as the world spun around me.

I heard screeching brakes and horns blare. People screamed, but their words meant nothing. Everything was a blur around me as I rolled down the street.

In the distance, I heard gunshots and felt bits of the street against my flesh as rounds blasted the street around me. Agony flared in my leg, I felt bone snap as my tumbling came to a halt.

A car sped past, horn blaring. Another swerved around me, cutting across the road between me and the sergeant's gun. Glass shattered as his rounds smacked into it. Cars collided behind him as they avoided me. Two more cars sped past, brakes squealing as they slid to a stop. Whether or not it had been the driver's plan, the cars blocked Thomas's shots.

All I could see was the top of the van, turning a corner a block ahead. Thomas's head stuck out from the back as they disappeared, his mouth opening and closing in curses I couldn't hear.

I sat up and tried to stand. Lightning flared in my leg. It was twisted back, my fibula sticking out through ripped pants stained with blood. I gritted my teeth and used the side of a stopped car to pull myself onto my good leg. Agony spread through me, turning my stomach, sending stars across my blurry, darkening vision.

I didn't have long. I knew they couldn't just leave me. Bystanders gawked at me as I hopped around the back of the car. The broken leg swung as I moved. It knocked into the car's bumper causing pain like nothing I'd ever felt before. I doubled over on to the trunk, vomiting across the car.

Tears blurred my vision. My limbs were sluggish, slow to do what my brain was screaming at them to do. Hands brushed against my shoulder, then jerked away. I expected to see Thomas there, a pistol in his hand. "No!" I shouted.

"Is okay!" A man's face I didn't recognize appeared in my fading vision. The man's wrinkled face was a mask of fear, his deep brown eyes filled with concern. "I help, yes?"

We stared at each other for a moment as I considered his words. By this time, more of the bystanders had closed in, surrounding us, asking questions, yelling at friends to call the police.

"No," I said, my voice nothing more than a hoarse whisper. "No, police."

The man nodded. "Yes, I help—"

The explosion shook the city. The deep, reverberating boom rolled across the street like an enormous thunderclap, breaking the sky. A second later, a second explosion ripped across the sky, the blast wave blowing out hundreds of windows in its path. I felt the warmth as it hit. It moved me, actually pushed me but I felt the old man's hand hold firm, his grip stronger than I would have thought.

Smoke and debris covered the street, rolling toward us like a charging army of destruction, coating vehicles and people in dust and ash.

Blocks away—I could barely see it, my vision blinking in and out—an enormous pillar of smoke rose above the buildings, silhouetted by a pale blue, early dawn.

A hitch-pitched whine cut through the cacophony as a rocket touched off, spiraling up from the site of the blast.

"Come," the old man said, giving me an encouraging tug on my arm. "We go, yes? Safe?"

Again, I looked into his eyes, looking for any sign of malice, and saw none. I nodded. "Yes, safe."

CHAPTER 46

The Doris
JumpLane Transit
10 Apr 2607

Fischer worked the muscles in his jaw back and forth as Sheridan finished his story. The whole thing sounded like a crazy holo-thriller. There was a part of him that didn't want to believe it, but the recordings from the Marine's link backed everything up, substantiating every detail.

The fact that Young was behind something like this didn't surprise Fischer in the slightest. He actually felt vindicated for keeping his hatred for the man burning all these years. The thought of slapping restraints around his wrists and hauling him off to prison filled Fischer with a satisfaction he'd never felt before. The fact that he'd be able to honor the memory of so many brave men and women by putting him away only bolstered his resolve.

Sheridan adjusted his position on the bed, grimacing. He let out long breath. "Finally."

"Meds starting to work?"

"Rashi was a hell of a field medic," Sheridan said, smiling. "But without meds... I thought getting shot and breaking a leg was painful, damn."

"I bet. I'm sorry this happened to you," Fischer said. "You and the rest of your team. Truly, I am."

Sheridan nodded. "Thanks."

"When we get back, I'm going to nail that smug bastard to the wall. He'll be lucky if he doesn't get a firing squad for this."

"I hope they miss all the vitals. Just let the fucker bleed out slowly, painfully."

"One hundred and ten percent agree," Fischer said with a smile.

Sheridan's eyes started to droop, his head lulling forward a bit. Fischer stood and put a hand on his shoulder. "Rest now. We'll get you home and fixed up before you know it."

Sheridan grabbed Fischer's wrist. "I want to be there."

"I'm sorry?"

"When you arrest Admiral Young. I want to be there."

Fischer knew that probably wasn't possible. Sheridan was definitely going to need surgery, not to mention a hell of a recovery, and Fischer didn't have that time to wait. He briefly considered telling the man as much, but as Sheridan's eyes began to droop again, he pursed his lips and nodded. "I'll make it happen."

CHAPTER 47

Regional Office,
Alliance Security and Intelligence
Blue Lake City, New Tuscany
14 Apr 2607

Jackson Fischer stood near the back of the landing pad, watching the shuttle descend through the clouds over Blue Lake City. The overcast morning, the dreary dampness that permeated through everything, contrasted sharply with the anticipation he felt at what he was about to do. Unconsciously, he felt the butt of his pistol with the inside of his elbow, reassuring himself that his weapon was where it needed to be. The potential for the arrest to turn violent was an ever-present possibility, regardless of who the target was, but in this case, Fischer thought he'd actually prefer the apprehension to go sideways.

"You okay, Fish?" Chief Carter asked under his breath, low enough that the arrest team behind them wouldn't hear.

Fischer inhaled through his nose and nodded. "I'm fine."

"Remember, we aren't trying to make a spectacle out of this."

"Whatever happens here will be squarely on his shoulders," Fischer said. "Just how he likes things. He'll get full credit."

"You don't have to do this," Carter said. "We can have them take care of everything."

Fischer shook his head. There was no way he was going to miss out on the opportunity to see his face. Not after everything he'd been through. Not after everything he'd seen. "I said, I'm fine."

After escaping with Private Sheridan, Fischer had not only concealed his return, but the very existence of Sheridan as well. He wasn't going to take any chances now that they had their case put together. The pieces all fit, and the picture they'd created pointed to one man. There was no way Fischer was going to let him worm his way out of it.

Carter had put together a small arrest team and planned on filling in the Director after everything was said and done. The newsfeeds were filled with conspiracy theories and rumors of a brewing conflict with the Pegasi, not to mention the outcry of URT lobbyists blaming the Alliance for the hundreds of deaths and billions of credits worth of damage done to Calibri City. One misstep now, and all those embers could spark into full-blown fires, engulfing everything and everyone in their path. Fischer hoped today would be a start to containing, and eventually, extinguishing those fires.

Eliwood, standing to Fischer's left, said, "He's waited a long time for this, Boss."

"This doesn't have anything to do with any of that," Carter said.

"Sure it doesn't," Eliwood confirmed.

But it does, Fischer thought. "This has everything to do with everything."

The shuttle flared, and the engines kicked up gusts of wind. Fischer's heart pounded as the shuttle settled on its landing struts.

It was everything he could do not to charge forward and rip the hatch open. Despite the fact that the landing pad was twenty levels above the ground, Fischer couldn't help but worry about escape routes. There was literally nowhere for Young to go, and even so, Fischer was terrified of him getting away.

The shuttle's ramp whined as it folded down, clanking against the pad. Exhaust plumed out from vents under the winds, rolling away from the shuttle, evaporating several meters away.

Admiral Marcus Young appeared at the top of the ramp wearing his dress blacks. His uniform impeccably tailored, ribbons aligned perfectly, the Second Fleet Command Shield gleamed on his right jacket pocket, even in the dreary weather. His brown hair and beard were both expertly trimmed. If not for his weight, which was out of regulations by at least thirty pounds, he would've been the image of the quintessential Naval Commander.

Young was halfway down the ramp before he caught sight of Fischer. His expression shifted from confidence to obvious irritation. "You've been relieved, Agent, you have no business here. Chief Carter, you will remove this man from the building at once. He has no place in my investigation."

Carter stepped forward. "Admiral Young, Agent Fischer is very much in *my* investigation."

The directness of Carter's tone seemed to take Young by surprise. Fischer thought he saw a flash of confusion appear on the Admiral's face, but the brief hesitation was quickly replaced by amusement. "I don't have time for games, Agent Carter. Your message said that you had new evidence in the case. I am here to collect it and be on my way, I have important matters to attend to."

"It's *Chief* Carter, and I'm sure you do," Carter said. "This won't take long. Fischer?"

Fischer moved forward. He felt the arrest team move with

him. He kept his right hand tucked behind his hip, concealing the cuffs. He reached forward, almost casually, and took hold of Young's wrist as he spoke. "Admiral Marcus Young, you are under arrest for treason, conspiracy, theft, and murder in connection to the events relating to the deaths of Alliance Marines, Embassy personnel staff, and Stonemeyer civilians."

Young tried to pull away, but Fischer's grip was solid. He twisted Young's wrist down and sideways while stepping around the Admiral, bringing his arm to the small of his back. Young arched his shoulder's and gasped in pain as Fischer slapped the first cuff on and reached for the other arm.

"What the fuck is this?" Young blurted out, still trying to twist away.

Eliwood stepped up beside him, taking hold of Young's arm and helping Fischer secure the cuffs. "He just told you, asshole."

Two of the arrest team members moved up either side, each taking one of the Admiral's arms as Fischer and Eliwood stepped away. Fischer stopped in front of Young, not bothering to conceal the smile spreading across his face.

"Do you have any idea who I am?" Young asked, trying to twist free. "I order you to release me! You have no authority over me!"

"We do," Carter said, joining Fischer and Eliwood in front of the Admiral. "And the evidence against you is substantial."

"You have nothing against me," Young said. "And your careers are over. All of you. You have no idea who you're fucking with."

"We know exactly who you are," Fischer said, "and we're not going to allow you to destroy any more lives." He stepped up and pulled the Second Fleet Shield from Young's tunic, then held it up in front of Young's face. "You aren't worthy of this command. You're not worthy of that uniform. You've disgraced yourself and the Navy and the Alliance you swore to serve."

"You have no idea what it means to serve," Young said. "You jumped ship as soon as things got a little tough. That's right, I remember you. I remember a brainless Lieutenant who couldn't handle being told he was wrong, who couldn't handle the pressure of following orders. You have no idea what it means to sacrifice for your world. I've sacrificed my entire life for this Alliance and I won't be talked to like I'm some dog on the street. Release me, now!"

"That's kind of an insult to dogs, don't you think?" Eliwood asked.

"You've *sacrificed* enough lives," Fischer said. "That's over now. You're done."

"Get him out of here," Carter said, jerking his head toward the building's entrance behind them.

"Yes, sir," both guards said in unison, roughly shoving the Admiral forward.

"You're making a huge mistake," Young shouted. "The security of the Alliance is at stake and you can't see it. None of you can. You can't imagine what it takes to ensure security for our citizens. You have no idea what it takes!"

Young continued to chip his teeth as the guards walked him off the pad. They were joined by four more at the entrance and all six escorted him inside.

"Does he ever stop talking?" Eliwood asked.

Fischer let out a long, relieved breath and shook his head. "No. No, he doesn't. He's completely convinced of his superiority. In his mind, there's literally no one else who can do what he does. He can't conceive of any scenario where he'd be wrong."

"So what now?"

"Now," Carter said, "we put this entire thing together and walk it up the chain. There's still potential for a lot of people to get burned by this. It isn't something we can just leave in the winds."

"Burned?" Fischer asked. "These people were trying to start a war. They were supplying weapons to a foreign insurgency trying to overthrow the rightful leaders of the planet. This wasn't some accidental encounter with a hooker, or a Senator buying drugs or defrauding the government. People lost their lives over this thing. Good people."

Carter pointed at Fischer. "Exactly, my point. This isn't small potatoes. This is one of the biggest cases this office has ever seen. It's definitely the biggest I've been involved in, which is why we need to handle this with kid gloves. We fuck it up and the entire thing comes crashing down around us."

"You want me to lock down all the files?" Eliwood asked.

Carter nodded. "Yes. Priority access only. You, me, Jackson. Anyone else must be cleared and read-in fully."

"We need to keep that number to a minimum," Fischer added.

"Agreed. I'll need to bring Director Nixon in, but a lot of the leg work can be done without a full read," Carter said. "And trust me, this isn't going to be any easier. Matter of fact, I'd be willing to bet it gets worse before it gets any better."

"Right, so I get *how*," Eliwood said, "but I don't get *why*."

Carter frowned. "What do you mean?"

"I mean why did Young want to start a war. I mean, he's not starting one with Stonemeyer—they barely have the resources to secure their own system. The only other logical explanation, then, is he was trying to provoke the Pegasi, but why? We've been at odds with them for years."

"Exactly," Fischer said, "We've been at odds, not war."

Carter nodded. "Right. We've had our conflicts here and there, but nothing like all-out war. I'm pretty sure neither side really wants that."

"Okay," Eliwood said, "but let's say he wanted to start a war anyway, why not just take Second Fleet, sail into one of their systems and blow the shit out of them? Why all the games?"

"He's got to have authorization from the President for that," Fischer said. "He just can't start shooting for no good reason."

"Not only that," Carter interjected, "but the President needs the Protectorate on his side as well. And you know damn well those bureaucrats aren't going to allow anything like that unless it's absolutely necessary."

"They can barely tie their shoes without oversight," Fischer muttered.

"I have a meeting with Director Nixon and Admiral Hunter in an hour to brief them both personally," Carter said. "What about our star witness?"

Fischer slid his hands into his pants pockets and looked down at his shoes. "He's safe."

"At some point, you're going to have to tell me where he is."

"At some point."

"Admiral Hunter's not going to be very happy about not being able to see his Marine," Carter said.

"Until I'm satisfied Sheridan's life isn't in danger, he stays in the dark. No one gets to see him without my personal approval." Fischer locked eyes with Carter. "No one."

"I can hold them off for a while, but…"

"We just need enough time to present the case, once we do that, I'll give him up." Fischer stepped away from his partners.

"Where are you going?" Eliwood asked.

Fischer turned, walking backward across the pad. He laughed. "I'm going home to beg for forgiveness and hope Carissa doesn't murder me in my sleep."

"Good luck," Carter said.

"Luck has nothing to do with it."

"Maybe you can tell her that you just prevented the Alliance from going to war and saved countless lives in the process," Eliwood suggested.

"Trust me," Fischer said. "When she sees the credit account

and I tell her what happened, war will be the least of my concerns."

———

This concludes Edge of Valor, but *Echoes of Valor*, the second book in the Valor Series picks up the story, and the war has just begun!

———

- Marcus Young was just the tip of the iceberg. Can Fischer unmask the rest of the conspirators in time to prevent a war no one wants?
- Can Sheridan push past the demons he'd acquired on Stonemeyer?
- The Holloman Alliance is in the midst of change and the questions remains: Will the Alliance hold together or fall to chaos?

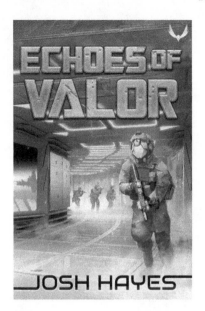

Find out what happens next!
Pre-order *Echoes of Valor* now!

JOSH HAYES is a USAF veteran and retired police officer turned author. In addition to the Valor series, his work includes Stryker's War (Galaxy's Edge) and The Terra Nova Chronicles with Richard Fox, as well as numerous short stories.

His love of military science fiction can be traced all the way back when he picked up his first Honor Harrington novel, as well as a healthy portion of Tom Clancy and Michael Crichton.

He is the President and host of Keystroke Medium, a popular community for writers of all levels, which produces weekly content including live YouTube broadcasts, craft discussions, and author interviews. www.keystrokemedium.com

When he's not writing or podcasting, Josh spends time with his wife Jamie and his four children. You can find out more about his books at www.joshhayeswriter.com.

Join his Facebook Fan Club: www.facebook.com/groups/joshhayes/

Receive his newsletter: www.joshhayeswriter.com/free-books--more.html

SPECIAL THANKS TO:

ADAWIA E. ASAD

BARDE PRESS

CALUM BEAULIEU

BEN

BECKY BEWERSDORF

BHAM

TANNER BLOTTER

ALFRED JOSEPH BOHNE IV

CHAD BOWDEN

ERREL BRAUDE

DAMIEN BROUSSARD

CATHERINE BULLINER

JUSTIN BURGESS

MATT BURNS

BERNIE CINKOSKE

MARTIN COOK

ALISTAIR DILWORTH

JAN DRAKE

BRET DULEY

RAY DUNN

ROB EDWARDS

RICHARD EYRES

MARK FERNANDEZ

CHARLES T FINCHER

SYLVIA FOIL

GAZELLE OF CAERBANNOG

DAVID GEARY

MICHEAL GREEN

BRIAN GRIFFIN

EDDIE HALLAHAN

JOSH HAYES

PAT HAYES

BILL HENDERSON

JEFF HOFFMAN

GODFREY HUEN

JOAN QUERALTÓ IBÁÑEZ

JONATHAN JOHNSON

MARCEL DE JONG

KABRINA

PETRI KANERVA

ROBERT KARALASH

VIKTOR KASPERSSON

TESLAN KIERINHAWK

ALEXANDER KIMBALL

JIM KOSMICKI

FRANKLIN KUZENSKI

MEENAZ LODHI

DAVID MACFARLANE

JAMIE MCFARLANE

HENRY MARIN

CRAIG MARTELLE

THOMAS MARTIN

ALAN D. MCDONALD

JAMES MCGLINCHEY

MICHAEL MCMURRAY

CHRISTIAN MEYER

SEBASTIAN MÜLLER

MARK NEWMAN

JULIAN NORTH

KYLE OATHOUT

LILY OMIDI

TROY OSGOOD

GEOFF PARKER

NICHOLAS (BUZ) PENNEY

JASON PENNOCK

THOMAS PETSCHAUER

JENNIFER PRIESTER

RHEL

JODY ROBERTS

JOHN BEAR ROSS

DONNA SANDERS

FABIAN SARAVIA

TERRY SCHOTT

SCOTT

ALLEN SIMMONS

KEVIN MICHAEL STEPHENS

MICHAEL J. SULLIVAN

PAUL SUMMERHAYES

JOHN TREADWELL

CHRISTOPHER J. VALIN

PHILIP VAN ITALLIE

JAAP VAN POELGEEST

FRANCK VAQUIER

VORTEX

DAVID WALTERS JR

MIKE A. WEBER

PAMELA WICKERT

JON WOODALL

BRUCE YOUNG